Praise for Helen Moorhouse

NEWSPAPER AND MAGAZINE REVIEWS

"Compulsive reading . . . a brilliant first novel, guaranteed to send shivers down your spine" – IRISH INDEPENDENT

"If a ghost story can be measured by its ability to scare the daylights out of you then this is very good indeed . . . Not for the faint-hearted"
– SUNDAY INDEPENDENT

"A classic chiller" – THE IRISH TIMES

"Helen Moorhouse has a fresh, original voice. She has created a satisfyingly scary page turner" – THE IRISH EXAMINER

"Read it" – SUNDAY WORLD

"Helen Moorhouse has applied skill, knowledge and respect to every word in this book, creating the connection between the past and the present and making the squeaks and scratches in our homes take on a whole new meaning!" – THE EVENING ECHO

"Satisfyingly chilling from start to finish, this is a deeply haunting book from an exciting new author" – WOMAN'S WAY

"If you enjoy a good ghost story, have a foible for romance and new beginnings or if you just like to curl up with an unusual tale, then *The Dead Summer* is the right read for you" – SUBURBIA MAGAZINE

"Thoroughly enjoying this suspenseful tale" – NEW BOOKS MAGAZINE

"Atmospheric" – U MAGAZINE

ONLINE REVIEWS

"An excellent debut. I had tingles down my spine as I read this and I couldn't read it fast enough" – BOOKSHELF.COM

"A chilling and sometimes heartbreaking read . . . fans of Linda Kavanagh will love this new author" – CHICKLITCLUB.COM

BOOK TRADE REVIEWS

"*The Woman In Black* has met her match! Deep within this terrifying and sinister tale lies a sad story of loss and regret. I could not put *The Dead Summer* down" – EASON REVIEWER

"I would recommend to anyone who enjoys gothic, ghostly and atmospheric stories. It has a similar feel to that of *The Lovely Bones* by Alice Sebold, *The Little Stranger* by Sarah Waters, *The Place of Secrets* by Rachel Hore and *House of Echoes* by Barbara Erskine. I look forward to more from this author and more of this type of book from Poolbeg"

– WATERSTONE'S DROGHEDA REVIEWER

AUTHOR REVIEWS

"An exhilarating, enthralling and spooky read. A great debut novel that leaves you eagerly awaiting the next one" – LINDA KAVANAGH

"A poignant historical thread is woven through this story of a haunting" – MARTINA DEVLIN

Sing Me to Sleep

HELEN MOORHOUSE

WARD
RIVER
PRESS

Published 2014
by Ward River Press
123 Grange Hill, Baldoyle
Dublin 13, Ireland
www.wardriverpress.com

Copyright for typesetting, layout, design, ebook
© Poolbeg Press Ltd

1

A catalogue record for this book is available from the British Library.

ISBN 978-1-84223-628-4

Typeset in Sabon

Printed by CPI Group (UK) Ltd

www.poolbeg.com

For DM. The best person I have ever known.

"In this big world I'm lonely, for I am but small,

Oh angels in heaven, don't you care for me at all?

You heard my heart breaking for it rang through the skies,

So why don't you sing me lullabies . . ."

Kate Rusby

Part One

Jenny

JUNE 1998

Jenny

I'm sitting at my kitchen table. It's Saturday morning and it's raining, a steady downpour, noiseless except for the steady drip-drip of water from the gutters just outside the back door. It's a nice rain. A stay-indoors rain. Even though it's June, the kitchen lights are on and it's cosy – there's a warm smell of coffee and toast and Ed's popped on the new Moby album. The washing machine is humming gently in the background – a gentle swish-swish sound. Adds to the atmosphere. Makes all this a moment.

I'm watching Ed do his usual Saturday-morning routine – standing at the countertop and going through the week's post in detail. He's always done it: stood there with his diary by his side, filling in any appointments that have arrived, filing the bank statements, binning the junk mail.

Sitting beside him on the work surface, helping, is our daughter, Bee. She'll be three in a couple of months. A fireball of energy at home, all ginger curls and green eyes and porcelain skin. Outside the front door of 17 Pilton Gardens, it's a different story – she's a serene little thing, silent and angelic. She's ripping up the envelopes for Ed as he empties them of their contents and flattens them into piles: bills, statements, correspondence, notifications.

I can't help but laugh as he wrestles a still-sealed C4 envelope from her hand.

"Bee!" he exclaims. "Give that back to Daddy – I haven't read it yet."

Bee giggles and tries to tug it back. "But I'm helping Daddy!" she counters. "I'm the Ripper, you said! I'm Bee the Ripper!"

Ed responds by tickling her exposed armpit, then nestling his head in her warm little neck and blowing a loud raspberry, at which she shrieks with delight, relinquishing the envelope and grabbing his arm, making a scrabble-handed tickle gesture of her own.

Making sure she's secure, Ed withdraws from her, smiling, and returns his attention to the envelope.

It's then that Bee turns to the kitchen table and sees me. I'm sure of it. A smile plays on her lips. "Mummy," she says softly.

I smile back.

At the same moment Ed opens the envelope and groans softly before being momentarily distracted by Bee.

"Mummy," she says again. Her eyes are completely focused on me.

Bee can see me.

Ed follows her stare to the kitchen table where I sit. He sees nothing of course. "Please, Bee . . ." he begins, and I see the start of tears in his eyes.

Please don't, Ed. Not in front of her. Not again. But he can't seem to help it.

My name is Jenny Mycroft, née Adams, and my husband can't see me because I'm not there. Because I died in a car crash on the 23rd of December 1997.

I watch as he takes my daughter, our only child, in his arms. He is crying silently into her hair while she struggles to look back at the table where I am sitting. Except I don't think she'll be able to see me now. Because the moment has gone. Because it's all broken.

I watch as my husband slumps down to the floor where he sits with his arms wrapped tightly around little Bee. A sob escapes him and he is helpless. And I am helpless too. I long to put my arms around them both. To somehow touch them, but I can't because I'm not really there.

And then I see what has fallen to the ground from the envelope with which they struggled in their little game and I know why he's crying. It's a wet Saturday morning in June and my husband has found, among the week's post, a letter wishing to know if I would like to renew my subscription to House and Home Magazine *for another year. It's such a simple thing . . .*

"Jenny," *I hear him whisper into Bee's neck.*

Her skinny little arms have snaked around his neck and she's hugging him back. It's not the first time that she's done this.

"Jenny," *sobs Ed again, helplessly, into Bee's neck.* "Why did you leave us? Why did you go?"

For all he knows, there is no one there to hear him. A louder sob escapes, his whole body surrendering to the tears, shuddering, convulsing with distress.

And there is nothing I can do. I didn't want to die, Ed. You have to believe that. But I'm here now and I'm not leaving. Please don't cry. I'm not going to leave you this time. Not ever.

NOVEMBER 1989

Ed and Jenny

Jenny Adams pulled her chunky mustard cardigan closer around herself. Another late night at college and she was freezing again – the heating in the library would have been switched off at six, of course. Some of her friends had gone to proper uni. With proper study facilities. Heat. A library in an actual building instead of 'temporarily' in a Portakabin. But no, not Jennifer Adams. Well, it wasn't possible just now, was it?

She *could* have gone to Cambridge of course, she knew that. But The Eleanor Darvill Academy of Art and Design in Chelsea offered courses that were just as good, the prospectus said. Jenny's History of Art lecturers were among the finest in the British Isles, apparently. And it was, according to the student information officer, easily accessible by Underground and bus, therefore saving extensive accommodation fees. And there were the grants for tuition and materials. Which didn't go amiss.

It had all made sense. Jenny's dad had begged and pleaded with her to go down to Cambridge but she knew, and he knew, that this – attending Darvill's – was the best thing all round. Who would look after him if she went away, for heaven's sake? She shuddered at the thought of what might happen to him. In his pyjamas all day every day – the grey ones with the burgundy stripes that he wore under an ancient blue sweater – and the slippers that had holes in the soles. Mum had bought them for him. Like the sentimental old fool he was, he refused to part with them, despite the numerous replacements he had been given at birthdays, Christmases and on Father's Days. He hadn't been in much of a mood for new things since he'd come home after her mum's funeral and announced that he couldn't go on. Eight years before.

It had been up to Jenny to take care of him then. Who else was there? At eleven years of age, she had made sure that he had porridge for breakfast, even though it went untouched six days out of seven. School had been close enough for her to pop back at lunchtime and make them both a sandwich and then she did her best to cook a meal every evening. In some cases it had been just beans on toast, if, say, she'd had a lot of study to do, or, later on, some coursework for her portfolio to complete. She'd always made it up to him though with a stew or some fresh fish the day afterwards.

She'd try her best to get him out once a week as well. Sitting silently through Chelsea matches in the freezing cold while everyone around them cheered and chanted. She even dragged him to the pub every now and again. It wasn't much fun, sitting there drinking Coke while he stared miserably into a pint of bitter . . . and people were inclined to avoid John Adams since his wife had passed away and he'd gone a bit funny. But it got him out of the house and if it meant she had to work a little later into the night to get her homework done, then so be it. It was Jenny's job to take care of her dad now.

Of course part of the idea of going to Darvill's instead of moving away to uni had been so she could be there for him in the evenings, but lately that hadn't been working out so well. She'd gone and selected medieval art as one of the course modules – and there was only over a thousand years of art to cover with that one. The paper on 'Animals in Medieval Art' that was due by the beginning of December, a subject with which Jenny was quite frankly struggling, was going to be the death of her, she was sure. At least Darvill's had a pretty big library – even if it was freezing and portable – where she could do some of the research in peace and quiet.

And Darvill's was where she found herself on a Thursday night in November, starving, on her way to the canteen to see if there might be something she could eat before it closed for the night.

Jenny looked at her watch – her mother's. Seven thirty, it read. She hadn't eaten anything since lunchtime when she'd had a small sandwich. No wonder her concentration had started to stray. Her thoughts flashed to her father as she pulled open what had originally been the servants' entrance of the great Georgian house in which Darvill's had been established in the 1960s, and made her way along the dark, tiled corridors to the original servants' quarters where the canteen was housed. Jenny wondered if her dad had eaten anything at all that day and immediately worry set in. She'd better hit the road home soon, she thought to herself as she walked, her second-hand Doc Marten boots squeaking out every second step on the red tiles. She'd be out again tomorrow night, she realised. Friday nights were her long shift at Movie Kingdom – she needed every penny that she could make from that job. She had to save for Cambridge, because they'd said they'd hold the place open for her and she was sure that she'd be able to take it soon, that maybe in the next while her dad would finally come right and get back into the land of the living. It was all a question of being patient. After Christmas maybe. And that was only a month away.

A quick snack, she thought, then another half an hour on bloody tapestries of unicorns and she would get off home. She'd videoed a travel documentary that her dad might like. He loved Monty Python, used to love listening to the records when she was younger. Maybe he'd enjoy seeing Michael Palin go around the world in eighty days?

Jenny could hear a TV set as she turned the final corner on the route through the college basement and walked through the open archway into the canteen. She knew its layout with her eyes shut. The kiosk, closed by now, just inside the door on the left, which sold single, polystyrene cups of coffee, chocolate, newspapers and cigarettes. Beyond that, running the length of the wall was the service area where, behind a glass screen, food was kept warm in bain-maries over the course of the day.

Jenny picked up a sticky red-plastic tray from a pile and slid it along the metal piping of the tray rack, peering in to see what was left. There were chips and there was curry sauce. That was enough for her. She ordered and then accepted the steaming plate from a white-clad server that she didn't know. Norma, the usual dinner lady, jovial, cheeks red with broken veins, always finished at half past five on the dot. Jenny then slid her plate along to the cash register, where she helped herself to a glass of tap water from a scratched old glass jug while she waited for the server to follow her so that she could pay. She fished in the pocket of her faded dungarees for her small red purse and counted out the one pound ten needed to pay for the snack. One pound for a plate of chips and ten pence for the sauce. Every student at Darvill's knew this price. Along with forty pence for a cup of coffee and fifteen for a Tunnock's teacake. The diets of the college students were pretty basic.

Once she had paid, Jenny slid the purse back into her pocket and glanced around her at the small, low-ceilinged room laid out, refectory-style, with Formica-topped tables and mismatched wooden chairs, eight per table. A cluster of them, however, had been pulled into a semicircle under the TV, which perched high on a shelf at the back of the room. There were students there, some on the chairs, some lounging on tables or leaning against the supporting columns that were dotted throughout the room, all of them with their eyes fixed on the TV. Jenny scanned them all and realised she knew none of them.

And it was at that moment, as she glanced up at the TV, that Ed Mycroft, the front two legs of his chair in the air as he leaned back and rocked, turned and did a double take at the tall girl in the faded denim dungarees, the red-and-white striped top and the vile mustard cardigan, her auburn hair pulled to one side over her shoulder in a simple, thick plait. Her skin was pale and unblemished, her eyes among the most vivid green he had ever seen. She was holding a plate of curry chips and staring at the TV, like everyone else. Her nose was a little too big, her eyebrows a little too thick, her lips pale pink and pursed shut as she concentrated on the screen. Ed's first thought to himself was that she looked nice, but when he thought about her later – when he couldn't *stop* thinking about her later – he realised that for some reason the layout of her face, the combination of features, made her the most beautiful creature he had ever seen and that that was the precise moment he had fallen in love with her.

For Jenny Adams, it was the TV that mesmerised her. She had given up watching *Top of the Pops* after she came to Darvill's – she was never home on a Thursday night in time to watch it any more, so there was something comfortingly familiar about the crowd clapping around the presenter as she introduced the next band – one of two Manchester bands that night, she said, and the obligatory crowd cheer went up. And when it started, the song was like nothing that Jenny had ever heard before. A man with a distinctly simian appearance, wearing what looked like a pair of pyjamas on backwards, was swaggering backward and forward, waggling his microphone and singing. To his right was a guitarist wearing a top covered in crosses, swinging his head from side to side in time to the music. To the left, the bassist had his hair slicked back into a ponytail. The drummer wore a white sunhat. The song chugged along, guitars chickering, the singer's voice low, a constant wah-wah sound throughout creating a rhythm that couldn't be ignored. Jenny stared, transfixed, as she began to feel every beat of the song and had to try hard to stop herself from moving in time. As mesmerising as it was, she was still far too self-conscious for that.

It took her a while to notice the young man with the dark brown hair in a sort of pudding-bowl cut who was staring at her, his chair about to topple over. She glanced at him, glanced back at the TV, glanced back at him. His face was solemn at first, but as the chair suddenly jerked back too far underneath him and looked like it might finally fall, and he grabbed at the nearest table, grimaced, and righted himself, his face broke into a broad grin. He'd just saved himself from looking very foolish, thought Jenny, trying to look back at the screen – trying not to smile herself – but being drawn back to his face. She thought at once that he had too many teeth – but as his floppy hair fell onto his face and he beamed at her, unable to stop himself from giggling at his near escape, Jenny couldn't help but smile back, feeling her cheeks go red as she did.

She looked down at her feet and smiled again, before turning away to walk toward the table she had mentally selected. Where she could eat her chips and then disappear back to the library to get her work done. She was stopped in her tracks, however.

"Great tune, innit?"

She glanced back at the group under the TV, at the boy with the hair and the teeth who had finally spoken to her. Jenny glanced back up at the TV set. The singer was still waggling his mic, absorbed in the music. It was a great tune, she thought. Better than great, in fact.

"They're brilliant," she admitted, her voice small.

The student nodded, smiled again and glanced back at the TV. "Stone Roses," he said. "They've got an album out – you should get it." He smiled again, his mouth closed this time, the smile sincere.

Jenny smiled back. "I will," she said, nodding, and made another attempt to reach her table.

"What's your name?" she heard him say.

Later, Ed would admit that he couldn't bear to watch her go, and that he cursed himself at not being able to think of something wittier to say.

"Jenny!" she called back over her shoulder. He was nice, she knew, but she wished he'd just stop talking to her right now. A few heads had turned to look in her direction which made her feel very uncomfortable and, besides which, she wanted to listen to the end of the song in peace, to feel the music again.

The boy responded by smiling again. "I'm Ed," he replied. "Ed Mycroft. See you around?"

Jenny Adams took a moment to look at him again and suddenly felt herself very much *there*, in the canteen at college with a rather good-looking boy smiling at her and the best song she had ever heard in her life playing in the background. It was a moment that neither of them would ever forget. Or would ever want to.

"All right," she replied and this time walked away, a new feeling that she couldn't quite understand running through her veins, almost unnoticed. What Jenny Adams didn't realise at that moment was that her future had begun.

1997

Jenny

Ed always looks tired these days. And he gets home from nursery with Bee far too late. She's only little – she can't cope with a twelve-hour day. And she needs time with her dad, but they never seem to spend any time together in the evenings. He doesn't bath her as often as I'd like him to. But she goes to sleep by eight o'clock and thankfully she sleeps through now. For a long time there were the night terrors, and not even Ed could console her when she had one of those.

He's not looking after himself at all. He should eat more veg for starters. But I know he's exhausted after the long days at work. The peppers in the sweet-and-sour pork he seems to survive on will have to do for the moment.

Then he tries to work a bit – turns on the computer and starts fiddling away. That used to drive me nuts when I was alive.

That feels strange.

When I was alive.

He still does it though. Doodles away – all those complicated animations that he's so good at. I know his heart isn't in it at the moment, but he tries, bless him. And his bosses at Brightwater Animations are patient with him, under the circumstances.

I always sit on the armchair just inside the living-room door while he works, waiting for him to finally wrap everything up, and make himself a hot drink before lying down on the sofa. And then I watch Ed as he watches Newsnight. It's then that I miss him most, inches away from his face, the light from the TV flickering blue on his features. Some nights he just falls asleep there and wakes in the early hours of the morning. Most times he drags himself to bed then. Sometimes he doesn't bother. A few times he's cried because he thinks no one is looking. But I am. I'm watching over him all the time.

Well, not all the time. I'm not always here, in our house. When I'm not here though, it's not like I'm anywhere else. Not like I'm anywhere at all, in fact. I seem to just cease to be.

Finding myself with Ed, with Bee, in our home, is something that just happens – like waking up suddenly, thrown into a scene as it unfolds. I wish that I could control that but I can't. When I am here, I just am. That's how things are at the moment.

When Ed falls asleep, that's when I get the urge to go to Bee. Sometimes I kiss Ed goodnight. He can feel something, because he always bats me away, like a small fly or a cobweb. I wish he knew it was me. I miss him.

With Bee, I can cover her in kisses and she never minds. She sleeps so soundly now as I sit there in the rocking chair beside her bed. The one I used to hold her in to rock her to sleep with a lullaby when she'd wake from a bad dream. And sometimes there didn't need to be a dream – I'd just rock her and hold her and lavish kisses on her and smell her hair and touch her cheek and sing her back to sleep.

I miss my little girl. More than I'd miss my own heart.

Watching her like this, I see so much that I would have missed if I were alive and asleep in the other room. She'll shuffle in her sleep on occasion, and sometimes talk – she's asked for all sorts – a puppy, a dragon, Barney the Dinosaur – and then she turns over and drifts off again.

And as I watch her, the house gets darker and quieter and settles for the night but I stay on watch. I wish I could sleep in my own bed of course. I wish I could have a cup of tea, or a glass of wine, or a packet of cheese and onion crisps. I wish I could watch EastEnders or switch on Mark and Lard in the morning but I can't. All I can do is be. And watch. Watch my family and make sure that they're okay.

1992

Ed and Jenny

"Jen."

"Mmm?"

"Wake up, Jen."

"I'm awake, Ed. What do you want?"

Jenny batted away Ed's hand as he tugged repeatedly on a lock of her hair with his right hand. The fingers of his left were entwined in her left fingers, his left arm holding her underneath her back as they lay curled together on the double bed, with its faded sheets, in the holiday apartment in Cefalù. They were fully dressed, back from lunch at a restaurant outside the Duomo and warm with local wine. Through the open balcony doors at the foot of the bed a warm Sicilian breeze was blowing over them, gently lifting the hem of Jenny's dress and letting it drop again. Ed wiggled his bare feet against it and sighed contentedly as he shifted his arm from underneath her and propped himself up on it to look at her for a moment.

There was no change in the girl he'd seen in the canteen that November night. Jenny was like that. Constant. Steady. Hardworking. Old before her years, sometimes. Dependable. Three years now she'd been in his life. Had it really been that long, Ed wondered. And how had he managed before her?

Not long after they had first encountered each other in the canteen, they met by accident on a cold Saturday afternoon at Stamford Bridge. After that, they had almost hunted each other, each gaining enough knowledge of the other's daily routine to orchestrate another chance meeting. Their first proper date had been to see a special screening at Ed's college animation club of Pink Floyd's *The Wall*. Ed had watched the movie – for the fifth time by his own declaration – in rapture. Jenny, however, had watched Ed and realised that she liked him far more than she'd thought she had, far more than she'd decided she was going to allow herself to.

On the bed in Cefalù – their first proper holiday if you didn't count the disastrous weekend to Whitby – she opened her eyes for a second and then closed them again lazily, as if she thought better of it. "I'm snoozing, Ed," she grinned and he smiled back, running the forefinger of his right hand around the outside of her face and then down the centre, along her nose, bringing it to rest on her lips. Jenny responded by snapping at it and catching it gently between her teeth for a moment before allowing him to remove it. Ed smiled, rolled onto his back, propped himself up on both elbows and looked out the balcony door. The net curtains blew in the breeze, framing a perfect shot of the beach: the Mediterranean spread out before them, cobalt blue against the cloudless sky. The scene was a still life – last night's bottle of wine, empty on the balcony table, along with the two glasses that they had used while they talked late into the warm night with its soundtrack of crickets and the faint rush of the tide on the beach below. The green plastic deckchairs on which they had sat still faced each other, ready for more conversation.

"Do you know why we're here, Jen?" asked Ed, thinking how pleased he was that they were. It had been difficult to convince Jenny to set aside her responsibilities for a week.

Jenny rolled away from him on to her side and sighed as she spoke. "Because we're celebrating the super-duper new job for you and finally being released into the wild out of Darvill's for me?"

There were still four days of their holiday left before Ed returned to London to start as Junior Animator at a company called

Brightwater Animations. They'd plucked him straight from Darvill's – a friend of a friend of one of his lecturers was the managing director of the company and, in casting a net around his contacts for talent, he had snared Ed, who had created quite a buzz with his final-year project. "They said they wanted to snap me up before Disney came and got me," Ed had boasted jokingly. Jenny had rolled her eyes at the joke. He'd cracked it every time his new job had been mentioned. She was thrilled for him, of course she was. But whenever Ed's future cropped up in conversation, she was beset, against her will, by a niggling fear of what awaited her when she got home, when this paradise holiday was finished.

There was no prospect of a bright career ahead for her, she knew. History of Art students didn't get snapped up quite so quickly as incredibly gifted young cartoonists. Instead, she had the prospect of a full-time job in Movie Kingdom ahead of her – either that or unemployment. What niggled at her most, however, was the fact that she didn't even know what it was that she actually *wanted* to do.

"In answer to my question, you're partially correct," said Ed.

Jenny shifted again. She'd forgotten that there was a question, reminded as she was of the little concerns that she was trying so hard to keep from her mind. The Mediterranean breeze again teased the soles of her feet through the open balcony doors. She scowled suddenly. For once, she didn't *want* to talk, didn't want to break the spell of the siesta they had enjoyed. She just wanted it to last forever. To just be here, with Ed by her side, just being . . . content. For a moment before Ed started the conversation she had drifted off completely, having pushed even her father from her mind for a few minutes. Suddenly reminded of real life, she worried whether Mrs Thompson from next door was actually doing as she had promised and checking in on him every other day. Was he eating? Had he washed? Jenny suddenly felt cold, lying on her side, her eyes closed tight. She felt the weight on the bed shift as Ed lay back down beside her and folded his arms behind his head.

"You're only released into the wild until the term starts at Cambridge," he observed casually.

Jenny opened her eyes, the spell in the room that she had tried to recall now well and truly broken.

"You may as well know that I'm not going to Cambridge, Ed," she sighed. "You know I can't . . . my dad . . ." The sentence was left unfinished, the conversation one that they'd had a thousand times before.

Ed didn't say anything but Jenny felt the change in the air and she squeezed her eyes shut tight again.

There was silence for a few moments.

"Let's not talk about that, Ed, okay?" she pleaded, still with her back to him. "Let's just forget about everything except the good stuff till we get home, okay?"

Silence again.

"Okay," Ed grunted eventually.

Jenny could sense that he wasn't happy about that proposition but that he wasn't going to argue with it this time. She allowed herself to sink back into the bed again and sighed with relief.

They fell into silence again. A long silence, but one that thankfully seemed to clear the air. After a while the room began to feel, imperceptibly, light again.

Ed wiggled his feet in time to a tune in his head and the mattress, not the firmest that they had ever slept on, jiggled underneath them both. He paused for a moment and then began again, wiggling his feet harder, knowing that it was irritating Jenny who was suddenly forced to put her hand out to steady herself, to prevent being jiggled off the edge.

"*Ed*!" she giggled. "Stoppit! You're *ruining* my holiday!"

The overreaction made him guffaw and the two of them laughed aloud together for a while, each giggle leading to another. As it died down eventually, Ed moved his head on the pillow closer to Jenny's, so that his crown touched her temple.

"You're meant to ask me why I said only *partially* correct," he said, reverting to their previous exchange.

"Why did you say only *partially* correct?" sighed Jenny as if going through the motions. Still she lay with her eyes shut, revelling in the warmth of the afternoon as if she was lying in a bath, unwilling to break the physical spell of that feeling.

"Because there's something else that I thought we could celebrate while we're here." Ed's voice had grown soft, yet serious.

Jenny continued to ignore it, and him, in her effort to drift back to her former state of complete relaxation.

There was silence again.

"Jen."

"Mmmm?"

"Wake up, Jen."

"I'm *awake*, Ed. What exactly do you want?"

"I want to marry you."

There was a long silence. A silence as Jenny allowed the statement to sink in. A silence where she couldn't turn to look at him because she felt dizzy with shock and emotion, where her mind filled with a thousand questions. But only one answer.

"All right then."

The air felt electric suddenly, but they remained silent. They could think of no words. Instead, Ed closed his eyes and turned so that his face was buried in the back of her auburn hair. He pressed himself against Jenny's back and she, in turn, pressed back against him. She reached out with her right hand, until her fingers found his, and they twined their hands together tightly, resting them on Jenny's thigh. Ed pressed his face even further into her hair and inhaled deeply as a tear made its way, unbidden, down her cheek, unseen by the man with whom she had just agreed to spend the rest of her life.

"I love you, Jen," Ed whispered, just about able to manage the words. There were so many ways that he could think of to express his joy but he could barely speak.

For a moment, Jenny was silent.

"Ed?"

"What?"

"That's all right then," she said, too overwhelmed with emotion to manage anything more. She had wanted this – this togetherness – to go on forever. And suddenly, with one small question, she felt like it could.

SEPTEMBER 1ST, 1998

Jenny

*Ed doesn't even cast a glance at the photo as he walks past me –
sort of through me, actually – with the tray of orange squash that
he's carrying outside for the party. None of those kids outside will
touch it – I know them of old. They all want fizzy drinks and
sugary stuff and he's giving them squash and cheese sandwiches. If
I'd been here the menu would most certainly have been different.
And there wouldn't have been a bouncy castle either. Bee's too
small for a bouncy castle and it's her party. As it is, only her
cousins, Tyler and Marcus, are on it and they're engaged in a game
of jump-kicking. If Ed lets her on with that happening in the
background I'll do my best to jump-kick him.*

*I turn my attention back to the photograph. In it, Ed's beaming
straight at the camera. He looks so happy. My head is bent a little
as I duck, using my bouquet as a shield because Betty and the other
crone – I mean Ed's sisters, of course – are chucking rice about. But
you can see I'm smiling too, clinging on to Ed's arm, my new ring
visible. And there, just behind me, slightly out of focus, visible only
from the nose down is Guillaume. Smiling too of course. Like it
meant as much to him as it did to us. Bloody Guillaume. But let's
not think about him, eh?*

All the other photographs are in an album upstairs somewhere.

19

At the time I said that I didn't even want a bloody photographer but Ed insisted. Not all of them were memories to treasure, mind, but I'm glad now that we went ahead with one, if only so that Bee can see us as we were.

I didn't frame any of the others – just Ed and me. The photographer was very trendy and we asked him for just reportage shots, but of course Ed's mum and dad and the coven had had a 'quiet word' as they're all so fond of doing and my final selection contained quite a few formal Mycroft family portraits. Many of them without, shock horror, the bride.

Eileen – Ed's mum – has one framed in the hallway of their house – Ed, in his suit, with his buttonhole that she insisted he wear even though I specified that there should be no flowers other than the bouquet, flanked by herself and his dad, Frank, and gathered around them his sisters, Betty and Vicky. I can never understand how these people could be related to my lovely Ed. Betty's all right, I suppose – a complete busybody, but practical to have around for Bee – but Vicky? Well, she almost makes me glad to be dead.

Betty's here, of course – it's her two little ninja thugs monopolising the bouncy castle. And Vicky's breastfeeding Matilda-of-the-Mystery-Paternity in the corner, telling all and sundry how breast is best while they try to avert their gaze from the fact that the breast she's feeding with isn't the only one that's on show. And there's my poor little girl, my Bee, in the thick of it, clinging on to a biscuit and seeking Ed out in the crowd while Betty's eldest, six-year-old Sasha, bends down right in her face asking over and over again if she wants to play dolls, to play picnics, to play cars. I want to pick up my daughter and take her away from the child's good intentions. But I can't, so I look back at my wedding picture. The only one I was proud to look at. But not any more. I hadn't been for some time, in fact. But we were happy in it, me and Ed. Despite everything.

Natalie's here too. She doesn't even have a kid to bring so I'm surprised that she's turned up. Then again, she's been popping over a lot since my funeral. Food here, little outfits for Bee there. It's good of her, I guess, even if her motivation is a bit of a mystery – I mean it's not like we were ever friends or anything. Just colleagues. Still. She's good to Ed and Bee and I guess they need all the kindness they can get.

The rest of the guests are made up of a small posse of mums from Bee's nursery. They don't really want to be here, of course. Don't have a clue what to say to Ed – they chat about the birthday and Bee and the weather and so on, but they shy away from him a bit, like they might catch death off him or something. I'm sure that they don't realise that they do that to Bee too. Thankfully their kids are a little kinder and even if Bee just stands and stares at the others, watching, just like I do, they still try to call her into their games and don't bother about her when she doesn't. And, bless her, sometimes she does.

Happy Birthday, dear Bee, I think – very hard. As if somehow she might hear me, as if she might suddenly turn and smile like she did before. Please see me, I beg, my voice silent and useless as I look at the people who have turned up to consume my husband's food and drink and who mutter about how tragic it all is out of Ed's earshot. I watch them gather around the dining-room table to blow out the candles on the cake that Betty brings through from the kitchen. Three of them. Three years since she was born. And instead of me being the one helping her to climb onto a chair at the table, instead of me being the one to blow the flames out for real over her shoulder, the task seems somehow to have fallen to my beaming former work colleague, Natalie, who cheers along with everyone and then plants a kiss on my daughter's cheek. My soul aches at the thought that that should have been me.

I hate this. Seeing this – all of this – that should have been mine. This is hell.

OCTOBER 17TH, 1993

Ed and Jenny

"Say 'Brie'!" shouted Dom, the photographer, waiting at the bottom step of the registry-office entrance for Ed and Jenny to descend. He didn't have to: Jenny couldn't stop smiling and Ed broke into a broad, proud grin as she linked his arm with her left hand and glanced briefly at him. Then, just as she made to descend, she ducked as she was showered with handfuls of rice thrown by Betty and Vicky. She instinctively raised her small bouquet of calla lilies over her head as a defence. She laughed, and Dom snapped and there it was. Their wedding day. Ed and Jenny. Mr and Mrs Mycroft.

Ed didn't think he'd ever seen Jenny look as pretty as she did in her buttercream dress that she had, out of the blue, designed and made for herself. It suited her height perfectly – cinched in at her small waist, the long chiffon sleeves covering her arms against an October chill, the skirt tumbling to just above her knees, the sweetheart neckline framing her mother's silver locket. The wine-coloured flowers made a bold contrast against it and the cream shoes added easily an inch to her height, but it merely made them stand shoulder to shoulder, Ed in his navy-blue suit, his pudding-bowl haircut now cut tightly to his head.

Jenny's hair hung loose on her shoulders, clipped back on one side with a sparkling antique hairclip studded with fake rubies and with three teardrop-shaped pearls dangling down into her auburn hair. Ed's mum had been shocked when she'd heard that the wedding gown would be homemade and that there was to be no veil, for starters. But then again a lot about Ed and Jenny's wedding had shocked Eileen Mycroft and her whole family. Looking around her on the steps of the beautiful nineteenth-century building, Jenny couldn't help but feel a small twinge of triumph as she took in the small gathering – Ed's parents, sisters, their spouses and dates and offspring, her dad, Guillaume, and Tanya, Jenny's cousin and bridesmaid, in powder-blue. She couldn't help but steal a glance at her mother-in-law that was filled with triumph. If Eileen Mycroft had had her way, Jenny knew that she'd now be standing on the steps of a vast, modern church with one hundred and fifty guests of Eileen's choosing lined up in rows behind her with a photographer standing on a ladder before them all, instructing them to wave. Jenny knew that her dress would be white with a train, her veil long and held aloft by one or both of Ed's sisters who would be dressed in identical cerise pink, Eileen's favourite colour. Of course, if Eileen were to *really* have her way, Ed would be hard at work at his desk at Brightwater and Jenny Adams wouldn't exist.

She could see that Eileen's grin for the camera was fixed and insincere, her teeth gritted, her eyes narrow. Jenny reached the bottom of the steps and suddenly beamed, turning her head to kiss her new husband on Dom's instructions. Eileen was going to hate the reception.

It had been a long road to get there, to get to the bottom of the steps of the Wellington Place Registry Office.

From the start there had been so many objections. Their age, first of all. Even Guillaume had brought that one up, but only briefly. Ed had told her about it later.

"You're twenty-three, man," he'd said to Ed over a pint. "Why don't you just, I dunno, move in together? Although even *that* seems a bit, well, serious, to be honest."

Ed had shrugged his shoulders at the friend he had just asked to be best man.

"I love her, Gui," he'd replied simply. "I just want to be with her all the time."

And Guillaume had shrugged in return. "Look, I know you love her. I love *you*, man. And I want you to be happy. Just saying – twenty-three is awfully young to be getting hitched for good."

Eileen almost had to be revived with smelling salts at the news. Normally, when something displeased her, when an issue needed Eileen's opinion, she would look at them both in silence and then request one of her 'quiet words' with Ed. On the announcement of their engagement, however, as they stood in her kitchen, tanned and happy from their Sicilian holiday, she'd looked at them both in dismay, as if waiting for a punchline, and then promptly burst into tears.

"You're too *young*!" she'd wailed, as if that was simply an end to the matter. "You've only just finished college for heaven's sake! You're a *baby*, Edmund. *Too* young by far."

And when she'd eventually accepted Ed's quiet determination that a wedding was most certainly going to happen, it was time to release so much more that she'd kept in reserve.

"What do you mean a *registry office*? What's the *matter* with you, Edmund? Insisting on jumping into marriage is one thing, but not in a *church*? Is that even *legal*?"

"*One* bridesmaid? *One*? What are your sisters supposed to do? Stand there like they're not part of the family? How will anyone know that they're your *sisters* for heaven's sake? We are your *family*, Edmund! *We* are the most *important* people in your life!"

"*Recorded* music? What about *hymns*? Whatever will my friends think if there are no hymns to sing?"

"Edmund, I simply cannot believe that you *refuse* to invite my friends . . ."

When she'd heard that the guest list comprised only her immediate family, the witnesses and Jenny's dad, Betty was the one dispatched to have the 'quiet word'. Yet Ed had stuck quietly to his guns all the way through the preparations. It was Jenny's day, he kept telling himself, even though a part of him agreed secretly that, yes, a church would be lovely, and, yes, of course his mum and dad's friends, and his cousins, and his work colleagues and their college friends were a vital part of his life, but he stayed strong and firm for the first time ever against the usually unbeatable team that his mother and sisters made. "Our day, our way," he kept telling them, over and over again. For Jenny. Because he adored her and this was what she wanted.

On the day, the service was brief and perfunctory, the bride and groom handsome, and the mood in the air one of such love that even Eileen Mycroft felt it, although it pained her to do so. Standing on the steps of the registry office with the leaves beginning to turn brown on the trees, and a chill wind blowing, Jenny and Ed looked into each other's smiling faces and kissed again, this time not for the cameras but for each other.

At the reception, they danced together for the first time – to Jenny's choice: 'There is a Light That Never Goes Out' – oblivious to the other guests as they told each other what a pleasure, a privilege it would be to die by the other's side. They followed that with Ed's favourite – Satchmo with 'All the Time in the World'.

Because that's what we have, thought Jenny as Ed pushed her gently away from him in order to twirl her around and then pull her back against him, and she flung her arms around his neck, both of them lost in each other, smiling. Ed nuzzled into her cheek as they circled slowly on the dance floor of the upstairs function room of the King's Arms – a venue that made Eileen Mycroft physically itch, but Ed and Jenny didn't care. As they danced, Jenny watched the room spin slowly round her from where she rested her head on Ed's shoulder. The long table with its white linen cloth, still strewn with the remains of dinner for fourteen; Guillaume's smirk as he made an exaggerated 'care to dance' gesture at a blushing Tanya before they took to the floor to join in; the disgruntled expressions of Ed's sisters and mother as they watched the dancers; the complete disinterest of both their fathers, sitting in a corner, deep in conversation about Chelsea FC.

This is perfect, thought Jenny to herself and smiled, raising her left hand again to look at the two rings that now lived on the third finger. *Mrs Mycroft*, she thought to herself, and closed her eyes, contented, squeezing Ed tighter as a thrill of excitement ran through her at what the future – what everything beyond that day – would bring.

SEPTEMBER 1ST, 1998

Jenny

It's Natalie who's looking at the wedding picture now. I don't know what she's still doing here – all of the guests are gone and there's really nothing left to tidy up after her so-far efficient performance.

Ed's sitting on the couch, breathing a 'phew' because he's finally got Bee to sleep, no easy task since Betty's thug ninjas were slipping her fizzy cola bottles all day. And there was no sign of their blessed mother to help when the colas all came back up again, was there? I look at Ed, feeling a certain sense of liberation from being in this state. I want to shout at him, "I hate your bloody family!" I want to say, "My child has gone to sleep crying and ill on her third birthday because you let them take over!" Instead I just watch, as always. What else can I do?

Natalie is standing there with the photo in her hands, silent. Why the hell is she looking at it?

"God, she was beautiful!" she says suddenly.

I see Ed jump. Like he'd forgotten she was there, even though she's standing only two feet away from him. It takes him a moment to register who she's talking about and then he sees the picture in her hand as she turns to look at him. His face falls in a funny way. Like he doesn't want to talk about it. But Natalie's not taking the hint.

"What colour was her dress?" she asks, gazing at my picture like she and I were long-lost sisters or something, instead of two office managers who worked in a video-shop chain.

I look at Ed who is just staring at this woman that he doesn't really know.

"Oh," he says, realising that Natalie wants him to respond. He looks from her to the photograph, shifts uncomfortably on the couch and makes an 'I don't know' sort of face. "White. Cream, maybe . . ."

Back to Natalie who is back staring at me like she can't take her eyes off my beauty. Like I'm the Mona Lisa *or something.*

"You look so happy," she sighs and looks back expectantly at Ed who doesn't know what to say.

He just looks back at her, sort of helpless.

Natalie shakes her head and replaces the picture on the bookshelf where it always lives, normally covered in a layer of dust. "What am I thinking of, Ed?" she tuts. "It's been a long day and I'm sure you don't want to talk about . . . it."

He shrugs again, embarrassed at not knowing what to say, on the spot now because he actually doesn't want to talk about anything *but is too polite to say that. He'll have a whole conversation about something he doesn't want to talk about purely not to offend Natalie. Just like his dad might. Just like I would have, to keep the peace.*

"You look exhausted, Ed," says Natalie, affecting some sort of sympathy. There's something up with her, I can tell. "Let me get you a glass of wine – or would you prefer a beer? Heaven knows we could do with something stronger than tea after the day we've had!"

Her laugh is sort of tinkly. I don't remember it sounding like that, actually. Ever. It follows her as she leaves the room, floating down the hall after her like pixie dust. She's obviously made the decision on what they're having already. I can hear her in the kitchen rummaging around for a corkscrew or a bottle-opener or something.

While she's gone, he glances over at the picture that Natalie just replaced. Our wedding day. Our memory. I long to touch him, to give him a hug. To be the one to go to the kitchen and get him some of that Italian beer that he loves and tell him that he did a fantastic job today, even though he didn't really.

"Red all right?" tinkles Natalie from the hallway, and appears back in the living room, carrying two goblets of wine.

Ed hates red. I know this, so I expect him to refuse, but he takes it from her and says thanks and takes the tiniest of polite sips before setting the glass down on the floor beside the couch.

Natalie, meanwhile, sinks down on the couch beside Ed and takes a generous slug from her glass. I watch as she slips off her navy-blue court shoes and curls one leg underneath her, her long, cotton polka-dot skirt spreading itself over the couch. She's reapplied her lipstick too – where did she find the time to do that? I imagine it's called 'Venus Flytrap', or 'Vampire's Dinner' or something.

She holds the wine aloft with one hand and fiddles thoughtfully with the pearls at the neck of her silk vest for a moment.

"Was it a great day?" she asks, draping herself over the back of the couch.

I can see her intentions clearly now. I am not cold in my grave and this bitch, this praying mantis, is daring to make a move on my husband. Don't you dare, I think. Don't you bloody dare.

Ed has leaned forward on the couch, his elbows on his knees and his hands clasped loosely together. In order to see her properly, he has to turn his head to look over his left shoulder.

Natalie, draped like a piece of fabric, nods at the wedding photograph, and raises her eyebrows at him to indicate that she means our wedding. This registers with Ed and he looks back at it, finally realising what she's talking about. He sighs heavily.

"It was a funny old day," he says suddenly and for the first time ever I feel a little funny too about what he's going to say.

In fact, I don't want him to say any more.

"Jen was – well, you knew her too – she was so stubborn when she wanted to be," he says. "Could really dig her heels in about stuff."

Stop, Ed, I think. Just stop now.

Natalie tinkles again. "Oh, you've never said a truer word, Ed!" she replies, her lips folding too far back over her teeth and shaking her head in an 'oh you!' fashion at my husband.

To my disgust Ed laughs along with her. I want them to stop. For Ed to stop being so stupid in falling for this, and for Natalie to just get lost before I get any madder.

"I've never said this to anyone, but I would have loved a church wedding," he says suddenly and if I had a heart to stop, it would. What the hell is he talking about?

Natalie raises her eyebrows interestedly, as if he's just announced some new advance in science or his intention to walk on Saturn. Again Stupid Ed nods in response, as if he's said something really interesting.

"I would have," he says again.

Shut up, Ed.

"The whole day, for something that was meant to be so simple – it was just such hard work."

I stare at him, dumbstruck. It was your bloody mother who made it hard work, Ed! That and those harpies that you call your sisters. Wasn't it? Besides which, you said that it was perfect, that it was everything that you wanted. And if you hated it so much, why couldn't you tell me? Or keep it to your bloody self? Why tell Natalie, lounging on the couch like a spaniel waiting to have her bits tickled? I don't think I have ever felt so angry, or so betrayed. Why doesn't he go take my wedding dress out of the wardrobe and use it as loo roll?

"Didn't you have a say?" Natalie, pipes up, glugging back her Montepulciano like it's iced water and thrusting her bosoms out like two cakes on a plate.

And what does Ed do? He shrugs. Shrugs his weakling shoulders, his noncommittal look spread all over his face. Like all of a sudden he can't say any more. Like he hasn't said enough as it is. Like that shrug doesn't speak volumes.

There's silence then, between the two of them. Ed staring at the picture with some stupid, hurt-puppy expression on his face. And Natalie, that bloody Black Widow, staring at Ed like he's a dessert trolley waiting to be attacked. Licking her lips and swigging the booze until it's gone. Letting a little burp out and giggling like a Japanese schoolgirl. Covering her mouth with her big red claws like she's been to finishing school or something.

And then Ed drops a bombshell back into the room.

"I adored her, Natalie," he says, without tears, staring at my picture with eyes that have grown soft. To hell with you, Ed, I

29

think. How dare you do that to me? How dare you use the word 'adore'? I've never been adored. You've never said that before. You shouldn't adore me – are you remotely aware of that? You shouldn't. And there's no one left to tell you why, to tell you how much you should hate me.

Natalie isn't sure what to do. She looks at the floor, where she's placed her empty glass, looking like she's hoping the wine fairies have refilled it while Ed's been declaring his love for me. He stares at the picture like she isn't there, and she doesn't know what to do. And then he sits back sharply on the couch, again ignoring her, and he raises his hands to cover his eyes as I have seen him do so often since last Christmas. He stays like that, silent for a long time. Like she doesn't exist. Then he lowers his hands, opens his eyes and stares ahead of him, still oblivious to her presence. I can see in her helpless eyes that she's decided it's now or never. Make it never, bitch. Make it never.

Except it's now. She picks her moment, breathes in deeply and throws herself across the couch, raising a mannish hand to cup Ed's face on one side, pushing out her thin lips, trying her best to touch his with them in a gentle and alluring way. She misses, gets the side of his chin. If I wasn't so mad at them both, I'd laugh.

Except I'm getting madder because, instead of pushing himself away, Ed jumps in surprise, and then for a moment, just a moment, he responds. His face turning in towards Natalie who now looks like a fish stuck to the side of a tank. And he kisses her back. It's only for a moment, but he kisses her. A surge of rage goes through me.

This is what it would feel like, I realise suddenly. Betrayal. The rage grows . . .

It's at that moment, when I am filled with this fury, that I do it. That I make the crash which makes them jump apart. That I smash our wedding photograph into pieces somehow. That I shatter it so that the glass of the frame looks like a spider web for an instant before the whole thing crashes to the floor.

I did that, I realise. My anger did that. Because the memories that it gives me – the feelings it makes me feel – are too much. It's all too much – everything that Ed has said, the things that I didn't know about our wedding, the fact that he still adores me, the fact that a tart, under the guise of being my friend, has come to my house, drunk my wine, kissed my child, joined in like she belonged – all with the sole intention of getting her leg over my husband. If I could take a breath I would.

The two of them jump apart and look simultaneously at the floor where the picture has fallen. The room's gone still now, the chemistry between them as shattered as the glass frame. I am sick with nerves that it will repair itself and continue. I watch them both: Natalie looking annoyed but composing herself, turning her sucker lips back for more – Ed, alarmed, looking at our shattered wedding photograph and then back at Natalie's face. I can't be sure, but I think he recoils a little. He pushes his body away from the approaching onslaught of her upper torso and magnetic lips and coughs politely.

"I think you should stop, Natalie," he says.

Relief washes over me.

Natalie's eyes grow wide, and she retreats a fraction of an inch but she soon regains her composure and recommences the slow attack, lips pursed, breath growing short. I despair of her. She embarrasses me. Back it up, lady, I think. The boy said no. And then he says it again.

"No, Natalie." He's being kind, but firm. "It's not . . . I don't . . . feel this is right . . ."

That does it. As effective as a smack in the face. My former colleague sits up sharply, back ramrod straight. "What do you mean, Ed?" she says, her tone a little more demanding. "I mean, you were there with me a moment ago. I felt the energy." The voice softens toward the end of the sentence. There's more energy where that came from, I think.

Ed sits up straight himself now, trying to increase the distance between them, discomfort apparent on his face. "That was a mistake, Natalie," he says kindly again. "Look, Jen's not . . . I mean I can't, it doesn't feel right . . . and Bee . . ." his voice trails off as he glances upstairs. Trying the not-in-front-of-the-children approach.

She's persistent, Natalie, I'll give her that, I think as she tries a different tack.

"Ed, I know you've been through a lot but . . ." breathy whisper, "Jenny's gone."

It has no effect on Ed. In fact, he takes this as his cue to remove *himself physically from the situation and he stands up sharply, pushing past her long legs which have tried to entangle themselves in his.*

"I think you should go, Natalie," he says quietly, standing up.

He is rewarded with a look of outrage.

He responds with a frown. The face is one I know. The one that says he just doesn't want to talk about this any more.

I look back at Natalie who is virtually spluttering with anger but holding everything together.

"Just leave, Natalie," says Ed firmly. "It's been a long day and I just need time to think. Just to be on my own. It's too soon after Jen . . ."

"Bloody Jenny!" she retorts, picking up her navy-blue jacket with the gold buttons where it's been slung over the armchair since the last of the guests left. Her lipstick is smudged and her breathing shallow, her face ugly with growing fury. "Saint Jenny!" she spits and looks around for her handbag. She's leaving all right, but not without a fight. "Saint Jenny, wonderful Jenny, beautiful stubborn Jenny who you adored. You'd want to get this into your skull, Ed – she's been dead a long time now and she's not coming back, so you'd want to get used to that, and move on sooner or later."

And with that, she's gone, flouncing out through the living-room door and through the hall beyond, her court heels clacking on the wooden floor. The front door slams loudly and then there's silence.

I look back at Ed who stands still for a moment and shakes his head to clear it before picking up the two wineglasses, one full, one drained, and heading out to the kitchen. How I long to talk to him! To ask him to quell the panic that gnaws at my gut after Natalie's words. When she said that he needed to move on. But you adore me, Ed, right? Even though you shouldn't. Even though I don't deserve you. You're not going to move on, are you? The thought has never crossed my mind up until now. That he could move on, see someone else – kiss someone else, make love with them – talk with them like we used to talk.

Because I'm not ready for that – how can I ever be ready for that when he doesn't know how sorry I am? When he doesn't know anything – when he doesn't know that I adore him a million times more than he adores me. When he doesn't know that I can't leave him. Ever.

1994

Ed and Jenny

Jenny, of course, wanted to be ironic about it – wanted to put the Toon Award in their new toilet.

"That's what Emma Thompson did with her Oscar," she'd told Ed matter of factly as they'd wrapped it carefully in layer after layer of bubble wrap. "Imagine Vicky walking in to have a poo and there's a *Toon Award* staring at her, as won by her baby brother!"

Ed had smiled faintly at the notion but had firmly put that idea away for good. "You know, she wouldn't know what it *was*, Jen," he'd said. "And neither would Mum – she'd probably try to scrape off limescale with it – or use it as a toilet brush or something."

Like an excited puppy, Jen suddenly paused in what she was doing. "We'll put it in the en suite instead – oh my God! *Imagine*, Ed!" She stared with wide eyes into the middle distance.

"What, Jen?" he'd replied, a smile forming on his lips.

"We're going to have an en suite toilet to have limescale *in*!" She clapped her hands together in glee as she piled more books into an already overstretched cardboard box before abandoning it to start filling another.

Ed grinned and placed the award carefully into its small moleskin pouch, setting it safely to one side. That done, he shuffled over to the box Jenny had just abandoned and removed the paperbacks that were about to spill over the top and slid them into another empty carton. Nearly there, he thought to himself, as he glanced around at the few belongings they had accumulated in their flat over the months they had lived there.

The Toon eventually travelled from the flat to their new home on Ed's knee in the removal van, for safety, and took up residence in pride of place on the mantelpiece. It was what, Ed knew, had enabled them to move. To get a mortgage. To buy their first house. *Our house*, he said to himself on the way, over and over again, as the van trundled past shops and down tree-lined streets.

Winning the Best Newcomer Toon Award 1993 was a real coup for Ed Mycroft. Out of nowhere, his creation – a rock-music-obsessed monster – had become an overnight success. It was a first for Brightwater Animations: a feature-length movie and a commercial success. With *Grimlet Goes Wild* making a killing at the box office, they were well in a position to award Ed with an enormous bonus. In fact, it would have been imprudent for them not to. "Can't let this guy slip through our fingers," his bosses had said. At only twenty-four, Ed was very hot property indeed.

Also at twenty-four, Jenny Adams-Mycroft worked, if not contentedly, at least with her trademark diligence and dedication, as a regional manager of the Movie Kingdom chain of video stores where she had begun her career as a student part-time. She'd kept her job, even when Ed had come home, stunned, to tell her that he had won one of animation's most prestigious awards and that his bosses had given him a very large cheque as a reward, with a promise of more to come.

"*Anything* could happen, Ed," she'd reasoned cautiously when Ed had proposed that she give up her job now that they could afford it. "And besides which, if I didn't work what would I do with myself all day?"

A shadow had crossed Ed's face when she said this. He knew what she could do, of course. Pursue her long-lost place at university. He could even finance setting her up in her own business, designing clothes, at which it had become clear she was inordinately talented. But he knew what would happen if he brought that up again and, this time, he left it for a change. He didn't want to spoil the mood.

"You can stay at home and housekeep our lovely new house that we're going to buy with all that lovely money," he'd offered. "And learn to drive the lovely new car I'm going to buy you to go with it."

Jenny had rolled her eyes. "Can we really afford a house and a car, Ed?" she'd asked timidly.

Ed had nodded in response, reassuringly. "Yes, Jen. We can afford a new car and a new house. And a pair of new Doc Martens for you if you like," he'd added.

Her face had broken into a grin. "Can I have oxblood ones, Ed?" she'd asked with a smile and he'd nodded benevolently. Jenny had patted his knee and stood up from the sofa in the living room of the tiny flat they had rented since getting married. "Thanks, Daddy Warbucks," she grinned. "Cuppa?" She took a step toward the door of the kitchen before pausing and turning to look back at him.

"Ed," she said.

"Yes, Jen. What would you like now? A golden watch? A stuffed pig? A Wonderbra?"

Jenny smiled and shook her head slightly, her new fringe falling into her eyes. "Being serious for a minute, Ed," she started, "I'm so unbelievably, incredibly proud of you that I can't even put it into words, you know."

Ed blushed.

"You're a bloody genius," she continued quietly, her gaze filled with love as she looked at him sitting on the floor, staring back at her. "And I admire you more than anyone I've ever known."

Silence fell and they stared at each other for a while longer before Jenny looked down at her feet. Ed continued to stare at her. "Thank you," he said eventually, quietly, taking her in. His wife. So beautiful. Their whole future ahead of them. They were going to be so incredibly happy.

Jenny coughed. "Right then," she said, snapping back to normal form. "Maybe you could put those millions to good use and nip down to the corner shop for something more exotic than a fig roll while I put the kettle on?"

And Ed suddenly found himself roaring with laughter at her, and feeling thrilled, feeling alive to his fingertips with the possibilities that lay ahead.

1994

Guillaume

Guillaume had seen Pilton Gardens before ever Jenny set foot across the threshold, before Ed had finally signed on the dotted line.

"Please come with me, Gui," Ed had begged his friend. "I just want a second opinion before I take Jenny to see it. She wants to put the bonus into a bank account and never lay a finger on it in case we're bankrupted suddenly. My round, isn't it?"

Guillaume Melesi – father Botswanan ambassador, mother French model – laughed aloud with his huge booming chuckle. He and Ed, his best friend since first form at school, had discussed this prospective house purchase over two pints already, and he had to admit that he was growing more than a little bored of hearing about Victorian red-brick semis and the potential for the garden, blah blah blah.

Guillaume stretched his six-foot-two frame to its full height and stood up from his bar stool.

"Okay, okay," he replied, showing Ed the palms of his hands to stop the pleading. "Just let me use the gents' and you get another round in and we'll go then – but this is a short visit, right? You and I are on a boys' night out to celebrate your big success – after we see it, then no wife or house talk allowed, geddit?"

Guillaume sloped off in the direction of the gents'. Not for the first time, he wondered what exactly Ed thought he was doing. At twenty-four years of age? In the prime of his life? Married? Tied down? That wasn't Guillaume's style. Marriage – that was imprisonment, and he had no intention of locking himself up and couldn't understand why Ed had. Why, when there was so much out there to see and do? So far he had spent two gap years touring France and Africa as a nod to his heritage; had dropped out of a degree in engineering and was currently taking some time out to think about exactly what it was he wanted to do next. Japan, he was thinking. Technology. Computers. Worlds of possibility . . .

His parents' wealth helped Guillaume immeasurably of course. Regular payments into his account kept him in the lap of luxury at their house in South Kensington while they travelled for nine months of the year. And the fact that his mum had been a model had meant he'd inherited very, very fortunate genes indeed.

Guillaume smiled coyly at a curvy blonde girl that he passed on the way to the gents', standing to one side to allow her to pass between two tables. The air virtually sizzled between them as she slid by in the tiny space and Guillaume was only too aware that she was holding her breath as she blushed yet maintained eye contact with him as she passed. He allowed himself a little satisfied chuckle as he continued on his way to the toilet. He could have her back at his place in five if he really tried – but that was too easy.

Three hours and four pints later, however, Guillaume found himself thinking that it would have been a much easier and more pleasurable way to spend an evening, as he found himself trying to count out change to pay a cab driver who had brought them to some mystery street somewhere in Fulham. That done, he turned and squinted down the lamp-lit street in search of Ed, who had wandered off.

Finally locating him, Guillaume hit the cab roof with the palm of his hand, indicating that the driver could go, and charged off toward where Ed stood. Once beside him, he steadied himself with a hand on Ed's shoulder before looking up to mirror what his friend was doing and stare intently at the house outside which they stood.

"There it is, Gui," slurred Ed, pointing at the house. "17 Pilton Gardens." The gesture, and Guillaume's added weight on his shoulder, unbalanced Ed and he staggered slightly to right himself. "That's our home!" he finished triumphantly. "Ed 'n' Jen's!"

Guillaume simply raised an eyebrow, as if to say: 'Is that it?'

The house looked like any other Victorian terraced house in the area to him – in the whole of London, in fact. Red brick, front door painted a chipped green, paint peeling from around the bay window of the living room, all of which looked onto an overgrown front garden with a rusted front gate.

"Isn't she beautiful?" slurred Ed with pride as he stared up at it.

Guillaume cast him a sideways glance and sighed.

Ed turned to face his friend and staggered again. Guillaume had been right. They should have come out here after that third pint, but what the hell. It still felt *amazing* to be here, showing the house off to his best mate. Ed breathed in deeply. The smell of a city evening was *intense*, he realised. He could hear distant sounds of traffic and the low hum of music coming from someone's garden nearby. A warmth flooded through him. This was going to be his home. His future, he acknowledged. For himself and his *beautiful,* talented wife.

Ed was high on triumph. He had never felt more of a provider, more of a man than he did at that precise moment, buoyed by the brotherhood he felt for his best friend at his side, and the copious amounts of lager that he had consumed. So buoyed that he glanced at his watch, which was a bit of a blur quite frankly, wondering if his solicitor might still be open so that he could get down there right now and sign the final papers.

"Isn't it a bit small, mate?" offered Guillaume.

Behind them, a curtain twitched in a house across the road at the odd sight of a tall and skinny white man and his very tall and well-built black friend peering up at No 17, hands on hips, and swaying on their feet.

Ed crunched his face to indicate that no, it wasn't small at all. "*Totally* deceptive," he managed. "*Massive* potential – we're going to do the garden, build an extension, attic conversion – the bloody *works*, man, The. Bloody. *Works*! Small on the outside maybe but, you know . . ."

"So, like a TARDIS," responded Guillaume.

"*Exactly*!" Ed snapped his fingers as though Guillaume had solved a particularly difficult puzzle. "Like a TARDIS, man. Small on the outside maybe but bloody *massive* on the inside when we're finished with it. Innit great?"

They stood in silence for a moment.

"Whatcha think, Gui?" asked Ed, looking up into his friend's face as Guillaume surveyed all before him.

"You *know* what I think, man!" replied Guillaume, shaking his head and slinging his arm around his friend, almost knocking him over. "You *know* what I think. Ditch the chick, mate. Come with me to the other side of the world and have an adventure. Learn new things – learn about *computers* and do some crazy shit and live a little. But you won't listen – you never have. Getting married, mate – that was a nuts thing to do. But if it's what you want, then Uncle Guillaume can't stop you!" He looked down on Ed in a fatherly way. "Do it, mate. Buy the damn thing if you want but don't say I didn't warn you!"

Guillaume suddenly gripped Ed's head roughly into the crook of his arm and playfully rubbed his crown with his knuckles. Then, as suddenly as he had grabbed him, he released him, shaking him off. It was time to move on to the next thing.

"Right," he said, clapping his hands together, the noise echoing down the leafy cul de sac. "Now, if you're gonna live here, we'd better do us some research." He looked right and left intently.

"What you got in mind, mate?" said Ed, taking a last look at the house he would buy, wondering silently how soon it would be before he'd actually have the keys, and setting off down toward the junction with the main road, which Guillaume had already reached with massive strides.

"The boozer, man," said Guillaume. "The local. And some chips. I'm bloody *starving*, mate."

"Good thinking," replied Ed and fell into step beside his friend.

"And some ladies. If I have to come and visit you here I'll need to check out the local talent. Life's too short not to have the lovely company of girls, Ed. A lesson you'd have done well to learn before you went and got tied down."

Ed grinned. "Only one girl for me, Gui, but I'll come with you for a look, eh? Make sure you don't get into any trouble."

Guillaume grabbed him in another headlock as they strode together down the road, all the while scanning the area around him, like an animal on the prowl. "Ed, mate," he said, "if I don't get myself into trouble tonight then this has all been a complete waste of my valuable time!" And with that he released Ed and pushed him playfully out onto the road, bellowing with laughter and striding into the night, hunting, as always, for adventure.

FEBRUARY 1995

Jenny

The steps of the Mayberry Maternity Clinic were icy first thing in the morning. Jenny knew this because she had slipped and almost fallen on her first visit there and it was at that precise moment that she realised how desperately she wanted her baby.

She and Ed hadn't been trying to get pregnant. They'd just stopped trying *not* to and she hadn't thought for one second that no sooner had the ink dried on the deeds to the house, that she'd be feeling queasy all day long and that her body would ache in places where she didn't know she'd had places.

She'd found out for sure early on a Saturday morning when she'd finally given in and taken the test out of her handbag. Sitting on the closed lid of the toilet, watching the line turn blue, was the most surreal moment of her existence.

"*Ed!*" she'd shouted suddenly.

She hadn't planned for this. In a split second she regretted calling him – didn't other people do this in a more romantic way? Didn't they present their partner with a pair of bootees or something? *Bootees*? Were they actually a *thing*? For a brief moment, Jenny panicked. What the *fuck* have I done, she thought to herself. And now what am I supposed to do? She called Ed again, the unmistakable feeling of panic clearly audible in her voice. His sudden footsteps on the stairs were heavy and rushed.

"*Jenny*! What's the matter? Let me in!" The door to the bathroom jiggled as Ed tried the handle. "Are you hurt? What's wrong? Jen! *Jen!*" His voice was filled with panic at the lack of response. After a moment, he heard the toilet flush, followed by the rattle of the bolt as she slid it back. Her skin was grey as she peered out at him silently. Slowly, Ed's eyes lowered to the plastic stick in her hand.

Later, as she sat on the couch in the bare-floored living room while he made her tea, she stared at her own wedding picture. At the slim, carefree laughing girl in it, taken the year before last – was it that long already? And that short? Had they only had a year of marriage together before this? For a moment, Jenny didn't recognise herself. A strange feeling crossed her mind that she was an utterly different person from the girl in the cream dress carrying the lilies. I want to be her again, she thought for a second. I want to be her, not me. Not this person. I don't want this to happen.

At once she felt guilty. She didn't, of course, want anything to go wrong – and she had no one to blame but herself. But she just didn't feel ready. At all. Would that change over time, she wondered. Would she actually grow to be happy about this?

"Are you okay?" asked Ed awkwardly as he handed her a steaming cup.

Jenny peered up him and nodded. No point in letting Ed know how she felt, she decided. It would pass. She was sure of it.

"*Wow*, Jen," he said, sinking down on the couch beside her. "I didn't think it would happen so *fast*." She said nothing, just sipped the tea silently. The two of them sat side by side, staring straight ahead.

"Nor me," she said quietly. Stay normal, she thought to herself. Don't let him know you're having second thoughts.

"*Jesus!*" he said again, breathlessly. "There's going to be a baby, Jen. *A baby.*"

Jenny felt helpless tears well up behind her eyes. Stop, Ed, she urged him silently. Did he think she didn't know that? Suddenly, she felt completely overwhelmed. By the situation – by Ed. She just wanted to be left alone, to forget about all this for now. To just turn on the TV and somehow block reality out. And yet she couldn't. It was really happening. Right now, in her body. Another person being made. A tiny, tiny person. *Her person.* For whom she would be always responsible. She felt ill. Christ, she thought. I'm barely out of college – I can't even get a decent job – how am I going to look after a baby? Jenny clenched her eyes shut as her head started to spin.

"A bloody baby," whispered Ed softly, in a daze of his own, strolling out of the living room and up the stairs.

It wasn't that they weren't pleased – after all, they'd made the decision for Jenny to stop taking the pill – but in retrospect she'd been totally unrealistic. Carried away by owning their own house, by being married. "Playing grown-ups" she knew Eileen called it, behind her back. It galled Jenny to think that somehow she was right.

And because she felt like this – the doubt, the terror – Jenny didn't expect to feel the sense of complete and total panic that hit when she noticed that she was bleeding when she went to the loo in work, three weeks after taking the positive test.

In the back seat of the black cab, Jenny shivered – partly involuntarily and partly because she was absolutely freezing. She noticed suddenly – as if waking from a daze – that she'd forgotten to put on her coat, such was her rush to get to the hospital.

Luckily she'd remembered to bring her handbag, and she thrust some money at the driver outside the Mayberry. It took an age for him to give back her change. *Come on*, she urged, her stomach throbbing, occasional dull, stabbing pains assailing her. I could be losing my baby, she admitted to herself suddenly. She was at once flooded with panic. I *know* I'm losing my baby.

Jenny fidgeted and was about to give up and simply disembark without her change, when the taxi driver turned slowly, leaned through the hatch to the back seat and slowly counted out her change into the palm that she extended toward him.

"Five, fifty, seventy and five!" he beamed at her, filled with the joys of a sunny morning and the promise of spring despite the cold. "Mayberry Maternity Clinic," he announced, looking out the window at the destination while Jenny scrabbled frantically for her belongings. "Best of luck, love – have a great day!"

Fuck you, Jenny wanted to say. Do you think that every time you drop someone off here it's all storks and bouquets? My baby could be dead for all I know.

Distracted by her venomous thoughts toward the cabby, she skidded as she stepped down from the taxi step onto the kerb. With a gasp she righted herself, paused for a second and then began to walk.

Without looking left or right she scurried across the pavement toward the façade of the cream-coloured, modern building that stood in its own piazza, surrounded by fountains. "We pay for the best," Ed had said. "We have the money, so we pay for the bloody best and make sure this goes right."

Well, it *isn't* going right, thought Jenny, crunching through a leftover patch of snow from the previous week's heavy fall, again distracted by rage.

It was then that she fell. So preoccupied with feeling angry was she that she failed to notice the ice across the shaded steps of the building. Before she was able to stop herself, she went down, her feet flailing underneath her and her hand grabbing frantically at the handrail but to no avail. Jenny fell square on her bottom, hitting the ground with a thump and jarring her coccyx, her teeth slamming together on impact. She was stunned silent for a moment, reeling from the shock. Suddenly, incapable of doing anything else, she started to cry.

What was the point, she sobbed to herself, feeling sore and strange and shocked. What was the point in rushing toward that door when the baby had to be dead? It was her own fault. Her just desserts. She hadn't wanted it enough at first and now she'd killed it.

It was the taxi driver who appeared from behind and helped her up. Jenny felt limp as he picked her up, holding her under her armpits, all the time clucking soothingly: "Are you alright, love? Saw you from the cab – can you walk? Can you put your weight on that leg? Is anything broken?"

Just my baby, she thought helplessly. My baby's broken. And my heart. Snot bubbled from her nose as she started to cry loudly at the thought.

The taxi driver was joined by an elderly woman with a tartan shopping cart. Next, Jenny became aware of someone in hospital scrubs running down the steps of the building and taking her arm as he called for help. Between them all, they helped her up the steps and into the shiny new building.

As she entered through the revolving doors, another rush of bodies milled suddenly around her – a wheelchair was summoned from somewhere and thrust underneath her. Jenny protested that she was fine, and that she could walk and made all those helpless noises that she always made when she felt someone was putting themselves out for her. But inside she felt like she was only watching. Like she was outside her own life, looking in, but not really there.

The examination room was warm, although she still shivered from a combination of cold and shock as she lay on the tissue-covered bed. The doctor stood with his back to her, fiddling with the screen on a monitor which was affixed to a complicated-looking scanning machine. When he turned to face her, his hands were gloved and the jelly that he spread on her stomach was cold. Jenny gasped.

"Sorry now, this will be a little bit cold," he said belatedly, applying his small scanning device to her skin, tugging down the waistband of her trousers before looking back at the screen.

Jenny lay there with her eyes closed. *I could just sleep here*, she thought suddenly. The room was dark and cosy, and it was nice to lie down. She could just pretend that none of this was happening. That she wouldn't have to get into a gown and into a bed and maybe have them do horrible things to her. What was it that they did in these circumstances? She took a deep breath to quell the panic growing again inside her. Just stay here, she thought. I just want to stay here. I don't want to see what he's going to show me.

"Now, we're not sure how far the pregnancy has progressed, Mrs Mycroft," said the doctor, concentrating on the screen and pressing the scanner more firmly into her stomach, putting pressure on her bladder. "And quite often at this early stage – if you're right about the date of your last period of course – it's not possible to see a heartbeat . . ."

Jenny forced herself to feel numb. Here it came. Here was the confirmation that it had happened.

". . . but by my reckoning, you're about seven weeks gone and the baby is showing a very steady beat there. Have a look yourself."

Jenny couldn't stop herself. Dizzy, yet entirely focused, she sat up suddenly, propping her elbows underneath to support her. The small screen showed a blob, and in the centre of it, a blinking dot. Steadily pulsing up and down rapidly. A blinking dot. A heartbeat.

"*My baby!*" gasped Jenny. She didn't know where that had come from. She had been trying her best not to think of it as a baby. She couldn't allow herself to think that it was a person – that it could be another human being. But as she saw the pulsing, moving dot, she whimpered, and sniffed loudly, unable to contain herself.

The doctor smiled. "I know, it can be very emotional the first time, but what I can tell you is that so far, so good. It's very early days, however, Mrs Mycroft, and pregnancy at this point can often be in the lap of the gods."

Jenny knew that. She wasn't a fool. Hadn't she *expected* to lose it? Hadn't she been sure that this couldn't be happening to her? She gazed at the screen as, all too soon, the doctor turned it off and hung the scanner on a hook below it. He was businesslike as he handed Jenny some thick blue tissue to wipe her stomach.

"But the bleeding . . ." began Jenny. "The cramps . . ."

"All very common at this stage of pregnancy," said the doctor, if not reassuringly, at least in a tone of voice that indicated this was a question he had answered many times before. "It's just your uterus stretching to accommodate the growing foetus. If you experience bright red bleeding then come straight back to us. That might not be such good news if it were to happen."

Relief washed over Jenny. She wanted to lie back down and cry a little more. To recover – no, to *savour*. She realised the doctor was waiting for her to leave, however, standing expectantly by the edge of the bed. Jenny duly swung her legs awkwardly over the side and slid herself off, at the same time trying to do the buttons up on her jeans while still holding the blue paper.

"Em, thank you," she said. It seemed inadequate after what she had just seen.

The doctor helpfully took the tissue from her hand.

"This is your first baby, is it?" he smiled.

Jenny managed a weak smile in response as she fixed her clothing. The base of her stomach felt sticky and uncomfortable where she hadn't managed to wipe off all the gel.

"Look, don't worry," the doctor said, placing a hand on Jenny's arm. "There's a strong heartbeat so, like I say, so far so good. Now make an appointment at the desk outside to come back for a scan in six weeks or so and we'll get an exact due date. And get yourself a coat and a hot cup of tea and take things easy. But not too easy – there's *nothing* wrong, so there's no need for you to do anything other than get on with your life normally. Read a baby book or two and find out what's going on. And above all, stay calm, Mrs Mycroft. And get plenty of sleep. You're going to need all your reserves. You're going to have a baby."

1999

Jenny

*And on the first of September that year you were born, I remember,
as I sit in the rocking chair in your room and watch you. Beatrice
Rose Mycroft. Bee. My Baby Bee. And as I held you in my arms
that night, for the first time, I knew that I could never leave you.
That you're mine. That you're me. A part of my very body. The sum
of my soul. And I still can't leave you, my precious little girl. I
cannot go anywhere. I cannot miss a second of you. My God, but
I didn't think it possible for a heart to ache this much.*

*When I watch you with your dad, when I see you play together,
it's just like I'm in the room with you, soon to be allowed to take
part in the game. I watch you laugh with him, my precious little girl
– you barely even think of me any more, barely remember that
there was once a lady who adored you. That you called 'mummy'.*

*I watch you both, and for a second I feel – no, I'm sure – that
I will be able to reach out and grab you in my arms and pull you
to me, to feel your skinny arms fold about my neck, to feel your
hair against my cheek, to feel your head in the crook between my
chin and my shoulder, where you belong. But I can't. I will never
be able to touch you, to hold you, to smell you, to kiss you ever
again, for all eternity – at least not that you will know. You will
never know me, my Baby Bee. I will never be able to show you this*

overwhelming love that engulfs me, that makes up my actual being. I am made of love, Bee. And it's love for you.

Look at you. Deep asleep. Lying on your back, your leg slung over the side of your bed, your mouth open, your breathing steady. How different from the nights when you thrashed about in your sleep screaming because I was not there, because your dad wasn't good enough for you, because you wanted your mum. How could I have left you like that, Bee? I am tortured by the thought that it was my fault you went to that place of horrors. How I wanted to climb inside your head and throw those thoughts away, to smooth your little brow and wipe away those tears.

I long for it to just be the night when you were born, your dad gone home to get some sleep and you and I left alone for the first time in the hospital bed. How I tried to drink you in as you slept, like you're sleeping now. How I touched your tiny, perfect face over and over, traced the shape of your eyes, your nose, your ears with my fingertips. How I held you, how I breathed you as if I was trying to inhale you back into my body.

But I left you. Suddenly and without so much as a goodbye. Ran out the door without a second look back. I can't forgive myself for that, Bee. I left you once but I won't do it again, I swear. Don't worry. Mummy's here. And I'll take care of you now, my beautiful girl, my precious Baby Bee.

OCTOBER 1995

Ed and Jenny

Jenny couldn't believe her eyes. She had seen Ed proud in the past
– at Bee's birth a month before, at the première of *Grimlet Goes
Wild*, when he won his Toon Award – but she hadn't thought that
this moment would rank up there with those greats. He stood at the
front door of 17 Pilton Gardens, hands on hips, chest puffed –
struggling, she was sure, to conceal a broad smile as he watched the
skip being gently lowered onto the road outside.

"The day comes when every boy becomes a man," she had
whispered in his ear from where she stood behind him. "And this is
yours . . ."

Ed had batted at her gently without turning, his eyes firmly fixed
on the rusting, yellow container emblazoned with the stencilled
phone number of the supplier along its side.

"'My First Skip' – not sure where you're going to park for the
next few weeks, however," she remarked wryly, taking a step back
before he made contact as he batted at her again.

The skip clanged loudly on the pavement and Jenny pressed her
lips tight against the laughter that longed to escape as Ed winced at
the noise and inhaled sharply through his teeth.

He shook his head and watched carefully, making sure that the
final contact between waste bin and ground was smooth, before

turning back to look at his wife. "Plenty of room for parking out there," he grunted, indicating the road that ran outside the house, its trees ablaze with the golds and oranges of early autumn. He turned his attention back to the delivery driver as he climbed down from the cab of the truck and began to unhook the skip.

Jenny snorted. "Not out there, there's not!" she laughed. "You leave for work at the crack of dawn every day but, trust me, it's like motorway services out there by half eight what with all the builders and painters and plumbers and delivery men and everyone else's bloody skips! Most people on maternity leave are woken by their newborns – with me, it's the Gentrification Squad every morning! This whole road is being flooded under a tidal wave of *trendy*!"

It was Ed's turn to laugh and he scrunched his face into a gurn. "Eeh bah gum," he began, "in mah day, we din't *'ave* wallpaper. We licked a bit o' th'Arrogate 'Erald and stuck it to t'wall wi' spit . . ."

Jenny gurned back. "*Walls?*" she shrieked. "You were lucky! We din't *'ave* walls. We lived in an 'ollowed-out toadstool, all seventy-seven of us – and in t'morning we'd 'ave to fight off giant slugs what would 'ave our breakfast quick as look at us. And then we'd 'ave to walk eight thousand mile afore our shift down t'mine began . . ."

"But you know we were 'appy in them days though we was poor," finished Ed with a giggle, just in time to revert to his normal voice as the delivery man made his way up the short front path to the door to request his signature on a clipboard, throwing a puzzled glance at the tall redhead who stood further back in the hall, helpless with laughter.

Ed waved him off with a smile before turning back to Jenny, grinning broadly as she composed herself. He reached out and wrapped his arm around her waist, pulling her closer to him as they both peered out the front door at the sun-dappled road outside. He pointed his free hand along to where Pilton Gardens curved slightly, at a house where another skip had residence on the pavement.

"Claw-footed bath," he stated flatly and Jenny dissolved into giggles again.

Ed joined her. "Saw it going in yesterday morning as I was leaving for work," he said, pointing then to another house further along the street. "New carpets Tuesday. *Victorian Floors Company* Thursday. Who knows where *that'll* end? And as for next door . . ."

Jenny placed a finger on his lips, still giggling. "And now us," she added, lowering her voice to imitate his. "Skip Saturday. What's next? Solar panels on Sunday? Fishtank Heaven on Monday?"

Ed responded by looking back out onto the road with a proud smile. "Can I help it if I found us a house in London's hottest, coolest, hippest, fastest-growing suburb?" he said, squeezing her to his side.

"And we've lived quite happily here for ages without a skip!" she replied. "You are sending us into hell, Mr Mycroft. Builders and dust and noise and disruption . . ."

"And swatches," Ed added mischievously. "And you like a good swatch, don't you, Mrs Mycroft?" Jenny feigned indignation but it was true. She had – foolishly, she knew – insisted that the house renovations be postponed until after the baby's birth, until things had settled down a bit, but now that Bee was here even Jenny had to admit that the time had most definitely come to make the improvements that Ed had longed for since the day they had first turned the key in the lock.

The house was fine for the two of them, she knew – the rooms habitable, if old-fashioned. Ed's plans were ambitious, too – another reason that she had insisted they hold back. He wanted new wooden floors throughout – in some cases the original floors of the house could be restored and where that wasn't possible he wanted authentic replacements. There was practical work to be done – insulation, for starters. Even Jenny had to admit that the thought of heading into winter with a newborn in an uninsulated house was unappealing. There was also some roofing work and plenty of plumbing to be done.

The small dining room behind the living room was to be converted into a study, the kitchen extended out into the long garden to open up into a glass-walled sunroom which would house the new dining area, the two bedrooms on the first floor modernised and equipped with small en suites and then the attic converted into a guest room. The thought of it all made Jenny slightly breathless – the mess, the weeks of work, the expense – despite the fact that Ed assured her that all was fine. She just wasn't used to this sort of thing, she had to admit. When she had grown up, they had to make do and mend – put up with the wallpaper which had last been changed sometime in the late 1970s. Her dad was a practical man, not aesthetically minded in the least, and Jenny had always learned to treat money with extreme caution – to work hard, to spend sparingly, to save. She couldn't conceive of the speed and extent of Ed's renovation plan – she had never *done up* anything in her life – and it made her anxious to think that it would all be done in a single swoop – and the chunk that it would take out of their – his – savings.

Deep down, however, she was buzzing with excitement at the thought of it all. A new home. A modern home – *underfloor heating,* Ed had said – a brand-new kitchen – a *study*, for heaven's sake! And it was to be her job to decorate.

Smiling, she released herself from the crook of Ed's arm and took a step backwards to peer in through the living-room door, retracing her plans and ideas for the room in her mind while simultaneously being unable to envision it any other way than it was now, as it had been since they had moved in, with the floral wallpaper and bare floor where Ed had ripped up the hideously patterned carpet on their very first night there. She would keep it neutral, she had decided. Ignore the current vogue for bright and vibrant greens and yellows and terracottas. Instead, she would keep her base colours pale and bring it to life with cushions and curtains, keep it free of clutter and ornaments and Constable prints, such as the type favoured by Ed's mother.

Jenny's mind turned to the garden out the back – a much bigger space than she had anticipated. She had plans for that too. And for the dining room where she envisioned family meals – dinner parties even, although she had never hosted such a thing in her life.

Her thoughts were interrupted by a small cry and she made her way along the hall and down the three steps that took her to the kitchen, where Baby Bee lay in her Moses basket. Behind her, Jenny heard Ed finally close the front door and turn to follow her down.

* * *

It took months for the house to turn from building site to anything even beginning to resemble the cosy haven that it would become. But it happened. Soon the house fell silent from the constant hammering, the drilling, the bustle of builders. And soon Jenny was hard at work redecorating.

By the spring of 1996, when Jenny's maternity leave finished, she reluctantly prepared herself to go back to Movie Kingdom with the knowledge that she had done something really special. She had created a home.

As expected, of course, Ed's family had hated it. His sisters sniped about how dull it was.

"It's so *boring*, Ed," sniffed Betty, looking around with a curled-up nose. "I mean no one has magnolia walls any more. And how could you like it so *bare*? It's like a bloody prison cell. Couldn't you brighten it up or something? Put a bit of colour here and there?"

Diplomatically Ed ignored her suggestions, thinking of her ochre-orange kitchen walls and her surfaces cluttered with candle-holders, porcelain angels and baby photographs. Yet he snorted with laughter when Vicky joined in the commentary – the last place that she called home was a flat-share in Camden, which she simply used as a dosshouse while she lurched from party to party. It had been only a matter of time before she had slunk back to Eileen, disillusioned by independent living and the fact of having to pay rent. It was much easier, she had observed, if you lived a busy life like hers, to stay somewhere that was nice and clean – and where there was someone who *liked* doing your washing for you.

Jenny tried to keep the invitations to Ed's family as few and far between as possible, which she knew rankled with her mother-in-law as John Adams ate with Ed and Jenny every Sunday. It made her feel better to feed him at least once a week, she had explained to Ed. Made her feel less like she had *deserted* him. Ed always told her not to feel guilty – that she was a married woman with a child of her own, for heaven's sake – but years of worry, of being his primary caregiver, were hard to cast aside. A roast chicken here or a joint of beef there didn't make up for it, she knew, but the least she could do was make sure that her dad knew that she still loved him and that she wanted him around.

Ed's parents, on the other hand, were invited to join them only once every couple of months, more for them to see Bee than to enjoy Jenny's housekeeping. "The Wendy House," Eileen called 17 Pilton Gardens. Ed's mother didn't know that Jenny knew that. And that Jenny knew only too well that she still resented the taking away of her only son – her baby – to "play house". Eileen resented every part of Jenny, most of all the fact that Ed, at the age of twenty-five, was successful and well off – and that it was Jenny who was the beneficiary of it.

Because of this, she also hated that Jenny worked, doing what Eileen liked to call a "good job". But she would also have hated if Jenny quit the "good job", because then she would have been simply "sponging off" Ed. Jenny knew she couldn't win with her mother-in-law. "Landed on your feet, girl," Jenny was told after Bee was born. As if their beloved baby girl was the final part of some greater plan to hook a wealthy husband, as if she had been created purely for the purpose of ensuring that he couldn't escape. It was exhausting, Jenny had to admit, to constantly endure the resentment and suspicion of her in-laws. Always to be damned if she did, and damned if she didn't.

Ed, too, was well aware of it, even though he was better equipped, after years of practice, to ignore it.

"You could really show her, you know," he mused one Sunday morning, the remains of a cooked breakfast pushed to one side and a Sunday supplement spread out over the kitchen table.

"Hmm?" asked Jenny, bending down to wipe rusk from Bee's face.

"My mum," said Ed, sitting back and looking at his wife and daughter with a smile, at his constant source of pride. "If she annoys you so much you could really rub her nose in it if you went off and did something you were actually really good at."

Jenny straightened and regarded her husband with furrowed eyebrows. "Like what?" she asked, genuinely puzzled.

"I dunno. Something that you really loved – if you changed your career, I mean."

Jenny frowned. She hated this argument. It wasn't the first time they'd had it.

"But I *do* like my job," she protested, and turned away, back to the counter-top where she was making Yorkshire Puddings for her dad who was due in an hour.

Ed sighed heavily. "Come *on*, Jen!" he snapped. "We have this conversation a thousand times a year. When are you going to do what it is you actually want to do for the rest of your life? You can't stay in your bloody student job forever."

Jenny felt herself tense, felt her heels literally digging into her shoes. "I'm doing absolutely fine where I am, Ed. The money's good –"

"We don't *need* the money, Jen!" he protested. "The *Grimlet* sequel is out next month and –"

He stopped speaking suddenly as Jenny slammed a wooden spoon down on the granite counter-top and turned to glare at him.

"*All right*, Ed!" she said through gritted teeth. "I *get* it. You're a massive, bloody, roaring success. You're doing what you've dreamed of since you were a boy and I'm some sort of *loser* who doesn't meet your expectations."

Jenny turned back to the mixing bowl while Ed stared at her, open-mouthed. Silence reigned in the kitchen for a few moments, eventually broken by Jenny, her voice trembling. Ed felt his stomach sink. He'd gone and pushed this conversation too far again. He hated it when she cried.

"I see you when I meet your colleagues, or when we have to go to those work dinner things and meet your contacts. 'And what do you do, Jenny?' they ask, and you butt in and say that I work in the movie industry too, and then you brush over what it is I do and get immediately back to what it is *you* do. I'm an embarrassment to you, Ed. I don't know why you bloody married me."

Jenny's voice grew loud and Bee, playing on the floor, looked up at her mother, sensing that something was wrong. Her chin began to wobble and, although she seemed to try to suppress it, she couldn't, and a long wail came from her mouth, her eyes filling instantly with tears. Jenny pressed a hand to her own forehead and ignored her.

"Is that what you think?" said Ed in a small voice. "What you really think?"

Jenny shrugged, continuing with the food preparations. "It's the truth, isn't it?" she replied over her shoulder. She wanted this conversation to stop. And stop now.

Jenny jumped as Ed shoved his chair back noisily and bent to pick up his daughter who was by now sobbing. All the time he kept his eyes on his wife, watching her half-heartedly reach for a carrot and the vegetable peeler and begin scraping it directly onto the counter-top. He jigged Bee up and down, pushing her head gently into his shoulder where her wails became muffled, but no less intense.

"I can't believe you," he said softly.

Jenny continued to work the vegetable peeler furiously.

"I am so fucking *jealous* of you, Jen," he hissed. "You have talent dripping out of your pores – you always have done. But you're either too lazy or too scared to do anything with it. Since we met – we should *never* have met in fact. You should have been at bloody Cambridge but you wasted your place. A place I would have *killed* for!"

"I couldn't go to Cambridge," she snapped in response. "My dad –"

"*Balls to your dad!*" shouted Ed ferociously.

Bee jumped and resumed the crying which had almost stopped. Ed rolled his eyes at what he had just done, and shushed her again.

Jenny stopped with the vegetable peeler suddenly, her shoulders heaving as she took a deep breath and stared ahead of herself at the cream butcher-shop-style tiles on the wall.

Ed knew what her face would be like, her chin jutting outward, her eyes like steel. It didn't stop him however. "Your dad is a grown man and I think you going to Cambridge would have done him more good than every bloody Sunday dinner put together that you've cooked for him in your life. It might have made him appreciate you for one thing, and made him stand on his own two feet for another."

Jenny remained silent.

"And don't you think it would have made him proud to see you in a cap and gown, graduating? From *Cambridge*?"

Jenny tried to bite back the tears but couldn't. "*No*," she whispered. "He needed me here, with him. Not flouncing around a fancy college just for the sake of it. My degree from Darvill's is as good as anything I could have had from Cambridge."

Ed sighed again, exasperated. "Jenny, I'm not even going to continue to argue about Cambridge because you *know* that the whole Darvill's experience wasn't a patch on what you could have had – that they don't even belong in the same sentence. And as for your degree? Art History? How does that qualify you to make sure that there's enough bloody copies of *Goldeneye* on the shelves on Beech Road, and that the returns policy in the High Street branch is being adhered to?"

Jenny turned sharply. "Please, Ed, I'm good at my job – do we have to do this again?"

Ed stroked the back of Bee's head and lowered his voice as she nestled into his shoulder, sleep imminent. "Yes, we do, Jen. What about your wedding dress? It was beautiful – that woman walked up to us on the street outside the registry office and told you that she wanted one just like it. Why didn't you tell her you could make one for her, just like you'd made that one?"

"It was my bloody wedding day, Ed," retorted Jenny. "I was hardly going to offer my sewing services while my wedding photos were being taken, now was I?"

Ed shrugged as much as he could with the dozing child in his arms. "It was hardly Westminster Abbey, Jen, was it?" he said.

Her face grew red again but he continued.

"I've seen those little sketches you do," he blurted.

The redness in Jenny's face rushed to her cheeks. She'd thought she kept her notebooks secret.

"I don't know much about dresses but they're not shoddy from what I can make out. Why don't you ever follow up on them?"

Jenny puffed, her argument revived by being able to cast the notion aside. "They're just doodles – just something to pass the time."

"Right. Just doodles," he agreed sarcastically. "You can sew though – ever think of trying any of them out?"

"I'm too bloody busy with Bee and my job and this house to even think about stuff like that, Ed," she replied. She rolled her eyes to heaven.

"Precisely – this house! Look at what you've done here. What about interior design? You could do a course –"

"Oh Ed, just shut up. I've got a headache and my dad's here in an hour and nothing's ready," she whined, her hand again clapped to her forehead. "Just leave me be. Stop bloody bullying me to be what *you* want when I'm perfectly happy with what I am."

Ed stared at her. Slowly, he shook his head, sighed, and turned on his heel and left the room. He couldn't talk to her any more. Just couldn't do this again.

And instead of calling after him, Jenny stayed with her eyes clasped shut, wishing that the conversation had never happened. Wishing that he would leave her alone. Since they met, they'd been having this altercation in various different ways. Him nagging at her to design clothes, to study interior design. Her batting him away at every opportunity.

With a sigh, Jenny Mycroft wiped away the tear that leaked from her eye. The tear that signified how unhappy she was that they were arguing when everything was so perfect for them. Except it wasn't, was it? Jenny sniffed, and turned back to what she was doing for a Sunday lunch she no longer cared about. And she wiped her eyes with the back of her hand again because she was, deep down, so very unhappy because Ed was absolutely right.

1999

Jenny

I never let on to Ed, of course. Too stubborn to let him know he was right. But it was all in my head. I had it all in theory all right – in spades. My imagination would leap ahead, taking an Olympic-style long jump over planning, hard work and straight to success. Incredible success. Something like being Princess Diana's favourite designer, or the woman behind an Oscar dress that the whole world was talking about.

1996. Bee was barely a year old and I knew that I should take Ed's advice. To just bloody well listen to him – but I didn't, did I?

I bought a sewing machine. Bought a sketchbook too. And started to draw even more than I had before. Proper designs. Dresses. Mainly dresses. Beautiful, floating garments in colours like teal and sapphire, corals and baby pinks, buttery creams and asparagus greens. In silks and cottons – fitted at the waist, skimming the hips, fabric cut to flare deliciously when the wearer would turn or twirl. There wasn't much call for them back then, of course. Everyone clumped around in combats and parkas and cropped tops, piercing their bellybuttons, trying to look like All Saints.

I didn't do a single thing with them, however. Instead, I made it all about Bee. I immersed myself in her. Her every movement from the time she woke, through each feed, each nap, each game. I cooked for her, I washed for her, I made her my universe. And now, watching her as I am, as usual, from the rocking chair in her room, I am so glad that I didn't waste a second I could have had with her, even though all of that precious time was spent as a buffer against actually facing up to doing something with my life. I don't regret a second of it now, that her life was mine, her every breath one that I shared.

From downstairs, I hear Ed moving about, opening drawers, rustling paper. In an instant, I am there, in the living room. With Ed who has so far managed to hold it together tonight. He's been watching TV – some David Attenborough thing.

I watch him for a moment. He's sitting on his armchair, his habitual seat in the dark room. I stand behind him, wondering if he can feel me in any way – if he even has the slightest inkling that he is not alone. If he does, he doesn't let on.

He's sketching. As he often has, trying to come up with new ideas. I glance over his shoulder to see what he's been up to. It's a new character. A little dinosaur, wearing dungarees and with red hair. Underneath it, he's scribbled the word 'Jen-o-saurus'.

It's for me.

The pang of longing to be able to touch him hits me again. I watch as he flops the sketchpad onto the table and his pencil with it, which rolls on landing, making a quiet 'tick, tick, tick' sound as it rotates as far as the edge of the table and then disappears silently over it onto the rug beneath. Ed seems not to notice as he pushes himself out of the chair, taking a moment on standing to gently stretch, straining his neck away from his shoulders and rubbing the base of his back absent-mindedly. That done, he takes a step toward the far right-hand corner of the room. No sooner has he hit 'play' on the CD player but I am suddenly and completely transported back to the time that I had been contemplating only moments before. To 1996, when Bee wasn't yet a year old. When I kept house and played mum and wore trainers and sketched in secret lest Ed should find out and nag me even more than he did. When I deliberately hid the sketches because I was too afraid to do anything with them.

Ed skips through the tracks on the album he's picked until he gets there. To 'Wonderwall', of course. The song that meant something to everyone back then.

To us it was pacing the floors with Bee through a period she had where she refused to go to sleep alone. Ed played the CD in the room as he paced, I sang along to it as I nursed her. I long to feel again her head grow heavy on my shoulder as she eventually – and inevitably – succumbed to sleep as I crooned in her ear.

And at that moment, in the present, Ed closes his eyes and throws his head back, inhaling deeply, as if cleansing himself with a breath. I wish I knew what was in his head. Wish I could stand beside him and rest my head on his shoulder in turn.

And I wish, beyond wishes, that I hadn't been so scared. That I had fought off that all-consuming, crippling fear. The fear that kept the sketches hidden away from the world, the fear that had kept me out of Cambridge, the fear that made me turn inwards. The fear of getting it wrong, of being embarrassed, of feeling again like Penny Jenny – the poor kid with the second-hand uniform in school.

Because if I hadn't been so afraid then I might still be here with him. Just him.

And not anyone else.

MAY 1997

Jenny

For all that he was her husband's best friend, drinking partner, sporting competitor, best man and almost-brother, Jenny Mycroft knew very little about Guillaume Melesi.

What she did know was that she didn't really register on his radar. That he was very much Ed's friend, not hers, that if she vanished off the face of the earth, in fact, he would barely notice. When Guillaume was around, everything had to be about Guillaume – his interests, his experiences, his views, his opinions. There was certainly no room for anything that a drippy little pen-pusher like her could say to interest him.

Deep down, it suited her that since the autumn of the previous year he had been absent on one of his adventures. So when he finally arrived home and accepted Ed's invitation to a dinner party, dressed in traditional African costume, with his booming voice tinged anew with an affected accent, she groaned inwardly.

He was the first to arrive – Ed had asked him to come along a full hour before the rest of the guests and Jenny had answered the front door at his loud knock. He had completely ignored her as he'd entered, of course. Strutted past her, dressed head to toe in a peacock-coloured smock over matching trousers, a blue kufi hat on his tightly cut hair, dominating everything around him as he entered. On seeing Ed, his smile grew warm and the men embraced like long-lost brothers.

Ed's joy at seeing his friend after so long was palpable, and Jenny stood to one side, watching them slap each other on the back and share greetings as if she didn't exist. Guillaume's enquiries were addressed only to Ed, his tone haughty, reminding Jenny of how much she actually disliked Ed's best friend.

Guillaume wanted to talk at length about his travels. Two months in Paris "in the château of my grandparents" as he called it, followed by just shy of six more in Botswana and South Africa.

"I needed to reach my soul, mate," he told Ed as they opened a beer on the patio, the doors of the sunroom wide open where Jenny could overhear them as she prepared dinner in the kitchen.

"Needed to feel the voice of my people inside me."

Jenny sighed.

It was a scorching hot Friday evening, the start of the bank holiday. Jenny watched as the men became completely absorbed in conversation and, with a glance at the kitchen clock, decided to nip upstairs to freshen up.

Despite Guillaume's presence, Jenny felt the excitement of a summer evening as she headed back downstairs to prepare for the arrival of the rest of the guests. She knew she looked pretty and fresh, dressed in a sleeveless lilac sundress that just skimmed her knees. Her hair, still wet from the shower she had taken earlier, was held in a messy bunch by a clasp above the nape of her neck and she had applied only light foundation and a swipe of lip gloss. Bee was at Betty's for the night and Jenny felt prepared for the evening, relaxed and ready . . . and then, once tonight was finished, three days of freedom ahead and a scorching weather forecast. She loved bank holiday weekends.

What she wasn't prepared for, however, was the figure that stared up at her from the bottom of the stairs. Vicky Mycroft – dressed in the shortest of short black skirts, revealing deeply fake-tanned legs, with a sharp, glossy new haircut – glanced up at Jenny as she descended, stretching her burgundy lips into an insincere smile. To anyone who didn't know her, Jenny mused, she looked at first glance not dissimilar to Victoria Beckham. It was really only when she opened her mouth and started to speak that the impression of anything posh was well and truly banished.

"Vicky," said Jenny, finally reaching the bottom step and extending her hand to her sister-in-law, who was being helped from a black velvet bolero jacket by Ed.

"All right, Jenny," she replied, unsmiling and cocking her head slightly to one side as if it were a confrontation rather than a simple conversation. She made no effort to take the proffered hand. Instead, she glanced down at it as if to question what Jenny thought she was doing with it.

Jenny withdrew her hand and instead clenched her fists by her side, digging her fingernails into her palms as she saw Vicky's mouth twist into her trademark smirk that indicated a tiny victory. One up for Vicky.

Jenny took a deep breath as Ed brushed past her absent-mindedly and opened the door to the understairs closet where he hung the jacket.

"I didn't realise you were coming along this evening," continued Jenny. A statement rather than a question.

"Vicky rang when you were upstairs," said Ed, as if it sufficed as an explanation.

Jenny's expression remained stony, her eyes fixed on her sister-in-law, unsure of her next move.

"So just now, then?" she managed.

"Ain't a problem, is it?" Vicky cut in suddenly. "Ain't I welcome to come round my big brother's for a bit of nosh of a Friday night? Ain't no 'arm in that, is there?"

Jenny's mouth twitched.

"No. It *ain't*," she replied, unable to resist the sarcastic emphasis on 'ain't'. She had no idea where Vicky's accent came from. She had grown up in the same household as Ed, after all, yet persisted in speaking like a latter-day Eliza Doolittle.

Ed stepped back out of the understairs cupboard and closed the door, stopping to look from his sister to his wife, his face plastered with an unwitting grin. He clapped his hands together and rubbed them.

"Right then," he smiled. "Shall we go through? The sun is lovely on the patio."

Jenny sighed. He'd opened his first beer the instant he'd come in from work and was an absolute lightweight when it came to booze. Now, he was babbling. An indication that he had drunk enough to feel that all was well with the world and, most dangerously, that he liked his family. Jenny knew there was no point in pulling him aside at this point to castigate him for inviting Vicky.

Instead, she politely stood back a little and indicated that Vicky should follow her brother down to the kitchen and beyond into the garden.

Jenny allowed Ed and Vicky to walk ahead of her, observing Vicky's unsteady path as she negotiated the steps down to the kitchen with caution. Ed wasn't the only one who'd started early, she observed to herself and suddenly collided with Vicky's bare back as she made a sudden stop at the bottom step and turned with a glare, trying her best to maintain her balance.

"Here!" she barked, thrusting the bottle of Faustino which she held in Jenny's direction. "Make yourself useful. Open this, would ya?" And, with that, she turned again and proceeded to follow Ed unsteadily through the kitchen and out through the patio doors.

Jenny glared after her and rolled her eyes as Vicky reached the threshold between the house and garden and came face to face with their other guest, who had helped himself to another beer from the bucket filled with ice while Ed had answered the door.

"I don't think you've seen this man in a while," Ed said, indicating Guillaume who stood and extended his hand to Vicky. She grabbed it, as much for support as in greeting.

And then Jenny heard her voice change, from the hissing harpy who had ordered her to "make herself useful", to something that could pass for smooth.

"Guillaume, innit?" she responded breathlessly. "Ain't seen you round in a long time – been on holidays?"

Three hours later, Jenny was exhausted. The guests had arrived in a sudden burst and instead of the sedate evening that Jenny had planned, they all seemed in full bank-holiday party mode. The food had been consumed merely as soakage and, as dusk fell, Jenny glared at Ed as he reappeared through the kitchen doors with a tray of tequila shots.

She tried to shift in her seat. It was difficult when she was jammed in between Ed's new assistant, Tim, and Vicky, who stank of CK One, and whose voice was growing louder all the time.

Jenny glanced around the table at the company, trying to remember everyone's name. With Tim was a mousy girl called Emma. On the far side of Vicky sat a purple-haired woman called Bella and her girlfriend, Fran, who had consumed the lion's share of the bread and was now lustfully eyeing up the remains of the raspberry roulade. Ed, with his face growing redder by the minute, was squeezed in next to Dom, their wedding photographer, and his wife Tess. And then there was Guillaume. Ten of them, at the garden table and benches that could just about seat six. There was barely room to move.

As the evening progressed, however, Jenny found herself relaxing. It would be too much of a shame to stay anxious in such a setting. The garden smelled of fresh grass and night-scented stock and the occasional whiff of lavender floated in on the breeze. Suddenly, Jenny yawned and as she did so wondered if she could maybe get everyone to take their glasses further down the lawn in a while. She could pull out deck chairs and leave them to lounge around in the warm night. Maybe then it would get dark enough for her to slink off to what she realised was her much-longed-for bed.

She glanced around the table. At least everyone else looked like they were enjoying themselves. People sat close to each other, picking at leftover bread and cheese, the hum of conversation ebbing and fading as the evening drew in around them, softened by the glow of the candles she had arranged all around the seating area. The patio itself was lit with tall candles in storm lanterns, and coloured fairy bulbs glowed above their heads, strung around the edges of the sun parasol that still remained open over the table and into the branches of the magnolia tree just above.

After a time, Fran and Bella excused themselves from the table and strolled a short way toward the end of the lawn. Jenny heard the click of a cigarette lighter as they sparked up behind her. At the sound, and the first fragrant waft of marijuana, Tess, too, jumped to her feet with a "Ooh, do you mind if I join you?" and soon the gentle hum of their voices came from the direction of the plum tree in the corner, down near the rear entrance gate as the joint was passed around between the trio.

The movement away from the table of the women lessened the crush of bodies nicely and there was almost a palpable sigh of relief as the guests spread out a little further and claimed an inch or two more personal space.

Jenny turned her attention to Guillaume, who was sitting back in his chair, his eyes closed momentarily. She watched for a moment, drawn to the sight of lamplight from the French windows falling on his cheek. She observed him as he raised his glass to his lips and took a small sip, savouring the wine in his mouth before swallowing, his Adam's apple bobbing up and down with the motion. He had removed the kufi hat and the bright blue of his tunic contrasted with the dark brown of his skin in the fading light. Jenny jumped as Vicky's voice suddenly broke through the silence. She realised that for an instant she had forgotten that everyone else was there.

"So where you travelled to, Guillaume?" Vicky demanded loudly, picking up her glass, sloshing the liquid from side to side violently as she raised it to her already stained lips.

Jenny was unexpectedly annoyed by the way that Vicky mispronounced Guillaume's name. '*Gee-yum*,' she called him.

"Ed says you been away for a proper long time?"

Guillaume turned slowly, opening his eyes to look directly at Vicky. He didn't answer for a while, instead taking his time in leaning, replacing his glass on the table with his right hand while slipping his left into his pocket, and shifting his position slightly so that he could see her better.

"I've been to my homeland," he began, his voice deep and coated with wine. He spoke slowly. "To Africa."

Vicky stared back at him, taking advantage of the extra leg space to swing one bony knee over the other and push her chest out slightly.

"Was you doing charity work then? Helping the starving and the poor and all that?" she asked, swinging her foot slightly under the table. Jenny could feel the vibration underneath her on the bench.

Again, Guillaume stared for a moment before replying.

"I'm from Botswana originally," he explained calmly. "It was a journey of discovery, seeking out my roots, my family heritage. I also spent some time in Cape Town – my parents live there now."

Vicky responded by taking another slug from her glass. The leg-swinging grew more violent and Jenny resisted the urge to reach under the table and grab Vicky's knee to make her stop.

Vicky held her confrontational pose as she stared back across the table at Guillaume, trying to think of a response.

She didn't have to, as it happened. Ed, flushed from the beers and wine, piped up instead.

"Gui, man, tell Jen where you were staying and who else stayed nearby while you were there? You're gonna love this, Jen."

Guillaume looked at his friend for a moment and then at Jenny dismissively. She stiffened as he turned his attention to her. For some reason, she felt a little panicked. For a moment, she wished that she could be like Vicky, could draw herself upwards, set her jaw in a firm line, thrust out her chest. Instead, she glanced nervously at the others around the table who were staring at Guillaume, and sank slightly back against the cushion, wishing that she could sink further into it.

Guillaume looked down at his hands and then back at Jenny.

"I had the pleasure of seeing the Princess of Wales at a party while I was in Cape Town," he said dismissively, reaching again for his glass and swirling it against the candlelight before taking a generous swig. His face showed distinct disinterest in a response from Jenny.

Jenny coughed lightly and felt her cheeks colour. "Diana. Wow!" she managed, before focusing her attention on shifting in her seat. Without realising it, she sat on her hands. A spark of annoyance ignited in her at her own discomfort. At Ed for bringing it up. She loved Princess Diana. Pored over pictures of her. She couldn't help it – the woman fascinated her. So much so that she was in the habit of designing dresses with her in mind.

An awkward silence fell over the table, broken only by Vicky's voice after a moment. "So what's with the costume?" she said suddenly, pointing at Guillaume, a hint of tipsy laughter in her voice.

At that moment, the atmosphere changed again. Ed flashed his sister a glare which went unacknowledged. Jenny glanced at her from under her lashes – she was still too embarrassed by the awkward moment that had just passed to look up.

Guillaume, at whom the remark was directed, froze midway towards reaching for his glass. Slowly he raised his eyes to Vicky, his expression cold.

"This is traditional African dress," he responded in a low voice. "What on earth made you think it was a costume?" There was no humour in his tone – in fact it was filled with even more contempt than the glare he had given Jenny a moment ago.

Jenny looked at Vicky and saw her squirm slightly. Something in her relaxed, the heat taken off her for a moment. She secretly even began to enjoy it a little. Like when someone else in school gets into trouble and you're thankful it's not you, she thought.

"Well . . . it ain't exactly from Jack and Jones, now is it?" Vicky responded, showing no discomfort, staring brazenly at Guillaume who glared at her.

"No. It's not."

From the corner of her eye, Jenny saw Ed try to warn Vicky off with a long-practised look. The intended recipient, however, never even acknowledged it. Instead, she continued to return Guillaume's cold expression with defiance.

"Ed said your dad worked in an embassy or something, am I right?" she asked.

Guillaume nodded.

"So he's a diplomat, then?" continued Vicky.

Sometimes she did this, Jenny acknowledged. Showed that somewhere along the way she had actually listened, that something had gone in and that she had a deeper understanding of things than she let on. The fact that Vicky wasn't a quarter as stupid and inattentive as she came across was what made her dangerous, in fact.

"That's right," replied Guillaume, casting a glance at Ed as if to ask why exactly his sister was prolonging this moment.

There was something about the timing of the response when it came, about the exact beat on which Vicky delivered it, that turned the air electric for a moment. The guests who remained at the table felt it. There was a collective intake of breath. Even the smokers under the tree paused in their chatter for a moment and stared back at the scene.

"So he's a diplomat then," Vicky confirmed. And paused. "Not the fucking Lion King?"

There was silence for a moment. Jenny couldn't be sure but she thought she saw something run through Guillaume, like a bolt that hit him. She cringed, sure that he would launch into some attack, and then, knowing Vicky, she'd respond by standing up and shouting profanities at him, jabbing the air with her French-manicured nails, her accent slipping, her language growing even coarser.

Instead, he laughed.

With a slow rumble that started in his belly, Guillaume opened his mouth wide and bellowed. There was sudden relief in the air as the other guests nervously joined in – a feeling that a crisis had been averted. As if the king had forgiven the jester and wouldn't cut his head off after all.

And as Guillaume belly-laughed, throwing his head back, his broad shoulders shaking as he did, Vicky stared at him, as proud as Punch of herself. And she allowed herself a giggle, checking the others with a glance to ensure that they had witnessed it too. One up for Vicky, again.

And Jenny watched her as the expression grew into one of smugness, and her posture relaxed and became even more flirtatious as Guillaume's laughter subsided and he leaned across the table in Vicky's direction, catching her eye, suddenly interested.

Jenny saw the look that passed between them as Vicky copied him. And in an instant, she realised there was something there, that electricity flowed between them. And much as she didn't like her husband's best friend, and much as she didn't like her sister-in-law, she suddenly realised that what she didn't like the most was the prospect that something was going to happen between them. Jenny Mycroft was amazed to find that she didn't like that most of all.

NOVEMBER 1998

Jenny

There is a fanlight over the front door of 17 Pilton Gardens. And on winter mornings, when the sun hits a certain angle, it throws a beam of light down the hallway and onto the top step down to the kitchen. And it's here that I'm standing on a nippy November morning. A Monday. Watching my husband sit at the kitchen table.

And I am absolutely livid.

What on earth does he think he's doing? What was so hard about keeping it all together, if not for his own sake but for Bee's? She is in nursery. He drops her off every morning, regular as clockwork. And then comes back home and does this until it's time to pick her up again.

I want to hurt him. I try to stare so hard at him that I burn a message in through his stupid, thick skull. How could you be so foolish, Ed? How?

He looks up, suddenly. Looks straight at the beam of light that the fan-shaped window sends down the parquet tiles of the hall. Looks right at me. I wonder for a second if he can see me – I stare harder, think harder – I so want to talk to him right now. So want to smack reason into him and then hold his hand and talk and see if this can't be fixed somehow.

He doesn't look well. His eyes are bloodshot. He's still being ridiculous about sleep – I've gone past sympathy for him at this stage. It's been almost a year for heaven's sake. And he's got Bee to take care of. He can't just fall apart. Wander around like something undead – which, technically, from my viewpoint, he is – eating crap, not bothering to wash or clean his teeth or change his socks or anything.

He's unshaven, too, verging on having a full beard which makes him look like he's been held hostage somewhere for years. I'm married to bloody Brian Keenan. Or at least I would be if I wasn't in this stupid half-life place, whatever that is.

He looks back down at his coffee again. As if he thought he saw something, but didn't actually. That stupid, stupid man. With everything before him. All that success that he had when we met first, when we left college. All he had to do was doodle on a post-it and his bosses were turning it into a film franchise. For heaven's sake, before I died they had been talking about creating action figures from some of his characters. Collectibles.

So what's this? This before me. So far from an action figure as to be virtually compost? He's like a tree with damaged roots. A stump that's just letting the ivy grow all over it. This is my husband. Smelly and unshaven and tearful and broken.

And unemployed.

It would have helped of course if he'd been able to make it into work every now and again. He did make a start, I'll grant him that. Going through the motions, working every hour he could manage in fact.

And then he pretty much just stopped.

The crying in front of the TV got worse after a while. And he finally caved and gave up sleeping in our bed, dragging a duvet down to the living room – a duvet that he hasn't changed since Betty stormed round one weekend about a month ago and changed it for him, actually – and making the sofa his bed, leaving Bee to bump down the stairs on her bum in the mornings to find him there, telling him to "Wakey wakey!", not knowing or understanding, of course, that he might only have dropped off half an hour beforehand.

And then he took a holiday. Straight after Bee's birthday. Some time off, he told the crew at Brightwater. They were very understanding – how could they not be? Ed Mycroft? Newly widowed cash cow wants to take some time out? Take all the time you need, mate.

Except what didn't seem to get through Ed's thick skull was that they didn't mean it literally. He took the holiday – told them he was taking Bee away for a couple of weeks, off down to the coast, sea air, ice creams, cockles and mussels alive alive oh and all that. Except he didn't of course. He just hid out at home, dropping Bee to nursery each day as normal. Ignoring the phone. Ignoring his parents, his sisters – everyone.

Ed took a holiday all right. A holiday from the civilised world and when eventually the three weeks were up, he didn't feel up to it, he said. Had a little headache. So he took some sick leave. And still Brightwater said nothing. Told him that if he felt like it they could help arrange someone to talk to. A gentle nudge, despite the fact that they were giving him more breathing space.

And now, here we are, with winter approaching, and none of their nudges have worked. His boss, calling unannounced for a "little chat"; his mates from the office – Tim, for what he was worth – Gavin or the other one – the one with the little beard – Fred. One by one they were ignored or dismissed at the front door with the excuse that he was too busy looking after Bee at that precise moment. And of course when they came back, he was wise to them and hid.

I can't blame them, of course. You can't have an employee – even if he is your star employee – suddenly decide that coming to work isn't an option any more. They've called it 'suspended' but we all know it for what it really is. Fired. They did their best to help, after all.

But nothing can help this man. This helpless man with no job and a dirty beard and greasy hair that's skimming his collar.

And a little girl who is so helpless and who depends on him and trusts him and needs him and loves him.

So why can't he provide for her? Isn't she enough to make him want to go on? He was the strong one, after all. It's not like I was so amazing that he can't possibly manage without me. Especially not when I . . .

This isn't good enough! I long to shake him by the shoulders! How can he forget about Bee? He is everything that she has. He is all that she has. He needs money to feed her and clothe her – it's not good enough that she goes to nursery wearing the same clothes for days, little dinner stains appearing day after day until the staff there are kind enough to pretend that she's covered them in paint or spilled some water on them and then change her – usually into some other child's spare clothes. It's embarrassing to see her coming in the door dressed in something clean, something fresh.

Most of all, Bee needs an example. She needs someone to get up in the morning and dress himself in clean clothes and make her toast with jam and tickle her and get her to help him with the post like he did up until that day in June when that stupid magazine subscription reminder arrived; the subscription that I can never renew for a magazine that I barely even read. He'd managed to just about hold it together until then. Why not now? Why is it getting harder for him instead of easier?

Bee needs a dad, I think, forcing the thought at him with every limited resource I possess, in whatever being this is that I am. Forcing, forcing. Staring and looking and thinking and wishing.

And I knock the coffee cup over.

It's as much energy as I can muster. And that's all it is. Energy. And what use is it?

Oh, that I could muster up his job back! And his self-respect.

Ed gets a shock. He jumps backwards and looks around him and then at the cup, the contents of which are slowly draining over the side of the table onto the floor. And then at his hand. Which was nowhere near the cup, but it's the only way that he can make sense of it: that somehow he knocked the cup over himself.

I'm sorry, I think, and try to force that at him too, but I can't make thoughts appear in his head. Only useless things are in my remit nowadays. Mind you, that's all I was capable of when I was alive too.

Get it together, Ed, I think longingly. This mess has gone on far too long and I don't just mean since I died.

I watch as he slopes over to the sink and picks up a cloth. He has absolutely no idea what to do with himself, I realise. He is just existing. He is a shell, a shadow, a putty man instead of the artistic, vibrant boy-in-a-hurry that I married. I want that man back. For Bee's sake of course. She cannot have a putty man for a father. He cannot do that to her.

JULY 1997

Ed and Jenny

Jenny Mycroft leaned on the doorpost of her open back door and gazed out at her garden, listening.

It was ablaze with early July sunshine, the reds and yellows of her flowerbeds vibrant, the purples of the lavender borders strong against the greens. She inhaled softly and held the breath, allowing herself to tune in intently, to listen to the complete silence that surrounded her. Outside, there was the faint chirrup of birds, the buzz of bees around the lavender plants.

Inside, there was nothing. It was as if the silence were thick, as if it was in itself an entity. She held her breath until she could keep it inside her no more and then exhaled deeply before glancing at her watch. Eleven, she noted. Bee was in nursery; Ed in work; no one likely to call; no one nearby to call *to*. The house had been vacuumed, dusted, polished and tidied by half past ten. Jenny turned and swept the kitchen with her eyes. There must be *something* to do, she thought frantically, desperately trying to engage her brain. But nothing came. She sighed – a sigh which turned into a groan of sheer and utter boredom. Yesterday had been like this too, she remembered. And tomorrow would be as well . . . and the day after . . .

And she had no one else to blame for this except herself.

And Ed, of course. Getting his way as usual.

It had been a wet Thursday, she remembered. She had been delayed at a regional manager's meeting and had thought she would never be able to escape. The day had been marked with minor disasters: muddy *and* laddered tights, a broken heel tip, her hair in a frizzy mess from the rain. She couldn't find the hotel where the meeting was to be held and had entered the meeting room late, tugging her skirt down to try to disguise the ever-widening hole at her knee, to a stony response from everyone else who had made it on time . . . and . . . she had managed to mark the laminate meeting-room floor with a series of small, irreparable indentations from her untipped heel.

Jenny still cringed as she recalled it. Stepping back from the open back door and into her kitchen, she pulled a mug from the cupboard and spooned in coffee, blushing still at the memory.

It had been close to nine that night when she had eventually made it home and into the shower to wash away the day. Once in her dressing gown, she had sunk into the sofa and gladly accepted the tea that Ed made her. He sat beside her on the arm of the sofa.

"I mean, it wasn't as if my suggestions were completely without foundation," she ranted loudly at him, her voice filled with the outrage that she knew she should have expressed in that stuffy meeting room. "I told them *expressly* that in the past week we'd had specific requests for *La Cage Aux Folles* and *Cyrano de Bergerac* in our branch alone and that our other branches were getting similar enquiries."

Ed suppressed the urge to giggle at how high-pitched her voice was growing with each sentence. He rubbed her back in a slow, circular motion in an attempt to calm her.

"And do you know what he said?" she hiccuped, turning to face her husband full on.

He banished the smirk, but with some difficulty. "What?" he queried softly.

"That stupid *idiot* Reynolds from Head Office looked at me like I'd run over his cat with a lawnmower and told me that there was no need to clutter up space with 'foreign muck' – he did the inverted commas with his fingers – can you believe that? He announced right there and then – representing a chain of video stores – that *no one* likes to read and watch a film at the same time and to direct enquiries like that to the appropriate English-speaking version. To *The Birdcage* and bloody *Roxanne*!"

Ed couldn't hold it in any longer. He suddenly laughed aloud, raising his hand in an apologetic gesture. Jenny opened her mouth in an expression of complete disbelief and whacked him, not so gently, on the arm.

"I'm sorry!" he spluttered. "I'm so sorry!"

Jenny looked close to tears again. "Not even *you* take me seriously, Ed," she wailed. "Why do I bloody bother?"

Ed settled, and looked down at her from his perch on the arm of the sofa with a bemused grin. "But that's just it!" he said. "You *don't* have to bother! You don't have to *do* it!"

Jenny frowned and looked away from him.

"You don't have to do it, you know that," he repeated. "You *know* that we're fine for money – please don't accuse me of gloating when I say that – I don't want to have The Row again. This time, just hear me out."

Jenny closed her mouth on the protest she had been about to make. In any case, it was a half-hearted one. She was tired, sore, humiliated and putty in his hands.

"Why don't you give up that awful job with that stupid name-badge and having to work on the counter at lunchtimes so that the part-time college kids get to go to Pret for an hour, and then you get stuck with a sandwich at your desk because you're a regional-manager-slash-dogsbody and you have all the paperwork to do? Why don't you just make a change? I mean, we're *lucky* – we have money – we wouldn't have to take Bee out of nursery and that would leave you all day to do things at your own pace – no pressure – to figure out what it is you want to do, whether it's finally designing stuff or house interiors or stuffing envelopes – I won't interfere. At the very least, why not take a month off and think about it, for heaven's sake? They owe you a ton of leave and you don't owe them a single thing."

Ed let a silence hang in the air for a moment, suppressing the excitement that he felt growing inside him. He could see Jenny softening, relenting. She had never done that before.

"I might like to spend a bit more time with Bee," she replied quietly, avoiding Ed's gaze as she said it.

Ed gauged his timing, waited a moment before speaking again. "You'd never have to wear *tights* again . . ." he said hesitantly, a slight smile to his voice.

She smiled back, catching his eye for a second before looking away again, her face filling with mock indignation. "But, Ed, tights are so lovely and comfortable and sexy to boot – why would I never want to wear them again?" She paused and then said, this time almost playfully, "I suppose I *could* just give up, couldn't I?"

Ed nodded enthusiastically. "Do it," he urged. "Start afresh. New job or new career or whatever you want to do – just do *something*. Learn to drive or do a course in origami or get some pigeons or run a flea circus – just get out of bloody Movie Kingdom and start your life – Jenny's life! Not our life, or Bee's life or my life – *your* life!"

He reached out and took Jenny's left hand, which was nearest to him, and squeezed it. "You're brilliant, you are," he said, gazing down into her eyes.

She found it hard to return the stare, found it almost too intense.

"You're brilliant at something – we just don't know what it is yet. So let's find out, eh?"

She looked back at him, searching his face for a hidden agenda. "No pressure, you said," she began.

He nodded emphatically.

"And I do it at my own speed, right?"

Ed crossed his heart and hoped to die, his forefinger held up in the air. "Tortoise or hare, whatever works," he assured her.

Jenny nodded then, slowly at first and then more emphatically. "I'll do it then. Will I? Will I do it?"

Ed nodded back vigorously, beaming as she spoke.

"I'll get out of there. Finally. Although what on earth will Dad say? He's from the 'get a job, keep a job' school –"

Ed interrupted her before she began to talk herself out of the decision. "Look – why don't we open a bottle of champers? Go mad on a school night? Celebrate making a change?"

And that was how it happened. That was how Jenny made her decision to leave the only job she had ever known and strike out on her own.

She poured the water from the kettle onto the coffee grounds and stirred, glancing out the back door at the garden again, the waft of instant coffee filling her nostrils.

And here she was – notice given, holidays accounted for, a swift drink down the Merry Maiden on her last day and a card filled with grubby fivers from the whip-round.

And now this.

A clean house, coffee breaks whenever she wanted, Richard and Judy on tap should she choose to watch . . .

And silence.

And the sinking sensation that she knew she should be doing something – she just had absolutely no idea what.

And, as did many other things in her life that she didn't know, the idea scared her. As the days stretched out in front of her, and with them what she perceived as the rest of her life, empty and silent and punctuated by coffee and daytime TV, Jenny Mycroft was filled, yet again, with fear.

AUGUST 1997

Jenny and Guillaume

Standing at her kitchen worktop, carefully assembling a cheeseboard, Jenny cringed – no – *winced* as the cackle cut the air yet again. Each time, there was a new added layer of hysteria, like Vicky was ramping up her 'amused' factor to fully prove to Guillaume, without a shadow of a doubt, that he was the funniest guy in the universe. And he, in turn, had seemed unable all evening to remove his hand from Vicky's knee, eventually snaking an unmistakable route up her thigh, taking her tight lycra skirt with it as the second bottle of red was finished. Jenny was glad of the few minutes' respite from the scene.

The whole thing was Vicky's idea. "Couples night," she had gone so far as to call it. "A bite and a bottle round at Ed 'n' Jen's."

"They've been going out over a month, now, Jen," Ed had shrugged as Jenny sulked furiously over the very idea of it.

"If they're going to be a proper couple then it's inevitable we'll be spending time together – I mean Gui is my best mate and Vicky's my sister – we can hardly just ignore them."

I could, Jenny thought firmly. I could quite happily let them get up to whatever it was they wanted, wherever they wanted and as often as they wanted – just so long as it wasn't anywhere in my immediate vicinity. Or preferably within a ten-mile radius of me, in fact.

As she carefully arranged some strawberries next to the Brie which was oozing perfectly, Jenny tried to figure out which of the pair she disliked more. Guillaume with his superior air and wandering digits, or Vicky in her tiny skirts with her shiny bob, cackling with that throaty voice that could shatter glass.

As if on cue, Vicky brayed with laughter at something Guillaume said in the adjoining room and Jenny dug her nails into her palms. She stayed that way until the laughter died away, and then took a deep breath before fixing a smile on her features and picking up the cheeseboard and cheese knives. The grin unmoving, she climbed the steps out of the kitchen and padded along the hallway toward the living room.

Jenny pushed the living-room door shut behind her with her shoulder and then knelt to place the heavy cheeseboard on the coffee table in the centre of the room, suppressing an urge to 'tsk' loudly as she noticed the glistening red ring on it where Vicky had plonked her wineglass directly on the dark wooden surface, completely ignoring her coaster. Jenny resisted the urge to wipe it straight away but itched to attend to it. It went against her upbringing to wreck something expensive through sheer thoughtlessness. She was suddenly unable to tolerate it and picked the glass hastily off the table surface and replaced it on the coaster, hopeful that the speed she had worked at would mean Vicky hadn't seen her do it. Jenny glanced up at her sister-in-law to check, and blanched as she was greeted by a cold and hard stare in response. She had been observed.

Vicky glared directly at her, her cheek twitching with barely perceptible involuntary rage for a second before suddenly transforming into one of relaxed enjoyment.

"What's this then?" Vicky bellowed suddenly, rapidly uncurling her legs from underneath her where she had tucked them on the sofa the better to fold herself against Guillaume's shape. "*Cheese*, Jenny? Are we having *cheese* then?"

Jenny stood up again and took a step back toward her armchair, watching her sister-in-law nervously as she did so before glancing at the men. Vicky's comment – and the inherent sarcasm, although for the life of her Jenny couldn't understand what fault she could find in a *cheeseboard* – had gone unnoticed by Guillaume and Ed who were deep in a discussion about football.

"There's a cheeseboard ready on the coffee table, folks," Jenny addressed her husband and his friend timidly, still very much aware that Vicky's stare was burning into her. There was something so unsettling about Ed's sister and her warped attitudes.

"*Gee-yum!*" barked Vicky, nudging her boyfriend with a sharp elbow. "*Cheese!*"

He ignored her, he and Ed laughing loudly, trying to outdo each other with witty retorts as they squabbled about the merits of Chelsea versus Man United.

"*Gui!*" cried Vicky suddenly – a particularly raucous shriek – her face distorted as she barked for attention.

It worked. Guillaume turned away from where he had been fully engaged with Ed, his face puzzled. Vicky glared at him, her teeth grey, her lips stained from the red wine as if she had been eating liquorice, her eyes narrowed into slits and her pointed nose scrunched up in outrage.

Jenny blinked and looked away, embarrassed.

Vicky extended a talon – painted black tonight – in the direction of the food. "There's cheese," she said bluntly, continuing to stare directly at Guillaume.

He, in turn, stared back for a second too long before following with his eyes the direction of her extended finger toward the cheeseboard and then back again to her pinched-up face.

Watching from under her lashes, Jenny knew that at that moment something in their relationship had changed. Something had passed between them that was barely noticeable, but it was a gearshift.

Guillaume nodded at Vicky who rearranged her features under his glare. The curl in the nose loosened, the snarl subsided, the eyes opened a little wider all of a sudden, as if to return her expression to what she thought was its original beautiful form. But still, there was a loud silence between them, an awkward electricity.

It took Ed to break it. Jenny wasn't sure if he did so intentionally or not but she couldn't have been more grateful.

"This looks great, Jen," he said, shifting position so that he was on the edge of his own seat, looking at the tray and rubbing his hands for emphasis. "Is that *Wensleydale*?" he asked, his attempt at the Wallace character even worse than usual. "*What a nice bit of cheese!*" he continued, pushing his upper teeth out and rolling his eyes.

Jenny cringed, but smiled at him gratefully for managing to change the vibe in the room.

"Man, that was a *shocking* Wallace!" announced Guillaume, finally tearing his gaze away from Vicky.

In an instant, Vicky's expression switched to one of dismay then to yet another one of simmering rage as she watched Guillaume turn his back on her.

Ed smirked back at Guillaume and slid off the couch onto his knees, walking the short distance to the coffee table on them before relaxing his bottom on his heels to peruse his favourite snack.

"There actually *is* Wensleydale," offered Jenny with a nervous laugh. "And some Brie and Red Leicester – that one you've got your knife on is a Somerset goat's cheese, Ed . . ."

"What's that one?" Vicky piped up, suddenly interested, leaning in earnest over in the direction of the board, her chest thrust provocatively outwards as always. She stole a sideways glance to check if Guillaume was watching. Instead, he was oblivious to her, holding a grape between his teeth while rotating it with his tongue as he waited for Ed to finish scooping soft Brie onto a cracker so that he could take his turn. She turned back suddenly to glare in Jenny's direction.

"Is it supposed to look like that?" she sneered. "All gone off and stuff? Isn't that *mould* on it? And what's that one with the red bits? Like *veins*? Like your legs'll look in twenty years I'll bet, Jen!" She laughed uproariously at her own joke, looking at her boyfriend and brother to join her, scowling when they didn't.

"That's a Stilton," replied Jenny quietly. "And the veiny one is a Port Wine Derby . . ." Her voice fell away as she realised that her sister-in-law wasn't looking for an explanation, but was mocking her yet again.

Vicky bent closer to the table and threw one bare leg over the other, leaning her elbow on her knee. She glanced again at

Guillaume who was mock-fighting with Ed, duelling childishly with their cheese knives over a cut slice of Leicester. Displeasure flashed across her features and she scowled.

"Only, well, a cheeseboard – it's a bit old-fashioned, though, innit?" she sneered, turning her attention back to Jenny. "A bit like what Mum wheels out at Christmas with a glass of Harvey's Bristol Cream – isn't that right, Ed?"

Her brother shrugged. "Suits me fine at Christmas too, sis," he said through a mouthful of oatcake and Stilton.

"Only I'd prefer something a bit *classier*, me," Vicky continued. "A bit trendier – like a mini-burger maybe, or a chicken satay on a stick . . ."

She was interrupted by a groan of pleasure from Guillaume and her eyes flicked away from Jenny in his direction, excited suddenly that she had said something that caused such a reaction.

He rolled his eyes as he savoured what he ate. "Man, I just bloody *love* goat's cheese! When I was back in South Africa, yeah? – I took a tour of the wine country – my God, but there was this winery just outside Paarl – they had their own herd, man – produced *the* most amazing cheese I have ever tasted. There I was, sitting outside on their sun terrace, with a glass of their own Chenin Blanc, eating this cheese – Pearl Mountain Winery – that's what it was called. Ay-*may*-zing. You gotta go, man."

Ed hung on his friend's every word, nodding in approval. Vicky tore her glare from Jenny's direction and stared at the two men, all of a sudden looking blank, as if she had been stonewalled, excluded forcibly from a club that she could never join. Jenny watched her, suddenly realising what the problem was. Vicky was trying to break into a circle that was unbreakable.

The tight circle made up of Ed and Guillaume.

It was then that Jenny also realised that Vicky couldn't bear for Guillaume to pay attention to anyone but her – and since they had arrived, Guillaume had slipped into his familiar way of being completely wrapped up in Ed. Of course. Jenny had realised a long time ago that the two men were best left alone but Vicky didn't have this insight. And she was jealous.

"Oh, here we go," she sighed dramatically. "Africa, Africa,

Africa – always on about Africa, aren't you, lover?"

If she hoped the endearment would draw Guillaume back to her, she couldn't have been more wrong. Instead, it was as if her mention of Africa – as if intoning the magic word three times – somehow reminded him of something and he turned his attention even further away from her to grab his coat which was slung behind him on the sofa.

He held it by the collar in his left hand and rummaged through the pockets with his right, fumbling and searching everywhere until he retrieved his prize.

"Man – Ed, you have *got* to listen to this – it's the one I was telling you about, yeah?" he said, thrusting a CD case at his friend who stuffed a cheese-laden cracker into his mouth, his cheeks bulging as he wiped his hand on his jeans and accepted the case.

"What's this?" he muttered, spraying crumbs down his polo shirt and flicking them off absentmindedly with one hand while examining the proffered gift with the other.

Jenny watched Vicky as her face contorted at a rapid rate. Disgust at the crumbs, disappointment and frustration as Guillaume again took the conversation in a direction away from her. She slumped back onto the sofa and stared into space, her expression sullen.

"What *is* this, mate?" Ed asked, holding the case close to his eyes at first and then at an exaggerated distance to emphasise the fact that he couldn't make out his friend's handwriting on the amateur recording. Guillaume ignored him, pumped with passion about his subject.

"Tuareg music, man, from Mali. I picked it up when I was in Africa."

Vicky's eyes rolled dramatically and she tutted loudly, to no avail.

"These guys are rebels and refugees – just listen to the rhythms – that beat – this is the music of the desert, my friend. Put it on. *Put. It. On!*"

Ed acted instantly, pushing himself to his feet and shaking out the pins and needles before crossing to the CD player on the bookshelves behind where he had been sitting. He pressed 'play' and the room was instantly filled with sounds of drums and guitars, the beat infectious. Guillaume threw his head back and laughed aloud, clapping his hands in obvious joy. Ed, perennially reserved, stood listening, his chin in his palm while his index finger beat out the time on his cheek.

"Don't encourage him," Vicky hissed suddenly at her brother, drawing her feet back up sharply underneath her on the sofa and arranging her seating position so that she faced away from Guillaume. She looked disdainfully over her shoulder at him as he moved his arms, eyes shut, in time with the music. "All he wants to talk about – bloody Africa." she hissed, not once taking her eyes off him. Guillaume remained oblivious. "So in love with Africa he's missing all the good stuff under his nose here in London!"

Guillaume continued to ignore her. Jenny glanced from Vicky to him and back again, remaining silent.

"So where did you get all this lot, then?" demanded Vicky, turning her attention back to Jenny. She pointed at the now depleted cheeseboard – a mess of crumbs and grape-stalks and strawberry hulls. "Your *cheeseboard*, that everyone seems to love so much. Where might one get such amazing *cheese*?"

Vicky glared again at Guillaume, and then back at Jenny whose eyes widened as she tried to figure out if Vicky was making some sort of joke. It was soon clear that she wasn't.

Jenny cleared her throat and looked nervously at Ed before replying. "I bought it all today – there's a market nearby on Wednesday mornings – all this stuff is organic and fresh from people's farms and stuff . . ."

"And how was you able to get to a *farmer's market* on a Wednesday morning? Pull a sickie, did you?" demanded Vicky. "That's hardly responsible, is it? Fine way to go about losing a job, if you ask me."

Ed interrupted her from his standing position behind Jenny in front of the CD player. "Says the girl who's managed to hold down her current position for a whopping – what is it, three months now?"

Vicky glared at her brother. "I work in retail, Edmund," she sneered. "It's a field where there is high personnel turnover."

Ed snorted. "You mean you've never stuck at anything any longer in your life." He looked back at Guillaume. "Gui, I'm not sure I'm crazy about this stuff . . ."

"Actually I've given up work," blurted Jenny suddenly, regretting it instantly. She hadn't wanted Ed's family to know yet, not until she'd figured out what she was going to do next. It had only happened a couple of weeks before, after all.

Vicky reacted as if she had been shot. "You've *what?*" she demanded.

Jenny threw another glance at Ed. "I've – *we've* decided that I should take some time out," she muttered quietly.

Vicky turned suddenly red and pushed herself upright on the couch, all the while glaring at Jenny.

"To do what exactly?" she demanded. "Sponge off my big brother? My mother's always said this was your plan, what with our Ed doing so well for himself. She was right – she knew this day would come and here it is. Little Miss *Retain her Independence* shows her true colours at last!"

It was Ed who stepped in. "Steady on, Vicky," he said, in disbelief at his sister's outpouring of vitriol. "It was my idea actually. Jenny didn't want to give up work – but we decided together that it was the best thing for us and Bee. It's nothing to do with you, or Mum for that matter."

An awkward silence fell across the room, apart from the jangling guitars from the CD player. When it eventually broke the silence, Guillaume's voice was rich and positive. And directed at Jenny.

"Congratulations," he said firmly. "I think that's absolutely bloody great news. I *love* it when I hear about people shaking off The Man, striking out on their own."

"It's great, isn't it, Gui?" agreed Ed.

"Absolutely bloody fantastic, man. Breaking free from the shackles and all that."

Jenny blushed.

"So what you gonna do with yourself then, if you're having a '*break*' as you call it," spat Vicky.

Buoyed by Ed and Guillaume's support, Jenny felt more able. "Oh, I don't know just yet," she shrugged nonchalantly. "Learn to drive, probably. Do a course in origami – get some pigeons, run a flea circus – who knows?" She finished the sentence with a grin and a glance over her shoulder at Ed. They exchanged a smile.

"A flea circus! *Loving* it!" guffawed Guillaume suddenly, clapping his hands loudly. "Seriously, Jen – hats off! A toast to you!" He picked up his half empty wineglass and raised it in her direction, keeping his eyes fixed firmly on her as he took a generous slug.

Jenny smiled back, making rare eye contact with her husband's friend. An eye contact that she suddenly found difficult to break. For a split second, she felt the others fade from the room, the music go quiet and her stomach lurch in a disconcerting way.

The spell was broken by Ed clinking his glass loudly against Guillaume's.

"See, Jen? I told you that *some* people would agree with me that it's bloody great, didn't I?" he said, taking a moment to direct a pointed glare at his sister who limply lifted her own glass in toast and then made a point of slamming it down again on the table, deliberately avoiding her coaster yet again.

"Unlike, however," Ed continued jokingly, "this bloody music! Sorry, Gui, but it's a thumbs-down from me. I'm in a little bit of a Radiohead mood, actually, if that's okay with everyone?"

Without waiting for an answer, Ed crossed back again toward the CD player and pressed 'eject' for the second time. Vicky groaned loudly but Ed ignored her and went about inserting *OK Computer* into the vacant CD holder and pressing 'play', before turning sharply and flicking Guillaume's CD rapidly back in the direction of its owner who made a fumbled catch. Guillaume replaced the CD into the case that Ed had left on the coffee table and smiled at Jenny.

"Does he make you listen to this miserable droning all the time?" he beamed jokingly, nodding at Ed as he did so, holding her in the same, intense stare as before.

"I like Radiohead," mumbled Jenny awkwardly, trying her best to ignore the sensation of heat as her colour rose, like a schoolgirl being spoken to by the teacher on whom she has a crush. She didn't know what possessed her to suddenly take a deep breath and fix

Guillaume with a stare of her own. "But I liked your music too," she said boldly. "A lot, in fact."

Guillaume held her stare and responded by smiling a lazy grin – like a sleeping tiger, she thought. And Jenny smiled back. Not quite sure why, but not quite able to stop herself either.

1999

Jenny

And that was how it began.

I'm alone upstairs just now. Ed is in the kitchen, preparing lunch, and Bee is playing in her room. I can hear her singing to herself. She gets that from me, I think. At least, I like to think that. Being dead, as I am, I like to grasp what I can that connects me to her – apart from the genes. As she gets older, I see that all of her mannerisms seem to come from her father. Starting a sentence with a long 'well . . .' when she can't think of what to say next, the way she rests her chin in her hand to think or to listen intently. There is little left of me.

I was a choir girl all the way through school. Until my mum died and I couldn't do it any more. It made me too emotional to carry on so I gave up. Made me think of her so much that I couldn't sing a note for fear that I'd cry – and I had to stay strong. For my dad, myself, for everyone really. It pained me when people would sympathise with me – when they'd make that 'oh-my-God-I'm-so-sorry-for-your-loss' face. It embarrassed me – worse, it made me feel sorry for them. They were right – it was my loss, not theirs. So it shouldn't make them feel bad. And I'd be at pains to let them know this. Would cast it aside with a flick of my hand, reassure them that it was fine, that I was fine, that it was all hands on deck at home and sorry, no, I couldn't go to the disco, or get to hockey practice any more or pop down to the precinct on Saturday. I couldn't bear being felt sorry for, being watched sympathetically in case I fell apart – the spectre at the feast. Which is ironic, considering my current status.

When Mum died, I had to change my priorities. I had a house to look after, and my dad – not that my schoolmates could really understand that – but I just couldn't drop everything at the slightest invitation. So people stopped asking.

So when I got to college, to Darvill's, I had a blank slate, a fresh start. And people there took it that this was just the way I was, and left me to it.

Such responsibility I had. It must be why I found it easy to look after Bee. Well, since I'd lost mine, I'd had to be a mother, didn't I? A sort of mother to my father. Which wasn't right – but if I didn't do it, then who would have? And all of my life, up until that summer – the summer before I died – it hadn't bothered me. I wouldn't say that I was happy, but I was okay – willing to accept that this was the way that things were. I was fine with the missed nights out with friends – girlie nights of nail-painting and too much cheap wine – the dates that never happened.

I was fine with the fact that my own company was the best I could hope for.

Unaware, truly, of how much I had missed.

Which was maybe why I didn't fight those feelings that hit me like a freight train that summer. I would have dismissed them out of hand before but maybe there was something different about that year – something I couldn't control, something I didn't expect – the wind blowing a certain way – or something I saw on TV or in a newspaper that triggered my subconscious into realising that pieces of my life were void and blank. Maybe it was just pent-up normal teenage-girl stuff that I had denied for years that needed to escape – a rush of hormones, or passions or desires or whatever it is that girls are supposed to experience, that I had sat on, like an overfull suitcase, while I kept house and tried to keep my father sane. Maybe that was it. Maybe I had just denied the insanity that screamed through my bones at having to take on all that responsibility because my surviving parent had relinquished his? Maybe it was all of those things that finally bobbed to the surface, that blew the lid off the suitcase and scattered pieces of me everywhere. Whatever it was, for that short time – it can't have been more than a month or so – I was a different woman.

Take my wardrobe, for starters – that's where I am now. Looking through my wardrobe in the corner of the room that Ed and I shared. He won't so much as open the doors. He did once – but he closed them as quickly. It must have been something silly like a scent, or the sight of a pattern or a fabric possibly. Or maybe it was all the new stuff. Things he'd never seen before. The things I bought that summer of 1997. Abandoning my jeans and band T-shirts for smart linen pants, baby-doll dresses and shifts; ditching my trainers for pumps and wedge-heeled sandals; hanging up my perennial parka for smart blazers; acquiring little black numbers – things that showed my legs – which weren't bad, of course, but they weren't something that I'd shown off since I was six; skirts and scarves and accessories – finally taking Ed up on his offer to spend some of his hard-earned cash.

It was insanity of course: what was I thinking, spending someone else's money? Before then, it would have been inconceivable, but for those weeks it was like I had a desperate longing, a thirst to change – to change everything about myself. As if scales had lifted from my eyes and I saw myself for the dull, frightened, uninspired, frustrated, unkempt thing that I was. I wanted, for the first time in my life, new things, shiny things, pretty things – I wanted to be new and shiny and pretty. To walk a little taller, stand with a little more attitude. I wanted to take Jenny Mycroft and shake her until the old one fell out and I could kick her to one side with my foot and replace her with the 1997 model: deluxe, polished, new and improved.

I don't know if Ed liked it or not. He never said. In all honesty I never asked – one half of me told myself that I didn't actually care what he thought – that my re-invention was entirely my business. The other half didn't want to hear his opinion in case he didn't like any of it. In case he wanted the old me back, and at that time such a thing was unthinkable. New Jenny could never go back to the frayed ends of denim and canvas trainers, to the Nirvana T-shirts and combats.

I think that the haircut might have been a step too far, however. He loved my long hair. And home I came in the middle of August one Saturday afternoon with it all gone, chopped into the tightest of tight pixie cuts. The hairdresser had swooned at my audacity, had tried to talk me into a 'Rachel' – all the rage at the time – but I wanted none of it. New Jenny didn't do things by half. And Ed, being Ed, hated it – I could tell – but he was too diplomatic to say.

There was one person, of course, who loved it. Who said he loved the way it framed my face, and made my eyes look enormous and deep and all-knowing. Who said it made me lighter and taller and look like some sort of shape-shifting wood creature. And yes, Guillaume could speak like that when he wanted to, in such a way that it never sounded like the total bullshit that it actually was. What Vicky so elegantly called the "knicker-drop talk".

Maybe she had more to do with it all than I let on, of course. Vicky – my nemesis – was part of the reason that I wanted to turn myself inside out and into something new. And as I stand here and look in my wardrobe – the low-cut tops, the short skirts slit high up the thigh, the tiny crop tops with spaghetti straps – I think I must have actually wanted to look like her.

To look like Vicky because some warped element of my subconscious knew that Guillaume liked – or had liked at one point – how Vicky looked. And I wanted Guillaume to like me.

All of it was fast and it was slow at the same time. After the night in our house, when Vicky's behaviour finally revealed just some of the nasty black filling underneath the shiny shell, after the ridiculous cheeseboard debacle, after I had announced that I was finally leaving my dead-end job, Guillaume seemed to sit up and see me in a whole new light for some reason.

In retrospect, I see myself in one too. A great spotlight that shows me for the fickle, shallow, undeserving cow that I am. After all, at 7 p.m. that evening, I had hated him, hated his pretentiousness, hated how everything about him was so contrived – the sudden yearning for Africa, his clothes, his hair, his ever-changing accent, the stupid hat. I hated how groomed he was –

when not in his native stuff, he wore black trousers and sharp black shirts, trendy leather jackets worn with caps and scarves – he could even look good in linen. I hated the fact that he didn't have to work because his parents were so wealthy they could afford to keep him in his lavish lifestyle.

And then by 10 p.m. he was my co-conspirator, bonding over some tenuous appreciation for the same obscure album – partly out of spite on my part because I knew Vicky hated it and I wanted to get my own back on her for trying to humiliate me the entire evening.

I am ashamed of myself now. Because in my boredom, I somehow turned toward him like a flower to the sun and virtually simpered.

And it grew from there.

And then it crossed a line.

I turn sharply on hearing a noise behind me in the bedroom and see her there – the person whom crossing that line has hurt the most. A pang of guilt and regret and shame rushes over me – it's difficult to explain, but the human, living feelings that we experience don't leave us in death. If anything, they are sharper, stronger, more painful. She is standing there, staring right at me. She isn't scared – but I know that she can see me. My heart flutters with excitement, with possibility, with anticipation. If she can see me, then maybe she'll say it. That word that I haven't heard in so long. That word that I physically ache to hear. That I would sometimes bat away when I was alive with a 'what now' or 'not again' but in this death, this aching void where I am so tantalisingly close to her yet cannot even speak to her, to hear my daughter say "mummy" would make me burst into light and explode with joy. Since I am dead, the good emotions are more powerful too – just so much rarer. Say it, I think. Say the word . . . I am longing . . .

But when she speaks, my being prickles with agony. It is physical. I can feel where my limbs used to be and they are made of pain. My head swells and fills with darkness and my heart, my poor heart that doesn't beat, is made of dark things like longing and shame and horror.

She sees me all right, but when she speaks, it is to say the word "Lady".

She doesn't recognise me any more. She no longer knows the face of the person who loves her fiercely and with an unimaginable strength – stronger than any other soul will ever be capable of. She has forgotten all trace of the first face she saw when she entered this world.

My soul – if that's what it is – is screaming. She no longer knows me. Something is broken and I long to be her mother again. To be connected so closely that I barely tell where my child ends and where I begin.

"Lady," she says.

And I weep and weep and long to take her in my arms and hold her to me.

AUGUST 31ST, 1997

Jenny and Guillaume

Afterwards, Ed made her feel bad about it. And Jenny knew that she had overreacted, but then again, so had half the world.

How could she not as they repeatedly showed Diana smiling on the TV, splashing down the log flume at Thorpe Park with the boys; her wide-eyed innocence on her wedding day in that dress that was far too big for her; those shots of her taken on the *Jonikal*, alone, perched over the waves; William in her arms, when she wore that tent-like green dress with the sailor collar, leaving hospital after he was born; Harry, framed against a red coat in the same scene two years later? When she was a mere twenty-three years old – younger than Jenny had been when Bee was born.

It was the constant playing of 'Candle in the Wind'; the childhood pictures – balancing on a wall at Althorp in a black leotard and straw hat; no older than Bee in a white dress on a red checked rug; wearing a floppy black hat, displaying a hamster to the camera . . .

By the time Ed roused for breakfast on the morning of September 1st, 1997 – Bee's second birthday – Jenny had seen these photographs and a million more on Sky News over and over again.

"She's dead!" she wailed, confusing Ed at first as he searched his own mind to see who it could be. "*Diana!*" Jenny pointed to the TV, her eyes red from crying, her cheeks puffy.

She had expected some sort of sympathy, but it didn't come. Instead, he looked from her swollen face to the TV screen in alarm, observed the mountain of tissues littering the cushion beside her on the couch, spilling over onto the floor. She was pale with exhaustion, her arms wrapped around her knees which were drawn up on the couch in front of her, as if to provide some form of comfort or protection.

"Have you been sitting here *all night*?" he asked, incredulous.

Jenny nodded, a fresh batch of tears brimming behind her eyes, partly at his reaction, partly at the scenes unfolding on the rolling news as she spoke, scenes of sobbing visitors arriving at the gates of Kensington Palace with their floral tributes.

Ed looked back at his wife, his expression a mixture of irritation and concern. "*Jen,*" he said. "You've been up all night – no sleep, am I right?"

She shook her head, failing to contain a tear that slithered down her cheek. She sniffed.

"On the night before Bee's birthday – when we're taking her out for lunch with my family? You've had no sleep whatsoever?"

Jenny sniffed again, a muffled sob escaping. "I don't know if I *can* today, Ed – I mean, I'm not sure if anyone can . . . she died in a car accident . . . in Paris. The car was being chased by paparazzi . . . they crashed into a pillar . . . Dodi died too . . ."

Ed shook his head in disbelief. "Jen," he said bluntly. "Seriously. A celeb dies and you've gone to pieces?" He glanced toward the baby monitor in his hand as Bee stirred in her bedroom. "That's Bee awake now. You'd better get upstairs and get an hour's kip before she sees you."

A wave of panic rose in Jenny. "She's not a *celeb*, Ed – she's a member of our royal family – a young mum – like me – and she's *dead* – don't you get it? Those boys – her children . . ."

But he had raised his eyebrows in disbelief and turned to go upstairs to retrieve their daughter.

On the TV screen, 'Candle in the Wind' struck up again as another montage of scenes from the life of the beautiful, thirty-six-year-old princess began to play and Jenny succumbed to a fresh wave of grief.

She knew that Ed was right, of course, yet she just couldn't seem to stop.

She managed to get through the day, somehow. She had thought that going out to a restaurant would make her feel worse but somehow it made her feel better, more part of things to get out onto London's streets. It made her feel less alone, less ridiculous for grieving so deeply for someone that she didn't know because, as far as she could see, she wasn't alone. The waitress was red-eyed; people passing on the street were ashen-faced with shock. Headlines on newsstands screamed of it: "*Diana Dead*".

After Ed's family – who were of much the same opinion as he was – had left them at the pizza restaurant and gone home, Ed, Jenny and Bee had made their way back to Pilton Gardens by taxi, accompanied by Guillaume who carried a bottle of champagne under his arm, his idea of celebrating a child's second birthday.

When they arrived, however, Jenny simply resumed her position on the couch while Ed put a tired Bee to bed, and immediately returned to rolling news, hungry for more, unable to stop herself. When Ed came back downstairs he nodded in the direction of the kitchen to Guillaume and they disappeared to the garden beyond, closing the back door behind them to sit outdoors, leaving her thankfully alone.

The Princess's body was returning home, she learned, collected by Prince Charles and her sisters earlier that day from Paris. Jenny's eyes filled with tears again as she caught up on all she had missed. The coffin, in the car, being loaded into the plane – coming home to her boys. And the waves of grief that were spreading throughout the world – waves of inexplicable grief like the one she was feeling now.

It was dark outside when Jenny heard the back door open and shut again. Her eyes barely flicked away from the TV screen. She was aware, from the corner of her eye, of shapes moving silently past the open living-room door on her left, but she didn't look, couldn't bear to tear her eyes away from the screen. Plus, she couldn't bear the fact that Ed would look at her like she was insane, and undoubtedly Guillaume too, despite the entente they had reached between them since the ill-fated 'couples night'. He had called a couple of times, in fact, unexpectedly. With more of his African music, which they had listened to together, surprisingly relaxed over coffee. Not any more, however, Jenny thought. Not when he, too, saw the madwoman who couldn't stop crying for the dead stranger.

She jumped suddenly, as she felt a weight at the end of the couch furthest from her. She didn't turn. What could Ed possibly want to watch for? Why couldn't he just leave her be?

She was surprised then, to note that it wasn't Ed who had sunk nervously onto the sofa, but Guillaume, and he was looking at her with real concern on his face. Jenny was puzzled for a moment. Ed was nowhere to be seen, but a tell-tale creak from the hall indicated that he was at the turn in the stairs. Moments later, she heard their bedroom door creak shut.

She turned back to the screen, too embarrassed and upset to speak. She continued instead to flick channels between the BBC and Sky in case there was, at any moment, something new. The boys, perhaps – they were at Balmoral, with the Queen – told the news when half asleep. A fresh brew of tears brimmed over Jenny's lashes as she thought again of them. Of how it would be if that were Bee. If Ed were to wake Bee to tell her that she was gone. The tears plopped silently onto her cheeks and rolled down.

Gui's voice was soft when he eventually spoke. "You all right, Jen?" he asked.

Jenny took a deep breath, tried to compose herself before replying. She'd tell him she was fine. And she was. It was just awfully sad, but what would he care? She found herself unable to speak, her throat constricted by the fresh flow of tears, which had grown stronger now, sadness exacerbated by kindness from another. She nodded vigorously, in the hope that it would reassure him and he would go away. Ed was gone to bed, so surely Guillaume must be heading off on his way home?

"I don't think Ed gets it," Guillaume continued, nodding his head toward the TV screen.

Jenny's eyes flicked in Guillaume's direction and then back at the screen again. She must look a sight, she knew, with her swollen eyes and downturned mouth. She remained silent. A lump was wedged in her throat and she couldn't trust herself to speak. She longed for Guillaume to just leave her alone so that she could sob silently and not embarrass herself any further. But he didn't move. If anything, he seemed to edge a little closer to her. She was stunned when she felt the touch on her arm and looked down to see his hand there, his Breitling watch on his right wrist, where he always wore it.

"I don't think you're nuts or anything," he whispered, leaning his head forward to try to make eye contact with her. There was a hint of a smile in his voice. If anything, it made the lump in Jenny's throat bigger. The hand on her arm squeezed. "I feel like crying myself, truth be told," he said.

Suddenly, she turned. Jenny frowned at Guillaume, studying his face, assessing whether or not he was mocking her.

Under her direct gaze, it was Guillaume's turn to look away. He nodded at the screen, at a shot of the coffin being carried across the tarmac at RAF Northolt, draped in the Royal Standard.

"She's home then," he said simply.

It was enough. The sob released itself from Jenny's throat in a great release. For the whole day she had endured Ed's disbelief at her response, the jibes from Vicky who had spent all of lunch making sarcastic remarks and inappropriate jokes, Ed's mother who had stared sniffily at her daughter-in-law, scoffing at people who were clearly stricken with some level of grief at the news, insisting that they should just "pull themselves together".

Jenny leaned towards Guillaume as he reached his arms out and pulled her to him.

"Hey, hey," he said comfortingly.

Her eyes stung as she closed them, squeezing tears out onto Guillaume's impeccable navy linen jacket. Jenny became aware that she ached. Her face, her jaws sore from clenching against tears she felt it wrong to shed, yet were unstoppable; her legs and back throbbing from where she had sat slumped for hours. Her head – most of all her head – with that terrible, dull, crying headache. She felt overwhelmed as Guillaume rested his chin on the top of her head, drawing her in to him and rubbing her back with his left hand, while stroking her hair with his right.

The darkness of the embrace comforted Jenny at first. And his smell. A mix of expensive cologne and champagne on his breath. It was a grown-up smell – for a moment, she felt safe, like someone else was in charge. She sniffed deeply and pulled away a little, using her hand to wipe her eyes as the tears abated momentarily.

"I'm so sorry, Gui," she mumbled, embarrassment creeping back in. She widened her eyes, trying to compose herself, and rubbed her nose with the sleeve of her cotton cardigan.

All the while, Guillaume didn't move, watching her with concern.

"I feel awfully stupid," Jenny finally managed to whisper. She glanced back at the TV and then down at her hands, stretching her legs out in front of her, pointing her bare feet with their pearl-polished toes to relax them. "I mean crying over someone I didn't know. I don't know what's come over me – you must think I'm so awfully silly."

Guillaume looked down on her tear-streaked face, his expression soft. He swept a hand lightly over her cheek and through her cropped hair, cupping the back of her head with his palm, forcing her to look at him.

"Stop being ridiculous," he whispered.

Jenny's stomach lurched. He did think her foolish. This was some way to bring her to her senses – something Ed had asked him to do.

"I know it's ridiculous. I'll pull myself together – maybe I'm depressed or something . . ." she began.

Guillaume shook his head, his eyes still fixed on hers. "That's not what I mean," he said. "You've every right to be upset. Jeez, *I'm* upset, but I just don't think it would be cool for me, of all people – with my street cred and all – to show it."

He smiled and Jenny managed to grin back at him. Still, he held her close to him and continued to stare at her face. She began to feel less abashed about what was upsetting her and more conscious of how terrible she must look. He must be staring at how impossibly swollen her face was, how unnatural her appearance must be after hours of crying over a complete stranger.

"I don't know what it is either, but she . . ." he glanced at the TV screen, "she touched something in everyone. I'm not ashamed to say it. That time I saw her in Cape Town – she was so beautiful – she *glowed*. And that bravery – walking out into a field of landmines? Hugging an AIDS patient to show you couldn't catch it? It's shit like that I admire. It's strength. And that lady had it in spades . . . and now she's gone so what's it all for?"

Jenny's eyes widened at Guillaume's words. She had never heard him speak like that. She had never heard him say a sentence that didn't feature the word 'man' at least twenty times, but then again, she hadn't spoken to him much one-on-one except in the last few weeks and even then it was mainly about music. There was something in Guillaume's words that was soothing, something infectious about the sentiment.

Jenny found herself nodding. "It's her kids," she began. "William and Harry. I feel so sorry for them but I can't help myself feeling sorry for *her* too – she adored them so much. And now she's gone and she's going to miss them growing up – growing into men and living out their lives and getting married – she's going to miss all the hugs and the laughter and the fun – she's so *young*. She didn't deserve to die. She could have done so much with the rest of her life and now she's gone. In the blink of an eye . . ."

Guillaume responded by nodding in agreement and sliding his arm around Jenny to pull her to him in another embrace. They sat awkwardly like that for a while, Jenny pulled uncomfortably toward Guillaume, too awkward with the situation to rearrange herself because that would mean pulling herself closer to him.

They stared wordlessly at the TV together for a while. The coverage rolled on. The scenes from the tunnel where the crash had happened, vox pops from around the country to reinforce the devastation of the people, messages of sympathy from heads of state, the growing sea of flowers and cards and candles and tributes at Kensington Palace. Scenes from her life. Her engagement day, the sapphire and diamond ring, Charles saying "whatever love means"

And as they watched, Jenny found herself become increasingly aware of Guillaume's bulk beside her. The intoxicating smell of him. She glanced in his direction more than once, at his chest muscles under the T-shirt he wore. She knew that he ran, that he lifted weights. That he teased Ed about how the heaviest thing he lifted in a day was a pencil. She allowed her gaze to run down his left arm which now rested on his knee. At the darkness of his skin, the smoothness of his hairless wrist running down to his long fingers with his pink, manicured fingernails. She turned suddenly back to the TV, re-focusing on a montage of Diana's early romance with Charles. Running to her car to escape the paparazzi pack outside her flat, the cotton skirts, the Sloane Ranger collars. But for the first time in twenty-four hours, Jenny was unable to focus on the Princess of Wales. She was too distracted by her companion. In a way that was familiar, yet completely new. In a way that she knew she, as a married woman, shouldn't be feeling. She shifted in her seat.

Guillaume, who had been absorbed in the screen, or so Jenny thought – until he told her otherwise later – jumped as she moved.

"You all right?" he asked, for the second time that night.

Jenny hesitated. She wasn't actually sure.

"I've dreamed of designing something for her," she blurted suddenly.

Maybe that was why she was so upset? Because, by now, in the sketchbook that she kept hidden at the bottom of her wardrobe, were pages and pages of sketches of clothes, all worn by a tall model with short hair and an elegant gait. Dresses for daywear, evening dresses, hats even.

"For Diana," she confirmed. She didn't know why she was saying this. "I sketch clothes. For Diana. And I might make them – I don't know. I'll see," she babbled nervously. "Don't tell Ed . . ."

In retrospect, she wasn't sure exactly what she was telling Guillaume not to tell Ed. Whether it was, in fact, about those aspirations or something else. Whether it was about the look in his eyes that seemed to drown her, that absorbed her in his dark brown eyes. Or whether it was the longing to kiss him.

To which she gave in.

A sudden, perfect, tentative, forbidden kiss. The first kiss. A kiss that may have been born out of a desire for comfort, from a need for human contact but which would lead to so much more.

That, truly, was when it started. The beginning of the end.

AUTUMN 1997

Jenny and Guillaume

Four months. Four short months. That was all that it lasted. Such a short space of time that cast such monumental ripples.

Jenny knew that she was lying to herself, telling herself over and over that she had tried to resist it – but she hadn't. Being with Guillaume – the secret moments, the meticulously arranged rendezvous – she hated herself for them, but she never tried very hard to resist.

Like a wave, the affair lifted Jenny out of something – some fug in which she was stuck, the rut which she had created for herself. It carried her along in a sea of sparks and excitement. It gave her a dull ache of longing and anticipation in her stomach when she wasn't with him, and allowed her to absorb herself fully in the moments that she was, so that time spent in his arms, inhaling his scent, feeling the delicious smoothness of his skin, seemed to fly at the speed of sound.

But there was also the *time*. Having the affair took up so much of it. Planning where and when to meet next, travelling to and from the forbidden assignations. Thinking about when the next moment would come to steal a phone call.

Had Jenny thought for a second as she hurtled through the autumn of 1997 into its winter that these months were the last of her life, she would have come screeching to a halt to make them last. As it was, every day felt like it lasted just moments. One minute the leaves on the trees along the pavements of Pilton Gardens were gold, and the next they were gone. There was scant time for illicit evening walks on the common nearby on the pretext of getting some exercise once Bee was asleep, before it grew dark in the afternoons and smoke from chimneys curled into the night sky and the meetings switched to out-of the-way wine-bars or hasty visits to Guillaume's new flat in Notting Hill, ostensibly meeting old friends.

It was all about time. Precious time.

Lying in Guillaume's arms with the last rays of afternoon sun travelling down the rumpled sheets of his bed, Jenny often longed for more of it. More time to snooze, to make love, to talk. Because they talked all the time. Sometimes about music, about art, about fashion – but mainly about themselves of course. About how it had been between the two of them before September 1st. About how Guillaume had at first perceived her as dull and unworthy of his friend, but how she had come alive before his eyes that summer. About how she resented him and his relationship with Ed, how she felt insignificant around him before all of this started. And Guillaume would rush to contradict her and tell her how wonderful she was, and then Jenny would reciprocate and they would forgive each other for their initial impressions, wondering how on earth they could ever have come to them.

They acknowledged Vicky's existence occasionally – Guillaume still saw her, but not as often, or as intimately as he had before. "I'm letting it die," he told Jenny, and she believed him. She had seen how he had looked at Vicky, how their relationship had turned on its head that night over "The Stilton Incident", as they referred to it. It was one of their favourite tales, their war stories.

They talked about that spark that had flared between them that night after the Princess of Wales had died. Over and over they recounted it, each time uncovering a new feeling, a new way of describing the attraction, feeling it anew every time they had the conversation. And as long as they stayed firmly on the subject of themselves – how amazing each one thought the other, how dizzy their passion made them feel, how the very longing for the other made the air they breathed sweeter – then they didn't have to touch on the one subject that hung between them like an invisible curtain.

Ed.

Because Ed was Real Life. For Jenny anyway. And she knew that Guillaume loved her husband too. That was what made thinking about him so inconceivable. Their betrayal was so enormous, Jenny knew, that to cope with it – to carry on through the days – she had to do her utmost not to think about him at all when she was with her lover. Her lover who made her feel so alive, so filled with ideas and inspiration, so creative. She sketched daily – pages after pages of designs. She devised games and activities with Bee that she thought up on the spot. She made the house in Pilton Gardens even more perfect than it had been before – adding touches here, finishing things there. She even began to take driving lessons. It would make sense to finally be able to take her dad places, she reasoned with Ed. And to be able to bring Bee to all of the activities that were to come over the years. He agreed with her – the practicality of it wasn't something to be ignored and he had encouraged her to learn for years. But if she thought about the real reason – that if she could drive herself, she could get to Guillaume faster and more often – she would have been so ashamed that she might never have sat behind a wheel.

But she didn't think. Because Jenny Adams, for the last four months of her life, was a woman who could split herself in two. She was Janus. One head was the perfect wife and mother, a creative force, someone who was absolutely making the most of her life – all of these things she could do on one hand, because of the secret that fuelled the other – the fire of the taboo passion that she kept hidden from the world that she saw through her second face, the clandestine nature of her life force fuelling her everyday motions and behaviour. And all of it combining to make her feel like a better, more complete person. There were times, in the autumn of 1997 when Jenny Adams-Mycroft, cresting on a wave of her own importance, fired up with lust and fuelled with the adoration of a man that she physically craved, thought that she could potentially be the perfect woman. Whichever Jenny Adams-Mycroft that woman actually was.

2020

Jenny

It seems such a cliché to wonder what I was thinking – but what was I thinking? It seems a cliché to say that I had everything – but I literally had everything. That autumn, when I started taking driving lessons, Ed even bought me a car for heaven's sake. And I let him.

I had everything I could ever want – my beautiful home, my gorgeous girl who I look at now that she is an adult with such pride and sadness, my every desire fulfilled.

And all that love. Because the love that Ed possessed for me was greater than the moon and the stars and the universe combined. Bee and me – together we were the axis around which he revolved. We inspired everything that he did from the moment he took his first waking breath each day to the second he closed his eyes and fell into a dreamless sleep at night.

It has taken the filter of a lifetime apart for me to see all that. To fully understand the vastness of his love for me. His contentment at our togetherness. He wanted us to be everything and more. He thought that we could be invincible.

And clearly through the filter of time, and the complementary filter of death – of this constant watching and observing and understanding more day by day that I have done over the past twenty-three years – I have come to understand that I took all of that away from him. His job, his life-path, his plans, his dreams, his vision for the future. For our future.

It was my own stupid fault that I lost the life that I could have had with him. I took it all away from myself, and away from him. All that love that he had invested. All the love of which he was capable, that grew inside him every day of his life – I destroyed it.

If I hadn't acted rashly and stupidly to try to change things for myself, to add some spark to a life that I had made dull for myself, then I could have had that life. And Bee could have had a mother. And Ed could have been with the woman he loved, as we had agreed in that registry office with his disapproving family looking on.

Except for a time she didn't exist any more.

It is the greatest regret of my death that I gave in to those urges that summer. That I acquiesced. Not to Guillaume. He knew no better. It was in his nature, after all, to seek and pursue. Even if I had lived to go with him, as he had asked, it would never have worked.

No, I gave in to myself. I gave in to boredom, to the fear. Rather than go and seek what was missing out of my life – like Ed wanted me to do, like he gently encouraged me to do all of our years together – not bullied me as I liked to believe. But rather than go and try to fulfil myself I went for the instant hit, the cheap shot and took what presented itself to me on a platter. All of that fizz and excitement, all that fun that I thought I was having.

It was absolutely nothing except a diversion, something to defer reality. And to stave off boredom.

I thought it made me a better person, a different one. But it didn't. I can see that now. It made me a horrible person. A person who was a liar, a duplicitous cheat. A person who was hiding. Hiding from herself behind the haircut, the clothes, the thrill of keeping a secret lover.

But I wasn't that person. Not deep down. I was just Jenny Adams. Penny Jenny. Scared of failure. Scared to poke her stupid head over the top, lest it be blown off before she could even see what was out there.

Shame I didn't cotton on to that at the time of course, all things considered.

DECEMBER 8TH, 1997

Ed and Jenny

Ed glanced at Jenny. "Jen?"

"Yes, Ed?"

"Let's bunk off today."

"What do you . . . hang on . . . *shit!* I am terrible at this, Ed – why on earth am I bothering to learn? I nearly ground the gearbox out that time!"

"Just calm down, Jen. And watch the language – Bee can hear you. Now start to slow down well in advance of the lights – and change down through the gears gradually . . . that's it."

Jenny followed Ed's instructions and they sat in the car – the Volkswagen Polo that he had bought her to learn to drive in – as it juddered, Jenny's foot held inexpertly at biting point, waiting for the red light to turn amber.

The morning was still dark, even though it was close to nine o'clock. Stopped in traffic at the brow of a hill, Jenny could see for yards ahead, the red tail-lights of car after car, the clouds of exhaust fumes being chugged into the frosty morning air. The houses around them were white-roofed and passing pedestrians walked gingerly, their expressions nervous.

Ed reached out to the radio and turned it up slightly. It was the first time that year. The first play of 'Fairytale of New York'.

Unexplained tears prickled at the back of Jenny's eyes as she was drawn into the moment that was all around her, seeing London go about its business on a frosty morning, smelling the coldness in the air, gripping the wheel with her knitted gloves, Ed in the seat beside her, and Bee, beautiful Bee, about to have her third Christmas, strapped into the car seat in the back, her woollen hat pulled too far over her eyes, copper curls escaping from underneath. Jenny glanced at her in the rear-view mirror and felt that rush of love that never failed to catch her by surprise when she saw her daughter. All of this played out to the opening bars of the song, just before Shane McGowan growled that it was Christmas Eve, babe.

The low rumble of traffic intensified suddenly, as the stationary train of vehicles began a slow crawl again. Jenny's Polo jumped a little and she tutted loudly, hands flailing between wheel and gearstick, trying to figure out what next to do. Ed reached out a hand and rested it on her thigh to calm her.

"Calm down, love. You're doing fine. We're nearly there."

Jenny obeyed, taking a deep breath and pulling herself back together. She hated this. Driving, that is. But it had to be done. She stopped the thought before she could finish it, before she could reinforce to herself the reason why. Not in Real Time, she subconsciously chastised herself.

"So yeah, whaddya think?"

"Hmm? About what – *speed up, mate, for heaven's sake!*"

"Bunking off. Aren't you listening to me?"

Jenny bristled. "Ed, I'm *trying* to get us to nursery and then back home in one piece on the frostiest morning of the year so far. So no, I'm not exactly listening to you. What do you *mean* 'bunk off' anyway?"

Ed smiled. "See? I knew you were listening. All that 'women are better multitaskers than men' stuff *is* true – watch, that guy is prone to braking quickly – we don't want to skid into him. What I mean, Mrs Mycroft, by bunking off is just that. Do you know that I have never rung in sick in my entire life and looking out the window this morning I thought, why not today? Why don't we drop the Beezer off as usual and then, instead of heading back home and me going to work, why don't we go shopping? Have some fun for a change?

Please, Jen – can we bunk off today? Can we? Can we? Will you play truant with me today?"

Baffled, Jenny dared herself to take her eye off the road ahead for a millisecond and glanced to her left to see Ed grinning broadly. From nowhere, Jenny felt a jolt. Felt her heart leap. For some reason, caught in the early morning light, Ed looked just like he had that evening in Darvill's when Jenny had seen him for the first time. She was filled, momentarily, with the most unexpected surge of love.

She returned her eyes to the road and in an instant the feeling had vanished. True to form, the car in front had stopped suddenly again and Jenny suddenly felt her own car slide out of her control. She impulsively jammed her foot onto the brake.

"*Easy!*" Ed shrieked, sitting bolt upright. "Don't panic! Pump the brake gently! That's it. Slowly, slowly . . ."

The car slowed to a halt. Jenny's heart, however, didn't. It pounded. She could feel it against her ribcage, banging against her chest. Her breath came in rapid bursts and she gripped the wheel for her life.

"For *fuck's* sake, Ed!" she barked suddenly.

"Jen!" he chastised her. "Just stay *calm* – there's no need to panic – we're fine."

"It was *your* fault," she growled. "If you hadn't been banging on about Christmas shopping and bunking off and acting like a total *idiot*, then I'd have had my eyes on the road and that would *never* have happened."

She knew she was lashing out. She didn't care. She was too pumped with adrenalin, her nerves tingling at the prospect of what might have happened.

"O-*kay*, Jen," Ed responded harshly. "Steady on. I didn't get out and forcibly give you a push into his rear end. And anyway, we're fine. We're all fine. That right, Beezer?" Eyeing Jenny nervously, he half-turned to see his daughter who was absorbed in a plastic fish that was her current constant companion.

Jenny took a deep breath and concentrated deeply as she gingerly edged the car another few feet forward.

"Look. By the time we get back home, it'll be almost lunchtime anyway at this rate. What is *happening* with that traffic this morning? Tell you what . . ." He stole another glance at his wife.

"What, Ed?"

"Do you a deal. When we get to nursery, how about we swop places and I drive? I've decided that I'm going to have a terrible cough today anyway so I'll need to do something to keep my mind off it. And it's not Christmas shopping I'm thinking of, although it *is* Christmas-related. So why don't you shift over to the passenger seat and let old Ed-ster take over and have a bit of fun for a change? Whaddya say?"

Jenny remained silent as she finally indicated left and turned slowly into the cul de sac where Bee's nursery nestled behind a protective screen of trees. She could see it ahead of her now, the large iron gates wide open, a few straggling cars negotiating the turn-space out front. She was flooded with relief as she drove through them and pulled up beside the grass verge.

"Agreed, then?" said Ed, not giving her a chance to reply, bounding instead from the car like an eager Labrador and whisking Bee out of her seat before Jenny even had a chance to think about it.

"*Bye, Mummy!*" called Ed, bending down at the passenger door which he had left open, Bee held in his arms waving frantically with a mittened hand.

"Bye, Mummy!" she echoed, and Jenny smiled broadly at the sound of happiness in her voice.

"*See-la-later!*" prompted Ed, and Bee mimicked him.

"Love you, darling!" called Jenny after them as Ed turned hastily, slamming the passenger and rear doors shut with his foot and charging off up the driveway to where small children, wrapped in colourful coats, hats and gloves, hand in hand with parents, filtered in through the door and then moments later the parents filtered back out again, their offspring carefully delivered.

Jenny watched them go until they disappeared inside. When she could see her husband and child no longer, she allowed herself to slump back against the headrest, overwhelmed momentarily by a wave of exhaustion and emotion.

For a moment, she stepped outside of herself. Alone in the car for an instant, Real Time Jenny allowed Other Jenny to come to the surface. New and Improved Jenny. Except from this angle, with the smell of Ed's aftershave lingering in the car and the sound of Bee's voice echoing in her ears, Jenny couldn't imagine why she thought Other Jenny was New and Improved.

And it was getting so complicated. Guillaume. Asking her that question. Saying that he was desperately in love with her. Saying that he wanted them to be together all the time. Talking about a new life together, in Africa, of all places. Cape Town. But he would take her everywhere, he promised. Exotic places like Zanzibar and Mali and out into the desert with the Bedouin. They'd have such adventures together . . .

Jenny gazed at the scene before her, taking in everything she could see on the freezing cold December morning. The white hoarfrost on the grass, on the roof-tiles of the nursery building – a converted Victorian villa. Grey brick against the grey sky, the black branches of the bare trees thrust upward. It was beautiful, yet stark. It was where she should be. It was Real Time.

But Guillaume offered her Other Time. Heat, colour. For a moment she imagined sinking into a hot bath against the freezing cold of the morning, just escaping from it. As it stood, she could barely feel her fingers and the cold that entered her body through her feet had spread all the way up her legs.

Jenny shook her head. It wasn't a possibility, of course. A total non-runner. She tried to banish the thought. She belonged here. With Bee. With Ed. With Real Life. Not with Guillaume, in that Technicolor world that seemed to exist when they were together.

Jenny caught sight of Ed emerging through the doors of the nursery, pulling his black coat around him and standing back with a smile to allow another parent to enter. Jenny watched as they chatted briefly, politely, for a moment. Watched how Ed smiled at the child – slightly older than Bee, she thought, from what she could see. And then she watched his familiar step back across the car park, looking from left to right, his artist's eyes taking it all in. Finding some beauty, she knew, in the grimness of the day. And there was beauty in it. She knew that. But she just suddenly didn't want to see it any more. She wanted to scream in fact. Scream at the situation. Scream at Ed. Scream at the choice that she felt she had to make. That she felt she should be able to make without hesitation.

She should be able to do the right thing, she knew. There was no other option for her, for heaven's sake. She belonged here. With her family. Taking care of people. Doing the right thing. Like she had done all of her life. *Choosing* to do the right thing.

Except that was it. She wasn't sure that she could. And that thought terrified her to the core.

2020

Jenny

That day. December the 8th, 1997. That perfect Christmas day. In my memory, it all blends together like a cheesy montage from a TV show. Ed and Jen's Christmas Special, *it should have been called.*

We went to a market first. Near Notting Hill – near Guillaume's flat, in fact, which Ed had been to often, yet which we had never been to together. To which I knew the way like the back of my hand. I remember that I bit my lip hard in case I said something that revealed this fact, somehow. And I remember that I was glad when we turned this way and that and I grew lost again and didn't have to pretend any more. And when we got there, to the Christmas market, I had nothing to hide because Other Jenny disappeared back inside and Real Jenny, wife to Ed, mother to Bee, took over.

They'd play Wham's 'Last Christmas' over that part of the montage. Ed and myself browsing through rows and rows of thick firs and spruces and pines, bickering affectionately – Ed in favour of something misshapen and miserable-looking and I, as always, desperate for our Christmas Tree to be perfect.

And then as we finally made our choice and paid and they wrapped our tree in mesh to deliver it later, I saw another tree. A smaller one this time. And fell in love with the idea of seeing it greet me just inside the front door of our home. Fell in love with the idea of it being there to welcome Bee home from nursery. Envisioned this one decorated in gold, green and red. Candy canes. A golden star on top. So we bought that one too.

And then we took ourselves to a stall selling carved wooden figurines and hand-painted baubles and we chose some to take home, both of us conscious that these would become part of our family history. That for every year for the rest of our lives, they'd be part of it all, part of the fabric of our Christmases, right through Bee's life and beyond – to grandchildren, perhaps. It was right there, as we watched the stallholder box up these things that we both had a vision of what the future should be for us. Of traditions that we were creating now. For Real Jenny it all became crystal clear.

The next part of the montage would show us in a café nearby, warming ourselves with a mid-morning drink, Ed insisting on getting marshmallows in his hot chocolate. He was like a child that day, I remember. His nose red, a bobble hat that he had discovered in his coat pocket pulled down over his ears against the biting cold. I can see him now as he was then, across the holly-patterned paper tablecloth from me, the very scent of coldness coming from his skin as he waited for the drinks to be brought down to us.

The song would still be festive, of course. 'Have Yourself a Merry Little Christmas', perhaps.

For a time, we were perfect. We were just Ed and Jenny again.

We held hands across the table. Around us sat builders – everywhere builders, because it was boom time – eating fry-ups, devouring doughnuts and steaming cups of tea and coffee. And amidst them we sat, a vision of young love in woollens, giggling together. At shared jokes that we hadn't thought about in years. At the prospect of Christmas – we talked about what we'd cook for Christmas day, about what to get Bee for under the tree, about what we'd leave out for Santa the night before – Ed wanted to create fake reindeer footprints across the kitchen floor with some brown paint and a stencil to make Bee believe that Santa had really been here. I reminded him that, at two, she might well not appreciate the effort, but he swore he would do it anyway. "I want it perfect, Jen," he said. Over and over again.

And in the cocoon of that greasy spoon with its fogged-up windows and the hiss of the coffee machine, I did too. I wanted perfection. And as Ed tentatively mentioned that maybe we should think about creating something else, Real Time Jenny was in full agreement. I absolutely was. As I sat there, holding my husband's hand, warm and safe and happy, I too desperately wanted another baby. I suddenly wanted the bubble of deceit that I had allowed to form around me to just go away. I wanted Real Life. I wanted a new year and a fresh start. I wanted all of those things that I had always wanted, but had somehow forgotten in the frenzy of the past few months. I wanted a place to be. A slot to fit in. A family.

We drove home to 'Driving Home for Christmas', cheesily enough. But it was perfect.

It was only on the final leg of the journey that the joyful Christmas music stops in my imaginary montage.

When we drove past the accident.

It was late afternoon and the temperatures had remained low all day. Someone had skidded at a junction into a parked car. There were flashing lights everywhere. Policemen in high-viz vests waved the traffic along, tried their best to keep it moving but to no avail. Everyone wanted a look.

Until, of course, they stopped all of the traffic. A grim-faced WPC made sure that nothing moved and then turned her attention to the ambulance, the doors of which were being closed. Slowly.

It drove away, taking its place in the traffic that the policewoman had cleared for it, but it was clear that it was in no rush. There was no siren. No flashing blue light. There was nowhere to hurry to, nothing to hurry for.

Because it was too late.

Ed and I were completely silent as we drove past. I couldn't bring myself to look at the scene. Kept my head down, trying to ignore the ambulance ahead. Nothing to see here, after all. My head was filled with not only the horrors of the actual scene, but the horrors that I hadn't witnessed.

And that was the end of Ed and Jenny's Christmas Special. We drove on in silence, the rawness of what we had witnessed waning somewhat as we reached home. Ed silently helped me to carry in the spoils of our day before leaving to collect Bee from nursery and pick up a pizza.

And I did mundane things. Put the heating on, put a match to the fire, closed all the curtains, turned on all of the lights. By the time my husband and daughter arrived home, I had all but blocked the image of the car crash from my mind.

But I shouldn't have, should I? Because I should have seen it for what it was.

Signs and portents, I should have been thinking.

Signs and portents.

DECEMBER 13TH, 1997

Jenny and Guillaume

It was Other Jenny who hosted the party. She wore a long, straight, black strapless dress, slit to the thigh, offset with an antique costume necklace and drop earrings, sultry red against the black. She gelled her hair back, swept red lipstick across her lips and smoky kohl on her eyes. She could tell that her husband didn't like it much but, possessed by some wickedness, she hadn't dressed to impress her husband.

After she and Ed had spent the day shopping together, after they had decorated their home for Christmas, after they had decided to host this party for all of their friends – the last one for a while, they decided, while they moved on with their family life – somehow, the boredom had returned inside her. More long days spent around the house, staring at the sparkling decorations that should have filled her with excitement but instead seemed lustreless. Despite the plans they had made, left alone while her husband went out to work and her daughter filled her days with paper craft and finger-painting in nursery, for Other Jenny the prospect of Christmas just wasn't enough.

It hadn't taken long for the thoughts of Guillaume to start stirring again. But she'd had to wait as he was away again, this time in the north of England somewhere, doing lord knew what. Not much longer, however.

As the guests for the party began to arrive in twos and threes and she greeted them at the door, welcoming them indoors and taking coats and umbrellas, showing them down the steps to the kitchen, Jenny was impatient. Because there was only one guest that she wanted to see. She couldn't give a toss about the rest, moaning about how cold they were, *oohing* and *aahing* at how beautifully the house was decorated. She was driven by a thirst, she knew: a thirst to see only one person. To have a long, deep drink and satisfy herself. It had been two weeks. Only a fortnight, but she felt as if tonight she would see him for the first time.

She missed his actual arrival – she wasn't sure how she hadn't heard the bell ring – but the first she was aware of him was when she caught sight of him standing at the top of the kitchen steps, scanning the room. She was standing by the tree in the sunroom, topping up someone's drink, when she registered that he had arrived. She was calm and cool, seamlessly pouring the wine, playing the perfect hostess, although it had taken every last shred of willpower in her to tear her eyes away from how gorgeous he looked bathed in the flicker of candlelight.

No sooner was the drink poured, however, the bottle righted, than she turned to stare. And found the room around her swimming, all of the voices around her fading into a hum, mixed with the sound of the festive background music. And it took only a moment for him to find her and stare back. It was a delicious moment. Fizzing with that electricity that they shared. It was lust and longing and physical desire. It was wrong, and it was right. It was at once dreamlike and still real. And then it was broken, everything shooting back into sharp focus by the appearance at his side of Vicky, dressed in red. Jenny came to, just in time to hear Noddy Holder scream that "*It's Christmas!*". And at that moment, she detected the worry that flickered through Guillaume's eyes which still held hers. And she knew that everything was not right.

It was easily an hour of crackers with pâté, vol au vents and Brie and cranberry parcels. An hour of topping up glasses, of chatting about Christmas plans. An hour of aching separation before she made her way toward the kitchen where Guillaume stood. He was silent, Vicky beside him, deep in conversation with a woman that

Jenny recognised as the new receptionist at Ed's work. Vicky hung there, hanging from the crook of his arm, making him list awkwardly while he paid her no attention at all. Instead, his eyes were glued to Jenny as she walked toward him.

Jenny fixed him with a meaningful look as she reached him. A look of longing, but also of confusion. '*What's the matter?*' she tried to ask with her eyes. He shook his head faintly.

Jenny's stomach flip-flopped, both at the very sight of him and with concern at the lack of breezy banter laced with double meanings that he normally managed in these public situations. She'd usually respond by more or less ignoring him, answering only where necessary with brief sentences, the hint of a smile on her lips the only giveaway as to the true nature of their relationship. Tonight, she cleared her throat and impulsively touched Vicky's hand to draw her attention.

Vicky turned and her face fell when she saw who it was.

"All right, Vicky?" piped Jenny. She had to get in there first, to stay positive, to rise above whatever jibe Vicky would come up with.

"Jenny," came the brusque response.

"Mind if I borrow Guillaume for a mo?" Jenny enquired breezily, without consulting him. "Only I've got a new CD that I think he might like. Here – why don't I top up your glass, and – tell you what – leave you this bottle."

Jenny flinched as Vicky suddenly whipped her arm out of where it was hooked into Guillaume's and covered her glass with her hand.

"I'm fine, thanks," she bit, and then coloured. "But . . ." she turned to the woman beside her, "Maria here might like some more, wouldn't you, Maria?"

Jenny shrugged. She was too absorbed in the task of getting Guillaume out of the room, too excited at the prospect of whatever the next illicit moments would bring to take any notice of Vicky's odd behaviour.

"Suit yourself," she smiled, handing Maria the bottle. "Gui?"

Without another word, Jenny lightly took Guillaume's arm, smiling directly up into his face – a smile that was rewarded by a frown and a cautious look. She guided him toward the steps up to the hallway, standing back to allow their next-door neighbour to pass down the hall between them, smiling politely. Once he was gone, in the cool of the space, she turned the handle to enter the room on her right and strode into the darkness of the little study, holding the door open for Guillaume to enter and then closing it quickly behind him, leaning against it to prevent anyone coming in.

"Turn the light on," she heard Guillaume hiss.

"No," she bit back. "Come here."

Her breathing was ragged as she anticipated his lips. Where would they fall? Her lips, her neck?

She was disappointed.

"Jen, I'm serious," he replied. "Turn on the light for a moment. I really need to talk to you. It's important."

She complied, leaning still against the door and reaching out to feel for the switch. The harsh light of the bulb made her wince. And it made her see clearly that the worried expression was still on Guillaume's face. A flash of disappointment, of annoyance flared in her. What did he want to talk about? What was so important to him that he would dare to use this wonderful, secret, illicit time for something more than kissing or touching or breathing each other in?

She watched as he lowered his bulk onto the swivel-chair that sat in front of the desk opposite. He rubbed his face with his hands, pulling them together as if in prayer and looked directly at Jenny.

"I need to say this to you, Jen," he began, his voice grave. "It's so important. I just want you to know that everything – *everything* – that I've said to you over all this time is true. I am in love with you, yeah? I didn't mean to fall in love with you, and I don't want to hurt Ed, but I cannot get you out of my head. I want to be with you all the time. I want to spend eternity with you. You understand that, don't you?"

Jenny nodded, unable to think of anything to say. Of course he didn't love her. He couldn't. This was an affair, Not Real Life. Wasn't it?

"I meant it when I said I wanted you to come away with me and this is the last chance I'll have to say it to you before I go, okay?

Now listen to me. I swear to you that I mean every word of this. Tomorrow, I'm going back to Manchester, okay? I've just promised an old friend up there that I'll help him launch his new company but then that's it. I'm going. And I want you with me.

"I've booked two seats on a British Airways flight to Cape Town on the 23rd – my parents have moved house and I've promised to spend Christmas with them – but I *need* you to come with me."

He paused for a moment.

Jenny remained frozen, her back to the door, wide-eyed as she listened. This was Real. But it couldn't be, could it?

Guillaume took a deep breath, ran his fingers across his hair and continued, his expression pleading.

"The flights are from Heathrow – I get back from Manchester that morning. If you meet me at the flat that afternoon we can go together. Don't bring too much because we're going to make a whole new start there. Do you get me?"

Jenny didn't. Couldn't take it in. And as if it wasn't difficult enough, she was suddenly disturbed by a loud banging on the door behind her. She felt the wood vibrate against her bare back as she stood there, staring at Guillaume in complete shock, unable to take it in.

"*Gee-yummm!*" came the voice from the hallway.

The handle of the door rattled as Vicky turned it back and forth violently. Obviously he had been out of her sight too long.

"*Gee*," she whined. "It's time, I reckon – are you in there?"

Jenny reached out to the handle and made to remove her weight from the door when Gui shot over to her side. He covered her hand with his for a moment and leaned in so close that Jenny was sure the kiss that she had longed for up until a moment ago was about to come. She found herself oddly grateful that it didn't.

"Whatever she says tonight," he whispered, nodding toward the closed door, "I need you to know that I mean everything that *I* just said. Do you understand me? *Whatever she says . . .*"

With that, the handle was turned so forcibly behind Jenny that she was forced to pull her hand and her body weight away from the door. She moved quickly as Vicky pushed it open and peered around, her face livid.

"What's going on?" she snapped.

Jenny blushed, and turned her head away to examine the bookshelves on her left-hand side. To her relief, a CD sat on top of a pile of papers at eye level. "There it is!" she chirped loudly, ignoring Vicky's demand. "I told you it was in here, Gui." She grabbed it and turned to him, aware that her face still burned but there was nothing she could do about that now. Brave it out, she thought to herself. "It's absolutely brilliant. I'd never heard of them before but the guy in the record shop said that it was amazing – I do hope you like it."

Vicky gave a 'tsk'. "Bloody African music," she snapped and grabbed Guillaume's arm, no longer interested in what Jenny had to say. She swept from the room, dragging a reluctant Guillaume behind her.

Jenny followed meekly, relieved, yet her mind raced.

She stood in the hallway behind them as Vicky perched herself on the steps leading down to the kitchen, unintentionally preventing Jenny's entry. Jenny's head still swam – the sound of Vicky's long nails tapping faintly on her wineglass, her raucous voice calling for quiet and calm, shouting that she had an announcement to make, was distant to her.

It was only when Vicky announced her pregnancy to the room of people who barely knew her and Guillaume leaned against the wall just behind her, his body angled so that he could look at Jenny who still stood, alone in the hallway, and mouthed the words '*I mean it*', did Jenny finally understand what he meant. And understood also that yes, frighteningly, he did mean it. Every part of it. Every single word.

DECEMBER 23RD, 1997

Jenny

Jenny stared at the clothes strewn on the bed. Other Jenny's clothes. Tops and skirts and wedge heels. Don't bring much, Guillaume had said. His words echoed in her head – they had done since the night of the party. The night of Vicky's bombshell. And his. The night that she finally understood that he was serious when he said that he wanted to escape.

Jenny had fretted since. All the signs – all good sense – pointed to the fact that she should stay. She should stay and make her own baby with a man who adored her, to build the future that they had planned. Not to run off across the world with a man who wouldn't stand by a woman who was pregnant with his child – even if she were Vicky.

Jenny thought that she might go out of her mind as Christmas drew nearer. Why on earth couldn't she decide? Why was it even a choice? Stay with Ed and everything that she knew and loved or go with Guillaume?

But wasn't what she knew and loved *all* that she had ever known and loved? Rainy London, Tubes and buses and the corner shop and Pilton Gardens? Wasn't there a huge world out there that she should see? That she owed it to herself to see? Didn't she deserve some spice, some excitement? Didn't everyone think that she had settled too young? That she had never lived a life outside her comfort zone? And in a way, didn't she owe it to Ed to let him do the same?

Jenny's head ached with the argument that she had fought inside herself ever since Guillaume had planted the idea within her. Was she smothered here? Was he right? Shouldn't she take a leap? Take a breath? Gasp in all of the air that the world had to offer? All the passion that a man like Guillaume could bring her? Had brought her since that summer evening when they first connected? A man like Guillaume who could desert his unborn child . . .

Jenny's eyes strayed to Bee. Her own child. Sitting cross-legged on the end of Jenny's bed, clumsily wrapping a scarf around her little neck. It took Jenny a moment to realise what she was doing. She reached out and gently untangled the scarf from the toddler's neck and pulled it gently from her hands. The chiffon fabric slipped through Bee's groping fingers and her face crumpled as Jenny stuffed the scarf into the top drawer of the bureau beside her.

A large tear rolled out of one of Bee's eyes, followed by another. Jenny's heart sank. She longed so badly, ached, to bend and cuddle her. But she couldn't let herself. Couldn't allow herself to smell the baby scent of her, to feel the softness of her cheek wet with tears. It would be too much to bear. Not when the task ahead had to be completed. Not when it made Jenny feel so . . . *impure*, she realised. Her perfection as a mother sullied forever by what she had done to her daughter. She reached out instead and stroked the copper curls as soothingly as she could.

"There now, silly," she crooned. "You can't play with dangerous things, you know that."

Bee responded by pulling herself away from her mother's touch as quickly and as forcibly as she could and, sliding off the end of the bed, pelted out the door in the direction of her own bedroom. Jenny watched her go: the shape of her little legs encased in the bright pink tights under the little denim pinafore, the way that her body propelled her across the landing, surefooted, the arms held out at either side to give her balance. By the time she was halfway across, Jenny knew that the confiscated scarf was forgotten and that Bee was absorbed in the movement of her own body, the air rushing through her fingers. Jenny smiled as Bee flopped to her knees and then stood up again as quickly, bounding into the bedroom in three jumps and disappearing behind the door where her soft toys lived.

She could take her, she thought, and immediately banished the idea from her mind. It was too upsetting. Taking her or leaving her, whichever. Jenny felt the flood of tears at the back of her eyes for the tenth time that day and squeezed the lids shut to hold them back. A sob escaped her throat. She had to leave her here. It was best for her, and that was the most important thing. Stupidly, a part of Jenny ached and throbbed at the thought of being separated from her daughter. The dust would settle eventually. The future would happen, life would go on.

Jenny glanced at her watch and tutted in frustration, picking her bag up off the bed. Where the hell was Betty? She had promised to be here at two, yet now it was half past. And Jenny knew that she didn't have much time. The check-in time at the airport was five, Guillaume had told her in the Christmas card he had sent from Manchester the previous week. It had pleaded with her to meet him at his flat – showered her with messages of love and devotion, promises of fresh starts. Jenny had fancied that she had caught a whiff of Guillaume's scent as she took it out of the envelope and then it was gone. She had ripped the card up and thrown it in the open fire, of course. Not because she didn't long to reread the words in Guillaume's scrawled handwriting, but because she couldn't bear for Ed to find it. Not only to keep the secret safe, but to not break his heart completely.

Lovely, loving and loved Ed. Husband and best friend. The best person she had ever known. Jenny banished the thought from her head. No. She had to do this. There was no point in thinking about him like that now. No point and no headspace.

The doorbell 'binged' suddenly. It spurred Jenny into action and she fled out the door of her room. She paused for a second as she heard Bee croon a tuneless dirge to her dolls and her heart contracted fiercely. Not now, she forced herself. Best that she just go, as quickly as she could. It would be easier that way.

And best not to engage Betty in conversation apart from a brief hello. Best to grab her coat and run as fast as she could, to shout that she'd see everyone later and that there were mince pies in the oven. They had baked them together, Jenny and Bee. They were the last scent she breathed from her home as she slammed the front door of 17 Pilton Gardens behind her, inhaling the freezing cold air as another heavy frost had already begun to settle.

She had planned to take the Tube. It was a five-minute drive to the station. And she was confident enough of driving the route once traffic was light, even though she was taking a risk in driving on her own having not yet passed her test.

Jenny unlocked the car door and clambered inside without a backward glance, slinging her bag on the passenger seat. Betty's lateness had delayed her by . . . Jenny glanced again at her watch . . . three quarters of an hour. That left no time to spare. She needed every second if she were to get there, to catch him on time.

And if it hadn't been for the slow crawl of cars that formed a tailback all the way to the turnoff for the precinct, Jenny might have stuck to the original plan and parked on one of the side streets near Fulham Broadway station, got on a train, changed at Kensington, and made it to Notting Hill in twenty minutes or so.

But that's not what happened.

Because in order to make sure she made it on time, in order to make sure she kept to the first stupid decision she had made, Jenny Mycroft made a second, even more stupid one, and kept on driving.

And that was the end of the end.

2020

Jenny

The belongings, the personal effects that were sent back to my broken-hearted husband all those years ago were as follows:

One watch, gold.

One wedding ring, plain gold band.

One engagement ring, gold and diamond solitaire.

One leather handbag containing purse, diary, tissues, child's handmade Christmas card and other sundries.

Umbrella.

And nothing else.

There was nothing else that was fit to go to him. Nothing that remained unharmed after the fire began, ignited by a spark from the engine in the pool of petrol that spilled out onto the road. Not the manuals in the glove compartment, not the thankfully empty car seat in the back.

It was my own stupid fault, of course. Inexperienced driver tackling Christmas traffic in slippery conditions. A drunk driver coming from a Christmas lunch . . .

They said afterwards that there was nothing I could have done to stop it happening.

But there was.

I could have caught the Tube, stuck with the original plan.

I could have not gone.

I could have stayed at home and baked even more mince pies with my beautiful, wonderful daughter. Or sung carols, or watched The Snowman, or just gazed at the sparkling lights of the tree and smelled her smell and stroked her hair.

I could have just telephoned Guillaume – I didn't have to see him. There was no need. It was just some warped sense of propriety that made me think I should tell him in person.

I could have stayed away from him in the first place, of course.

I could have snuck off to bed on the night of that dinner in summer, like I had planned to do and then I'd never have seen him in that light, in that new way.

I could have done all of those things that Ed wanted me to do. I could have gone to Cambridge, could have taken a different path.

I could have stood up to the fear instead of thinking that escape was the best route.

There was plenty I could have done to stop it actually.

But I didn't, did I?

And so, on December 23rd, 1997, two days before my baby's third Christmas, with my whole life ahead of me with a wonderful man, I died.

I left them.

Which was exactly what I had finally made up my mind never ever to do.

Part Two

Rowan

JUNE 1999

Ed

John Adams died in June 1999, in solitude and silence, much like he had lived out his remaining years after the death of his beloved daughter, Jenny.

Apart from the kindnesses shown to him by his son-in-law, her broken-hearted widower, and the absolute adoration that he felt – but didn't seem capable of showing – for his granddaughter, Beatrice Rose, there was nothing of interest on earth to John Adams. He had outlived the first love of his life – his wife, his Rose – by exactly eighteen years when he finally decided that enough was enough. The death of his only child had finished him. He lasted a mere eighteen months after the car crash that claimed his first and only daughter.

And then his heart simply gave up.

But in the death of John Adams, which was barely marked by anyone, there was redemption. Because finding his father-in-law's body slumped across his bed was what turned Ed Mycroft's life around. The moment was a revelation.

Ed had looked around the room with a fresh perspective. At the sparse, functional furnishings, the outdated wallpaper, the clothing neatly folded and slung over the back of a chair, the single ornament – a photograph of the woman who would have been his mother-in-law had he not been only eleven when she died, her arm slung casually about the shoulders of a girl no older than that. The girl who became his wife. The smiles of mother and daughter were identical, their hair sweeping across their faces in a seaside wind.

In John Adams' fridge were a single pint of semi-skimmed and a sliver of bacon, curled dry at the edges. A layer of dust covered the surfaces in the living room, which hadn't changed since the days of Band Aid and the miners' strikes. His wardrobe consisted of three pairs of trousers, five shirts and two knitted sweaters. And the suit that he had worn to his daughter's wedding, and in which they buried him.

His funeral service was simple and short. No one spoke – hardly anyone came, in fact. Ed placed a Chelsea scarf in his coffin before they closed it at the funeral home, whispering that he hoped it would keep him warm.

And then they buried John Adams beside his wife and his daughter.

That was a family gone. That was that.

But it was enough for Ed Mycroft who turned the key in the lock of his home at Pilton Gardens on the day of that funeral and saw his home – really saw it – for the first time since the day in December 1997 when, incapable of making his own way from work, he had been brought home by a kindly WPC to where his sisters and his mother scurried about his house, ashen-faced and oddly silent.

Since the day a year before when he, too, had given up.

Seeing his home – their home – as a slightly messier reflection of the one where he had found the sad and lonely corpse of his wife's father triggered something in Ed Mycroft. He stopped at the entrance to the living room, stared at the décor – Jenny's décor – in dire need of freshening-up, and thought for a moment that he might be bowled over by the flood of emotions that rushed like a tidal wave from wherever he had kept them at bay. It wasn't the obvious mementoes like their wedding photograph. It was the cushion on the couch that Jenny used to clutch to her when she watched TV, the thick church candle in the holder on the hearth – it suddenly struck Ed that the last time the wick had been trimmed and the flame lit was the night before she died; it was the Patricia Cornwell

on the bookshelf that she had never finished. It was as if his brain
was equipped with some sort of radar that picked out these items
solely. Eventually Ed Mycroft's breath was taken away and finally
he broke completely.

Not the everyday, functioning brokenness that he had sustained
for almost a year now, the brokenness that had confined him to the
house, that had lost him a stone in weight – and his job. Not the
dull veil that had hung over him, blocked out the real world, kept
function to a minimum other than that which sustained himself and
his child. None of these things, in fact.

Instead, it was as if that veil was ripped off his eyes and he
suddenly saw everything in the sharpest relief. And felt pain so
intense that his knees buckled and in the privacy of his own living
room, with the living reminders of his dead wife all around him, he
howled in grief and agony and desperation and misery. He cried
like he couldn't stop, gripping the doorframe beside him to keep
himself from collapse. Memories stabbed him like knives driven
into his heart. He mourned their time together, her passing, and he
raged at the future that had been taken away from him and from
Bee. He had never felt such despair in his life. He hadn't thought
that it was possible.

And when the tears had finally stopped and his back teeth ached
from where he had clenched them together, when he had actually
made himself physically ill, vomiting out more of the blackness and
pain that he suddenly realised was all he had inside him, Ed
Mycroft made a decision. That he was going to have to do
something about all of this, or else risk being found slumped dead
across his own bed at the precise moment that his heart had finally
given up. That he was going to have to function. That he was
somehow going to have to keep swimming through this soup that
he was in, through no fault of his own. And more importantly than
that, he was going to have to carry his daughter on his back, like a
proper father; like a decent human being.

And with no idea how to do any of this, he reached for the
phone book and picked out the first grief counsellor that he could
find within a three-mile radius.

And thus began the time he spent with Dr Phyllida Rice. Who

repaired him as best she could to carry on. Who helped him repair the breaks to the best of his ability.

She encouraged him to talk to others. And he found Betty's husband, Mike, a willing ear in return for a hand on the allotment that he worked. In Guillaume's place – Ed had given up trying to locate his friend – Mike was a steadying hand and a good companion. And somehow it worked. The fresh air, the companionship, the constant talking and thinking. It didn't fix him – Ed knew that he was completely and entirely unfixable. But it helped him to cope.

And by New Year's Eve, the big one, the one where everyone was going to party like it was 1999, Ed Mycroft felt well enough to face the world and went out to celebrate with his brother-in-law, leaving his precious daughter in the care of her aunt.

As he shaved and washed, applied some hair gel and the Hugo Boss aftershave that his mother had bought him for Christmas, he brushed away a tickling sensation at the end of his nose which he thought was a fly, or a cobweb but which was, of course, the tender touch of the person who watched over him at all times – that of his dead first wife.

And then, out on the town, in a haze of fireworks and bottled beer and Auld Lang Syne and relief that the world didn't end on the stroke of midnight, he met his second.

He just didn't know it at the time.

NEW YEAR'S EVE, 1999

Rowan

Rowan Sutherland liked horses; she liked hot baths smelling of rose oil; she liked her laundry to be dried outdoors; she liked autumn, and the feel of velvet against her skin, and the smell of wet dog; she liked the countryside.

There were few things in reality that Rowan Sutherland actively disliked. She just wasn't a 'disliking' sort of person.

One of the things that she did dislike, however, was living in London.

Another was noise.

Another was New Year's Eve.

Therefore, finding herself spending the evening of December 31st, 1999, in a nightclub somewhere near Leicester Square – she couldn't be sure of the exact location – was Rowan's idea of hell.

She wasn't sure exactly why she had accepted the invitation of her downstairs neighbour and friend, Claudia, to come along on "the biggest blowout of all time" but at approximately 10.30 p.m. on Millennium Eve, Rowan found herself nursing a beer, guarding it with her life – not in case someone should take it from her, but in case someone should think that she required another one – and peering across a sea of bouncing heads that moved as one to 'Rendez-Vu' by Basement Jaxx. Everywhere she looked there were party hats, streamers, poppers, blowers, people wearing tinsel on their heads. Claudia wasn't too far away, engrossed in dancing with her friend Jon, and she had somehow managed to obtain a pair of giant spectacles in the shape of '2000' which flashed on and off as she moved. Rowan wondered how it had come to this and sighed, taking another tiny sip of the beer as Claudia caught her eye and pointed a warning finger at her, a warning that she'd better be having a good time or else.

This wasn't what Rowan had planned. It was to be solitary, the transition from 1999 to the new millennium. Locked in her flat with a triple bill of *Jean de Florette*, *Manon des Sources* and *Cinema Paradiso*.

She glanced at her watch. Round about now, Gerard Depardieu should have been relentlessly carting the water back to the farm on the donkey, sweating against the sun and the hardship. Every hint of 'Happy New Year' and threat of 'Auld Lang Syne' should have been eliminated, the curtains drawn against fireworks, plenty of Judith's leftovers to get through and maybe a glass of sloe gin. The intention had been that not even a threat of a Hootenanny would get past her front door. And then she would go to sleep with earplugs in, blissfully unaware of the time, of ships tooting on the Thames, of Big Ben chiming, of revellers converging on Clapham High Street nearby.

The tune changed to one that Rowan despised but couldn't get out of her head. She found herself clenching her fists as the familiar notes and the nonsensical lyrics – *I'm Blue, Da Ba Dee, Da Ba Dah* – rang out across the club and the tempo of the dancers changed and a cheer went up. She rolled her eyes. For this she had left the Quantocks behind her, thinking that it would spare her the festivities planned in the village at home. If she had stayed in Somerset – much as she longed for a brisk New Year's walk along the country lanes near Judith's Acre – then it would have been unavoidable, so she had decided to come back to Clapham to lock herself away. Judith hadn't approved, of course, but there were times when Rowan knew she had to stand firm and this was one of them, even though the old lady looked so uncharacteristically forlorn on the platform as Rowan's train had pulled out. Rowan had steeled herself, however, reminding herself that as much as she respected the crazy old hippy, her grandmother's bidding wasn't actually law.

Yet somehow, she had accepted an invitation to share a single celebratory drink with her downstairs neighbour on passing her open front door on her way back from the video shop. And somehow, that had led to a quick change of clothes before heading down to the Coach and Horses nearby. And then on to a wine bar somewhere that Jon recommended and after that she got a bit lost but there was a pizza involved – thankfully – and then somehow they had ended up here. In something that to Rowan, with her love for meditation and solitude, was like a circle of hell.

She was disappointed with herself. Her sole resolution as Christmas turned into the dreaded New Year celebrations was that she would see in the Millennium alone. And already she had broken that one. Things didn't bode well for the year 2000.

Rowan noticed suddenly that Claudia and Jon had vanished into the crowd and she searched for them desperately for a moment, suddenly completely alone in a sea of strangers. To compound matters, two men were sidling up to the high table where she stood fiercely guarding their coats and drinks and Claudia's Gucci bag. Rowan felt her heart begin to pound and her palms grow sweaty. It was the familiar sensation that struck her when a stranger approached. She made a point of looking into the sea of partygoers around her again, this time to pointedly ignore the approaching men rather than to specifically try to find her companions – not without, however, keeping the pair within her peripheral vision. She couldn't risk herself completely.

The first thing she noticed about the one who leaned in to speak to her was his smell. It was delicious. She was taken aback by the cleanliness of it, the masculinity. Normally she hated the smell of men. She had to know them very well, to trust them before she could tolerate a masculine smell. She much preferred the sweet warm odour of Judith's goats, or the scent of Schubert, her old pony. Safe smells. Comforting smells.

The fact that she had to ask him to repeat himself three times over the music made her even more aware of how pleasant the scent was, however. As it happened, he was merely asking if he and his friend might share the chest-height table – if they could place their drinks on top and their coats underneath, much as she had done. Rowan nodded politely and stared back out into the crowd again, as if completely fascinated by the dancing, which had shifted a little in tempo to fit the beat of Prince's '1999'. It made her feel a little calmer.

Much as she hadn't intended coming here in the first place, the last thing she intended was chatting to a complete stranger, but when her new table-companion had stood there for a good ten minutes, moving awkwardly to the music and ignoring his friend who was avidly checking texts on his phone, she couldn't help but be polite and respond when he leaned over with his lovely scent and asked if she were actually enjoying herself. In fact, she couldn't help but laugh because it was the last thing that she was doing. And by his tone, this sweet-smelling stranger felt the same way. She turned, smiling, and studied his face briefly, noting that he had a very nice smile too. And once she had seen him smile, seen him wrinkle up his nose in distaste at the nightclub in general, seen him point comically at the ceiling where a net of balloons awaited release at the stroke of midnight and make an exaggerated face of dread, she couldn't help but relax a little. He was safe, she decided. Inasmuch as anyone was ever really and truly 'safe'.

His friend whose name was Mike, apparently, didn't say much – he also looked entirely out of touch in his surroundings. He was even wearing cord trousers, she noted, and he kept his eyes firmly glued to the screen of his Nokia 3210 as he mutely shuffled off in the direction of the bar, noting that his glass was empty. It wasn't their first drink of the evening by a long shot, she concluded. The man with the nice smile was decidedly squiffy, too.

"I've come here by mistake," he confessed, leaning against the table.

The line reminded her of another of her favourite movies, *Withnail and I*. She wondered if he were aware of the reference he had just made.

"Me and Mike – he's my brother-in-law – we were only going down to his local and somehow we've ended up at an orgy." He looked around him again, an exaggerated look of confusion across his features. "And we've no idea how to get out so he just keeps buying drinks, and texting his missus, and I'm just wondering how I'm ever going to get home!"

Rowan smiled again: "Me too," she responded – leaning closer to his ear to repeat herself when he indicated that he hadn't heard her. "I'm meant to be at home with a DVD triple bill, but somehow I'm here and I have no idea where my friends have got to."

She glanced out again at the dance floor, slightly worried now at the fact that she hadn't seen Claudia and Jon in so long. Her companion leaned in again to speak and she turned back to him, angling her head so that her ear was near his mouth in order to hear him better.

"In that case, do you mind if I chat to you till Mike gets back?" he asked. "That way we don't look so out of place either. My name's Ed by the way."

Rowan eyed him with mock suspicion. "All right then," she replied. "I'm Rowan."

She smiled faintly and was rewarded with a beam from Ed in return. "Fantastic!" he enthused, energetically shaking her free left hand with his. As he did so, she noted the flash of gold from the third finger in and felt somehow safer at the sight of it. Yet also, oddly, disappointed.

The conversation began with their origins – he was a London boy – Fulham born and bred, he announced. When Rowan shared the name of the coastal village nearest to where she lived he laughed uproariously.

"*Watch-et*?" he barked in disbelief, laughing again. "*Watch-iiiit!*" he warned, jokingly.

Rowan couldn't be cross at him – not at his animated face, his broad smile with all those teeth that could have verged on horsey but somehow didn't. His eyes were brown and crinkled at the edges when he grinned. His face lit up so much when she told him the name of her village that she tried another couple – Nether Stowey, West Quantoxhead, Sampford Peverell, Kilve. He particularly liked the idea of Wimbleball Lake, but before she could think of any more they were interrupted as Mike returned with a bottle of Cava and three glasses which he deposited on the table before pointing at the phone, holding it to his ear and indicating that he was going outside to actually speak on it this time. Rowan watched him bumble meekly in the direction of the exit and felt momentarily sorry for him. He looked as out of place as she felt.

When Mike had disappeared, Rowan turned back to glance at the dance floor, yet paused as she caught sight of Ed. He was staring at the bottle on the table before him and despite the multicoloured lights she couldn't help but notice that he seemed paler than before. He was silent too. Tangibly silent. The lovely jollity, the giddiness of the moments before Mike's return seemed to have deserted him and then he blinked suddenly and looked back at Rowan, that lovely smile spreading across his features again.

"What harm can it do, eh?" he said and invited her with a sweep of his hand to join him in a glass, setting about pouring before she could argue.

Rowan glanced at her watch, and was shocked to see that it was five minutes to midnight. That familiar panic set in with her, the desperate sensation that something would go hideously wrong once the clock struck twelve – unfounded, she knew. Around her, other revellers were whooping and cheering as they lined up their own drinks in preparation for the inevitable midnight toast. A flicker of panic ran through her. What was she doing here? She shouldn't be here – shouldn't celebrate. Should be somewhere safe . . .

A feeling of dread filled her as the crowd around them chanted what she always thought of as a doom-filled countdown.

"*Five, four, three, two, one . . . Happy New Year!*"

Up went the cry and panic gripped Rowan. She wasn't ready for it. She wasn't prepared for that split-second threshold that took her without her consent from an old year into a new one. She tried to calm herself as she gripped the glass that Ed had handed her, and rigidly raised her hand to her mouth to take a slug.

It's all just a matter of minutes, she reassured herself. Nothing has changed except the calendar. Stop giving it so much significance. This was why she hated New Year so much. The forced jollity all leading up to a moment that inexplicably made her panic, that made her feel like a puppy around fireworks. She turned suddenly to look at Ed. He must think her odd, she reckoned, panicking even more. Completely ignoring him like that, ignoring New Year like that.

She was relieved, however, to find that he, too, was in a world of his own.

That he was, in fact, crying.

That two long streaks of tears rolled down his expressionless face as he stared out at the crowd, now jumping on each other to hug and embrace and kiss before wordlessly organising themselves with crossed arms to sing 'Auld Lang Syne'. Silently, the balloons were released from above and the sound of the partying crowd all around them was punctuated with gunshot-like bangs as they burst for one reason or another.

But none of the silver and white balloons that floated gently down between Ed and Rowan made a sound. Watching them fall around him, in fact, Rowan was reminded of swirling snow. And it felt as if everything around her had gone silent for a moment.

It was Claudia who broke it by suddenly reappearing, who reintroduced the noise and the hubbub to Rowan's consciousness as Europe's 'The Final Countdown' blared out.

The following morning, as Rowan lay in her own bed in her own flat, peacefully alone and in the silence of her room, she didn't remember the exact order of things after that, other than the fact that the night had been quite good, actually. That she had talked more with Ed who ceased crying so suddenly that she wondered if she had actually imagined he had been doing so in the first place. There had been more champagne – and even a little tipsy dancing, she was sure.

And there had been the kiss.

The odd, dry-lipped, innocent kiss that she had shared with Ed as they bade each other farewell. As New Year's Eve kisses went, it made the word 'chaste' seem reserved. But as she thought about it – about closing her eyes at the inevitability of it and then at not feeling some passionate, damp, fake embrace close in on her – Rowan felt a small thrill. It had been pure, she remembered. There was no ulterior motive to it. That man – that nice, kind, sad man, had simply kissed her for no other reason than to share a kiss.

She hadn't got his number, however. And he didn't have hers. So that was it. She would never see him again. Which made Rowan feel sad as she lay in her tartan pyjamas on the morning of January 1st 2000, unable to sleep, retracing the night over and over again in her mind, replaying it in case she remembered something that she had forgotten.

What she couldn't forget all day was what Ed had said to her as they had finally said goodbye. He hadn't had so much fun with another human being in a long time, he'd said. *Not since his wife died.* And it was when Rowan thought about this that she understood the tears at midnight.

And it made her all the more regretful that she would never see him again.

MAY 2000

Jenny

He's started to change things around a bit. First him, now the house. Odd things. New cushions – new paint on the walls. I heard him mention new curtains to Betty and 'doing something with Bee's room'. I'm not sure where the money's coming from for all of this. I might be dead, but I'm still conscious of making ends meet, even if there's nothing I can do about it. And it's not like he's in a position of vast wealth these days.

He's changed though. Less like the putty man that he was. A better father to Bee and that's the most I can ask for – not that he was bad, just distracted.

And I worry does that mean he's over me? I have no right to be bothered by that, I know, not after what I did. And I know he's not even thirty yet, and he has a life to live and if I'd been diagnosed with a terminal illness I'd have had that conversation with him where I'd have encouraged him to move on and find someone new and be happy for himself. Mind you, I'd have been lying.

I don't think that's what's going on though. Apart from the odd night out with Mike, he's always here, here for Bee, here where I can keep an eye on him. I don't know what else to do, after all.

If I hadn't been so stupid and so selfish then I'd be the one doing all this house makeover business. I'd be taking care of Bee, getting her organised for school – I can't believe that my baby's starting school already. But if I were still there, I'd be in charge of the ship and he'd be doing god-knows-what – having an amazing career, bringing Grimlet to Hollywood, earning stacks of cash for himself.

Not that that ever mattered to me.

With this amazing hindsight I have now, I know that all that really mattered was how happy he was. How fulfilled. How he used his God-given talents to their absolute best.

I seem to think about God a lot these days. All that's still as much a mystery to me as ever – it's not like I've met Him or Her or anything but I do wonder a lot. Mainly if this is it? If this is forever? Me and my family – me watching over them? Trying, somehow, to see if I can make it up to them for that terribly stupid thing I did, that awful mistake that blew them apart.

Maybe this is God. Maybe God is where I want to be the most – with them. And that's not so bad after all.

Well, apart from missing them. Apart from sitting on the stairs watching as Ed playfully chases Bee up and down the hall and she passes within an inch of me and I reach out what I think is my hand to touch her, but she feels nothing. I forget sometimes. Forget that I'm not actually there, that I'm watching, watching, as if through a pane of glass.

She doesn't see me any more, of course. She doesn't remember me. Then again, if I had simply left her, if I had gone to Cape Town that Christmas, she wouldn't have remembered me either. So I have to content myself with trying to be as close to her as I can, as often as I can and sometimes to brush her cheek with . . . something . . . with my energy . . . when she's asleep – and watch her nose curl up in response. Sometimes, I can even see traces of her baby face, the face that looked up at me from her cot each time she woke and I went to her. That look that said she was amazed and delighted to see me – the look that made me feel like I was the greatest thing on earth. Mostly it's gone too, but sometimes I see it and I'm plunged right back to then. To before.

How could I have contemplated it? Even for a second, how could I have thought of leaving her? How could I have fallen so hard for Guillaume? Or did I just fall hard for the situation? The excitement? Something to lift me out of that rut that I had got myself into – that wasn't caused by Ed, or leaving my job, or having a baby – that was caused by me, me, me and my stupid boredom and lack of guts. God, but I make myself angry when I think about that. It's not even as if Guillaume actually loved me – he couldn't have.

The anger makes me do things, sometimes. Physical things, I've noticed. A lot more than before. I've knocked over some books from the shelves in the living room, for starters. Popped open a DVD case for Bee because I was so frustrated that I couldn't help her do it in person. Broke a couple of glasses, knocked a picture off the hall wall.

And I shifted a chair – that was a big one. It was stupid stupid Vicky's fault. She's got a new look these days. Gone is the sleek, manicured Posh Spice look that she cultivated in the olden days, before she had her baby.

Her little red-haired, pink-cheeked baby girl.

Little Matilda who is almost two now. A hideous little thing – I can say that now I'm dead and I don't have to worry about offending anyone – with eczema and brown bruises from falling over, although she hasn't been walking long. Too fat and lazy to get up off her baby backside and bother to learn, I should think – much like her mother who has embraced what they apparently call 'Pramface chic' wholeheartedly.

I suppose it's not fair to criticise Matilda – she doesn't know any better after all and it's not her fault that her mother feeds her rubbish and never encourages her to move. But there she is. Poor little pink Matilda, with her skin ailments and her three discernible words.

Bee is slightly repelled by her, slightly afraid, the poor thing. She tries to be kind but it's difficult because Matilda's nose is never wiped, and no one pays her any attention so she's a starer – and if she senses for a second that she's going to get love in any shape or form, she latches on and won't let go. Just like her mother in that respect. I do actually feel sorry for her, the poor snot-covered little mite. She's not the brightest button in the box. And as the Mycrofts all have brains to burn – although what they choose to do with them has been their own affair – I can only assume she takes after her dad, whoever he was. Because it also doesn't take the brightest button in the box to work out that it wasn't Guillaume. It was never Guillaume. And while Vicky cried desertion throughout the rest of her pregnancy, cried that Guillaume could never have loved her at all (which was true, of course), I wonder did she know all along that he hadn't sired her offspring?

And I wonder now does he know? Guillaume? Because no one's heard from him. Since the day I died.

I assume that he knows that I'm dead. Or does he? I know that Ed tried to contact him a million times on that awful day but by the time that Ed was informed about the crash, Guillaume would have been in the air – Cape Town bound – with his mobile turned off. And from what I can see from Ed, he never turned it on again. And that was the last that anyone heard of him.

He hasn't come back, hasn't made contact with anyone – which is pretty low considering that when he left he thought he'd almost stolen Ed's wife, along with impregnating his sister. And considering the fact he was convinced that he loved me truly.

I don't know if he knows about Matilda. And her pinkness. I don't think he can because Vicky ranted with amazing regularity that she was sure he must be dead too because he'd never have left her with their child on the way. He has never made any contact with her to find out about the child, has never paid a penny in maintenance.

It's as if he, too, died.

And if anything, his desertion, Matilda's birth and the clear evidence that he could not have been her father has made Vicky even more horrible than she already was; it has made her past redemption.

So horrible that when she reduced Bee to tears at a false accusation, when she called her names and accused her of stealing Matilda's Smarties, when she made Bee feel ashamed and naughty and confused over nothing, I summoned up so much anger that I moved a chair. Just a little bit, mind – it didn't shoot across the room or anything – but it did move just enough for Vicky to think she'd misjudged the distance she needed to cover to plonk herself down on it. Just enough that she fell on her backside and hurt herself.

I am not totally powerless after all. I will still do everything in my limited powers to fight for my beloved Bee, my heart, what's left on earth of my soul.

And maybe what's left of me. Because Ed is getting over me. He's applied for a new job – he's been seeing that Dr Rice woman for quite some time now – he cooks, he cleans – he even whistles the occasional tune. And he doesn't cry any more – not much, anyway. Which is a good thing, I know. But so much is slipping away from me right before my eyes, and moving a chair can do nothing to solve it. I feel that I am growing further away from them. That I am drifting off their radar. That before long I'll be forgotten.

I've been forgotten by Guillaume already – that's clear. But I cannot bear it if they move on from me – if Ed and Bee forget me.

And worse, if I am trapped here to watch it forever.

JULY 28TH, 2000

Rowan

Rowan glanced at her watch for the third time that morning. Immediately, she berated herself silently for doing so. It was only five minutes since the last time she'd done it, for heaven's sake. It was still only nine thirty. That wasn't going to change significantly any time soon.

She straightened her back, rolled her neck along her shoulder blades left and right, and tapped her fingers impatiently on her desk. She should focus, she knew. But it was difficult. The sun was beaming down outside the office. Even though no natural light shone into the reception area, she could see it through the long glass panes of the salesroom every time one of the team wandered in and out to her desk for messages and faxes with none of their usual sense of urgency, relaxed by the sunshine of the day and the promises it brought: lunch outdoors, ice creams for an afternoon break, a cool glass of wine in a sun-soaked beer garden to celebrate the end of the day, the end of the week.

It was one of those Fridays. Casual clothes, a longing to be outside before summer ended forever and time at a virtual standstill. She wished suddenly for it to be one of those frenetic days when the hours would fly, when the phone barely ceased and she hadn't a moment to catch her breath or make a cup of tea, and the sales team were snapping at each other to get things done before the arrival of a deadline and the designers rushed up and down the stairs to and from the enormous open-plan studio above, bathed in the natural light of the atrium on the floor above.

Rowan glanced upward, as if somehow she could magically see, through the white, stippled ceiling above her, all that daylight and blue sky and puffs of clouds that the designers could see if they wanted. She'd look up all the time if she worked up there, she thought to herself. Open spaces inspired her, made her drawings come to life. Although the chances were that she wouldn't be getting up there any time soon. Since starting work as the receptionist at Grafix Designs three months previously, her hopes of rising through the ranks to become an actual designer, from the humble beginnings of the reception desk, were fading by the day. Her heart sank a little as she saw for a moment a bleak future for herself. Two months shy of her thirtieth birthday and here she was, sitting day in and day out in a cheap suit that made her itch, answering calls for other people and unable to figure out how to break through.

Her lack of qualifications didn't help, of course. She was barely even qualified to be a receptionist, come to think of it. She decided to look further into taking a graphic design course. She was good at drawing – it had always been her strength. There had to be a way to make a career out of what she was good at after all. She'd just have to find it. And at least she had her little sideline at home to keep her sane. To keep her from being just a bad receptionist.

For today, however, her only thoughts were of dashing out the door as fast as she could. Through the tourist crowds and down to St Paul's Station. From there, Central Line to Oxford Street – change – Bakerloo to Paddington – and then into the queue for the six-thirty to Taunton. No time for delays or hanging about. More than anything, she wanted to be on that train out of London that evening. Back to Somerset. Back to all the fresh air she could breathe, all the sky she could manage to see at the one time. Back to Judith's Acre.

So engrossed was she in imagining how it would feel at the exact moment that she would disembark the train in a delicious evening breeze at Taunton station, that Rowan failed to hear the squeak of the reception doors opening and the soft stride of a new arrival across the plush carpet. It was only when she heard a light cough that she roused herself from her trance and straightened herself to greet the person who stood there.

He was vaguely familiar, she realised. His hesitant smile was warm. Lots of teeth, Rowan noted, out of the blue. When he spoke in greeting, his voice was soft.

"Hi," he said quietly. "I'm here to see Rob – I've got an appointment at ten?"

"Take a seat," she responded with her habitual smile. "I'll just ring upstairs for him."

With curiosity she watched from the corner of her eye as he sank into one of the leather chairs to the right of her desk and placed the laptop bag he was carrying on the floor at his feet, glancing back at her and frowning as he did so. Who the hell did he remind her of, she wondered again, the question nagging at her as she dialled an upstairs extension and waited for a man with a deep Welsh accent to answer over the speaker with his habitual "'Hoy 'Hoy!" Rowan rolled her eyes and squirmed. Although it was a preferable greeting to his prolonged "Wasssuuuup?" she thought.

"Rob, your 10 a.m. is in reception," she said briefly, making to cut him off as fast as she could but not before he managed to respond with an "Alroight, moi loverrrr!" in his crude approximation of her accent. Rowan coloured immediately and smiled politely at the waiting man who grinned back, a hint of sympathy in the smile.

"Funny guy," he remarked quietly.

Rowan smiled softly back for a moment before returning her attention to a sheaf of pink faxes on the desk before her just as Rob Thompson, Head of Design, bounded through the doors of reception like an eager puppy and thrust his hand at the man who was here to meet him with a loud "All right, mate! Wonderful to see you – come upstairs!" and in a matter of moments they were both gone, leaving Rowan to rack her brains in peace.

She was still pondering the question of who the new arrival looked like when she fled to Postman's Park at lunchtime. She knew she should probably work through, particularly when she was due to finish early, but the day had grown even quieter. Three quarters of the sales staff had disappeared off on imaginary calls and the total silence of the phone made Rowan believe that every single one of their clients had done the same. There were so few sunny days, she reasoned to herself as she grabbed her tub of hummus and the sticks of veg that she had placed in the kitchen fridge that morning. Surely bunking off for a half an hour on one of them wasn't a cardinal sin?

She assumed that by close of business there would be no one left in the office at all, in fact. By then, work, such as it was, would have shifted to a pub near St Paul's – the one with the big beer garden, she imagined. While she flung herself as fast as she could down the steps toward the musty, dank air of the Tube tunnels, freedom finally within reach.

The sun on her arms felt blissful and she took a moment to savour it as she emerged from the building out onto the street. She made her way down to the small park where she often sought sanctuary and ate lunch, and spotted that a favourite patch on the grass was free. In a matter of moments she was settled, her lunch arranged before her and forgotten, her water bottle untouched. It was her sketch pad that was her complete focus, balanced on her knees, her pencil skimming the blank page rapidly as she immersed herself in her true passion. Drawing.

Rowan remained like this for a solid fifteen minutes, frantically sketching on the paper, as if somehow purging herself with a frenzy of activity. Only when she had stopped suddenly and looked up to the sky, made a roll of her neck along her shoulders and took a deep cleansing breath, did she notice for the second time that day, the familiar man from the office, only six feet or so from where she sat, yet somehow she had missed him completely up to now.

She observed him for a moment. Sitting on a bench, a half-eaten bread roll in its wrapping on the seat beside him. He was doing the exact same thing she was. Sketching.

His pace was more measured, she noted, his hand more hesitant and careful about putting the pencil on the paper than hers, his concentration deep. He analysed the work that he did as he did it, stopping every now and again to hold the pad aloft and sit back from it to gain a different perspective.

It was in doing this that he happened to glance over the pad he worked on and caught Rowan staring at him. His response was to feign surprise at seeing her, and then smile again. It was that smile, along with the sudden breeze that brought with it a familiar scent that made Rowan realise finally who it was she was looking at.

It was Ed, she realised with a start. Ed, from New Year's Eve. Ed of the balloons and the tears and the kiss.

And he remembered her too, it appeared, as he stared directly at her, his eyes growing wide and his mouth making the shape of some words in her direction. "*It's you,*" he said, nodding, as if he too, at that precise moment, had just realised who she was.

Rowan could think of nothing else to do except smile herself and mouth back, "*It's me.*"

Without realising for a second how familiar that walk would become to her, Rowan Sutherland watched as Ed Mycroft gathered his belongings and strode the short distance between them to sit awkwardly beside her on the grass and smile again, neither of them entirely sure where to begin.

SEPTEMBER 2000

Rowan

Since the arrival of Ed Mycroft on the design floor, Rowan found herself, every day, looking forward to lunchtime. If she cared to admit it to herself, she had actually started to look forward to going to work. There was something there to interest her now. Something that was more than the isolation of her desk, the constant bleeping of the phones, the ridiculous headset she wore, the demands of the sales team and the taunting mystery of the upstairs floor which she was only allowed to glimpse. Where she longed – or at least thought she longed – to work.

Ed worked up there, of course. He had been an animator, he told her as they sat on their favourite bench in the park between one and two each day. He had worked for a pretty big animation company once, had created a character – nothing special really, but it had done quite well for him, he said, before brushing off the subject to talk about something else.

They ate together outdoors most days. Lunch hour became precious to them and they spent it talking, exchanging their back stories. At least some of them.

There was one thing that Rowan burned to talk about, yet it was a subject that he avoided at all costs. Because after almost three months of knowing each other, Ed had still to make any reference to the dead wife he had mentioned on New Year's Eve. Rowan knew that they had both been drunk but her memory of him saying this was completely clear. She had replayed those words over and over in her mind ever since when she had thought about him and she burned to know exactly what had happened. Had he really been married? How did she die? And what sort of woman had married him?

It had taken him until the end of August for her to find out that he had a child. A daughter, he said. Bee was her name, short for Beatrice. The revelation had surprised Rowan. And unnerved her a little. Because ever since New Year's Eve and that lunchtime in the park back in July, she had known that she was intrigued by Ed Mycroft. Attracted to him. Interested. More interested than she had been in any man since . . . well, since college. Since then.

And sometimes he seemed to be interested in her, too. She would catch him staring at her from under his lashes and see him blush as he looked away immediately, embarrassed at being caught.

And they seemed to have a real connection – they laughed easily together, they listened sympathetically to each other's rants. Rowan had felt, as the summer ended, that she had grown to know so much about him and, in turn, had told him so much about herself. She even had to go as far as to say that she felt completely comfortable with him, that he was entirely honest with her about everything that he had told her so far and as for what he hadn't . . . well, there was still time . . .

So once he had mentioned his daughter, Rowan felt as if she had been smacked in the face. It had never entered her head that such a thing might exist. A child. A daughter. It opened up a whole new element to him, an undiscovered area of his life that unsettled her and led her to wonder if there was much more that she didn't know.

Once Ed mentioned this little Bee to her, this five-year-old girl, Rowan found herself thinking about little else. It had been a Friday when he had told her that he was taking the following week off to get his daughter settled into school. And that had been it. Casually dropped into the conversation, as if he assumed it was something she knew already, and then left, floating in the air as he changed the subject casually to something else.

Rowan stayed at home throughout the entire weekend. Working on her little side project. Her website, her plan.

She had got the idea when she had overheard two women in the park the previous spring, discussing wedding invitations. Complaining about the lack of originality that they had seen in everything they had viewed so far, describing what they thought they might like. Rowan had listened intently. And had gone home and taken out her sketchbook instantly.

She was still at the very early stages of putting her plan into action, but her ideas for quirky wedding invitations had expanded to include birthday and Christmas card samples and now she was working hard on designing a range for newborns. Quirky, hand-drawn sketches, on sustainable papers with interesting colours and textures. She still had a lot of work to do, of course, on making the finished products. But when she had, she would launch her website and see if she couldn't put her talents to good use by selling a few here and there. Corkscrew Cards, she had christened it.

Ed had approved of the name as well as the concept.

As she sat in the sunlight that streamed through her front window on Saturday afternoon, Rowan burned as she thought of how she had told him all about it, trusting him to keep it a secret from everyone else at work, when all the time he had been keeping his own secrets, and now she didn't know if that trust could be reciprocated.

She knew nothing about him, she realised. He had sisters but she didn't know their names; he was from London – hadn't he said somewhere like Fulham? – but she wasn't entirely sure where; he had a child, but she had only just been made aware of this having known him for weeks. A child that was five years old, a child that he hadn't described so Rowan couldn't form a picture of her in her mind – and if there was anything that was guaranteed to rankle with her, it was that. She was visual. And at all times she needed to be able to visualise, and that was the problem with Ed Mycroft. She couldn't visualise anything about him other than what she could see before her.

He, on the other hand, she realised, knew everything about her. About Corkscrew. About the Quantocks – about Judith's Acre. He knew where she lived, who her friends were. He knew her route to Paddington Station every fourth Friday evening, and the train she took back from Somerset on a Sunday evening. He knew that she liked to visit Camden Market on a Saturday afternoon, that she secretly loved folk music and that her grandmother took her to the Glastonbury festival every year and had done since she was a child.

He didn't seem to know, however, how much more she wanted to know about him. And how much she was bothered – yes, bothered – by the idea of his dead wife.

Rowan rested her chin in her hands as she tackled the subject in her head.

His wife. Rowan didn't know her name, didn't even know how long Ed had been married, or how she had died. Did she even exist? Was it just something that he had said when he was drunk on New Year's Eve out of the blue? Some tasteless and unfunny joke? Did he have some sort of dark side to him that she wasn't aware of? And if this wife existed, was she the mother of the child? Of Bee? Had Ed shared a life with someone to the extent that he had started a family with them? Had he wanted more children? Did he want more? Could she trust him at all or what else was he keeping from her? And why did it matter so much?

Rowan suddenly flung the pencil she was holding down on her sketchpad.

She needed to get a grip, she realised. She was verging on becoming obsessed with Ed and experience had served to teach her that that was not a good idea.

There was only one thing for her do, she decided. To just forget about Ed Mycroft. For the time being anyway. Because he confused her. He made her head ache at the same time as making her heart sing. But without the facts, and the honesty, she had to admit to herself that she was really better off without him. For now, anyway.

She had a week to fulfil her promise to herself.

* * *

As Rowan entered the Grafix building on the following Monday morning, she remembered that he was on a week's leave. For a second her heart sank but as she climbed the stairs she resolved that she would block him from her mind and see what the week brought.

It was difficult at first but, on Monday, the clock had struck ten past one before she realised that it was lunchtime. For a millisecond, her hand hovered over Ed's phone extension to see if he was coming for lunch, before remembering that he wasn't there. She took a deep breath to banish the instinctive feeling of disappointment.

Maybe this was how it should be from now on, she thought. Did she really need a lunch buddy after all? Didn't it just encourage the other staff to talk about her behind her back? And she didn't need that. Being whispered about, having no control over what others were saying – behaving in a way that made her visible to them in the first place – that was all stuff that Rowan most definitely didn't need. It was the exact opposite of what she needed, in fact. The exact reason that she had left Somerset behind her.

Which was why, when Friday evening eventually rolled around, she dragged her heels as she made her way into the ladies' to freshen up on the dot of five. She never went to the pub after work but today, however, all staff were to attend – company policy. There was an announcement to be made, they had been told in an internal email. Grafix had 'Great News', it said, the fact emphasised by capital letters and at least ten exclamation marks. And there was to be a celebration attended by all staff (capital letters, 18 point size, bold red font) at 6 p.m. on the dot in the Choirmaster's Inn.

Rowan sighed as she looked at her reflection in the mirror of the ladies' and rooted in the bottom of her bag for her seldom-used make-up. She frowned as she started to apply a light foundation.

It didn't take long to apply her make-up. Her lip gloss in place, she reached around the back of her head and released the bobbin which held her hair tightly off her face and swore suddenly as it snapped in her hand. "Well, *shit* on that anyway," she whispered to herself, the ferocity of the curse somehow negated by the accent that Ed found so amusing.

Ed, she thought, as she rummaged in her bag for some replacement device with which to hold up the uncontrollable curls that had spiralled around her face. There was a name she hadn't thought of in, well, it must have been twenty-four hours at least. Rowan withdrew a hairbrush and began to struggle with her hair. That just went to prove that she'd made the right decision to block him out, she reassured herself. Clearly, Ed Mycroft didn't mean that much to her after all if she had forgotten about him after four days.

But when, less than half an hour later, she spotted him across the pub chatting to Rob, she had to go back on her word. Seeing him out of the context of the office, in a short-sleeved polo shirt and jeans, was completely unexpected. Like a thunderbolt, in fact. Like he was the only other person in the room.

And for Ed, it was weeks later that he finally admitted that he had felt the same when he saw her hesitant entrance through the double doors of the pub. Her hair like a blonde halo around her head, glowing with different colours as the sunlight shone through stained glass, her figure slim in the teal-coloured shift dress that she had worn for casual Friday. And his heart had leaped through the roof at the sight of her. And that for the rest of the night, as they celebrated Grafix's merger with another design company called Iconic, he realised that he wanted nothing more than to be with her.

And so, by the end of the evening, while Rob lined up shots on the bar and their colleagues danced awkwardly amidst the tables, Ed and Rowan were tucked away into a corner together, heads close to hear above the hubbub of the pub jukebox on which someone repeatedly played 'Tubthumping' – talking.

Really talking. About where Ed lived, about his family, about *Grimlet*, about Bee who had bravely watched her dad retreat from her new classroom on the previous Monday morning, the red waves of her hair skimming her shoulders, her chin wobbling slightly. Everything that Rowan had wanted to know, he told her without prompt or hesitation.

Almost everything. Throughout the course of the night – which didn't finish until well after closing time – he still didn't mention his dead wife, except when he described Bee on her first day at school, his eyes distant and misty at the thoughts, and he mentioned how much like her mother she looked.

Like Jenny.

At last, Rowan thought. A name.

There was more that she wanted to know, of course. But that was a start. The name. Jenny. Bee's mother.

And she felt sure that it was only a matter of time before she knew the rest, but that it wouldn't come until Ed was ready. And Rowan knew that she would be there when he was. That her gut instinct was correct. That Ed Mycroft was worth the wait.

DECEMBER 29TH, 2000

Rowan

The old lady's fingers looked gnarled from years of hard work as she accepted the cup of steaming tea. Adjusting it so that the handle was in her left hand and the base rested in the palm of her right, she nodded in the direction of a Viburnum bush. "That'll be your grandad, I'll swear," she observed in a voice barely above a whisper to her granddaughter, who took a sip from her own cup and hunched her shoulders against the biting cold of the winter's morning.

Together, the two women stood and stared at the robin which chirruped from deep in its little throat at regular intervals, its voice clear against the frosty air as it sang out over the farmyard. With a smile, Rowan stole a glance at her grandmother who watched the little bird intently, her eyes momentarily soft and filled with love and delight.

"All right, you silly bugger," she addressed the bird before turning to her granddaughter. "He'll be wanting us to trim the hedgerow again. Like bloody always. Impatient, he is. *Impatient, you are!*" She finished the sentence in a louder tone directed at the robin again, but without frightening him away. "Always so impatient," she repeated, and sipped noisily from her cup, removing it from where it nestled in her right hand to rummage in her pocket for a single cigarillo that had been plucked from the box she kept on the kitchen dresser to accompany her morning tea. She lit it using a tarnished brass Zippo lighter from the same pocket, keeping it in her bare hand for warmth once the cigar was lit.

The familiar scent of the rich, sweet smoke entered Rowan's nostrils immediately. She didn't smoke – had never so much as tried it, despite the constant urging from her grandma's friends to at least try a drag from one of their joints. The smell of the thin cigar, however, mixed with the pure air of the new day, edged with the tang of frost – to Rowan, at that moment, was heaven. It was home.

Yet for once, for the first time since she had come to live there, Rowan had spent Christmas longing to be somewhere else. With someone else. Over the past few days she had come to the realisation that yes, it was serious with Ed. Very serious indeed.

"Maybe I should go and get him some Christmas cake?" mused Judith aloud, taking a deep drag of the cigarillo and staring still at the robin. "*You'd like that, Emerson, wouldn't you?*" she called to the bird, which cocked its head in her direction as if listening.

"Judith," Rowan chastised softly. What would anyone think if they heard her, for heaven's sake? Talking to birds.

She was rewarded with a sideways glance, a raised eyebrow and the long, gentle exhalation of fragrant smoke.

"Who on earth is round here to hear me talk to a bird?" Judith asked drily, indicating the valley that spread out below them, picture-perfect white with rare hoarfrost and completely still. "Besides which, even if there were someone round to hear, they wouldn't expect any different from me," she sniffed, turning her attention back to the robin. "That right, my love?" she called out, smiling as she did so.

Rowan had never known Emerson Garvey, her grandfather. He had died from a brain haemorrhage the year before she was born, his body found on the ground outside the dairy by one of the farmhands. Dying as he did, he left his wife bereft. "I was a widow and a grandmother before I was even forty," Rowan remembered her saying once. It had stuck with her, had seemed so ancient when she was a child. It was only now, as she entered her thirties, that

Rowan realised just how young she had been. And how long her grandmother had been alone.

Alone, Judith had inherited the farm, which Emerson had called Judith's Acre in her honour, and had worked at tirelessly to make into a substantial dairy holding. Alone, she had rented out some of it and sold the rest, in order to leave herself with a manageable smallholding. Alone, she had dealt with the sudden death of her only daughter and son-in-law some eight years or so after losing her husband. And alone, she had opened her arms and taken her grandchild in to live with her in the untidy farmhouse, along with the chickens and the goats and the remaining ponies in the stables, the vegetables in the adjoining garden and the tomatoes and marrows in the greenhouse. Looking at the old lady in the morning sunshine, it suddenly dawned on Rowan that she had been alone for longer than she had been married. And she had done it, had managed. And Rowan had never wanted for anything from her in their entire time together.

"What are we doing out here, child?" grumbled Judith suddenly, turning abruptly to look back at the farmhouse which was badly in need of a coat of whitewash. She placed the half-smoked cigar between her lips at the corner of her mouth and slung the last of her tea into the grass of the ditch that bordered the farmyard where they had stood, overlooking the valley. "I know I like a bit of fresh air in the morning but that's enough for now. Can't feel my bloody toes."

Rowan glanced down at her grandmother's feet and smiled, rolling her eyes affectionately. "Judith, you've got your slippers on," she scolded. "And there's not much point in wearing a rug over a waxed jacket on top when you've got silk pyjama bottoms on below."

Judith shrugged. "Perhaps," she sniffed, throwing a grin over her shoulder at her granddaughter who still gazed out at the fields below, the odd curl of smoke rising here and there from a distant farmhouse.

Rowan could never tire of looking at this view. Whether it was rich with lush summer greens, or white as it was now, it restored and revived her every time she took it in.

She turned and fell into a slow step beside her grandmother as they crossed the short distance to the back door of the house which had been left ajar.

"Couldn't let a morning like this pass all the same though, could we?" Judith asked softly.

It had been their habit since Rowan was a child, since she had first arrived here and Judith would take her outside for her morning milk to try to take her mind off the fact that she was starting another day without her parents. Eventually it had become a happy event, undertaken religiously, even if it were a brief scamper across the yard in torrential rain just to peer over the hedge down to the murky scene below and then run back to the house again, screaming with laughter, and dodging puddles.

"It's a lovely one all right," Rowan agreed, linking Judith's arm and feeling the warmth of the thin body underneath the tartan blanket and the muddy jacket that had been slung on over her night attire. Judith had always been slender, as was Rowan. Rowan's unruly hair was the product of her father's branch of the family, however. The Ilkley Mop, Judith called it. Her own hair had been straw blonde and straight to her shoulders until the day that she had chopped it into a short crop following Emerson's death. And that was how it had stayed over the years, turning first to salt and pepper and then eventually to the platinum white that it had stayed.

The kitchen felt cosy as the two women stepped back through the door and shut it behind them. Rowan busied herself removing her grandmother's wellingtons that she had slid her feet into when carrying out the tea and Judith crossed to the porcelain enamelled sink, lowering her empty cup in, and running the tap over the still-burning end of the cigarillo, hearing it give a satisfying hiss as it was extinguished. She turned then and crossed to the door of the wood-fired stove which she had lit earlier, casting the butt inside and closing it again. All these movements, thought Rowan. All so familiar, yet nowadays so alien. Her heart was suddenly gripped with sadness and a hint of panic at the clear realisation that she really didn't live here any more. She took a deep breath, urging herself to get it together.

"You haven't said as much," said Judith suddenly, crossing to the fridge and peering in at the groaning shelves of Christmas leftovers, "but I'm guessing that you're not going to stick around for New Year again, am I right?"

Rowan's heart sank as she thrust her feet into the pair of slippers that she had discarded at the back door. Of course Judith was right, but she had put off telling her all over Christmas so that it wouldn't hang over them like a shadow, like it had done the previous year. There would be no big millennium celebration to avoid this time, of course, so there was no real reason for her *not* to welcome in 2001 at the Acre. But she couldn't, she knew. There was a special anniversary to be celebrated elsewhere. In a country house hotel in Berkshire, in fact, where she and Ed were to spend their first proper weekend away together. Rowan suddenly looked at her plans – the spa, the five-star restaurant, the four-poster bed – through Judith's eyes and at once felt disloyal and profligate. She wouldn't tell her that bit, she decided. Not if she wanted to be told firmly that it was far from spas that she was brought up, a fact she was only too well aware of.

Rowan cleared her throat. "I'm going to go back to London tomorrow," she replied, her voice small and timid.

She fully expected to hear the fridge door slam and its contents jiggle loudly as Judith's legendary temper blew into force. Instead, there was calm and the normal kitchen sounds as Judith removed the milk and shut the door gently behind her.

"Good," she replied.

Rowan looked at her in amazement.

"Not good that you're going, of course," continued Judith, filling the kettle, "but good that I'll have your room. The gang are coming up here to ring in the New Year, you see, and I'll imagine that there will be a few that won't make it back so I'll need all beds free for their old bones."

Rowan grinned in surprise. "Their old, stoned bones, you mean," she smirked.

Judith's friends were themselves the stuff of legend. Two couples – Ron and Jean, and Dave and Peggy – a widow called Susan and a widower by the name of Gunther – all folk who had settled in the area over the course of the 1960s and 70s and befriended each other over a love of red wine and knowledge of where to obtain the best marijuana. Rowan was suddenly very grateful indeed that she wouldn't be around on New Year's Eve. The Glastobuddies, as she liked to call them, were notorious for getting out of hand at parties – even though all of them were a long way past the first flush of youth.

Judith tutted, well used to her granddaughter's disapproval. "You know Susan only uses it for medicinal purposes. It's her back, you see . . ."

"You don't have to justify it to me, Judith," laughed Rowan. "It'll be the party of the century, I know. You folk will all party like it's 1969!"

"Don't be cheeky," Judith replied snippily. "Anyway, what are your plans, then? Staying in that little hole you call a flat in Clapham with a read-along film and a cup of Horlicks?"

It was Rowan's turn to frown. "You know I don't drink much, Judith," she bit back, folding her arms and observing her grandmother make another two cups of tea. It took at least four to get the day started, after all. "And I actually have plans this year. I . . . I'm going away, actually. For the New Year's weekend . . . with a friend."

There was a moment when Judith froze, but just a moment. A blink would have disguised it, but Rowan saw it as she watched her intently for a reaction. The silence that followed lasted a millisecond too long until Judith recovered herself enough to speak.

"That'll be nice," she managed. "I don't suppose it's anyone I know?"

Rowan sighed. "Look, I've met someone, all right? That's what you're trying to get out of me, isn't it? If it's a boy – a man – and it is. And he's lovely and kind and caring. He works at Grafix too – he's one of the designers – it's a really good job. And it took us ages . . . well, before it turned into something more than a friendship . . . which isn't to say that it's *much* more, but I think it might be . . . it *could* be . . . and I think it's time and I think I'm ready . . ."

Rowan's voice trailed off as she watched her grandmother desperately, waiting for a response. Judith, after all, was the only person who knew. Was the person who had picked up the pieces the last time. And there had been no one since then. Not a soul.

Rowan watched as Judith stood still for a moment, paused in the act of making tea, her back turned to her granddaughter as she leaned against the counter top and stared straight ahead.

"Happen you're right, Rowan, love," she said softly. "Happen you're right."

Judith turned, and Rowan marvelled for a second at the emerald green of her eyes in the sunlight that shone in through the window over the sink.

"I think it might be time," she continued. "But will you promise me something, love?"

Rowan nodded, tears pricking at the back of her eyes.

"You're a good girl, Rowan," continued Judith, a slight waver to her voice as she spoke. "And what happened before . . . well, you know that wasn't your fault, don't you?"

Judith nodded, unable to speak, bowing her head so that Judith wouldn't see the tears that ran suddenly down her cheeks.

The old lady continued. "Well, you just remember that, this time. And remember that you're beautiful and precious and that you deserve the best, you hear me?" She paused for a moment. "And Rowan . . . ?"

Rowan nodded again, raised her head a little to hear.

"You be careful this time. Just take care of yourself. And remember that I'm always here at the Acre, do you hear? Always here for you."

And with that, Judith turned back to making the tea, carrying on as if nothing had ever happened. Just like she had always managed to do.

MARCH 2001

Jenny

It's happened. A single knock on the front door and everything has changed. I'm filled with so many emotions – such heightened emotions. I am anxious, worried – I am in turmoil. It can't be happening. Cannot actually be happening. Is it too soon? Should he dare to do this at all? Did I expect it? Was I right to think it might never happen or was it inevitable?

Bee isn't happy either. Does anyone understand that? Has anyone actually thought of her at all and what she might be feeling? I am so angry with Ed – how dare he do this to her? How could he be so thoughtless as to land this on her like that?

What does it mean? Will everything change completely now? Will he leave? Will he take my baby away from me? Will he go away from me?

How could he be possibly ready? Only five minutes ago it seems that he couldn't get through the front door to get himself to work – and now this. It will not end well – it can't. It's too soon. Too soon.

Does it mean he has forgotten me? Is over me? Has he boxed me off? Put me in a compartment entitled 'the past'. Is that it – am I just something from his past now? Just a memory? Am I 'before'? No longer part of 'now'?

I cannot bear that. I cannot be just an occasional fond thought when I feel everything so fiercely still. It will pass, surely. It's just a thing that he has to go through. It's not the real thing. It couldn't be. Not this soon after me. It's just something that I will have to bite my lip and get through, while he learns, while he gets it out of his system and then I can have him back.

I just have to get through it – whatever it is with this woman who has come to our door.

MARCH 2001

Rowan

Rowan knew, from the first moment that she set foot inside the door of 17 Pilton Gardens, that she wasn't welcome. It wasn't something that she could explain – it was ridiculous, irrational, but from the instant Ed had opened the front door, despite the fact that he was there, grinning from ear to ear with delight at seeing her, she felt that she couldn't relax. She was overwhelmed by a feeling that to enter she would need to break through some sort of barrier. She had a real sense that she didn't belong.

It could, of course, have been that horrible child, she reasoned. Bee. Ed's pride and joy. Who had stuck her tongue out before screaming at Rowan to *"Get Out!"* and running to her bedroom where she hid for the duration of the visit. Until Ed had tried to force her downstairs to say goodbye which caused a tantrum of mammoth proportions. Rowan had been glad when the time came for her to slip quietly away, leaving Ed to calm his child who, with her red curls and screeching voice had reminded Rowan of Violet Elizabeth Bott from the *Just William* books.

So that was Bee, she thought to herself. The Big Meeting. She and Ed had openly been a couple at work since just before Christmas and Judith had been told at New Year.

Only Ed's family to go then. To make the official announcement.

That they were serious about each other – that they were going to give this a go. But first, a visit to Pilton Gardens – an address named after a Somerset Village – a good omen, surely? – to meet Bee. Queen Bee, she thought bitterly.

Rowan wondered if Bee's reaction might have been because of something she did, but she couldn't for a second think what that might have been. She hadn't said anything other than "Hello", hadn't been overly affectionate with Ed, hadn't tried to establish any form of supremacy or go to the other extreme and try to be instant best friends. Regardless of all the advice on how to deal with this sort of thing, that just wasn't her style.

Her heart was heavy as she walked away from the house, Bee's squeals still audible from behind the closed door. Was she destined to be the wicked stepmother, then? She wasn't even entirely sure that she wanted to be a stepmother of any sort, in fact. The part of her that so wanted to be with Ed had naïvely overridden any fears – any thoughts, in fact – of what meeting his daughter would actually be like. But seeing Bee's little face scrunched up with rage, her eyes narrowed with instantaneous hatred, her fists clenched and her knuckles white with tension – and all of it directed at Rowan – had been a sharp shock. Rowan had felt completely ill at ease.

But maybe that was the problem? Maybe she gave off that *vibe* and the child sensed it. Maybe Rowan emitted some low frequency of fear and Bee, with the ruthlessness of her tender years, took advantage of it? Maybe it was because Rowan couldn't, for a single second, not think about how uncomfortable the house made her feel in the first place and she somehow projected this discomfort? Or maybe it was simply that Bee was absolutely – and probably justifiably – horrified at the thought of her father taking love away from her and passing it over to someone else? Rowan sighed. Thinking about it like that, she'd probably have thrown a tantrum too.

She'd need to swot up on it, she reckoned. After all, it had been solely Ed and Bee for so long – five years now? And it was clear from the way he spoke about his child, from the way that he glowed when he talked about her, that Ed quite simply and quite unashamedly worshipped the ground that Bee walked on. And why wouldn't he? His only child, the last remaining link to Jenny. She could understand perfectly how every sentence he uttered to her finished with the word 'sweetheart' or 'precious' or 'darling'. She couldn't understand, however, why he allowed Bee to interrupt conversations constantly to demand information, food, attention, hugs. She couldn't understand why he suddenly walked off, mid-chat with Rowan, to make Bee a sandwich which she rejected instantly, flinging the contents on the floor. Couldn't understand why he didn't tell Bee to wait until he was finished speaking, or not to interrupt adults or to pick up her mess, like Judith had always instructed her. Rowan surmised that she had a lot to learn about children. And their parents for that matter.

She was due to return the following weekend – Ed had phoned her while she made her way home in the brightening evening, once Bee was settled.

"Take Two," he'd gently urged, as if selling her the idea. "We'll do it on her territory again but I'll have a word with her in between times. Maybe if we can get through lunch she might tolerate a trip to the park afterwards, what do you say?"

And Rowan knew that she had no choice but to say yes because, as off-putting as his child was, when weighed against the strength of the feelings she had for him, she found that yes, she did wish to try again the following weekend. And the weekend after, if needs be. She'd just have to get herself used to it all. Learn a bit more about how to manage kids. And brace herself for his house and that strange, eerie feeling that she had there. If she wanted to be with Ed, then she'd just have to get over the feeling that she wasn't welcome. The feeling that she wasn't even wanted.

SEPTEMBER 2001

Rowan

Jon had found it hysterically funny, of course, with that childish sense of humour of his. He'd even gone so far as to give her a copy of Hitchcock's *Rebecca* on DVD as a housewarming gift. Even Claudia expressed reservations.

Rowan had called her friends together to announce that she and Ed were moving in together in expectation of a celebration: of congratulations and best wishes. Looking at their concerned faces, she realised that she had most definitely thought wrong.

"It was *her* house, sweetheart," Claudia had observed over Jon's vodka martinis in her flat where they lounged around the pastel-painted living room, decorated like something straight from a Doris Day movie. "His wife. His *dead* wife. If that's not a bad omen for you guys . . ." She had left the sentence hang in the air.

Rowan had shrugged in response, sipping an orange juice. "I know it's maybe not the most romantic thing in the world," she reasoned, which was greeted by howls of laughter from an already tipsy Jon. "But it's practical. It makes sense." she had continued, once he had calmed a little. "My lease is up and if I stay then I'll face a rent hike. On the other hand, Ed's mortgage is low, so even if I pay a share of it I'll still be paying slightly less than if I stayed here. Plus, there's Bee to think about. She's lived in that house all her life – isn't it weird enough that she has to get used to a complete stranger moving in without having to be completely uprooted as well?"

Claudia and Jon had remained unconvinced.

"That's so dull, darling, I need to put the light on," Claudia had replied drily.

Rowan sighed. "Besides which – there's a whole room that I can use for Corkscrew Cards. Now that I've got that space, I can seriously think about giving up Grafix and working at that full time – I'm swamped with orders as it is and it will be far better for me and Ed if we don't live and work together. It gives me the opportunity to do something I love – to be my own boss. Doesn't everyone want that?"

"And I suppose you want to use his dead wife's forks and knives and teacloths – and sit on the furniture where she sat, and sleep on her side of the bed . . ." said Jon.

"Enough!" barked Rowan, uncharacteristically. "Now you're just being silly. It's not ideal, I know that. And we're buying a new bed, as it happens. But I love Ed and he loves me and this is called compromise. It's what grown-ups do in relationships."

"Except it seems to me that there's only one of you actually making compromises." Claudia's voice was low. And wise. As always.

Rowan had sighed again and toyed with her glass of juice.

"We are genuinely happy that you've met Ed, Rowan," Claudia continued. "But for what it's worth, I think that if you're moving in together, then a fresh start would be best . . . I *know* that there are complicating factors, but don't settle for anything that doesn't make you happy, do you hear? Don't settle."

Rowan frowned. They had a point, particularly Jon with his observation about living day to day with Jenny's things. Would it drive her mad? Wondering if everything she touched, everything that she used on a daily basis had been Jenny's? Had Ed's wife drunk tea from this mug? Lain her head on that cushion? Was Rowan's underwear drawer also Jenny's?

Rowan shook her head to banish the thoughts, took a deep breath and drained her glass of juice.

NOVEMBER 2001

Rowan and Ed

Rowan picked at a piece of lint on the hem of her dress and then rubbed her forefinger and thumb together until it floated to the ground and disappeared in the multicoloured rug. She then pulled the dress over her legs which she had folded underneath herself. For the tenth time since she had sat down fifteen minutes before, she glanced around the room. Three weeks she had lived at 17 Pilton Gardens now. Everything she owned had been unpacked, her belongings merged with Ed's. They looked a little out of place, she had to admit. She hadn't realised how much her tastes mirrored Judith's until they were taken out of the context of her flat and put against the modern, minimalist décor of her new residence. Beaded lampshades and heavy throws in velvets and brocades, collected at second-hand shops and brought from the Acre itself. The small jade Buddha that Rowan always kept in the hallway, the pair of admittedly ugly but much-loved ceramic cats that had come from her father's family in Yorkshire. All of it, out of place against what she knew to be Jenny's handiwork. It was a feeling that didn't serve to make her any more comfortable in the slightest in her new home.

She stood, abruptly, deciding that she needed to keep herself busy, that it was nerves that were making her anxious and negative. She swept from the living room and out into the hall, walking intently down to the kitchen and through to the sunroom where she studied the scene before her with satisfaction.

Rowan had laid the dining table with a rich gold raw-silk cloth and then added pale-green silk placemats and a matching table runner. In the centre was her pride and joy, the centrepiece that she had made from leaves collected on a trip to the park the previous day – vivid golds and browns and reds, arranged around a cluster of conkers and pinecones that Bee had grudgingly helped to gather with her.

At least there was an impasse between them at the moment, Rowan reflected thankfully. An entente cordiale, even. Bee's open animosity of those few months ago had now turned to a suspicious tolerance, much to Rowan's relief. It wasn't ideal – she still had to be on her guard with more or less everything that she said or did in relation to the child – but at least the tantrums had stopped.

Bee even tolerated time alone with Rowan now, occasionally suggesting that they play together, or offering to help out in the kitchen. Rowan had put her to good use a few times, allowing her to help to pack orders of invitations and envelopes, working together in the small study that was now the headquarters of Corkscrew Cards. And in doing so, she had found in herself a new understanding of the angry, bitter girl.

Rowan had begun to see Bee less as a tiny tyrant, and more as a terrified, motherless child, trying her best to make sense of the enormous change that was taking place in her life, trying to get used to a strange new mother figure – a mother figure being something that she had never known, or at any rate did not remember.

Which was something that Rowan understood only too well, something that was brought home to her while she paused to watch Bee examine a sample that had caught her eye while helping out one day. It was a birthday invitation, cream woodchip paper, decorated with dried flowers and a small cluster of red beads and paste jewels that glittered on catching the autumn sun through the window. "This is lovely, Rowan," she had announced, out of the blue, smiling suddenly for a moment before remembering that Rowan was not to be smiled at and returning to her habitual frown.

But for a second, Rowan knew that she had seen through all of the bluff, all of the front that the child could muster, all of the pretence, through to the real Bee. Through to a sweet, innocent little girl with magpie tendencies. And in that instant, her feelings for Bee changed. Her heart opened a little wider than she had thought it possible to do and she resolved to try a little harder – not just for Ed's sake, but truly for Bee's.

Rowan glanced at her watch again and then looked away from it with annoyance. She was nervous of meeting her partner's family for the first time, particularly with Ed's warnings that they could be difficult to manage ringing in her ears. At least the dinner table looked great, she admitted, even if she said so herself. And the food was prepared already – Judith's chicken pie, accompanied by creamed leeks and buttered carrots and a Queen of Puddings for afterwards.

It was one thing she could be completely confident about. Her food. Taught at Judith's elbow since she was a small child, she felt entirely at home in a kitchen. Silently, she leaned over the table and screwed the cap off the bottle of red wine to allow it to breathe. It was a good one, the man in the off-licence had told her. "Good grub and good wine," she whispered to herself, feeling a little better at the reassuring thought that she was well-prepared. Preparation was the key to everything, Judith always preached.

Suddenly, Rowan whipped around to face back in the direction of the empty kitchen. She was sure . . .

There was no one there. Nothing at all, in fact.

She breathed in deeply, and out again, realising that her heart was hammering against her ribcage with fright. That was the second – no, the third – time it had happened in the time since she had moved in. It was stupid Jon's fault that she was so jumpy. Stupid Jon filling her head with stupid notions about Ed's dead wife and stupid Rowan for letting her imagination run riot.

It was all just anxiety, she reassured herself. Anxiety at moving in with someone – at moving in with a man, with whom she was having a relationship, of all things. She'd never done that before. Anxiety at these feelings she had for him, the intensity and the suddenness of them, anxiety at having a child thrown into the equation. Anxiety about what others would think, at where all this was *leading*.

Rowan's body suddenly virtually convulsed with shock at the loud clicking noise which suddenly invaded her thoughts, coming from far down the hall. The front door, she realised, after a second. Ed. He was home. She heard the buzz of voices from the hallway, the thump-thump-thump of two sets of children's feet – Bee's and her cousin Matilda's – disappearing into the front room and the instant hum of voices and light-hearted music from the TV. Her body flooded with gratitude for a moment as she turned and saw Ed's beaming smile as he stood at the top of the kitchen steps.

Rowan beamed in return at him as he stepped down into the kitchen. It was a smile that soon faded, however, as she was greeted with the grim and serious faces of the people who followed him.

"Rowan, these are my parents," said Ed. "Eileen and Frank. And this is my sister Vicky. Everyone, this is Rowan."

"So pleased to meet you, everyone," she said lightly, her hand extended in greeting. A hand that remained extended into thin air for just a moment too long, before Ed's father reached in from between his wife and daughter and clasped it firmly, nodding his head at Rowan before awkwardly releasing the hand and turning to Ed to request the Sunday newspaper.

"I'll get it for you now, Dad," replied Ed, guiding his father back up the kitchen steps toward the living room where Rowan knew that the papers lay on the coffee table.

Immediately, she became uncomfortably aware that she was under intense scrutiny from the two women who now remained, facing her, still standing stiff at the bottom of the kitchen steps, coats and scarves on, waiting for something, or someone to take care of them.

Rowan took a breath and smiled. "Let me take your things," she offered. "It's a bit nippy out there today, isn't it?"

She was rewarded with silence.

Eileen Mycroft sighed as she unbuttoned her red coat and slipped it off with what seemed like unnecessary effort, passing it to Rowan who mumbled a "There we go!" as she draped the coat over her arm and accepted the scarf that followed. Rowan then reached out to take the black leather jacket which Vicky had removed carefully, watching Rowan closely as she did so, before thrusting it at her rudely.

"Don't put that jacket in the cupboard under that manky stairs!" Vicky barked suddenly. "It's designer. Put it somewhere that I can keep an eye on it."

Rowan was stunned and opened and shut her mouth again, unable to formulate a response. She glanced at Eileen, who was rooting through her handbag for something, completely ignoring her daughter's rudeness.

For a moment, Rowan contemplated saying something . . . but what? Telling Vicky to ask nicely and say please, like she might of Bee? Instead, she silently gathered herself together and carried the coats up to the hall meekly, where she draped them over the bannister, before taking a deep breath, steadying herself and returning to the kitchen.

"Would anyone like a drink?" she offered politely before noting that Vicky had made her way to the table and was already clutching a glass of red in her hand.

"Got one," she said flatly. "And could you make sure that them two don't disappear anywhere?" She nodded toward the door into the hallway where the voices of squabbling children could be heard. "Need to keep an eye on those two when they're together," she remarked drily, taking a large slug from the glass. "That Bee's a sneaky little biter when no one's looking. I ain't going home out of here with chunks gone out of me kid again. Ain't that right, Ma?"

Rowan's eyes widened at the words and she looked at Ed's mother to see if she agreed with this opinion. She knew that Bee was prone to tantrums and liked to deliver the odd kick here and there, but in all the time Rowan had known her, she had never shown signs that she might be rough with other children.

Eileen looked up from her handbag and directly at Rowan, giving an exaggerated shiver as she did so. "Could I have a cup of tea?" she asked, oblivious again to what her daughter had just said. "Only it's ever so cold in this room – always has been. In fact, I might have my coat back if you don't mind. Very parky. Have you got no heating on?"

Shocked, Rowan nodded and turned, retracing her steps to the hallway where she retrieved the red coat and returned it to its owner who slung it around her shoulders before silently making her way back up the kitchen steps toward the living room, followed by her daughter.

* * *

By the time lunch was over Rowan was exhausted. The demands and the criticism had been relentless.

"Take those filthy weeds off the table. Can't eat with them there!"

"Ain't that tablecloth very colourful, Mum? Like something you see in an Indian's house."

The food – the delicious pie and trimmings – was sniffed at, poked, analysed and commented upon, but not before a demand had been made for chicken nuggets and chips for Matilda who didn't eat "all that sort of creamy stuff". Preparing them – for a child who looked like she ate little else – delayed lunch by almost half an hour and Rowan bristled as she served up the food that had been reheated.

Even her own portion of nut roast couldn't go ignored. It was Ed's Dad this time: "You a tree-hugger then, love?" he asked loudly, pointing his knife, held like a pencil, at Rowan's plate.

She reddened as the others peered in to stare.

"Rowan's vegetarian, Dad," responded Ed. "She doesn't eat meat but she was very good to make you a lovely chicken pie, wasn't she?"

He was answered with a grunt as the old man shook his head, mystified at the prospect of someone who didn't eat meat, which prompted Vicky to wade into the conversation.

"Give over, Dad," she said through a mouthful of potatoes. "It's the twenty-first century now, for heaven's sake. Veggies ain't nothing new. And just 'cos we can't understand how they all think and that, don't mean that they can't eat nuts and leaves if they want. Ain't nothing to do with us if they're all pale and skinny and getting sick all the time."

And with that she poured herself the last of the red that Rowan had so carefully chosen, that she had commandeered instantly when they sat down to eat, leaving everyone else's glass empty. Rowan glanced around the table. Ed's mother had brought her cup of tea with her to the table although, in her favour, she had managed to shrug her coat off her shoulders. It still rested across the back of her chair, however, just in case. Ed's dad had requested a large glass of milk which he slugged from regularly as he stared into space while eating great shovelfuls of food and apparently tasting nothing.

The children had juice – Matilda had begrudgingly accepted it in the absence of anything fizzier, which Rowan firmly didn't allow in the house. Rowan couldn't help staring at the unfortunate child as she stuffed her mouth and then stared around the table at the adults as she ate, her red cheeks bulging, her mouth open in order to breathe, scratching at the eczema marks on the inner joint of one of her elbows and her hands. Rowan felt ashamed for staring. But more than that, she felt sorry for the child as she hunched over her food as if someone would steal it. She wore a dress which strained at the seams, emblazoned with the words *Hot Chick*. Her hair needed a wash and her shoes were scuffed, a pink bow at the toe of the right but missing from the left. Part of Rowan was slightly repelled, but a bigger part wanted to take Matilda off for a bath and a hair-wash followed by a plate of decent food and some cuddles. She glanced at Vicky, seated opposite her, whose eyes were glazed now after the full bottle of red, her expression increasingly disdainful with each tiny mouthful of food. Watching them, Rowan found that her own appetite was sparse. Who on earth were these people, she wondered suddenly, feeling for a moment as if she had left her own body and was an observer on the ceiling.

And there, in the middle of them, was Ed. Funny, clever, sophisticated Ed. How on earth could he have come from these people? How could he be one of them?

There was a sudden loud clatter as Eileen dropped her knife and fork loudly on her half-cleared plate and then gave an exaggerated sigh, intent on gaining attention.

"Oh, I couldn't eat another bite," she declared, glancing at everyone else's plates around the table. "Did you make all that yourself, Rowan?"

Rowan froze, a forkful of potato halfway to her mouth. "I did," she replied awkwardly.

Eileen rolled her eyes and exhaled with a "Phew!" She shook her head. "Very rich," she said bluntly. "Very rich. You shouldn't have gone to all that trouble for us. We wouldn't expect that. Jenny never did. Did she, Edmund?"

It was Ed's turn to look at his mother, swallowing deeply and reaching for his water glass.

Rowan glanced at him, nervously.

"Mum –" he began.

She carried on regardless. "Jenny knew how to make things easy for herself. When we'd come round she'd get all the grub from that lovely Deli-*catessen* on Fox's Road, didn't she, Ed? All of it in silver foil tubs – stews and the like. That's much more the type of people we are, isn't it, Frank?"

Her husband nodded, not lifting his eyes from his plate where he was scraping the last of his sauce off the completely cleared plate with his knife and then licking it with a flourish.

"They did the mash and everything. Lovely it was. Nicer than Marks and Sparks, even. And so simple . . ."

Ed's voice interrupted her, more insistent now as he glanced at Bee who was staring at the adults intently. "Mum, I'd rather you didn't in front of –"

Vicky cut him off. "She always had lovely clothes too, had Jenny," she observed.

Rowan looked on in alarm as she saw her turn to Bee to address her directly.

"Your mum was a great dresser," Vicky said, slugging the last drain from her glass. "Any more of this Ed?" She waved the glass at him.

"No, Vicky, I think you've had enough," he growled. "And I think you should all stay quiet on the other subject too. We've spoken about this before."

Vicky groaned loudly and banged the glass back onto the table. "Oh, keep your *hair* on, Ed," she whined.

Rowan stared at her, shocked and nervous. With her stained teeth and petulant expression, Vicky looked in that instant like a naughty child being deprived of liquorice.

"You'd swear she was a big bloody secret, your *wife*," she bit, "when everyone knows she was the bloody Love – Of – Your – Life. Capital 'L'. Irreplaceable, you said she was."

Eileen suddenly joined in, nodding her head in agreement with her daughter. "Vicky's right, Ed. It's important that my granddaughter knows about her mum and doesn't forget her, especially . . . now . . ." Her words trailed off as she nodded in Rowan's direction.

"Yeah, especially now," added Vicky sullenly. "Now that you've found a . . . well, it won't do for Bee to grow up and forget her *real* mum, will it?"

With that, it was as if the room came alive with voices. Rowan watched, open-mouthed in horror, as Ed began to shout at his sister, which made Bee dissolve into tears. The little girl suddenly slipped off her chair and fled from the table, out through the kitchen and up the hall. Moments later, Rowan heard the thump of her feet as she ran up the stairs and then overhead, after she had slammed the door of her bedroom.

At the table, Ed's mother tried to speak over both of her children, arguing loudly in Vicky's defence; shouting that Ed shouldn't be so quick to "move someone new in", especially with Jenny's memory so fresh, and expect everyone to be happy about it.

Before Rowan could fully take it all in, Vicky had then herself burst into tears, accompanied by loud, exaggerated wails. From this, Matilda took her cue to shriek with confusion and fear. Rowan instinctively reached out a hand to comfort her but that in turn made her scream louder. Rowan withdrew her hand sharply, looking fearfully at Vicky, confident that this would bring a fresh tongue-bashing, but nothing came. Vicky was completely absorbed in her own crying fit, her mother's voice still nag-nag-nagging at Ed while she reached out to try to comfort her wailing daughter. Ed, in turn, had fallen silent and instead sat there, trying his best not to explode again. Rowan could see by him that he was seething with rage. His father, all the while, sat in complete silence, with his hands folded across his chest, staring into space, as if somehow all of this wasn't happening.

Suddenly, something inside Rowan snapped.

"Ed," she said firmly, "don't you think it might be a good idea to go check on Bee?" She turned back again to Matilda who recoiled from her as if she was about to be struck. Rowan glared at Vicky for a moment, before turning back to the crying little girl. "Matilda," she said loudly, over her hysterical shrieks, "how would you like some pudding?" There was an immediate silence. "And some cartoons, maybe, eh? Some pudding in front of the TV for a little treat?"

Matilda nodded emphatically, a trail of snot dribbling from her nose.

Rowan nodded back and sat upright, turning her gaze back down the length of the table at the rest of Ed's family, as he meekly stood up and left the table to do as she had suggested.

"Right then," Rowan said loudly. "Myself and Matilda are going to get some pudding and then she's going to watch some cartoons. Shall I make some coffee?"

It was only later, when the Mycrofts had eventually left, and Ed had coaxed Bee from her room to give her a conciliatory bowl of ice cream, that Rowan managed to make her way to her bedroom and collapse, trembling with stress and exhaustion. What was she doing here, she asked herself. Why was she constantly facing a barrage of obstacles when it came to this relationship? Why was it so bloody *hard*?

First Ed himself, then Bee and now his hideous family? And Jenny, of course. Bloody Jenny.

Up until this moment, she had always believed that if something was good, then it was worth fighting for. But as she listened to the muffled hum of Ed's voice through the floorboards, talking cheerily to Bee, and thought again of the afternoon's events – of the horrible screeching voices, of the disapproval and downright ignorance of his mother and sister, the indifference of his father – she wondered if she were up for this. If she had it in her to persist with this relationship where it had become apparent that she wasn't wanted – not by Ed's family, not by Bee – not really, anyway – not even by the damned *house*. It dawned on Rowan suddenly that she was always going to be second best. Second fiddle, second in the race to a dead woman.

And in an instant she became aware that she had no idea how she could ever make it to be first. Something she wasn't even sure if she wanted to be any more.

NOVEMBER 2001

Jenny

I almost feel sorry for her. I should, I know I should.

I should be able to reach inside my soul, such as it is, and find something there that is human and kind and Christian and all that jazz.

I should feel empathy – those harpies gave me a hard enough time too, for heaven's sake – I should be able to identify with her, feel her pain, understand her discomfort.

So maybe that's why I'm still here? Because I'm a horrible, unforgiving witch who hasn't an ounce of the milk of human kindness running through her . . . well, not bones . . . being, then. Because a part of me thrills a little that they were so horrible to her with her nut roast and her creamed leeks and her handmade centrepiece.

I'm not happy about what they did to Bee, mind. God forbid that they should be the keepers of my memory. What they did today had nothing to do with me, of course. It was as downright nasty and low a piece of manipulation as I have ever seen and had I the power I would kill them for what they did to my little girl.

But if some good should come out of it, maybe it will be that that woman finally realises that she's not on an easy ride. And maybe she'll take her boxes of paper and her website and her lentils and her ugly things and just get off it?

That she'll realise it's hard. And that Ed will never be hers and that she cannot have Bee?

And maybe she'll just get the hell back to her life, whatever it is. And get out of the one that should have been mine.

NOVEMBER 2001

Ed and Rowan

It was after ten before Ed poked his head around the bedroom door and observed the scene before him. He was taken aback by the sight – he had thought that Rowan would be calmly meditating as she liked to do sometimes – after today, he could probably do with a little meditation himself.

But she wasn't. She was moving around. Silently, and intently. Packing clothes into a suitcase.

Ed thought at first that Rowan hadn't heard him enter, and he coughed quietly so as not to alarm her. But Rowan had. She responded by glancing briefly at him before crossing again to the wardrobe, removing an armful of dresses and skirts and carrying them to the bed, focusing her attention on removing hangers and folding the clothes vigorously before placing them into her case.

"I just got Bee to bed," Ed mumbled hesitantly, pointing through the wall in the direction of her bedroom, next to theirs. "She was okay after a banana split. Really tired actually. She conked as soon as her head hit the pillow."

He received no response. Not even a grunt of acknowledgement. Rowan continued her silent movement.

"Rowan, what's going on?" Ed managed to say.

Again, there was silence. Rowan paused what she was doing for a moment, then proceeded as before, but with a confused expression on her features. Ed watched, growing more nervous by the second, as she picked up a bundle of coat hangers from the bed and returned them to what he could now clearly see was an empty wardrobe.

Still silent, she turned her attention to a chest of drawers, removing a handful of underwear from the top drawer and crossing to the bed, bundling the lot into the case and turning back for more.

Ed couldn't watch any longer. He suddenly felt panic rise in him and he stepped toward her, grasping her wrist as she reached in again, pulling her gently, but firmly, closer to him, willing her to look at him. When she did, her eyes sparked with fear for a moment, blinked away in an instant to be replaced by confusion and anger. Ed saw that they were red from tears, her cheeks blotchy and flushed.

"Rowan, please, what's the matter?" he asked, loosening the grip on her wrist.

Rowan responded by sinking down and sitting on the end of the bed, clasping her hands firmly together on her lap. Ed sank down beside her.

"You're stressed because of today," he began gently. "I know – my family are a fucking nightmare. They are completely out of line and I'm so sorry about what happened . . . if I'd thought for a second they'd be that bad then I'd never have invited them."

Rowan's eyes brimmed with tears again as she met his eye. "You did nothing to stop them, Ed," she said, her voice breaking a little as she spoke. "You sat there and let them say all of those horrible things to me . . . to upset Bee like they did . . . and then you let Bee run off on her own. You're a grown-up – you're her *dad* – how can you let them behave like that in your home?"

Ed frowned and squeezed his eyes shut, shaking his head. "I know, I know. I don't know what gets into me when they're around . . . I revert to being six years old . . . I tie myself up in knots around them. Sometimes I say nothing, do nothing, because I'm afraid that if I do I'll actually *kill* one of them with my bare hands." He grasped Rowan's shoulders and looked her straight in the eye. "I swear to you that I won't let them do that to me – to us – the three of us, again. I promise. Please don't go anywhere, Rowan. Were you planning on staying with Judith for a while?"

Rowan swallowed hard, sat up straight. "No, Ed," she said. "I'm not going to Judith's – not 'for a while' – I'm *going* – leaving. For good." She had to stop herself for a moment, to control a loud sob that she could feel rising. She tried to stand, but Ed's grip held her where she was.

"What . . . what do you mean *for good*?" he whispered, his breath quickening, his eyes searching her eyes which wouldn't meet his. He raised his hands to her shoulders and squeezed them. "Rowan, come *on*. I've said I'm sorry and I *am*, I swear! They're awful but we don't have to see them. Or I'll have a word with them – that's what I'll do – they were like this with Jenny too . . ."

From somewhere, Rowan found the strength to stand up. She turned her back on Ed and walked over to the window where she stood, arms folded. She hadn't bothered to pull the wooden blinds shut and she peered out between them to the street light below outside the house. She could see herself, her own reflection in the glass.

"It sure didn't sound that way to me," she said suddenly, her voice low, as if she were trying to maintain control.

Ed frowned. "What do you mean?" he asked.

She remained silent again for a moment. Thinking twice before saying something and then thinking once again as was her habit, as her grandmother had instilled into her. She turned suddenly and pointed at the wardrobe.

"*Jenny's*," she said simply, her face like stone. She pointed to the chest of drawers: "*Jenny's.*"

She swallowed hard as she swept her arm around the room. "All Jenny's. Jenny's paint. Jenny's space. Jenny's house . . ." She paused, her breath heavy and her eyes filled with fire. "It certainly didn't feel like they hated Jenny, like she used to get the same treatment as I got today. And anyway, that's by the by . . . This, Ed – you and me – I've realised today that it *can't* work." She was speaking now in a hurried fashion, each word chasing the other as she stood there, her arms folded against her chest again, as if they were physically holding her together, as if she might collapse if she unfolded them. "It's never going to, so we may as well end it now and just move on. I'm packing to go back to Claudia's for a couple of days, to figure out where to go. I'll come back for the rest of my stuff – the Corkscrew stock, my computer –"

"*Rowan!*" Ed exclaimed, interrupting her flow. "What on earth are you on about?" His expression darkened and he, too, stood. "Don't you think this is a total overreaction? Don't you think that you're just taking things a step too far? I mean, my family are hideous but I'm not my family."

"How do I know that, Ed?" she barked in response. "How could you possibly be different from them? You were all born from the same womb, grew up in the same house, went to the same school –"

"Chose a completely different path in life," he finished, raising his voice to silence her.

It worked. A silence fell between them for a couple of moments. Ed waited to see would it last before he spoke again.

"Rowan, I am *not* – I can't repeat it enough – *not* my family. Now do you see why I held off so long before having you meet them? And yes – all of those things that you said are true – we came from the same house, but that's where anything I have in common with those people you met today stops."

He paused again, his eyes fixed on her face to make sure she was listening. Her skin had flushed on her neck and chest, the colour climbing up the underside of her chin. She looked frightened, angry, determined. And so vulnerable. Once he was sure he had her attention, he carried on, his voice calm, even though he trembled inside.

"My family is run by those women," he said. "And when they're together, when they're under the one roof, it's like they have some sort of energy, some *vibe* that they feed each other. My mother and Vicky are the *worst*. Growing up in that house was a nightmare – it was always filled with fighting and raised voices and insults between Vicky and Betty too, although you wouldn't think it of Betty now – not sibling banter – we're talking horrible stuff here – ripping each other's clothes up because one wouldn't let the other borrow something, or spreading vicious rumours about each other around school. They're *terrifying*. I swear to you, I'm not like them.

I was the only boy and it gave me the opportunity to back away, to get out of there as much as I could. I mean, it's not like my dad is much use – you saw that yourself. And yes, before you say it, you saw a trace of that in me today . . . but when I say that I revert to being six years old around them . . . it's horrible. I can't tell who's going to do the next most vicious thing and I tune out – just like my dad, except he's made it his life's skill because he *can't* get away.

"But I did. From the time I was small – football practice, the school band, extra art classes, an art club. I was lucky. My school was great – I could even stay there in the evenings to study rather than go home, which was a bloody miracle, because it meant I got all the right A-levels and then got to college. Once I was there, I'd stay at Darvill's to study and work on my portfolio too – as late as I could every single night – until the janitor would practically have to kick me out. And then I'd go hang at my friend Guillaume's until I thought they'd all be gone to bed and I could go home without having to speak to a single one of them. In turn, they called me Edmund the Swot – they jeered at me, and made fun of me. I got a reputation among my peers, my lecturers, my teachers in school as Mr Dedication. And it's stood to me – I know that. But it *wasn't* dedication. It was far from it. It was because I didn't have a bloody choice. I just couldn't bear being around *my own bloody family*."

Ed paused for breath, his eyes still fixed on Rowan. He couldn't be sure, but he thought that she had relaxed a little. He was wrong.

"But Mr Dedication went off and found himself the *perfect wife* . . . I'm sorry, Ed, I shouldn't have said that. I really don't mean to be disrespectful about your wife . . ." Rowan fell silent, her apology genuine. "I didn't mean to say that. But they obviously loved her – that was clear today."

She was stunned by his response. By the hollow laugh that he emitted.

"You couldn't be more wrong," he replied, his expression growing deadly serious as he looked her in the eye again. "They are *poison*," he whispered. "They *hated* her. They absolutely *hated* Jenny." He paused to scratch the end of his nose. "Betty was fine – but my mother and Vicky, they were like terriers on a rag doll with Jenny. Just like they were with you today."

"And how did Jenny cope? How *could* she have done?"

Ed shrugged. "I dunno . . . she reacted to them, I guess. She'd dig her heels in – get stubborn. Even more stubborn than she actually was and Jenny was like a *mule*. But my family somehow made her worse. It was awful. All that conflict – all that passive aggression and tension and waiting for something to kick off. It never really did – things might have been better if the air had been cleared by a big ding-dong – but that wasn't the game that they were playing. This was long-term tactical warfare. I know that Jen and I were young – maybe too young – when we got married, but we were pretty sure it was what we wanted. But our wedding, for example . . ." He rubbed his hands down his face. "It was awful: my mother versus Jenny, and I was caught in between. My mother wanted a church wedding; Jen didn't. If I'm completely honest with myself, I wanted one too – it sounds like a girl's fantasy, but I wanted to turn and see my bride walk up the aisle to me . . . look, you don't need to hear all that. In the long run it was Jen's way or the highway. We had our wedding at a registry office. A fifteen-minute . . . procedure . . . was what it took for us to be married – supposedly the greatest moment of our lives. The reception was in a function room over a pub which had sticky brown carpet and a jukebox. You could count the guests on both hands. And that's because for months, my mother and sister cried and screamed and tried to sabotage things to get their way. A few days beforehand, I caught Vicky on the phone to the venue pretending to be Jen calling to cancel everything. Jen never found that out – I never told her – their relationship was bad enough for Christ's sake. Anyway, on the day itself, they couldn't have behaved more badly. They commandeered the photographer. They never spoke to Jen. My mother cried out loud at the ceremony and Vicky dressed like a – like a *prostitute*. Thinking back, barely a second of it was the wedding day that I wanted, but I needed to – I *wanted* to make Jen happy.

"My whole life, you see, has been trying to keep people happy – and to distance myself from them, while keeping them too – they're the only family I have. Despite that, though, I couldn't wait to get away from them – to get them at arm's length – to move out and escape. And marrying Jen and buying here – buying this house, that's all that I'd ever wanted. But maybe I didn't do it for the right reasons . . ." His voice trailed off as the thought struck him, as if he had never realised this before.

"I can't live like that," Rowan said quietly. "I can't live my whole life prepared for battle. Waiting for the next landmine that they've laid for me to explode." Her voice grew angry. "You should have told me about this before, Ed. Should have warned me. That's not my kind of thing and you know that. I can't bear conflict – I don't know how to deal with it."

"But that's not true," sighed Ed. "You mightn't know it but the way you dealt with them – with me too – at dinner earlier – just going ahead and taking control, being confident – it completely floored them. It was a brilliant technique –"

"I don't want to have to employ *techniques*, Ed. I don't want – don't need to have to have strategies for how to cope with the people closest to the person that I love . . ."

She paused. Their relationship was still young, the phrase still fresh.

She uncrossed her arms and stepped back to the chest of drawers, continuing with her packing where she had left off.

Ed watched her with alarm, watched this new resolve that she seemed to have. "Please don't," he began, a tinge of panic to his voice.

It might have been the words, or the tone, but Rowan suddenly froze and raised her hands to cover her face. She couldn't hold the tears back any longer.

"I have to, Ed," she sobbed into her palms. "I can't do this. It's not just your family, it's you . . . it's your past . . . all the baggage. It's Bee – taking her on – I can't do it, can't be the *replacement* in her life . . ."

She paused to take a deep breath, lifted her face from her hands and looked at the ceiling as she desperately tried to stop the flow of tears.

"It's being *second*, Ed," she whispered. "Being the second – and whatever that brings – second best, second fiddle, second-rate – I don't know." She turned to look at him, her eyes filled with sadness.

"I just can't do this. Because no matter how far we go together, no matter what we do – as long as it lasts, I'm always going to be the replacement. And that's not good enough for me, Ed. I not only cannot live with you and Bee . . . I cannot live with Jenny."

There was a long silence between them. A silence that said it had to finish there. A silence that said even louder that neither of them really and truly wanted it to. It was Ed who broke it, his eyes filled with pain, and longing and love.

"Please, Rowan," he said, a new seriousness to his voice. "Please sit down with me for a little while. Because I need to tell you about Jenny."

They went downstairs and he made her tea. Camomile. Jenny had been a coffee-lover, he thought to himself as he boiled the kettle and drowned the teabag, steam rising around his face. He knew he shouldn't have allowed the comparison to the front of his mind, but he couldn't help it. Rowan's words, his family's actions – it had all ignited something in his mind, made the scar – if not re-open, then feel painfully tender again. And he knew he had to eliminate that pain.

Rowan sat at the kitchen table, her head in her hands. Once the tea was made, Ed placed it wordlessly on the table in front of her before opening the fridge and removing a beer for himself. It hissed as he opened it. With a sigh, he placed it on the table and he sank into the chair opposite her. It was moments before he spoke.

"When Jenny died," he began, "when I lost her, the world ended." He paused, eyes turned toward the ceiling, struggling for the next sentence. "I don't mean that in the trite way of love songs . . . like things got bad for a while but I knew that they'd be okay. It *literally* ended. Beyond the next day – the next hour in fact – there was no world, no time, nothing to me. I couldn't bear going onward, going forward . . . making a cup of tea . . . I wouldn't want to drink it because there was no point in sustaining myself. And the further down the cup I got, the more panic I'd feel because it meant that time was going forward and I didn't want that. I was being propelled through time against my will, away from where I really wanted to be – because I wanted nothing more than to go backwards. I hated everyone – they were pushing me on through time – and away from her, away from the minute I had left her that morning to go to work. I'd been in a hurry. I'd gone without giving her a kiss because I was eager to get out and get the day done with so I could come home and begin Christmas proper. I shouted 'Bye' from the front door and she shouted 'Bye' from the landing and that was it. The last words we'd ever say to each other."

He paused for a moment to swig from the beer, aware that Rowan's eyes were by now fixed on his face. He rubbed his temples with the tips of his fore and middle fingers and continued.

"I can't . . . verbalise the sorrow that I felt. I don't know if it's even possible. All of the words just seem so meaningless because they're so overused – lost, sad, broken-hearted – but take each word and make it stand alone – think about what it means – what it really means – and you've got a *fraction* of how I felt. I couldn't allow there to be a tomorrow – because it couldn't be yesterday – it wasn't *acceptable*. Yet tomorrow just kept on coming like an unstoppable wave. I felt like . . . you know, on a windy day when you turn a corner and a gust catches you and stops you in your tracks, and you're trying to push against it but *it's* in control, not you? That makes me angry and so did this endless 'things will get better', 'time is a great healer' nonsense that everyone was peddling – Christ, you should have heard the stuff that my family said. They just couldn't understand that my world had stopped. That everything I wanted from life was now no longer possible and that there was *no one* to blame for that. I couldn't believe that all of my future – my plans, had been taken from me. And I couldn't for the life of me see what to do instead – so I didn't do anything. I just got through that nightmare – Christmas, the funeral, birthdays, anniversaries – all of them the first one without her, all of those significant dates that I couldn't escape . . ." He paused to control his lip which had begun to tremble.

Rowan wanted to reach out and take his hand, but couldn't.

"I thought there wasn't any point any more. And for about six months I was fine – I functioned. I went back to work, put in all the hours I could, tried to do the best for Bee that I could . . . and then I broke. I couldn't see any point in anything. I didn't want anything – I got to the point where I didn't even want to go back in time any more. When I stopped counting the hours since she'd been here, when I stopped saying 'this time last week' or 'month' or 'year'. I stopped leaving the house. I lost my job – my career, really. I used up my savings, let the house go to pot – it only got a clean when Betty or Mum would call.

"And they wouldn't talk about Jenny to me – *no one* would. And I couldn't talk about her to anyone else either – it was just too hard to even say her name because I thought that if I did I'd open the gates to a dam that would drown me. But all the time I was drowning anyway. I didn't realise it until I found Jenny's dad . . . when he died. And I looked at him and thought what a blessed release it was for him because all he had ever wanted was to be with his wife Rose again, and all of Jenny's life had been spent trying to make it up to him for her death and that's partly why she was the way she was – all damaged and stubborn and indecisive – but still wonderful underneath. But when I really looked at him – when I looked at the layers of dust on everything around his house, and found his awful old sweater folded up neatly beside his bed – when I saw what was left in his fridge – something triggered inside me and it was like looking in a mirror except it was a reflection of a future me that looked back. That was the point where I decided that I had to take my finger off self-destruct. I suddenly saw that I had a whole life ahead of me – and that it wasn't just mine, it was Bee's too. And that was the turning point, as they say."

He paused for a breath, looking at the barely touched bottle of beer and running his finger up and down through the condensation. A part of Rowan longed to touch his finger with her own forefinger but she held back.

"I saw a counsellor for a long time afterwards," he continued, matter of factly. "I didn't tell my family that either – they'd have mocked me endlessly. My mother and Vicky would have said it was a waste of time, that things would get better by themselves, that I should just pull myself together. But I had to talk to someone – I realised that when I saw how alone John Adams had been for so long. That's what had killed him, I reckon. The fact that he had never shared the burden while at the same time placing a whole different one on the shoulders of his only daughter. I couldn't let history repeat itself. The counselling was the best thing that I could have done. Without it, I wouldn't be here today. Not just sitting here, trying to convince you how much you mean to me – because that's what I'm doing. But actually *physically* sitting here. She talked me back from the brink, not to put too fine a point on it. There was so often during that time that I wanted to just stop the world and get off – because everyone else was fine, just getting on about their business and I wondered why I wasn't – why I just *couldn't*. That's when I fell to pieces. When the grief wasn't anyone else's except mine. When there was no one left to share it with me. That's where the doc came in. And all the while I learned how to deal with the grief, I was learning about me too. About why I did the things I did through my whole life. That I probably married Jenny because I was so eager to be a grown-up, not to be the six-year-old kid who's getting his action man covered in lipstick because his sisters have bullied him into handing it over for their game. Not to be the guy who stays in college until the middle of the night just 'cos he wants to avoid the world of grief at home. I wanted to be a *grown-up* – to escape from them, like I said. And when I left college it all happened so fast. I'm the luckiest guy in the world, Rowan. I landed the job at Brightwater and the first idea I pitched them turned into Grimlet. And it got even better from there – awards, bonuses, more money than I knew what to do with – but I still wanted to play at being grown-up. That was the phrase my mother used to use and I hate to admit that she was right. Not that I was playing, you understand. I genuinely loved Jenny – I still love Jenny – but I've actually *become* a grown-up instead of playing at being one. I've learned what it is to *be* a dad, for example, rather than *wanting* to be one to have something of my own . . . do you understand?"

Rowan nodded and shifted in her seat.

"What I'm trying to say to you here is that yes, I loved Jenny. And I love this house because it was the first real, meaningful thing that I ever bought, and of course I love Bee beyond words. When I lost Jenny, I suffered so much because I was certain that I had lost all of my future. But that's just what happened. And there's nothing I can do about that now, even though it still hurts, just not as much, all of the time."

Ed cleared his throat, reaching his hand across the table to take Rowan's.

"But I am not that Ed any more. I've had to become a new make and model, a different person. I don't want to turn time back any longer. And the first time that I realised that – that I really realised it – was during the countdown on New Year's Eve 1999 – the night I met you. That's what I mean when I say I'm lucky. That was the first night out I'd been on since I lost her. And you were one of the first people that I spoke to – who wasn't Mike, of course."

Both of them managed a weak smile.

"And at the time," Ed continued, "I thought that the connection we had was just the one I was trying really hard to find – that it was something I was making up because it suited me. But my God, Rowan, I was *so* drawn to you then. And I never regretted letting anything go as much as I did you when I saw you heading off home that night, away from me. And I thought about you so often afterwards – looking out over London and wondering where you were out there and if I'd ever see you again. And then to find you, the day I started in Grafix – my first bloody job since I'd gone and lost myself the one at Brightwater. I swear that I'm not the fate and destiny kind of type, Rowan, but you have to agree that the odds of us meeting again were a million to one. But we did. And I can't help feeling that it was meant to be. And that's why I *need* you to stay with me. Maybe we've rushed into things, I know. That was a bit of the old Ed – impatient to get on with things, impatient to get to the good times – but I'll work on that, I promise. That impatience would have broken me and Jenny eventually and I can't bear that to happen to us."

"What do you mean, 'would have broken you'?" probed Rowan.

Ed looked down at his beer and scratched at the corner of the label. "I've never said this out loud to anyone before, but I have a horrible feeling that Jen and me . . . that we mightn't have lasted. When I met her, when we began, I was very eager to get to the good bits. To start the future, I guess – which is ironic when I think how long I spent subsequently trying to scrabble back to the past. But there we were, with everything I'd ever dreamed of – a house, a car, my fantasy job, a beautiful little girl. I wanted the good times to get better and better, instead of just enjoying them as they were, being patient – breathing in and breathing out and taking my time. But I wanted more, more and more – not money – *happiness*. Fulfilment. And I wanted that for Jenny too – we spent our marriage at a different pace to each other, and I was so breathless for her to catch up that I pushed her into things that maybe she wasn't ready for. When she died, a part of her wasn't happy. I knew that. And now I can look back and say that it was the part when I hurried her along to catch up with me. Where I wanted her to be as *ecstatically* happy as I was in order to make myself even happier . . . am I making sense?"

His and Rowan's eyes met across the table and held for a moment, his filled with pain and honesty, hers with confusion and sadness.

"I've been through so much darkness, Rowan. But finding you – and having you find me back – that's been a light rising over the horizon. And I swear that you're *not* second place – you're not *any* of those things that you're scared of being."

He paused, looking at her for affirmation, finally reaching his hand across the table to find hers.

He looked down at their fingers as they entwined and cleared his throat.

"I love you, Rowan," he said. "I really do. I wouldn't have asked you to be part of my messed-up, complicated life if I truly didn't – as screwed up as that sounds. And I'll do what it takes to make you realise that the life *we* have together is a completely new one. I absolutely love you, as the song says. And I am learning every day. And I want to be with you and only you. So go if you need to – to Judith's, or Claudia's or wherever. And stay as long as you need – as long as it takes. But please, Rowan, think about everything that I've said – I mean every word of it. And *please*, whatever you do, just come back."

NOVEMBER 2001

Jenny

In a little over a month, it will be four years since I died. Four long years. Four short years. Depends on which side of the mortal veil you are, I suppose.

The truly worrying thing is: how much time is there left? How long do I have to stay here and watch this nightmare play out? Trapped. Listening to my husband plead with another woman not to leave him? To hear him tell her how much he loves and needs her – and worse, for him to mean it?

To hear him say that he is over me – over the life that we had together, the life that we planned.

To hear him say aloud to her that he feels in his heart and soul that that life, those plans, would never have come to fruition.

This is what it feels like to have all of your hopes and dreams hit hard with a shattering blow.

Because I might be dead, but my dreams have stayed with me – after all, how could I have made new ones for myself?

And in my dreams – had I lived – this is what would have happened: we would have loved and cherished our beautiful little girl and given her a brother or a sister – both, perhaps. We would have had a dog or a cat or both of those too. Ed would have reached dizzying heights in his career and I would have begun mine

– something that I was good at, something that made me happy.

We were singing from exactly the same hymn sheet, after all. But Ed was right. We sang at a different pace. By the time I was tentatively humming the first few notes, he was full belt into the chorus. But I would have caught up, I swear I would. And we would have been as happy as he wanted us to be – in exactly the way he wanted us to be.

We'd have had family holidays, Christmases, birthdays – watched our little ones grow and grow until the day came that they would leave us for lives of their own. And though it would have broken my heart to see them go, my consolation was to be that Ed was by my side, and that we would still be as in love, if not more so, as the day we met.

He was always going to be there, you see. And I was always going to be there for him.

Except for the bit of my life where I wasn't, of course. The bit that ruined it all. My one selfish act that took me from him – that more or less delivered him into her arms.

That's how I saw it was going to be. It was going to be great. Me and Ed. Ed and Me. Ed and Me and Bee makes three . . .

Until I ruined it.

And now this – watching him replace me – this is my punishment, a greater punishment than I can endure, I think.

But I can't escape.

And I can never, ever forgive myself for my stupidity.

That life is what should have been.

And this – this is what is.

AUGUST 2009

Rowan

Sunlight danced on the facets of the diamonds, making them glisten as the hand of the wearer moved to show them at their best.

Rowan giggled as the waiter interrupted them with the two food-laden plates. "How lovely," she said, smiling, as she sat back to allow him to place it before her.

Once he was gone, Rowan shook her head to indicate disbelief, still beaming. "I'm so absolutely delighted for you, Clauds," she said sincerely. "The ring is *stunning*. You must be thrilled."

Claudia glanced down at her left hand and waggled her fingers, again catching the light as best she could to make the clusters of tiny diamonds on the band, either side of the pear-shaped centre stone, sparkle. She giggled and Rowan joined her conspiratorially.

It was a gloriously sunny afternoon. They sat outdoors at what had become Claudia's local since moving to Cambridge – The Commoner's Arms it was called, named for its proximity to Midsummer Common. Inside, it was cosy: inglenook fireplaces and original oak beams. But today they sat on the patio outside, savouring the feeling of sun on bare arms, soothed by the gurgle of the River Cam as it made its lazy progress by.

"It's just all a whirlwind, Rowan," observed Claudia, pulling her knife and fork from their napkin sheath and laying them either side of her plate while she smoothed the linen over her knee and examined the plate of fish and chips. "Robert's promotion and then buying the house. It's so much bloody work, by the way, Ro. Don't *ever* land yourself with a do-er upper. Bloody money pit too."

She slid a forkful of mushy peas between her lips and removed the fork with a flourish, taking a moment for an exaggerated, appreciative roll of the eyes. Rowan marvelled at how Claudia's lipstick always stayed perfect, her bee-stung lips never anything other than bright cherry red. Like her auburn hair, styled to perfection like a 1950s' housewife, and her wasp-like waist. As they had entered the pub, other customers had stared at the tall, curvaceous figure in the polka-dot sundress which flared from her waist to just below her knees, the sweetheart neckline perfectly showing off her pale white skin, a red scarf knotted at her neck. Rowan grinned as she considered her own clothes – a long, black cotton skirt worn with a black vest top and a short denim jacket, now slung over the back of the chair. Her blonde curls were cut to just below her ears, her arms laden with silver bangles, and a locket that had belonged to her mother hung on a long chain around her neck. They looked like they were from two different eras, she mused.

"Anyway," Claudia continued, her fork hovering over her plate as she decided between a mouthful of haddock or a fat chip, "it all happened about three weeks ago. It was a Tuesday evening, I think. I got fed up painting the bloody dining room – my hair was all spatters of Cinder Rose and I stank of white spirits – so I took a glass of wine down to the end of the garden and sat on the iron bench down there for a bit of peace and quiet." She leaned over the table as if she was telling a great secret. "Truth be told, Ro, the last person I wanted to see was Robert trudging down the lawn, but no sooner had I so much as had a slug of my Riesling than I spotted him, ambling toward me, looking all shifty." She rolled her eyes. "I *groaned*, Ro. Positively groaned. But down he comes and plonks himself beside me – and I have to admit to myself that even though he *is* annoying, he looks absolutely dishy in his ancient Springsteen T-shirt and long shorts – sort of like his own rebellious cousin if you know what I mean? Like we're in a TV show and they've changed the actor playing Robert to a slightly hotter one . . ." Claudia paused for effect and sipped her glass of San Pellegrino.

Rowan giggled at the thought. "I don't think I've ever seen Robert in anything except that leathery jacket thing and his jeans," she offered.

Claudia nodded in agreement, taking a bite from a chip and leaving the rest suspended on her fork mid-air. "That's because he doesn't *wear* anything else! He read a handbook once on how to be a trendy college professor and he's rocked that look ever since, despite my best efforts at reform – I mean, he'd look fan-bloody-tastic in a pair of skinny jeans, don't you think?"

Rowan clamped her hand over her mouth to prevent the mouthful of food she had just consumed spraying all over the table and her dining companion.

"And a pork pie hat," continued Claudia, thoroughly enjoying the effect her mental images were having on her friend. "Sort of like Pete Doherty meets the skinny one from *The Inbetweeners* – you know, the one who does the robot dancing. Anyway, he popped the question there and then – completely out of the blue. In retrospect, I think he only did it to re-incentivise me to finish the painting. I like to think that because he did it when he did he had to go off the following day and cancel the river trip in Paris or whatever the *real* plan was."

"Come on, Clauds!" laughed Rowan, used to the way that her friend constantly played down her relationship. "It sounds so lovely and perfect – I can picture it. Not Robert in the shorts, mind . . ."

"Please don't try," pleaded Claudia, her face straight. "Not while you're eating anyway. And yes, I'll stop now. I'll be good. It was absolutely lovely. It was a lovely, summery dusk and I could hear the river in the distance and see our lovely house – well, our house that will be lovely once we've worked our way through the Farrow and Ball catalogue and actually bought some furniture that isn't made out of books – and there were little stars just blinking in the sky and clouds of midges that weren't feasting on me for a change. And it was hazy, and it had that smell . . . you know, that lovely summery one? And I was ecstatically happy."

Rowan smiled gently at her friend. "I'm so thrilled for you,

Clauds. You deserve it, you really do. Robert is just lovely and you two are great together." They shared a smile for a moment before Rowan returned to her food. "On a more practical note, have you got a date set yet?" She looked up to see her friend colour.

"Ummm, not yet . . ." Claudia replied with an uncharacteristic lack of assurance. "There's a few things we need to sort first . . . the house, of course . . . and then there's my shop – I've found a great little premises near the High Street – there's tons of other antique shops around, of course, but I ran Fine Old Things in the heart of Camden for how long – nine years? So I *think* that I can make this one a little bit different."

She fell silent, turning her attention to the river as she stuffed a chunk of fish in her mouth and concentrated hard on chewing it.

"What's the real delay, Clauds?" asked Rowan outright. She had known her friend for too long to think that her silence was anything to do with the food or the view. "You don't have cold feet or anything, do you?" Concern filled her voice as she watched Claudia swallow hard and look back intently at her plate.

Claudia laid her knife and fork down slowly and cleared her throat as she looked up to meet Rowan's eyes.

"Well, I'm not sure how to put this," she said, her tone serious, in complete contrast to just moments before, "but we definitely have to give it six months or so before we think about it." She paused again, her hand straying to her stomach.

Rowan took a deep breath as the penny dropped. "Oh, Clauds," she beamed. "A baby! How wonderful – oh, come here!"

She clambered awkwardly off her bench and around the table to hug her friend. Claudia stayed sitting, her arms stretching upwards to receive the embrace. They were silent as Rowan made her way back to her seat, climbing again back over the bench and settling herself. She took a long drink. Partly to quench her dry throat, partly for something to do to stall for time while she took in the news. She also wanted to avoid Claudia's sympathetic stare across the table.

"I've upset you," said Claudia.

Rowan was quick to shake her head vigorously. "No, no, not at all, Clauds. *You* couldn't upset me. This is fantastic news – I didn't think it could get any better what with the engagement but this is just . . . the icing on the cake . . ."

Claudia rushed in. "I'm so sorry, Rowan – I wasn't sure how to tell you –"

"Clauds!" Rowan spoke over her.

Claudia fell silent.

"*Clauds*," repeated Rowan. "Calm down. Please – I am happy for you – so, so happy. And you must never, ever, apologise again for telling me something wonderful." She paused, her eyes moist. Claudia couldn't be sure whether happiness, like Rowan said, or sadness, put the tears there.

"A little baby," Rowan said, her voice wavering slightly as she spoke. "A beautiful little ginger-haired, 1950s' baby in an old Springsteen Babygro and a pair of wire-rimmed glasses . . ."

Claudia snorted, tears filling her own eyes as her friend continued.

"And you'll put him or her in some ancient bassinet thingy and Rob will read it Chaucer and you'll both manage to do a marvellous job and be incredibly happy and – and I am made up for you, I swear. Please don't think I'm not."

"I didn't want you to think I was rubbing it in," said Claudia, her voice quiet now. "I mean, you're drinking water today . . . a part of me hoped that we might have a double celebration . . ." The words trailed off as Rowan shook her head vigorously again.

"You know I don't really drink, silly. And no, not this time," she sighed. "But what matter? This is about *your* news – not my lack of it."

Claudia reached across the table and squeezed her friend's hand. "Have there been any more . . ." she began, unable to finish the sentence.

Rowan looked down at her plate of food, her appetite gone as she nodded. "Two," she said. "I made it to nine weeks on the second. Which was *hard* . . ." Her voice wavered again and she paused for a moment, biting her lip. "It was the furthest we'd made it, you know?" she said, sniffing and retrieving her hand from Claudia's to wipe it across her cheek where a solitary tear trickled down.

She sighed as she picked her cutlery up and forked at her risotto without eating a morsel. "Me and Ed . . . well, we've made a decision." She shrugged. "To stop trying. I don't think either of us can take it any more and we've faced up to the fact that it's just not going to happen at this stage. Medically, it was always unlikely but we've had enough, Clauds. From now on I'm going to devote myself to good works and charity and the children of my beloved friends – of which there are approximately one and that's yours." She grinned, a smile that was at once strong and wistful. "It's just not worth all the pain any more." She sighed resignedly.

There was silence for a moment.

"Plus," Rowan raked her food vigorously, "I have to concentrate on being a fantastic stepmum to that wonderful, well-behaved and placid scholar, little Bee, of course." She sighed again, but this time accompanied it with a roll of her eyes.

Claudia made another sympathetic face, knowing that there would be no more discussion on this, that the subject had changed.

"Oh dear," she said, taking the baton from Rowan, "what's she done now, the little hornet?"

"What hasn't she done? I love her – I really do – but she's just an absolute nightmare, Clauds. Sneaking out at night, getting caught hanging about at all hours – by the *police*. She's fourteen years of age! If I had done something like that at her age, Judith would have strung me up! I mean, her punishments were old school – she made me whitewash the outside of the goat sheds once for lying about going to the library when I actually went to the funfair, for crying out loud!"

Claudia sniggered. "Your grandmother is such a legend, Ro – you know that!"

Rowan smiled back. "In more ways than one, Clauds. More ways than one!"

"So what punishment did Ed impose?"

Rowan rolled her eyes. "I try to be patient with him, I really do. But when it comes to Bee he's *impossible*. Initially he was happy with a severe telling-off so I had to give him a nudge and tell her that we'd discuss her punishment and then *I* was the bad guy when she was sentenced to a month's grounding with no TV." She sighed.

"It's just always been the same old situation, hasn't it? He never disciplined her after her mum died because firstly he didn't want to upset her any more than she was already . . ."

It was Claudia's turn to roll her eyes. Ed's lack of stern parenting skills had long rankled with her.

"She was only little, Clauds!" exclaimed Rowan, laughing aloud. "She didn't need much in the line of discipline back then. In his defence, he hadn't a clue how to do it anyway. His mum let his sisters run wild, more or less. Whereas my childhood . . ."

"Well, when you come from Cold Comfort Farm like you did," giggled Claudia.

Rowan smiled back. "Precisely, again!" She sighed aloud. "Bee was fine for a while, but since she's hit proper teenage years what a nightmare child she is. So far this year there's been the drinking, the sneaking out, the bullying – although I don't think she was the ringleader of that particular incident . . ."

"You're very good to defend her, Ro," said Claudia sincerely.

Rowan replied with a shrug. "I don't think she's a bad kid underneath it all – it's just she had a bit of a tough start and Ed's had all his problems too and then I landed on the scene. It can't be easy for a kid that age who's never had a proper mum."

"*You* never had a proper mum," interjected Claudia, scraping the last of her mushy peas onto a chip.

"That's true," replied Rowan. "But I did have Supergran."

Claudia smiled. "How is old Jude, then? It's so long since I've seen her and her Queen of Puddings!"

Rowan wiped her mouth with her napkin and placed it on the table, pushing her unfinished lunch away.

"She's not so good, as it happens," she replied, resting her chin in her hands as she watched a punt slide lazily by.

"What's the matter?" Claudia asked, concern filling her voice. She had met Rowan's formidable grandmother a number of times and had become besotted with her, admiring her strength, her sacrifices and her kitchen skills.

"Well, it sounds a bit worse than it is, I think . . . I hope," Rowan replied, looking back toward her friend. "She found a dreaded lump a few weeks back. Unfortunately it's the nasty type but they got it quite early and she's lined up for surgery soon to remove it and then they'll do whatever else it is that they do – chemo, radiotherapy, whatever." Claudia made to sympathise but Rowan silenced her with a wave of her hand. "Oh it's fine, Clauds. You know what she's like – strong as an ox. She says her docs think that the prognosis is good – she's older, but she's very fit and healthy. And heaven knows that her skills at alternative medicine have practically made her into a witchdoctor. She's just pottering about the Acre as always, baking and taking care of the chickens and driving into town in her old jeep to cause grief to the local council about one thing or another – you know what she's like. She spends her days secretly wishing for another Greenham Common – itching to cause trouble, the mad old thing. I'm going to go see her next weekend anyway – make it two weekends away in a row that I'm free from the little Bumble Bee and unlucky number 17."

Claudia nodded appreciatively before smiling sympathetically again. "You're not having much of a run of luck, lately, are you?" she offered.

Rowan didn't reply for a moment. As always, her friend had hit an exposed nerve with kindness. She bit her lower lip for a moment as it wobbled, taking a deep breath to control her voice so that she could speak again.

"It'll all work out," she managed. "I think . . . only *think*, mind, that I can still persuade Ed to finally move out of Pilton Gardens and get a place of our own."

"If Pilton Gardens isn't your own place, having lived in it for eight years, then whose is it?" scoffed Claudia.

"You know what I mean," replied Rowan, concentrating hard on the one piece of optimistic news that she'd had lately – feeling the hope that had grown inside her since Ed had tentatively agreed to think about moving.

"It's for a fresh start. Since we've decided to stop trying for a baby we just feel . . . well, I think, anyway, we just need to be somewhere new. That it would do us good."

Claudia nodded in agreement. "About time too. I've always said that living in Jenny's house wasn't the right thing for you all. Maybe next time you'll trust Auntie Clauds. Ooh! Do you think you could persuade Ed to move to Cambridge? I'm sure we'll find him an artistic sort of job somewhere – painting our house, for example!"

Rowan grinned again as she shook her head. "I do love my Cambridge weekends, Clauds, but I think we'll stay in London for the time being. I mean we like it there – well, Ed does, and I'm happy to compromise with a new house. After all this time, I just think it could be really good for us. To get to know each other in a different environment – get a bigger garden maybe where I can potter a bit more . . ."

"I know, I know – get some chickens," laughed Claudia. "I really hope it works out, Ro. You and Ed have had a tough time these past few years and you deserve something good to happen, even if it's covered in shitty feathers."

The friends exchanged a smile again as Claudia signalled for the waiter to take their dessert and coffee orders. Resting her head in her hands again, Rowan looked back out over the brown water of the Cam and felt the peace that she always did while watching a river laze by.

As Claudia excused herself to head to the toilets, Rowan was glad of the few minutes' peace to absorb her surroundings, to be in the moment. To block out the voices of their fellow diners to a low hum and tune in, instead, to the birds on the trees nearby. To feel the prickle of heat on her skin and to visualise a weight lifting off her. If she decided to be happy, then she would be, she reckoned. Despite Bee, despite Judith's illness, despite reaching the realisation that she would never feel a child of her own in her arms.

Rowan took a deep breath and filled her body with warm summer air. Breathe the good in and the bad out, she thought to herself. It would be all right, she repeated to herself, centring her thoughts and her emotions in her chest before exhaling. Everything was going to be absolutely all right.

SEPTEMBER 2009

Rowan

Rowan had often wondered how Ed bore it, how he carried all that pain with him every single day of his life, how he lived a life of such loss. Until the day she realised that the life filled with loss was actually her own.

It had begun with her parents, when she was nine. The weather conditions had been appalling as they drove at speed through the Yorkshire Moors – rushing home to be with her because she had fallen ill with measles while they had been on a weekend break.

Then it had been her school, her friends, her ancient Labrador Izzy, too old to make the move from Yorkshire to Somerset where Rowan was to live with her mother's mother.

There was the loss of everything in college. Her course, her academic credentials, her future career in design.

All of which paled in comparison to the six tiny lives that had planted themselves in her body and one by one hadn't made it.

And now Judith. The woman who had herself lost love so young. Who had pulled her granddaughter to her as tightly as she could, without hesitation – raising Rowan, sharing everything that she had, to bring her grandchild to adulthood as best she could before resuming her own interrupted life when Rowan had grown. A free-spirited life full of creativity, of nature, of protest and persuasion.

Until the cancer had come. Not just a single lump in her breast, as she had first told Rowan, but many. Which had spread and grown unstoppably through her old body before she so much as acknowledged that something might be wrong. Because the person who believed the most in Judith Garvey's indomitability was Judith herself. She had no time for dying, least of all from cancer – a prolonged, painful process which would steal her dignity as well as her life. Much better to be hit by a truck, she said, or seized with a heart attack which would take her instantly. To just go when you were heading to the dairy for milking, painlessly, with no need for goodbyes. Just like her Emerson.

In the end, it came quickly enough. A month after her official diagnosis, Judith Garvey was dead.

They cremated her, as she had wanted, her ashes to be scattered across the Acre, the plot of earth that she had cultivated and loved for most of her life. Her very own place.

In that way she could be part of it always. Washed back into the earth so that she could finally become part of the grasses and wildflowers, the cherry trees in spring, the holly berries in winter. They sent her off with choruses of Dylan and Baez, to 'Swing Low Sweet Chariot', to a rousing chorus of 'All Things Bright and Beautiful'.

Ed read from a poem called 'A Song of Living' by Amelia Burr. So fitting, because of anyone he – and indeed most of the congregation – had ever met, Judith had loved life. It seemed fitting to think of her with her cheek pressed against the earth, like a drowsy child, finally returning to it gladly, as the poem said.

And throughout it all, Rowan tried her hardest not to shed a single tear, much as she wanted to. Because this was what Judith had asked her to do in those last weeks when she had realised what was happening. And when she went, when she finally slipped away, her final act of defiance was to make sure that Rowan was not in the room with her as she had been, day and night, for over a week. Because Judith did not want her granddaughter to see her die.

The tears came later. At the Acre, where they stayed the night after the cremation. When Ed had gone to bed, exhausted after the day, the long drive back to London ahead of him the next.

When she stood at the ditch, looking out over the countryside below, just as she had done with Judith since the first night she had lived there. Inhaling the scents that signified the end of summer and the advance of autumn. Seeing the stars under which her grandmother had retired night after night in this place that she loved.

It was as Rowan heard the silence that the tears came. For the first time ever, it felt all-consuming. And she felt so bitterly alone and anchorless because her beloved Judith wasn't sleeping upstairs, or busy in the kitchen. And because she never would again.

It was then, at that moment, all the familiar made unfamiliar around her, that Rowan's tears came in a flood – that she cried for so many things: for her mother and her father, for the children she could never have and for troubled Bee, the child that she did. She cried for her past – her history, her mistakes, her lost opportunities. Tears that wouldn't stop.

And most of all she cried for the loss of Judith. The woman she adored and revered.

And as she cried, Rowan prayed to the heavens for some of Judith's strength to go on.

AUGUST 8TH, 2011

Rowan

The sound of the front door opening, close to 1 a.m, made Rowan's stomach lurch. She had expected – feared – the doorbell ringing or, worse, a hollow knock. Ed jumped to his feet at the sound and charged to the living-room door, his hand reaching the handle at the same moment as the first step of the stairs creaked. As he flung the door wide, Rowan could see Bee's face, terrified and pale, frozen in shock at seeing her father and stepmother still up at one in the morning, clearly waiting for her.

"*In here,*" barked Ed, standing back to indicate that Bee should enter the living room.

She didn't move. She remained where she stood, peering out from underneath the grey hood which she had pulled over her head, one foot on the bottom step of the stairs, ready to begin her ascent. They stood like that for a few moments until Ed made both Bee and Rowan jump by shouting "*Now!*" in a voice more ferocious than Rowan had ever heard him use on his daughter.

Meekly, Bee withdrew her foot from the step and followed the instruction, walking with small, silent steps past him as he pointed into the living room where Rowan sat on the edge of the couch. As she passed him in the doorway, he yanked the hood back, revealing her beautiful auburn hair underneath, scraped back into a tight ponytail. Rowan noticed that Bee was wearing large, gold, hooped earrings and wondered where they had come from.

Bee came to a halt in the centre of the living-room floor as Ed slammed the door shut firmly behind her. Bee's eyes strayed lazily to the TV, which was muted on a news channel showing footage taken from a helicopter of a 140-year-old furniture shop engulfed in flames that appeared uncontrollable.

The screen then changed to shots of shops being looted: gangs of youths, dressed in hooded tops, just like Bee's, using every means at their disposal – litter bins, bricks, hands and feet – to break through shop shutters, to smash glass and run as fast as they could with their haul.

Bee watched the screen, transfixed, while her father stood behind her, watching her in turn. Rowan looked from Ed to the TV and back again, noting how white his face was, the slight tremble in his hands as he contemplated what to say. Rowan couldn't tell if it was rage or fear. She had simply never seen him like this before.

It was a couple of seconds before he reached out to touch Bee's shoulder, to turn her toward him, away from the TV. Instead of complying, however, she went rigid and refused to turn to him, pushing with all of her wiry strength to stay facing the TV and away from him.

"Where did you get those?" he demanded suddenly. "Those earrings? Where did you *get* them?"

Bee remained still, staring at the TV, her hands in her pockets, fiddling with her treasured BlackBerry. She set her lips in a thin line, a clear indication that she had no intention of answering the question.

"Beatrice," said Ed, his voice insistent – Rowan had rarely heard him use the full name before.

"Those earrings. You have ten bloody seconds to answer me or, so help me, I'll rip them from your *bloody* ears!"

A trace of a smile played across Bee's lips. "I'd like to see you try," she replied, in a quiet, defiant tone.

For a moment, Rowan wasn't sure that she'd actually heard what she'd thought Bee had said.

Ed had heard, however.

Bee's smirk wavered momentarily as he replied in a growl: "*Don't test me, Beatrice!*" he hissed. "Now tell me where you got those bloody earrings before I call the police."

Still she remained silent, staring with deep concentration at the scenes of opportunism, of destruction, of violence and flame on the TV.

The silence hung ominously in the air for slightly longer than Rowan could bear.

"Bee, where have you been till now?" she asked, her voice calm and soft. "*Please* tell me that you haven't been doing anything silly? That you haven't been part of – of this?" She pointed at the rolling footage of the rioting on TV, her voice filled with anxiety.

Bee responded by turning to Rowan, her face a broad sneer of hatred.

"Just shut *up*, you, yeah? Where I been and what I been doing ain't none of your business, d'ya get me, yeah? Ain't *nothing* to do with you. You ain't even my mum and you won't never be neither. Do you get that, lady? Do you?"

As she spat out the words, she bent closer and closer to Rowan's face until their noses practically touched and Rowan could smell her breath and feel spittle on her face.

Before she knew it, however, the teenager was yanked away by Ed, who had grabbed her arm and pulled her roughly toward him. It was enough to make Bee turn her hatred on her father, yowling in pain as she did so.

"Get *off* me, old man!" she roared. "You ain't got no right to do that to me, yeah? I'll get social services on you. Manhandling me like that. You hurt me! You could've broken my arm!"

Ed cut across her. "*Shut up, Bee!*" he bellowed. "*Just shut up!* Or if you're going to speak then speak properly instead of this absolute nonsense you're coming out with. You can bloody well start by apologising to Rowan for everything that's just come out of your mouth, do you hear me? *Do you hear me?*"

Rowan shrank back on the couch. She would never have expected this of Ed, of her partner who she had known and loved for nine years. She was sure that she knew him, knew what he was capable of. But not this.

Bee became even more incensed by his words. Drawing herself up to her full height, she lunged at his face with hers. "I ain't gonna do no such thing!" she roared. "She ain't my mum. I ain't *got* a mum, right? I never have done. And this . . ." she pointed a finger at Rowan without turning to acknowledge her, "*this* has been in my face for years, trying to be someone that she's not. Telling me 'homework this' and 'veggies that' and talking her hippie shit at me and trying to be my mum and she can't ever be 'cos *my mum is dead*. Do you *understand*, Dad? My mum is *dead* and this woman here is just giving me a headache, hanging off you, latching off us . . ." She turned suddenly toward Rowan again, her mouth gleaming with spittle, her eyes wide and her face red. "Why don't you just go away, right? Go back to fucking *Hippietown* or whatever hippie rock you crawled out from and leave my dad and me the *fuck* alone!"

It took a moment for it to sink in with Rowan that the loud crack that she had just heard in the room was the sound of Ed hitting Bee. Hitting his precious, beloved daughter. Hitting a fifteen-year-old girl across the face to make her stop. Ed's face was unknown to Rowan. The gentle, kind expression which he always wore was replaced by a grimace, his mouth set in a firm, hard line. It was an expression of rage. Of lack of control. The expression of a stranger.

Rowan's hands flew to cover her mouth which was wide with horror as she realised what he had done. And as she realised that his face showed no remorse either.

Bee's eyes were wide with shock and, as she looked back at her father, they filled with even more emotion – hurt, confusion. She looked like an animal that has been kicked by its owner.

And deep underneath, Rowan thought, she looked like a tiny child who has been rejected and hurt by the person it loves the most.

Suddenly, Rowan felt as if she couldn't breathe, as the scene slowed down in front of her and played out in slow motion. She had no idea what would happen next, but the one thing she did know was that things had just that second changed immeasurably, and that she felt completely overwhelmed by it all. She needed to be alone, to think, to reason, to figure out what she had just seen. These people – they were suddenly complete strangers to her. Bee – little Bee – transformed into something that terrified her. And Ed – her beloved Ed – turned into a monster.

Rowan's mind suddenly felt as if it would burst and in an instant she stood and made for the door. Neither Ed nor Bee made any move to stop her. The slap had somehow isolated them. Placed them into their own universe, isolated from any events outside the two of them.

With no idea what would happen next, Rowan fled, slamming the door of the living room behind her and hurtling upstairs as quickly as she could.

Once there, she made her way into her room. Although was it really her room, or just the room she shared at Ed's house?

Rowan's mind was a jumble as she shut the door behind her and stepped clumsily to the bed where she sank, pulling her legs up and wrapping her arms around them, burying her head in her knees for a moment.

From below, she could hear that the argument had started again. Ed's voice, deep and booming, and then Bee's, crying now, screaming at him in defiance. At one point Rowan was sure that she heard a scuffle. Bee trying to escape, she imagined, Ed blocking the way. She knew that she should go back down again. To try to referee, to mediate. To stop things getting out of hand. But they were there already, weren't they? She was out of her depth with this, the most serious thing that she had ever seen happen between the two of them.

She felt sure that tonight was some sort of turning point, however. That after tonight, things could never be the same.

She shivered. The air. It felt electric all of a sudden. Charged up, the hateful energy of the argument from below seeping through the floorboards underneath her. She should meditate, she knew, but meditation required relaxation and that, tonight, was impossible. Every impulse in her body felt alive.

She tried to soothe herself. Tried to take herself out of her body a little bit. Strained her ears hopefully to hear if the tone downstairs had changed somehow. It hadn't.

She found herself trying desperately to hear what was being said, her gut in a knot, suddenly terrified that something should come to pass between Bee and Ed that might not be resolved. That something would change between them and break them forever.

Rowan took a deep, cleansing breath, and looked around the room for something to focus on, to try to stay calm as the argument raged beneath her. Her eyes fell on a photograph she kept on her chest of drawers. Silently, she padded over to it and picked it up.

Her heart gave a leap as she turned it toward the light to get a better view of the familiar smile of its subject. Judith. Taken at the Acre over lunch outside. It had been a hot day, with a muggy, almost Mediterranean breeze. Judith was sitting, her empty plate pushed away from her, her hands folded on the table. She was wearing a purple, sleeveless top, her tanned skin – leathery from years of exposure to the sun – glowing brown, her shoulders dappled with the light that filtered through her straw hat. And that smile. Judith had been a stern woman when she wanted to be, but the smile spoke of the warmth that lay at her core, a warmth which especially Rowan, and her mother before her, had known so intimately.

Instantly, tears sprung into Rowan's eyes and she spun on her heel to look back at the empty room.

She felt suddenly as though she were drowning – as though she had already drowned, even. She felt as though she had left her body, that she was looking at someone else who she didn't know listening to two complete strangers arguing. Except it was her that was the stranger. In a stranger's house.

Rowan swallowed deeply and licked her lips, which she realised were bone dry. What was she doing, she wondered for a moment. Her stomach felt hollow and she could feel her hands trembling. Without thought, she aimed a kick at the chest of drawers – still the same as she had emptied on the night she tried to leave, so long ago. They had never got round to replacing it, to getting one that Rowan could call her own.

"You're always here, Jenny, aren't you?" she half whispered, half growled.

Silence.

Rowan's voice grew louder and filled with uncharacteristic spite. "You always have been, in fact. From the very first moment that I arrived here. Every minute of every day for the past nine years. Moving in here, falling in love with Ed – and he with me, Jenny, *he with me*. But things can't stay like this. This – right now – me, talking into mid-air like an idiot – it can't go on. It's convincing me more and more that something I've been thinking about is the only way to put an end to this. Because do you know what I've decided, Jenny?"

Rowan paused for a moment. She had no idea why she was holding a one-sided conversation with someone who couldn't possibly respond to her, but somehow it was making her feel better, making her feel stronger. She scanned the room around her, her heart thudding in her chest, her blood pumping with defiance.

"I've decided that I've had enough, Jenny. And this time, I'm actually leaving. Ed stopped me once before. And it worked . . . and I stayed and I've been happy with him . . . *you* know what it's like to love him. And believe it or not, I love your daughter too – your poor child who I've only ever tried to do my best by. And there she is, downstairs now, playing out a scene that I never thought I'd see. And I'm damn sure that you didn't either. So I'm *certain* now of what the right thing to do is. It's for me to leave. And to take them with me. You've tainted my life for nine years, Jenny Mycroft. Maybe more than even *I* realise. But I'm going to end that now. I'm going to take them and start a new life with them. I'm going to be free of this house and its hang-ups and its ghosts and its shadows and its history. And I'm going to start afresh with the man I love because he deserves a second chance. He loved you, Jenny, but you're gone. And Bee – she's in big trouble. Gangs, and possibly worse. She's rude and disrespectful, and falling behind at school. And more than anything – more than getting myself away from here, I need to take her away too if she's to have any future. *Any damn future at all*."

Rowan jumped and fell silent as the door to the bedroom suddenly burst open. Her mind went into overload for a moment, her reason suspended, until through the fuzz of the fright she recognised Ed's voice.

"Ro?"

She looked at him, took him in, this man who had been a stranger to her earlier. Restored again suddenly to the one that she loved.

"Who the hell were you talking to?" he demanded.

Rowan shook her head. "No one," she replied. "I'm just – just meditating. Look, Ed, we need to talk . . ."

"I know," he replied humbly. "So much talking. But right now I need you to come downstairs. It's Bee. She wants to apologise. She asked me to come and get you. She wasn't out in the riots – she's told me that and I believe her. The earrings are a loan from some chavvy friend of hers. Can you come down? She's really upset . . ."

Rowan nodded, a smile forming on her lips, a smile of relief. "Of course," she said, realising that she still held the photograph of her grandmother tightly in her hands. Gently she replaced it on the shelf and left the room. On the way, she glanced at Ed's bedside clock: 2.10, it read. Suddenly, she felt very tired. She took a deep breath and slipped past Ed who closed the door of the room behind them and together they made their way down the stairs.

AUGUST 8TH, 2011

Jenny

She hasn't the slightest idea, has she? Not a notion that while she has her imagined one-sided conversation with me – as she chastises me and gives it what-for and tells it like it is or whatever it is she'd call what she's doing – that I am standing with my nose no further than an inch from hers. That I am face to face with her, wishing that I had the power to hit her as hard as I bloody well could and knock her into next week with her threats and her nonsense.

What is she doing hiding in the bedroom anyway? What does she need, a licence? A ring on her finger to step up and get involved in what's going on? Does Lady Somerset think that it's none of her business what's going on down there? That after nine years she still isn't fully part of things? Not that I want her to be – don't get me wrong – I still hope that she'll sling her hook and leave my family alone, although the longer this ridiculous joke of a relationship goes on, the less likely that looks.

Without me – and without Ed having the sense he was born with – that curly-haired, meditating, candle-sniffing, patchouli-scented, lettuce-licker is the closest thing to a mother that my poor child has, lord save us. And what a fantastic job she's done. So busy at her make-and-do in the study that she's somehow managed to turn my daughter into some sort of delinquent, out till all hours, dressed like

Death without a scythe.

All the time, I am in that room with her, growing stronger from the energies that she's releasing. Not the positive ones, filled with light and hope and Quorn and whatever else it is that she likes to surround herself with. But real anger – and anxiety. She can't hack it. Isn't of any use to my Ed as he deals with Bee's total meltdown, leaving him to cope alone – I thought the whole point of them getting themselves together was so that they wouldn't have to be alone any more? I mean, what else can he see in her? That weak-willed, cheesy, sentimental, soft, daft bloody Wurzel . . .

She couldn't carry out those threats to leave if she tried anyway. I know she couldn't. She's too weak, too willing to keep Ed happy, to keep him buttered up so that she has a nice house, and a room to do her cut-out-and-keep in and so that she doesn't have to be out there, dealing with the real world.

Ed won't want to go anywhere, I know that, so she can threaten to leave and take them with her all she wants. He won't leave our home, which we bought and did up together, even though she's turned it into a shrine to Woodstock. Ed won't take our baby away from the only place that she's ever known, the home that we made for her. I know he won't. Because he won't leave me – he can't. Just like I can't leave him.

So if she needs to pack a case and leave alone – actually do it this time – then I'll be first on the doorstep to wave her off. Because my family are staying put.

They're staying with me, where they belong.

SEPTEMBER 2011

Ed and Rowan

Ed stayed as long as it took for him to serve his notice at Grafix. It was accepted sorrowfully, but not without a sigh of gratitude by company executives, money men who were relieved at the prospect of making one less person redundant as they struggled through the recession. Ed would not be replaced.

It was on a bright Saturday morning at the end of September that they loaded up Ed's car and Judith's old Land Rover, now Rowan's, driven back from Somerset for the task.

They took only their essentials, only what they really needed. Rowan was keen to leave as much of Pilton Gardens behind as she could. The anticipation that she felt at the prospect of the move, of a fresh start, of a whole new life, was overwhelming.

It hadn't taken much to convince Ed of the merits of her plan. He agreed that it was best for Bee, who was impressionable, keen to grow up before her time, easily influenced by those around her. Within a month of the move, she had begrudgingly settled at her new school. Her hooped earrings were confiscated for breaching the uniform code, her language and tone tempered by her new classmates who couldn't have been less impressed by the tough street talk which Bee tried out on them at first to make herself seem hard and in control.

Deep down, she was far from it. She had cried in her room – Rowan's old bedroom – as for the first week of their new life she had pleaded to be sent home to London. And for a time, Rowan had been sure that Ed would give in to Bee's wishes, that he would softly give in to his daughter's demands and head for the city again. For one thing, Rowan knew that there would be no redemption for Bee if they did that. For another, she couldn't be sure that this time she'd have it in her to go back with them.

She had prayed to Judith's spirit that Ed would stay firm. And was pleasantly surprised – and eternally relieved – when he did.

Within that first month of their new life, Bee had made a friend – Josie, who liked horses and sketching wild flowers.

Within six weeks, Ed felt brave enough to allow her to take the bus from the end of their road direct to school instead of driving her himself to counter her oft-repeated threat to run away back to London on the first train that she could get. At half past four each day, he busied himself in the garden, weeding, pruning and digging – keeping an eye keenly peeled, his heart in his mouth, until he saw her lurch in through the front gate, her rucksack slung over her shoulder, her headphones buried in her ears playing Florence and the Machine as loudly as she could tolerate it.

By the Christmas of the year that they left London, Bee was part of the stage crew for the school variety show and Ed's heart sang as he watched her take her bow at the end of the revue. She was dressed in the black jeans and T-shirt uniform that she had been at pains to select, anxious that it should be just the right *black* to remain unseen so that she could be really professional, so that she could be guaranteed to remain inconspicuous during scene changes. Ed watched his daughter as she smiled, the stage lights glinting off her auburn hair. He saw her mother in her, yet felt only a small longing for Jenny, just a tiny tingle of nostalgia and wistfulness. He was instead distracted by Rowan squeezing his hand hard, and beaming at him in the darkness of the school auditorium and he was immediately overwhelmed by her beauty, and by the joy and pride that she so clearly shared with him as they watched Bee take her deserved bow. Ed squeezed her hand back, feeling in that moment that he had made the absolute right choice for his family in moving to this place, which made him feel so complete.

And so inspired. He was drawing again – not just menu designs, or brochures or posters – proper, actual drawing. He had converted a place – an old shed – for himself into a rudimentary studio where he spent long hours absorbed in his sketches, and in the computer animation package he had bought on a nostalgic whim. And somehow he had designed a character. A small, red-haired tomboy character called Lila – a precocious six-year-old who lived on a farm with her pet fox, Vulpo, who had an inquisitive mind and went on magical adventures.

By that Christmas, as Bee worked hard with hammer and nails and paint on creating the sets for her school show, her father had finished a five-minute cartoon short – the first new character that he had created and brought to life since *Grimlet,* during those hazy days when he was the next big thing in animation. It wasn't as good as Grimlet, he knew, but then again, he hadn't animated anything for at least thirteen years, so he couldn't fail to be rusty and awkward with these new techniques. But still, it was better than he thought he was still capable of. Good enough to make him feel confident.

As for Rowan, she had to concede that she had never been happier in her entire life than she was in those first months when they settled into life at their new home – at her old one. At Judith's Acre.

At first – when they had first come here – she hadn't given a moment's thought to what their new life might actually be like – she had simply wanted to run away from London.

But life at the Acre had proved to be so much better than she had thought life could actually *be*. It was the simplest things that gave her most comfort – lying awake early in the morning and hearing the chirrup of birds outside their bedroom window as Ed lay snoring gently beside her.

Their days were full – as well as Ed's experimentation with his little character, and Rowan's Corkscrew Cards orders, the house itself needed work and repair and most of all cheering, as did the garden, all of it neglected throughout Judith's illness and since her death. Rowan liked to think that somehow she was still with her there. And that her spirit approved of their taking the Acre as their home, and of the work that they tirelessly undertook to bring it back to life.

Claudia and Robert and their children came for Christmas, laden with expensive gifts which were placed under the tree that Rowan had decorated with popcorn strings and dried orange slices and hand-baked ginger cookies, topped with a star woven from straw. Together they toasted in the New Year, Rowan delighting in the company of her godson Hal – almost two now – and his infant sister, Clemency – acutely aware of the passage of time, of the unpredictability of change, of missing those who had gone.

But she didn't greet 2012 with the dread that had filled her in the past. As the bells of the churches scattered across the valley struck midnight, and they stood in their habitual spot, overlooking the lights below the Acre, exhaling clouds of steam as they made a whispered toast to the New Year, Rowan and Ed exchanged the kiss that they never failed to share at this moment, the kiss that remembered the first time they had met, different people, in a different place.

They were happy, the three of them. Bee took drawing classes and spent hours swimming and walking the lanes with a boy called Seb who lived nearby, who was tall and in need of a haircut and who played fiddle in his brother's folk band.

Ed spent long and happy hours in his shed studio – gradually building up the stock of equipment he needed to bring Lila to life in better ways – but spent more time outdoors once spring arrived and brought long evenings with it. He was suddenly filled with a newfound passion there that he had never felt before: a passion for bringing things to life, for returning Judith's garden to its former glory. By Easter, much to Rowan's amusement and delight, he was seriously talking about chickens and bees and a couple of pigs.

And Rowan too felt her happiness grow as her business flourished and what she finally thought of as her own family grew in contentment. She felt reborn. As if somehow being here simply blew away everything that had gone before, throughout her entire life. Rowan finally felt free.

It was in May – an afternoon that glowed golden with sunlight and heat – when she walked through the ancient headstones of the churchyard where they had celebrated her grandmother's life when it came to an end, flanked by her best friend and her stepdaughter, her veil pulled over her face, to finally marry the man who had been her friend, her companion, her lover for the past twelve years. Rowan and Ed were joined in the church ceremony that they *both* wanted, attended by his family who remained subdued and respectful throughout, by their old friends from London and their new friends from their new, blissful life in Somerset. And by Judith's old friends – the Glastonbury gang who gathered annually at the stone circle in her memory – the pensioners who would introduce Bee to her first joint and send her home sick, and reeling, vowing never to touch the stuff again. All of them, gathered under one roof, singing 'Give Me Joy in My Heart' and 'Jerusalem', Ed's favourite.

And then that perfect summer's night in the marquee that they had set up at the Acre for a feast catered by Claudia's old friend Jon and the team from his restaurant. Where they ate spit roast, and danced along to Seb's brother's band. Where Bee got drunk on fruit punch and Ed and Rowan didn't notice because they were giddy on champagne and happiness.

At midnight, they watched the fireworks that they had arranged and when Ed and Rowan had waved the last of their guests off to bed and down the road, they retired to their own room to spend their first night as man and wife in the place that had made them happier than they ever could have imagined. Where possibility had become their friend again, where there were only fresh starts and memories to be made.

Where there were no ghosts from the past.

MAY 2012

Jenny

It's so very quiet here these days.

And dark.

I keep thinking that they'll come back – I mean, they have to come back – they've left all the stuff. The tables and chairs, the washing machine, the beds – everything. So they can't be gone for good. They've just gone for a holiday, haven't they? It's just temporary, and soon the house will be filled with voices again. Soon, my family will come back and take the dust sheets off the furniture and begin life again. They'll just do the normal stuff like go to work and eat their meals and watch TV and sit out in the garden. They have to.

I have to see Bee go to school, you see. I'm her mum, after all – it's my responsibility. I have to keep an eye on her while she does her exams to make sure that she works hard but still doesn't overdo it. That she doesn't binge on junk food or play on the computer when she's supposed to be doing essays, that kind of thing.

Because I can't be apart from her for long – she might be a teenager now, but she's still my baby – every mother says that, but it's only when you watch your own grow that you understand that no matter how old they get, they are still always your baby – the infant that you held in your arms is always somewhere, in a parallel place maybe but always just within reach.

She can't actually have kept her promise, can she? Old Roberta Plant. She just can't have done that to me – actually taken them away to be somewhere else? To live somewhere else? To have lives somewhere else? Away from me? Away from here? Away from where I can watch over them like I've promised to do.

She can't.

But there are days – like today – where I am cold and weak. And where the loneliness seems endless, like some night that will never have a dawn.

This can't be how it is now, can it? Because if it was hell on earth to watch them every day without being able to touch them, to let them know I was here, then what could this be? This silence? This longing, this feeling of desertion and sorrow and grief and worry – all of these feelings razor sharp, cutting my very soul to pieces?

I am not sure how I am still here – why I am still here if they are gone. But what I do know is that I don't want to be here any more if I cannot be with the people I love. I can't bear it – can't bear this limbo, this punishment. This death.

Has the time not come yet when I have finally done my punishment? Have I not served my time? Yet not only is there no end in sight, it's getting worse. And I cannot bear it any longer.

For the first time since I died I feel that I no longer deserve this. And I want them back because I am terrified of being alone.

Part Three

Bee

SEPTEMBER 2019

Rowan and Bee

Rowan found the key was stiff in the lock. It was a long time since the door to 17 Pilton Gardens had been opened regularly, since entry and exit were daily occurrences. Ed and Rowan had taken tenants at the beginning, shortly after they had moved to Somerset – a middle-aged couple had stayed for a year while their own house was renovated and then a young American couple in London on a three-year secondment. They were long gone now, and the house hadn't been regularly occupied since they had left.

Ed had stayed overnight there occasionally, just to keep things ticking over and to visit his family when he really had to. He had managed to evade pressure from his mother to allow Vicky and Matilda to set up home there, conscious that Vicky's lack of regard for anything other than herself grew with the years, aware that he wanted Pilton Gardens left in a habitable state. He had no desire for his sister to use it to entertain and house her constant stream of boyfriends, had no appetite for dealing daily with her inevitable constant demands and her destructive tendencies. He was content in his new life in Somerset and felt that there was no reason to bring stress on himself.

When Rowan finally got the key to turn and shoved the door open, disturbing the piles of junk mail on the mat as she did so – a smell of must greeted her, but nothing worse. There was no hint of damp in the air, just disuse and stale heat from the warm summer that had just passed. Nothing that a few open windows wouldn't sort, nothing that smells of fresh habitation wouldn't solve before long.

It felt odd to enter it again. This house where she had lived under a shadow for so long. She paused on entry, took in the familiar hallway around her, glanced up the stairs. It was just as they had left it eight summers before, the last time that Rowan had set foot inside.

She stepped forward to allow her companion to follow, to enter as she had done, to sniff the air in the same way, to cast her eyes around – at the heavy mirror where it had always hung, at the bare hall table, to peer through the living-room door which was slightly ajar.

Bee hadn't thought that the house would make her feel strange but, with that single step over the threshold, she was suddenly overwhelmed, as the sights – the familiarity – of her childhood came rushing over her. She glanced up the stairs – where she knew her old bedroom lay, where she would sleep from now on – those stairs that she had trodden up and down thousands of times – and suddenly had to bite down hard on the inside of her cheek as a completely unexpected wave of emotion washed over her. She kept her head turned well away from her stepmother, not wanting her to see.

Bee wondered if Rowan felt anything. When she had composed herself a little, she glanced at her stepmother, curious to see any sign of emotion on her face. She was suddenly struck by the fact that Rowan had aged. That there were defined lines radiating from her eyes, at the corners of her mouth, evident with the half-smile that she gave her before taking a tentative step toward the door of the living room, which she pushed gently to open it further. Her hair was still blonde, but an ashy blonde now, the curls a little dry and tired. Somehow, seeing her in the city made her look out of place – her tanned skin, the scruffy jeans and sandals, the habitual smock in bright colours. It was exactly as Rowan looked at home – *her* home, of course – in Somerset, but it was somehow wrong in Pilton Gardens.

Bee didn't *hate* her any more. All that rubbish she'd spouted when she was a kid, the disrespect she'd shown her, the hard time she'd given her – Bee blushed at the thought of it now. It didn't mean, however, that she was even yet entirely happy to be alone in her stepmother's company, even after all this time.

On the surface, Bee could be completely logical about her relationship with Rowan yet could never take it that little step further, could never fully feel what she thought she might be supposed to feel – companionship, kinship even. They were friendly, yet somehow still formal with each other – polite, courteous, careful – Bee couldn't quite put her finger on it. There was plenty about Rowan that still grated on her after all these years, too. Ridiculous things like her vegetarianism, the meditation which Rowan practised for hours on end. Bee tried her best not to be spiteful, to think well of Rowan, but there was always a part of her that held back.

It was all about control, of course, wasn't it? And Bee, deep down, felt that she just couldn't trust someone who on the outside seemed to be so relaxed – laid-back, at one with nature, all organic, and teetotal and free-range and so on . . . but underneath . . . Bee was sure all of this had to be a veneer. Rowan, after all, had always got exactly what she wanted, hadn't she? Ed, Pilton Gardens and then Judith's Acre. The successful husband, the life in the country – you had to have a strong character to successfully run your own business for years, too, after all – to keep it successful, to *grow* it in recessionary times. There was no amount of meditation could do that for you, Bee reckoned.

She had puzzled long and hard over her father's wife. It had to have been part of her plan all along – to eventually end up living exactly where she longed to live the most, where she fit in – while keeping her business going – and in the process managing to get Ed to go along with it all, despite the fact that it meant he'd had to up sticks from his home city and turn to building a whole new life for himself. Glancing again at Rowan – make-up-free skin, the amethyst that she wore as an engagement ring instead of a diamond, the slightly down-at-heel look she sported – when Bee knew for a fact that these days she was anything but – all of these things intended to show that Rowan didn't bow to convention, that she followed her own free path. Yet all of it was fake, Bee had concluded. It had to be. A careful façade put on by an inscrutable woman. For the millionth time in her life, Bee looked at her stepmother out of the corner of her eye and wondered just what really lay underneath.

Trying to free herself from the suspicious train of thought that she had a habit of falling into involuntarily, Bee inhaled sharply and focused on her surroundings, following Rowan along the hallway and down the steps that led to the kitchen and through to the dining room ahead. It felt like walking through a dream of her childhood suddenly, familiar things hidden under dust sheets as she passed, just waiting to be uncovered, to take her back. Bee knew that underneath everything would be as it was eight years ago when they had left. A charge of unease ran through her at the thought that to remove them might just transport her back to being fifteen years old and all of the feelings that went along with that – the resentment, the feeling that she didn't belong. She shuddered and then blocked them from her mind.

She watched as Rowan strode with what looked like no emotion across to the windows of the sunroom and began to pull the Roman blinds up, one by one. The room was flooded with light, suddenly, like a stage being set and Rowan was immediately transported back in time. There it was, the dining-room table, so ordinary, yet suddenly so evocative – the scene of so many Christmas dinners and family celebrations – of books spread out for study, sketchpads and charcoal – laid as a buffet for summer feasts, the double doors behind propped open with pots of lavender, curious bees and insects flitting in and out, carried on sunbeams. A hundred flashbacks washed over Bee suddenly, years of memory. She felt woozy for a second and thought that she might have to sit down.

"Windows could do with a clean," remarked Rowan suddenly and Bee jumped a little.

She had been absorbed in herself, in retracing the life she had here with those little memories, those little scenes. She hadn't expected her stepmother to speak, much less to break the silence with something so banal. A flash of irritation ran through Bee at

Rowan for breaking the spell of the moment but it was also mixed with an odd glimmer of gratitude to her for somehow normalising this strange momentous event. The new phase. The final stage of Bee's education, her degree in Art completed at the new university in Taunton and now her Master's in set design to be undertaken at Weatherall's Art and Design College in nearby Chelsea. It had been Ed's suggestion for her to move back into Pilton Gardens. Makes sense, he'd said. For someone to make use of the house, to breathe life into it again, keep it occupied while living practically next door to college. All provided she could find someone suitable to share with, of course.

"What time did the others say that they'd get here?" Rowan continued, fiddling with the lock on the garden doors. The sound of them opening made Bee's stomach leap a little at the familiarity of it. Something so ordinary – just a small clicking sound. But it released another flood of memories. How many summer mornings had started with her turning that key first thing, as soon as she had got up and slipped into shorts and T-shirt? How many mornings had she heard the door make that self-same sound before running outside into a new summer's day when she was small. Pushing her doll's pram outside or in later years pelting out to read a *Harry Potter* on a deckchair underneath the plum tree at the furthest corner away from the house. In an instant, she could smell it. The fresh aroma of a day already warm. She could feel the heat warm her skin, hear the bees in the rosebushes as vividly as she could hear her stepmother's voice.

Bee cleared her throat before replying, taking a moment to make sure that the words would come out in an even tone, without the wobble of emotion that she felt sure her voice would take on.

"Sasha said that it would be after work – she finishes teaching her classes at four. She's driving over with some of her stuff and her boyfriend's coming over with the rest later," she managed.

Rowan gave a barely perceptible tut of annoyance at the mention of Ed's niece's boyfriend. They had been very clear that Pilton Gardens was to be shared by the three girls only – that no boyfriends were to be allowed, but twenty-seven-year-old Sasha and her Aaron had been together since their schooldays and it was more or less a given among the Mycrofts that it was only a matter of time before they'd marry. It was highly likely that Sasha would not be a long-term resident of Pilton Gardens.

"And what about Matilda?" continued Rowan, taking a step onto the decking just outside the back door, peering down the garden, at the covered garden furniture and the overgrown bushes and flowerbeds, with a furrowed brow.

Bee snorted. "You know what she's like – so eager to move in that she's taken the day off work at the café. I'm surprised that she wasn't sitting outside in that beaten-up Mini when we got here!"

Rowan smiled and rolled her eyes pityingly. "Poor Matilda," she remarked, two words that still seemed to run together naturally. She stepped back inside, leaving the back door open to allow the warm breeze from the garden blow through. A butterfly fluttered behind her, made to fly indoors and then thought better of it, changing direction at the last moment.

"To think of what that poor child has been through," Rowan tutted. "And here she is, so excited about finally making her own way in the world. I really hope she can hack living away from home."

Bee rolled her eyes at the familiar refrain. Poor Matilda. "Matilda will be absolutely fine," she snapped. "Everyone thinks that all that neglect by Vicky has made her vulnerable but it's made her the complete opposite. She's as hard as nails. And so excited about finally going to university – even if it is to study Chinese. But more than that, she cannot *wait* to get away from living with her mother – finally."

The mention of Vicky sent a worried frown across Rowan's face. "I really hope Vicky doesn't see this as her chance to get a foot inside the door here. Your dad would go nuts. It wouldn't be the first time she's tried to move in."

Bee noticed the strong hint of the West Country in her accent, again seeing her out of context. The thought struck her that maybe Rowan hadn't ever been meant for this house – that she was never meant for anywhere other than Judith's Acre.

"I think there's a whole side to Matilda that you don't see, Rowan," Bee replied softly. "I think that she'd build a barricade at that front door before she'd let her mother move in with her again and, besides which, won't this give Vicky the freedom that she so craves to start her life as a trucker chick alongside Hairy Brian or whoever the Bloke of the Month is?"

Rowan giggled, the sound of her laughter unexpectedly loud in the silent house. "Sometimes I really think your father was adopted, do you know that?" she remarked, rubbing her hands together and striding back across the living room to glance into the kitchen. The Shaker units, which had been so up to date when they had lived here, were outdated now that the fashion in kitchens was for hard, gleaming plastic and chrome.

Bee grinned at Rowan's remark. It wasn't the first time that any of them had made that observation, including Ed himself.

Rowan busied herself by systematically opening and closing each of the cupboard doors, the washing machine, the oven, checking them all.

Bee joined in by groping behind the toaster to find the plug for the fridge which had been left open to air. She popped the plug into a socket. There was an instant hum and a glow as the light came on and Bee closed the door firmly.

"Wonder how he's getting on?" she said.

Rowan glanced down at her watch. "He's in that meeting right now," she remarked and looked at Bee, her face contorted in a mock expression of nerves.

"Do you really think they'll commission a full series?" asked Bee tentatively. It was one thing that they were entirely in unison on, she knew. Possibly the only thing. It would change Ed's life if the *Star Junior* channel were to broadcast *Lila and Vulpo*. "I mean it's brilliant, isn't it?" she continued, her tone confident. She truly thought her father's creation clever and funny, with an appeal to adults as well as children. "I mean Claudia's younger kids adore it, don't they? And they're just the right age."

The reference to Claudia's daughters reminded Rowan to arrange a trip to Cambridge sooner rather than later. For something to keep her busy as much as anything else. It would be odd with Bee away in college full time. While studying in Taunton, she'd driven home most nights, where Rowan made sure to have a hot meal waiting for her and her laundry done, despite Bee's protestations that she just wanted to stand on her own two feet. Rowan would need something else now besides her work to keep herself occupied – since she had taken on the two staff to work full time at the renovated studio at Judith's Acre, she had found herself less and less hands-on with Corkscrew Cards.

"We'll just have to keep everything crossed, won't we?" replied Rowan softly. She smiled broadly at her stepdaughter. "Right, then, shall we start to get stuff in from the jeep and get settled? I promised your dad we'd meet him for lunch in town after his meeting and then get us on the road home."

Bee frowned. "It's such a long drive. Are you sure that you won't stay tonight? I'm sure that Sasha could be convinced to stay at Aaron's and you could take her room – which is your old room, after all."

"Wouldn't dream of it, Bee," Rowan said firmly, pulling the dust sheet off the kitchen table and revealing the battered pine underneath. "I mean, we can't keep your dad away from Godiva any longer than we have to, now can we? She'd pine!"

Bee smiled back at the thought of the pot-bellied pig that followed Ed about the farm like a puppy. "You mean *he'd* pine!" she giggled.

"That's true!" responded Rowan, standing still for a moment and glancing around her reflectively.

"No, no – this house is a girl-pad now," she smiled. "You three girls don't need fogies like us about. I'm sure you'll all have unpacking and stuff to do tonight. Order a pizza, get a bottle of wine – christen the place. You'll have enough hard slog to do when college starts."

Rowan suddenly looked directly at Bee and caught her eye.

"Start your life proper," she said quietly. "Away from home. All the opportunities and the chances are there for the taking. Make this place your home again and start over."

Rowan smiled, but Bee couldn't help but notice that the corners of her mouth were turned down slightly.

"And be happy, Bee. You've only got one chance – so just be happy," she said, in a voice that Bee knew was tinged with regret.

SEPTEMBER 2019

Jenny

I'm a watcher again.

For a long time, I wasn't . . . what? Wasn't what – sentient? Awake? Aware? Active?

Whatever it's called, I feel as if I have been awoken from a deep sleep with a jolt – like someone has poured water over my face, or shouted loudly in my ear or switched on a hundred radios and a hundred TV sets at full volume and roused me into an instant state of glaring awareness.

It's that unsettling, that disconcerting.

Bright colours are so bright, light is blinding and sound deafening. It must be how a bewildered newborn feels. Startled, terrified, overwhelmed, curious.

It's a sensory attack – all of everything, all at once. And I am the one being born again – does it mean that in the space between I was properly dead? Is that what dead feels like? The nothing of deepest dreamless sleep?

The only thing that I do know is why I have awoken, why I've been reborn. And how odd that the person who is responsible for my rebirth is the person that I gave birth to in the first place.

I'm not entirely sure how it has all come about but she is here again. My Bee. My wonderful child, the substance of my soul. No longer a child skipping down the stairs, singing to her doll, her red curls bouncing as she moves – but a woman, laden down with knapsacks and books and heaven knows what else. Grown now, with no need any longer for my protection, you would think. But that doesn't matter. Just because she shouldn't need it doesn't mean that I won't give it. Surely if proof were needed then this is it – proof that my reason for still being here is because of her – to take care of her, to protect her – to pay her back for the childhood that I stole from her with my selfish stupidity.

And so I sit again by her bed at night and watch her sleep, and wait by the front door for her to return, and worry and care and wonder and feel anxious until I hear her key in the lock at night.

And revel in the sheer exhilarating joy of her presence, so close to me once again. My baby. My child. My daughter.

My beautiful Bee. Come back to me.

MAY 2020

Bee

Bee yanked her hood up as vigorously as she could and even went so far as to daringly pull it down in front a little to conceal the top of her face, instantly causing the small police drone to zoom closer to her. She frowned, walked a little faster. She was in no mood to co-operate with the London Metropolitan Police this evening. She couldn't remember the last time she had walked home through the city without the air buzzing with the remote-control drones, which hovered everywhere, fitted with cameras to keep close watch on the streets. Made you long for good, old-fashioned, intrusive, sneaky, quiet CCTV, she thought to herself.

Mind you, she could also see the advantages. Street crime – in particular the violent rioting that had come to symbolise summer in London's suburbs for the past four or five years – had reduced radically. Muggings, knifings, random assaults, public drunkenness, verbal abuse and gang activity had all but vanished in the areas where the drones had been initially trialled, causing the LabCon government to introduce them throughout the entire Greater London area, and plan for their introduction in all major towns and cities by 2022.

Tonight, however, as she made her way back to Fulham in the evening sunlight, she wanted to be alone, longed for privacy, yet knew that none was to be found, especially at Pilton Gardens.

It was Sasha's fault, of course. At the start she had been fine – well, tolerable – but it hadn't taken long before she'd started asking Bee to ask Ed, their landlord, to make improvements to the house – a small shed for storage, a new power shower – perhaps the kitchen could be upgraded? Soon, there was a new demand every other day, which Bee resented bitterly. As the eldest of the cousins, Sasha thought it was her business to oversee, to take care of the others. She saw herself as a self-styled mother, the lady of the house – which only Matilda tolerated, blissfully unaware of any underlying politics, so happy was she in her newfound state of independence, her ruddy cheeks permanently glowing. Bee, however, felt that Sasha had no business behaving like this, particularly as she couldn't shake the sense of ownership of Pilton Gardens that she felt. After all, it had been her home for fourteen years.

She knew that if she went back there now, Sasha would be holding court, with Aaron, who was a man oblivious to everything except football and the fast-becoming-obsolete fossil-fuel-run cars; Aaron who spent four or five nights out of seven in the house, loudly sipping tea and crunching on crisps; Aaron who Sasha hypocritically refused to buy or rent a property alone with until they were married. Bee was already counting down the days until the wedding, even if there was another year to go.

Sasha's dad would be there too, of course. Mike, the general handyman and dogsbody. Hen-pecked after years with Sasha's mother Betty, who, when her own children and those of her siblings had eventually reached adulthood, had somehow switched from being helpful to being plain interfering, her hands idle and itching for a face to wipe or homework to oversee. Mike's current constant presence at Pilton Gardens was because of an attempt to install a Universal Household Control system – at Sasha's demand, naturally. Doing it on the cheap, Mike had spent three nights so far trying to install the system through the old house alarm. So far, he had succeeded only in getting the OmniVac to start its nightly clean before anyone had gone to bed and they had spent three evenings with the device whirring around their feet, banging repeatedly up against them as it detected the dirt on their shoes as something it should clean up. To top matters off, Mike hadn't succeeded in disabling the actual alarm system and it had rung out for an hour during the night, bringing three police drones and two Community Co-Operation cars with it. Bee had stayed in bed throughout, her pillow pressed firmly over her face, counting to ten over and over.

Tonight, she knew that Betty was due round for her weekly catch-up, plus it was probable that Sasha's annoying brothers – Tyler, Marcus or both – would have joined Aaron on the sofa, guffawing loudly at the TV and salivating at the possibility of Betty's coconut cake, which Bee hated. It made her blood boil to think of them all. Why Sasha couldn't just go round her mum's and keep her family there, where they belonged, she didn't know. So much for Vicky trying to move in – she hadn't darkened the door once, whereas Betty practically left a toothbrush.

Bee longed for them all to leave. Just to leave her alone in *her* house. Where she felt safe. Where she felt – she knew it sounded stupid – looked after, somehow. Nourished and loved and protected. Returning to Pilton Gardens had sparked something in her that brought her back to childhood. And this she couldn't really understand.

To Bee, her childhood could be marked out in three phases. Death of mother, Crippling Depression of Father, Usurpment of Mother by Just-Tolerable Conniving Hippy Stepmother. There were other lesser parts too, of course – her father's troublesome, interfering family which was unfortunately the only family that she could ever remember having, and then things like the bullying she'd participated in at school, the difficulty in making friends except of the wrong sort. It had hardly been the stuff of warm, fuzzy memories, she acknowledged.

So why then did the house where she had experienced all of that feel like such a cocoon for her? And why did Sasha's invasion feel like such an utter, unforgivable intrusion?

An electronic female voice suddenly boomed through the air. *"Please remove your hood. Under London Metropolitan by-laws, concealment of the face is not permitted. We are grateful for your co-operation."*

Bee sighed and begrudgingly did as the drone bade her. More intrusion. By something that looked like a bloody toy helicopter. However, she knew the consequences. A young man in her class had refused to remove his scarf from around his nose on a cold day at Camden Market the previous winter and within moments of the drone issuing a third warning, a police car pulled up beside him and he was taken in for questioning. Another of the new rules allowed that: Suspicion of Hatred, Incitement and Terrorism it was called. The police tended to avoid using the unfortunate acronym but everyone else did.

Her hood down, the drone receded and Bee continued her walk in the ensuing silence, fumbling after a moment for her headphones. She tended not to wear them too often as it made it difficult to hear the drones approach and she disliked being taken by surprise by discovering one hovering overhead if she found herself on a quiet street. They were meant to be for the protection of all citizens but she could never quite be sure if they were there to keep her safe, or to ensure placid behaviour by making people feel suspect at all times.

She was disturbed by a man's voice calling her name just as she made to slide the flat disc of her headphones into her ears.

"Bee! Bee Mycroft, isn't it?" the unfamiliar voice called.

Instantly, the distant hum of the drone became audible again. The heat-seeking facility in the machine would have detected the second presence from some distance away and immediately begun to transmit the information back to the Central Information Centre from where they were controlled, on the top floors of what had once been Buckingham Palace.

Bee turned sharply, and sighed as the drone hovered overhead. The man caught up and fell into step with her, panting slightly from the exertion.

"Bee," he said. "I wasn't sure if it was you or not – I saw you coming out of the Tube – I'm Adam Wilson, by the way. Sorry if I gave you a shock there – not too sure if you remember me but I worked on –"

"*High Society*," Bee interrupted with a hesitant smile. "You're Head of the Costume Faculty, aren't you?" Of course he was, she thought. Adam Wilson, of all people. Of all the coincidences! She had encountered him numerous times before, not that he'd remember, of course. And not that they'd actually ever *spoken* – but he was certainly someone that she had thought about frequently. It had been almost six months since they had worked alongside each other, preparing for the Weatherall's Christmas musical, where all faculties of the college came together to stage a full-scale, West End style musical at a proper venue so that all of the disciplines could experience theatre for real.

It was also almost six months, then, since she had taken the plunge and pressed 'send' on the e-mail. When no response came at the time, she had been sure that she would never hear back from him. And while she had been disappointed, she had taken it as a firm sign that what she had sent him was never meant to be and had carried on plodding through the day to day.

"I don't think that we were formally introduced, were we?" Adam continued.

Bee shook her head slightly, her steps slow and awkward beside him, unsure if they should continue walking or just stop which, thankfully, they eventually did when Adam thrust out his hand and she shook it.

"You sent me some designs," he continued. "I'm not sure if I got back to you – it was all so frantic at the time and then straight after the Christmas break it's into exam prep . . ."

He continued to speak while Bee registered what he had said. He'd received them. Her designs. Those sketches that she had done. And more than that, he'd said he had meant to get back to her – somehow knew who she actually was, *remembered* her. She was at once overwhelmed at this and baffled as to why this man – with his reputation – was chatting to her on the street near her house. She tried to retain what he said, all the while making a study of his face up close.

She mustn't be intimidated by him, she told herself. For starters, he wasn't all that much older than her – by the looks of him maybe mid-thirties? She was, after all, one of the oldest students on her course at twenty-five.

His hair was a sandy-blond colour, cut short at the sides, a little longer at the top. He was a little bit feminine, quite *pretty* actually, she observed. His accent was cut glass – public school without question. He wore a pale blue shirt under a navy blazer over a pair of burgundy tight-fit jeans. His brown brogues were thick-soled. A tan-coloured satchel slung across his chest. All very consciously vintage. There was something old-fashioned about him in general, thought Bee. And terribly *British*. Terribly *theatre,* as the saying went at Weatherall's. She forced herself to tune back in to what he was saying.

". . . anyhow, I've always intended getting back to you about the sketches and I've just never quite managed it. Geoffrey Cameron pointed you out to me at the time – hard to miss you with the . . ."

His voice fell away and he pointed at her hair, the distinctive red curls now held tightly back in a ponytail.

Bee blushed with embarrassment. Her hair was filled with dust and paint, she knew. Her intention tonight had been to give it an overdue wash and then hide in her room for some peace and quiet while it dried. Her hand shot to her scalp and she swallowed hard, realising suddenly that her overall appearance – a pair of scruffy jeans and the ancient hooded fleece that her father used to wear – oh God, that he had wrapped Godiva in as a piglet, if she remembered correctly – was most certainly not what she would have worn had she been given a formal appointment with the man standing before her. Because this meeting – this chance encounter – was something that she had thought about often in the previous six months.

"I've been working on the end-of-year project," she managed, looking down at her appearance, before her voice trailed away. She felt embarrassed at how she looked – she had dressed that morning, after all, with only heavy woodwork and lifting in mind. No one on her course dressed any differently from this. What was the point with all of the dirty, manual labour that it involved? Yet still she felt dowdy and dirty beside Adam. It struck her suddenly how very *clean* he was.

"Oh gosh, the Grecian thing that Gerry's got a bee in his bonnet about?" finished Wilson with a smile.

Bee smiled back and nodded. She had thought it was just her

who had noticed that her course head's passion for *Antigone* verged on the obsessive.

"I had a peep in at the rehearsals at the weekend actually. Shall we?" asked Adam, indicating that they should walk again.

They fell into a slow step.

"It looks great," he went on, "but I have to say that I hate it when Gerry gets his choice of the end-of-termer. He always picks something Theban and the costumes are such a bore – really nothing that my crew can get their teeth into. It doesn't benefit them in the slightest when they go looking for *actual* work: 'For my final college assignment I pinned some sheets' sort of thing is all that they can come up with when it comes to the crunch."

Bee smiled. "You should modernise it," she suggested offhand, immediately regretting the words that had just come from her mouth. "Sorry – I didn't mean to – I meant just for fun – punks, or Goths or something . . ." She flushed deeply, glancing at Wilson who was a good head taller than her – which was unusual. She was relieved to see that he was smiling.

"That's not a bad idea," he mused, glancing at her with a grin. "Not entirely original – I've done it before and brought it into the 1920s – but punk – now *there's* a thought. Not very fashionable at all any more, punk. But what a challenge . . . all that *lovely* Vivienne Westwood stuff . . . Do you live around here somewhere?"

Bee nodded again. "Pilton Gardens." She pointed in the direction of her home. "I share with two of my cousins. Only just at the moment it's two of my cousins, my aunt, my uncle, their other two kids and a football-crazed lorry driver most of the time." She wanted to kick herself. Why would Adam Wilson care about any of that? What did he want with her anyway?

He stopped walking suddenly. "Sounds like utter hell," he remarked. "Look, to be serious for a moment – oh bloody thing!" He swatted at the ever-present police drone as if it were a fly, even though it was a good ten feet above his head. "I *hate* modern Britain, don't you?"

Bee glanced upward at the device, which remained static. She wondered if it would register Wilson's action as a threat and incur some follow-up? She glanced around nervously.

"I live around here too," he continued. "Just on Pinegreen Road – I assume you know the King Harry pub?"

Bee nodded. "I grew up round here," she said suddenly, feeling another irrational need to explain herself. "Used to be called The Gibraltar before . . . well . . . the whole *Harry* thing . . ."

"Shall we go for a drink there?" Wilson asked suddenly. "I mean . . . would you mind . . . I have something that I'd like to discuss with you. Sorry – all of this is a bit out of the blue. I'm a bit out of sync, having pursued you all the way from Fulham Broadway!"

Bee wasn't sure if she saw correctly but for a moment she could have sworn that Adam Wilson blushed.

It was contagious. She reddened, and lowered her head slightly so that he wouldn't see. There was silence for a moment before Wilson spoke again, his voice serious and quiet: "It's about your designs, the ones you sent . . . and . . . I can't bloody hear myself *think* with that thing up there." He pointed upwards at the drone.

Bee glanced at her watch. She would have preferred this invitation to come at a different time and in a different place. It was already half past eight and she looked like a builder's labourer. But then again, no one was expecting her at home. And the football on TV was likely to last for another while. And how long would she have to wait for another invitation to discuss her sketches – her *designs* as he'd called them – with Adam Wilson of all people? She smiled nervously.

"I'd be happy to," she replied, indicating that she would accompany him to the pub.

Wilson smiled, and stood back to let her lead the way.

* * *

Bee Mycroft lay on her bed that night with much to think about. Her tongue was still tangy from the Merlot but she didn't want to clean her teeth, couldn't face bumping into one of the other residents of the house on their way to the bathroom. And she needed to think, uninterrupted. Because the meeting with Adam Wilson couldn't, in fact, have been more timely for her. It was something that she had wanted for a long time now, she realised, but had been afraid to acknowledge it. After all, her dad was paying huge amounts of money for the set design course at Weatherall's – and she had sworn blind when she had finished at Taunton that it was what she definitely wanted to do as a career.

But more and more, from before *High Society* at Christmas, before ever she had sent Adam Wilson the speculative sketches of a pale blue dress with a tight bodice and flowing skirt, sparkling with hand-sewn diamante and pearl trimmings, before ever she had finally admitted it to herself, she had felt an inexorable creative pull in another direction. Toward clothing. Toward fabric and shape and bias and cut.

Bee wondered, if she had never found that sketchbook in the attic, might she have been content with hammering and painting and the occasional trompe l'oeil feature forever? But since the day she had come across it she had been intrigued. She had no idea who had placed it there, of course. Probably that American woman who'd lived there had left it behind and then forgotten all about it. But the sketches captivated her – all very out-of-date stuff, but beautiful. Elegant. Flattering. The smart styles and feminine appearance of the pieces sketched onto the same tall, short-haired figure. All of them an inspiration for the stuff she had started to doodle herself, and for the design that she had impulsively sent Adam Wilson.

He had loved it, he explained as they sat in the pub. It was head and shoulders above some of the stuff that his students were producing, he'd told her. However, he couldn't have included it in the show, simply because she was from Set not Costume, and he was bound by college politics. But he hadn't forgotten it and had since been intrigued by it, he said. She couldn't transfer courses at Weatherall's unfortunately, but if she was really interested, there were two other places that could work out for her. One being RADA, the other, however, a little less well-known. It was Bee's turn to be intrigued as Adam spoke in hushed tones of a college she had never heard of before. A small, exclusive place, he said. It had just been an art school for years, but in recent times had begun to specialise more and more in fashion design. Eventually, it had grown in stature – there were big names in fashion on the board –

all the oldsters, mused Bee, but big names indeed. Lady Beckham, Sir Gok Wan. There were rumours that Baroness McCartney might take up the chairmanship for the '20-'21 academic year. Which was when they were to introduce a course that Adam felt might be perfect for Bee – a degree in Costume Fashion Design – clothes that were theatrical in essence, yet not for use in the theatre.

The course was revolutionary stuff, he explained. Something unprecedented – modules in history as well as design and also practical stuff like needlework – hard, hard slog. Terribly exclusive too – only people of *real* star quality could potentially gain a place. There wasn't even an application process – applicants could only be nominated by professionals and experts in their field, and even then they would face subsequent rigorous screening before they would be whittled down to just twenty names in total.

Bee felt the world spin a little when Adam told her that he thought she had potential to be put forward as a candidate. That he thought that some of the quality that they required had shone through from the single piece that she had sent him – a quality that he hadn't noticed in his other students, even though they were full-time prospective costume designers. He'd gone through their stuff over and over, he told her. And yet was constantly drawn back to her single garment.

Would she be interested? he had asked.

At first, the answer was no. How could Bee possibly gain a place in something so specialist when she hadn't even studied basic costume design? Wouldn't she be best to take the Costume course and *then* apply? she had argued, overwhelmed by what she was hearing.

He refuted her argument vehemently. There were costume designers nationwide who would fight tooth and nail to get a place on that course, he told her – his own students among them – but also designers with *years* of training and experience. But this course wasn't just about costume design – it was about fashion, about trendsetting, about revolutionary design coupled with good old-fashioned mastery of skill – about *instinct*. It was about creating designers of the future, about lifting fashion out of the grey and black, shapeless rut that the obesity crisis of the last five years had created, and taking it back to being something glorious, something to be proud of, something that celebrated the human form. Bee listened, wide-eyed, as he spoke passionately, not just about the course, but about design, about fashion in general.

"I think you have it, Bee," he stressed. "They want raw talent after all, not the same old ding-dong that's being produced day in and day out on stages and high streets everywhere. They want *art*, not just expertise. They want *Hirst*, not paint-by-numbers."

He had asked for more of her work. Which she had in spades. She sketched and drew every spare minute that she could. For a moment Bee sent a silent prayer to the heavens in thanks for the fact that the only time that she got to herself in her own home these days was by locking herself into her room at night and drawing.

Adam had also requested some of her needlework – it was the real tricky area, he told her. No one knew how to sew any more, of course. It wasn't something that today's designers had to worry about with the advances in computer stitching programs and robotics. But if she could actually, physically, push thread through fabric then something that simple could be the key difference between her and another applicant. It would be worth it, even though it might be difficult to get the old-style equipment, he had suggested. And costly for that matter.

Bee had smiled when he'd said it, however, and now, lying on her bed, she pushed herself far enough up on her elbows to glance at the table which stood by the window, bearing the old-fashioned sewing machine that she had also discovered hidden in the attic. She wasn't sure how to use it yet but when she had opened the box it had seemed brand new, with instructions included, and she knew that she could find a good tutorial on the net. It was possible even that Auntie Betty might know how to work the damn thing, although she wasn't entirely sure that she wished to bring that on herself just yet.

Bee flopped back down on her pillow and stretched her arms above her head, running her fingers through her hair. She'd have to wash it in the morning now. And maybe she'd root out those new jeans that she'd bought in the sales, actually. No harm in sprucing up her image a bit for college. With so much at stake, it might be a good idea not to look like a total navvy, as her dad liked to call her, when she next met Adam as arranged. Tomorrow. After classes, when they would get to work on putting together her application and her portfolio.

Only another six weeks of set design to go, she thought to herself. And then a whole summer to work hard on getting shortlisted for the course at Darvill's. Adam had said he would help her – she wasn't sure why, other than the fact that he saw real potential in her for something different. It could all be a complete wasted effort, of course, but worth a try, he said, to have a place on the very first year of a course that he felt would become incredibly prestigious in the fashion world, something that all budding creative designers would aspire to. He really seemed to believe that a place in Darvill's College would be something special and he insisted that she had the talent, raw as it was.

Bee smiled. What a night, she thought to herself. New possibilities – what a lucky path that trip to the attic had set her on all those months ago. Like someone was looking after her.

Silently, she mouthed another 'thanks' heavenward. She had always avoided what she called Rowan's hippy tendencies, but had secretly agreed that showing the universe occasional gratitude couldn't do any harm. After all, what else could have somehow, fortuitously, brought Adam Wilson into her life?

AUGUST 2020

Bee and Adam

Why? Why did Rowan keep on doing that? Throwing those looks? Dumping plates on the table with a clatter? Frowning? Making those remarks? It was so unbelievably embarrassing.

Bee consoled herself with the fact that Adam didn't seem to notice. That instead he sat with his attention fully focused on Ed Mycroft who seemed oddly animated for a change, fully embracing the rare opportunity to talk at length about his animation processes. From what she could hear of it, Bee imagined that the conversation would bore her to tears – what little of it she could understand. But Adam was rapt, nodding in the right places, making appreciative gasps when required, asking interested questions. Bee couldn't take her eyes off him for a moment and a warm smile spread across her lips as she thought about how perfect he was, framed golden in a Somerset sunset as they sat around the dinner table in the fading light.

He sat alongside Ed, his arms folded and his legs stretched out before him under the table, reaching occasionally to sip from his glass, attentively refilling Ed's when required – which was often, Bee noticed. It was seldom her dad got the chance to relax like this, she thought. Chatting amicably over a bottle of wine, telling his war stories. Things had been like this at Pilton Gardens, he had told her once. When she was a baby. Dinner parties, impromptu get-togethers, friends and colleagues and fascinating folk gathered around the same dining-room table that was currently buried under a mound of Sasha's bridal magazines and fabric samples. Or out at the big table in the garden, which was in need of a coat of varnish these days. Bee looked at her dad. His hair was still thick, but completely grey now, his waistband straining a little after the huge meal, his skin tanned from the long hours spent trudging around the farm and through the nearby lanes with Godiva at his heels while he sought inspiration for *Lila and Vulpo*. She transferred the smile she cast at Adam to her father. She loved to see him like this, completely relaxed, caught in a moment, talking about something that he loved.

He was remarkably sociable when he wanted to be, she observed. Unlike the man he usually was these days at Judith's Acre. Always working or walking or reading something – silent and thoughtful. This – this sociable, affable character chatting in the evening sunshine, was who he was truly meant to be, she was sure. Bee wondered if he might have been like this all the time if he'd stayed in the city. The man who had entertained strangers at his old home in London, not the one who hid himself away from the world in the countryside. The man who had married her mother.

Jenny.

Bee had thought of that name often throughout her life but never more so than since she and Adam had become a couple three months ago. It was because they were serious, she supposed. Because suddenly, her mental plans for the future had expanded to fit two rather than just one. Because she wasn't alone any more – she was part of a pair – better than that, part of a *team*. Being with Adam somehow made her feel more complete – two heads were better than one, after all, and now everything she did involved him. She no longer had to make decisions all alone, like she felt she'd had to do all her life. They had worked at length on her portfolio for Darvill's and now it was ready. Everything was good enough, he had told her. The needlework was basic, but perfect; the designs were divine. She was ready. And next week, when she went before the selection panel, she knew that he would be waiting outside the interview-room door for her. He'd said that she was a shoo-in, or he'd eat his hat. The panel would most certainly be blown away by her. Bee's stomach flipped at the thought and she took another mouthful from her wineglass to calm herself.

More and more these days, she wished desperately that her mother was still here. For so long, it hadn't crossed her mind – her only memory of Jenny was a hazy one, from the kitchen at Pilton Gardens. She remembered a pale, tall woman, with hair colouring like her own, smiling at her from the kitchen table while she had been perched on the worktop with Ed. She was very young, she knew. Had to have been – her mother had died shortly after her second birthday, which was why the memory didn't make all that much sense. Bee sometimes thought that she must have dreamed the moment, yet still she clung to it for all she was worth. Apart from photographs and a watch, it was all she had to link her to the woman who had given birth to her.

Bee wondered if Jenny would have liked Adam. Her first serious boyfriend. Her grown-up partner, as she liked to think. She looked back again at him, lost for a moment in the way the light reflected in his hair. With the sun setting behind him, it looked almost as red as her own. Of course Jenny would. She'd have loved him. Everyone loved Adam, didn't they? He was kind, clever – brilliant, in fact. He was handsome, funny – he was perfect in so many ways, thought Bee lovingly. And perfect for her. Encouraging her, helping her every step of the way. He constantly told her how beautiful she was, how talented, how intelligent. With him, she felt complete. She wondered if that was how her parents had felt together? If Jenny had felt the same way about the man she married?

Ed didn't often speak of her, of course. What Bee knew about her mother had been gathered from odd snippets that he had told her occasionally, from things that her aunts and grandmother had filled in along the way. That Jenny, herself, was beautiful. That she was quiet and calm and dedicated to her family. That she was giving – sacrificing her own job for the needs of her family. Straightforward. Nothing like Rowan with her quiet – sneaky? – ambitions. Bee cast an eye across to where her stepmother was gathering the dirty pudding bowls and was suddenly roused from her stream of thought by the ferocious look that Rowan threw across the table at Adam. Bee sat up straight. What the *hell* was her problem?

Bee had known that Rowan was unhappy about Adam since she had first mentioned him. It was a mistake doing that, Bee realised now. Rushing down to the Acre the weekend after that fateful evening when he had followed her from the Tube. They had barely been apart – except for classes – after that. There hadn't been enough hours for them to talk together – to share, to admire, for each to greedily absorb information from the other, for the realisation to grow within them that it was unavoidable that they should be together. All of this Bee had blurted across the kitchen table to Rowan as the older woman kneaded bread and listened carefully to everything her stepdaughter had to say. What a mistake, Bee knew. Trusting Rowan enough to tell her all of that, expecting someone as deep-down cynical as her to understand.

"Isn't he a bit old for you?" had been Rowan's first question.

Of course it was. Her eyebrows raised. The old familiar way of showing that she didn't trust what you were telling her. Bee remembered it only too well from when she was a teenager. Rowan would give her that look and the next thing she knew, Ed would be hauled on board to dole out a punishment or issue a warning. Never Rowan to her face, of course. The second she saw the eyebrow lift, while the hands continued to pummel the bread, Bee knew that she should never have opened her mouth – at least not to Rowan first. She should have just told her dad straight away, given him the real version of events. Now her good news would be coloured by Rowan's disapproval. And it *was* good news. Any man would be pleased to hear it, Bee was sure – that his daughter had not only just been handed the biggest career opportunity of her lifetime, but that she was – for the first time – properly and truly and rightfully in love.

Bee watched as Rowan's gaze burned onto an unwitting Adam as she picked up the small tower of bowls stained with raspberry crumble with one hand and clinked together the four water glasses with the claw she had formed of the other, one on each finger. The hostile stare continued as Rowan made her way slowly round the table and broke only when she had walked past and carried on back into the house. Bee watched her go with an expression of disdain.

How *dare* she? That bloody woman. All her life Bee had tried to be fair towards her. Had tried her best to accept her. Had tried to overlook how different she was to herself and her dad, had tried to tolerate the changes that she made to their existence when she had come to live with them. It had been difficult, Bee remembered. They were doing fine all of a sudden – her and her dad. His depression had lifted and things were normal for the first time in her life. She remembered them being properly happy for once – and that was all that she had ever wanted – for the two of them to be properly happy. She knew that they could never have her mum back, but there were plenty of kids in her school who had only one parent and they were absolutely fine. She recalled being content at last. But then, of course, Rowan had to come on the scene, hadn't she? All curls and sketchbooks and that big stupid smile; all alone and searching for a mate.

Bee knew that her own behaviour in the earliest days had been extreme – and she had been harsh on herself for it since she had grown up and moved away from home – but since meeting Adam, since talking it all through with him, she realised that her reaction to Rowan's arrival on the scene had been perfectly normal. Rowan was an intruder, a competitor for her dad's affections, he wisely said. Things had been difficult between them because Rowan had *made* them that way. He'd even gone so far as to offer the opinion that Rowan might have seen *Bee* as a competitor for Ed's affections and that, too, made sense.

Bee suddenly burned with a resentment that she hadn't felt for years. How *dare* that woman, she thought again, fiercely. She was suddenly so hot, so fired up, that she looked at her boyfriend and her father across the table and expected them to stare at her, expected them to feel what she was feeling. But they didn't. They were oblivious, their heads leaning in closer to each other.

Bloody Rowan. All her life Bee had done her best to tolerate her, to understand her. And she didn't even have the courtesy to be polite to Adam on his first visit to Judith's Acre – which wasn't even

Bee's home. It was *Rowan's* home, where she had dragged her father to live so that she could have everything her own way.

Since their arrival on the early train that afternoon, Rowan had been nothing but rude to Adam. Coldly civil at first, in greeting, but after that she had pretty much ignored him, locking herself away in the kitchen to prepare their meal. And then she had disappeared for an hour, saying that she was going off to the village to get cream or something, but Bee was certain that it was because she could scarcely bear being under the same roof as Adam. Who was she to judge anyway?

The meal had been awkward too. Adam had behaved impeccably, of course – Bee was always impressed by how socially adept he was, even in the most awkward of situations – but he had to have seen the penetrating gazes that Rowan had thrown him across the table, had to have felt awkward as she quizzed him about the course that he taught and about the change of course – and college – that he was proposing for Bee. Why couldn't she just calm down and trust him, like her dad clearly did, wondered Bee furiously. After all, her father was the one with the *right* to be concerned or suspicious about her welfare, about anyone that she brought home. And he was clearly happy with Adam and his ideas. How funny that Darvill's had been the college that her parents had attended! Surely that had to mean something? For her to go to the place where her mother and father had first met? Wasn't that fate? Serendipity? Surely it held too much significance to be mere coincidence? Surely it was a sign that somehow meant the love her parents had shared was still alive – still somehow a force at work, far and above anything that had come from her father's relationship with Rowan?

She claimed not to be materialistic, but Rowan had to have some sort of issue with the whole money end of things, mused Bee, catching sight of her stepmother at the kitchen sink through the window overhung with wisteria. She had to have some problem with the cost of things – which Ed had instantly offered to help out with, naturally. The new course wasn't cheap – not to mention the materials that would be required – but they had resolved that earlier in the evening. Ed had promised to help out if Bee got a part-time job to sustain herself. If this course was what Bee wanted to do, and it was so difficult to get onto, then she deserved the extra investment, Ed had reasoned. Rowan had frowned at that, of course. But why? It wasn't as if Bee was asking her for money personally – and it wasn't even as if she was poor – that Corkscrew Cards business had done pretty well for her over the years. Yet no one had suggested even touching a penny of Rowan's precious stash – it was Ed who was volunteering to help out his only daughter – wasn't that a natural thing to do for a parent? He could well afford it – *Lila and Vulpo* had proven to be a huge success – the merchandising alone provided a very healthy income, not to mention the international rights. So if he wanted to spend his money on what he chose, then that was his business, reasoned Bee.

Was it the case, however, that more money spent on Bee meant less money spent on Rowan, or more to the point, on stupid Judith's Acre? She'd been rambling on for months now about turning some of the outhouses into self-catering accommodation. A sound retirement investment, Bee had overheard her say to Ed. For whom? For Ed? Or for Rowan who would at some stage get too old or too bored or too lazy to run her card company and decide that it was time to live off the fat of her land. The fat into which Ed was expected to invest his hard-earned income.

Yes, that had to be it. All about the money, as the old song went, mused Bee. And besides which – more to the heart of the matter – Rowan had always, deep down, wanted Ed completely to herself. She had never loved Bee, had never connected with her in a way that she felt sure she should. She couldn't even really like kids – too much competition. If she did, then surely she and Ed would have had one of their own, perish the thought?

No, Bee was a fly in the ointment – but not to worry – Rowan knew that she'd grow up and leave someday and then it would just be her and Ed, in a little country bubble of her making. Exactly as she wanted it. Well, that was how she'd have it then.

How dare she be rude to Adam, to be so judgemental and bitter and unwelcoming? Tomorrow, Bee would take Adam back to London and never visit this god-forsaken place again. She'd get her dad to come to the city if he wanted to see her – it wouldn't do him any harm to get out from under the thumb of that woman every now and again, after all. But there would be no more dealings with her stepmother. None. She could keep her selfish ambition and jealousy from now on. Bee had better things to do. A whole life ahead, where she could finally achieve the impossible and, with Adam's guidance and love, become a proper success, not some sort of crusty, accidental artist like Rowan was, living off the real success of someone else.

Bee stood up from the table abruptly, finally causing Adam and Ed to look in her direction. "I'm going to bed," she stated bluntly, and stormed off in the direction of the house without a glance backwards. She'd sneak into Adam's room later, she decided. And explain everything to him. She was too angry now – best if she didn't try to come up with a polite excuse.

Bee's expression was stony as she stormed past Rowan who emerged from the house, carrying a tray of coffee, just as Bee reached the back door.

"Off to the loo?" Rowan asked with a smile as she stood aside to allow her stepdaughter to pass. The comment registered no response, not even eye contact, in fact, and Bee stomped up the back step and into the cool darkness of the kitchen in silence. With a frown, Rowan watched her go for a moment, before making her way to the table where she dished out pottery cups and saucers and set the *cafetiére* down. She was relieved when, as she did so, Adam stood and excused himself, shaking Ed's hand sincerely and casting her a polite – if chilly – smile, before himself heading toward the house after Bee.

Rowan was left facing her husband who smiled contentedly across the table at her. Rowan grinned back. "You're pissed," she observed, and thrust the plunger down into the coffee, watching the displaced black liquid swirl around the sides. She leaned across the table and poured Ed a cup. "You'll need this," she remarked as she did, but he ignored it, the same silly grin plastered across his face as she had seen so often on evenings like this when they ate outside, warmed by sun, talking at the table until the stars emerged and it grew too chilly to stay put.

"Oi'm jest *content*, woman," he observed in his best imitation of her accent, with a sigh.

Rowan rolled her eyes at him and sat back in her chair, arms folded across her chest, looking out over the valley below where the first of the evening's lights were starting to twinkle. She glanced at Ed, still smiling, and felt a pang of warmth for him. She, too, was very content.

She leaned forward and poured herself a half cup of coffee. "What do you think of that Adam chap?" she asked tentatively.

Ed's eyes were closed as he leaned back in his chair. He shrugged. "Seems nice," he replied.

Rowan remained silent for a few moments, save for the scraping of her spoon around the base of the pottery cup as she stirred vigorously to gain his attention.

It had the desired effect. Ed sat up and looked directly at her. "You don't think so?" he asked, his eyebrows raised.

Rowan looked away from her husband and placed the spoon on her saucer, pausing to take a sip of the black coffee before replying.

"He's nice, all right," she offered, setting the cup back down but keeping her hands wrapped around it as she glanced back across the view of the valley below. "I still think he's a bit old for Bee though."

Ed continued to look across the table at her. "Only ten years or so," he replied, shrugging casually as he picked up his own cup. Rowan was right – he *did* need it, he realised.

"I suppose I just know so little about him," observed Rowan. "I mean, I know that he lectures in that costume design course, but with that extra ten years to him, he has to have some sort of past, doesn't he?"

Ed was quick to respond. "You don't think he's a *cad*, do you?" he spluttered. "With that accent and those clothes? Are you worried he might have gone *foxhunting* once or something?" he giggled.

Rowan ignored him. "I just think that he has to have had more . . . *experiences* . . . in his life than Bee does. I mean, she's been very sheltered since we left London, hasn't she? Local school, local college – even when she's made her big break back to London she's moved straight back into the house where she was born, practically. We've probably sheltered her too much, don't you think?"

Ed nodded thoughtfully. "There was a reason for that, remember?"

Rowan nodded in response. "I know," she said, sighing.

Ed watched the frown form on her face. "What's really up?" he asked, leaning across the table and reaching for Rowan's hand. "Spill it, woman, or you'll be up all night."

Rowan sighed again, and laced her fingers through Ed's. "I'm not sure I've thought this through properly or not . . . but I'm . . . *uneasy* . . . about all of this. Aren't you? Am I imagining things?"

Ed responded by continuing to look her directly in the eye. He might be slightly tiddly, but he'd learned over the years that two could play at Rowan's silent-treatment game. Eventually the other person always cracked.

"I don't know," she continued, thinking aloud. "When she told me about Adam first . . . I mean, alarm bells went off straight away. About that course first of all – there's something about it that isn't right, isn't there?"

Ed released his hand and pulled himself back across the table for another swig of coffee. "It's all legit," he shrugged. "I looked into it all myself – I'm not so stupid that I'd go and pay for a course that doesn't exist – and it's Darvill's – what a coincidence!"

Rowan smiled. "No. You're not stupid, love," she said softly. "But you *are* indulgent. Always have been when it comes to Bee." He made to protest but Rowan raised a hand to silence him, all the while smiling indulgently herself. "And I know that there's a reason for that too. But we've also always known that sometimes indulging Bee hasn't worked out for the best, now has it?"

It was Ed's turn to smile. "Hey, we wouldn't have moved down here if it wasn't for that, now would we? Every cloud and all that!"

"And I love that we moved here, Ed. You know that."

"And so do I," he said. "I've never been happier. It changed my life so much for the better."

Rowan smiled back. It was true that Ed had become a different man in the countryside. She had been afraid that he would wilt and wither once away from his home and his foundations, but instead he had flourished.

"I just think that maybe Bee is rushing into something and I'm concerned," she said. "It's only been a couple of months since she met Adam, but she's already talking about him moving into Pilton Gardens once Sasha moves out."

Ed frowned.

"I didn't say that to you because I thought you'd get mad, but it's true. She told me that the weekend after she met him." Rowan paused for the message to sink in. "That's how fast this is moving, Ed. And I'm worried that something will go horribly wrong. You know that Bee's like a freight train once she sets her mind to something and in the past we've always been able to avert disaster at the last minute but, this time, I don't know why, but I just feel like the crash is inevitable. And I'm worried for her. I know that we haven't always seen eye to eye – I mean, to this day I have no idea what Bee truly thinks of me deep inside. But she's my family, and I know that she's your *world*. I just don't want her getting hurt, that's all."

Ed took a deep draught from the cup of coffee, his own brow furrowed at the thoughts that suddenly sprang to his mind. "What should we do?" he asked. "Should we stop her? Forbid her from doing the course? Withdraw funding? What do you think?"

Rowan shook her head. "No, no. None of the above, Ed," she said impatiently. "I just think that maybe you should have a talk with her – on her own. Maybe I'll take Adam into the village or something in the morning – to the market – and you and she can go for a walk – show her the plans for the self-catering apartments or something. But maybe just try and get something out of her that doesn't solely revolve around the fact that Adam lives and breathes, and how wonderful he is and how his students think he's amazing and how Darvill's college is the best thing since sliced bread . . . Maybe just . . . I don't know . . . introduce a note of caution perhaps? Pull her back to the kerb a little bit? She'll take it from you – she'd just think I was interfering, but you're her dad. *And* you're paying for it after all . . ." Rowan's voice trailed off as she saw Ed's worried face. "Look, don't panic. I'm sorry – I'm scaremongering, aren't I? I don't mean to. I mean, she might not even get on this course if it's as tough as she makes out, and that will mean that problem might be solved. I don't want to belittle her talent but it's not like she has the slightest experience in fashion design, has she? And if she doesn't get on the course, then it might sort everything out. I don't think Adam will seem so glossy when she has to get a job and with him out of the way then she might, I dunno, go travelling maybe? See a bit of the world? Make some new friends, meet some new boys – have some adventures. Maybe she'll grow up a little bit. She's only twenty-five, after all. She has her whole life ahead of her."

Ed was silent, but he nodded in agreement across the table. "Twenty-five," he said after a moment, sighing heavily. "Where did the time go?"

Rowan laughed lightly. "Hark at you! You've gone all maudlin now. I should have left you drinking the wine until you nodded off, like you normally do!"

Ed smiled sheepishly in response and reached out to take her hand again. "I'll talk to her tomorrow," he said. "As always, my love, you have it figured out, don't you? Making sense of my life for me yet again." He raised Rowan's hand to his lips and kissed it tenderly. "What would I have done without you?" he said, quietly, and she squeezed his fingers. They sat like that, in silence, in the growing darkness, as the valley lit itself below, the lights of occasional farmhouses coming on, one by one.

While from just inside the darkness of the kitchen door, the chill of the evening creeping in around her bare feet, Bee burned with rage at everything that she had just heard her stepmother say. *That bloody woman*, she fumed as she grabbed the handbag she had come back downstairs to retrieve, stopping for a moment to eavesdrop as she heard her name mentioned through the still of the evening. *I was right all along. How dare she!*

Bee stomped back up the stairs, not caring if her footsteps were heard from outside yet hoping that Adam wouldn't appear at the door of his room. It wasn't that she didn't long to see him, to collapse into the arms of the only person that she felt truly loved her. But she felt too distraught to talk to him now. She needed to calm herself, to be alone. To be rational and calm before she spoke to him. Because if she spoke to him now – if she saw his perfect face filled with concern, and blurted everything out to him – then she felt sure that there was a chance she would leave that house right there and then and never return. A real chance that she would say something to her *father* that she would always regret.

No. She would leave all right. And never darken the door of Judith's Acre for the rest of her and Adam's life. But she would do so with her head held high, with her father's love for her intact, and with her stepmother's regret at meddling in her life assured forever.

SEPTEMBER 2020

Jenny

I do not like thee, Adam Wilson.

No. Absolutely. Not a jot. Not one little bit.

I want you to leave. Leave us alone, me and the girls. I've got quite used to it just being the four of us actually. Me, Bee, 'Poor Matilda' as they all call her and Sasha, always The Bride. I've got to know them all quite well, actually. Through watching, always watching.

I know that Poor Matilda is far from poor. That she's been squirrelling money away in secret for most of her life, ever since her first summer job as a kid in fact. Because she wants to go travelling. Not just travelling – she wants to go far, far away. Hence the degree in Chinese.

She wants to get as far as she possibly can. As far as she can get from her vile mother. She hasn't saved enough just yet, but she's working away every hour that she can in that awful greasy spoon that she hates so. Coming home, stinking of dirty chip fat and onion rings and lord knows what else – all the time working. And when she's not, she's studying her absolute hardest at her degree. She's actually clever, you see, despite what we all used to think. All those years being the victim of her mother's vileness have taught her to keep quiet and keep watch. And she has learned well from this.

Matilda might still have that unfortunate colouring that she's always had, along with those scars from her childhood eczema, she might act like she's a simpleton but she is far, far from it. She is wise, she is shrewd, she is quiet. She verges on sneaky, but that I can forgive seeing as how she has spent her whole life hiding firstly her most treasured possessions from that grabbing mother of hers and subsequently her own hard-earned cash. Her escape fund. And she has succeeded.

Matilda has brains. Brains to burn. She is astute and resourceful. And all of this wrapped up in the most physically forgettable, verging on unpleasant package that you'll ever find, with her terrible, cheap clothes, her allergies, her limp hair, her vast hips.

She'll do very, very well for herself, that child.

Add experience to what she has already and she will be unbeatable. She will have the art of surprise at her fingertips; she will attack quickly and coldly, when her enemies least expect it.

I suspect that she will one day be CEO of a very large company or hold high political office.

And that will show her mother, won't it?

I know that Sasha exists solely as an extension of that awful lorry-driver boy, that her only aim in life, her only goal, the only horizon that she can see is her wedding day to him. And she will make a very good wife for him, I'm sure. Just like her own mother, Ed's sister Betty, with her ruthless efficiency, her single-minded ambition. So long as that ambition relates solely to her personal wants. And Sasha wants. Good God, does she Want, with a capital 'W'!

She wants the perfect dress, the nipped-in waist, an up-do that will refuse to budge all day long. She wants her favourite pop songs in church – she wants the biggest church she can find, in fact, and no one will stop her having it. She wants the most tender beef and salmon on the menu, the immaculately choreographed first dance. She wants the bridesmaids to be that little bit less perfect than herself – that's why she's putting Bee in crimson and Matilda in something sleeveless, poor thing – so that they don't show her up. She wants the perfect honeymoon, the perfect house, perfect teeth, perfect skin – the perfect man. Well, we all can't have everything, can we?

Yet with the same dogged determination to have everything her own way for her wedding, she will apply herself on return from that perfect honeymoon to making sure that Aaron does exactly as she wants. And then she will make sure that the babies begin arriving in perfect order – she'll give up work, devote herself solely to the home.

And for what? I thought that would work too but I got pretty bored pretty fast, didn't I?

In an odd way, I admire them both – Matilda and Sasha. They are both determined young women who will, I think, go far for themselves, who know exactly what it is they want and are working hard toward achieving it.

Which is exactly what I didn't do when I was alive.

And exactly what my daughter seems unable to do now.

She thinks that she wants this course at Darvill's – how I thrilled and chilled when I heard the name of that place! – the source of my greatest happiness it was, although I didn't realise it then.

But I don't think she does want it.

And more worryingly, she thinks she wants this Adam Wilson character.

But I've been watching him as closely as I've been watching the rest.

And I do not like him, not one little bit.

I see how he checks out his own reflection every time he passes something that will show it to him. I see him preening and primping in front of the mirror, using the palm of his hand to tease back his hair into that odd flick he's so fond of.

I see him smoothing down his stomach and sucking in his gut when he thinks no one is looking. I see him checking his fingernails – his manicured fingernails – when he's alone.

I see the way he rolls up his nose at our house – it's a proper house-share house now, instead of the family showhouse that I worked so hard to make it. Everything is mismatched, three disparate tastes all thrown in together, washing draped over radiators, bridal magazines, textbooks, dirty coffee cups.

And Adam doesn't like it that way, making those faces of disgust when Bee has left the room and then melting into that fake smile of his when he sees her again.

I hate it when he does that. The face he makes is bad enough but what I hate the most is the face that she makes in return. It makes me look away to see it – the expression of sheer trust and devotion, the glow of happiness and expectation, the want and the desire to be with no one else.

I hate it because in it, in that beautiful woman's face that she now has, I can see as clear as day her baby face. And because I know what she was like then, I know that it is the very same expression with which she used to look at me.

And I cannot bear for anyone else to have that gift bestowed upon them. Particularly when they don't deserve it.

I don't know what Adam Wilson's game is, what exactly he wants from my daughter. I do know that he is always here. That he looks through all her little sketches and drawings – that he has even seen mine in that sketchbook Bee found in the attic – those stupid things I used to pretend to design for Princess Diana all those years ago.

I know that she tells him her thoughts and her dreams, her private desires, her hopes, her regrets, her loves, her hates – she gives herself entirely to him, and he takes, takes and takes some more. And what worries me is where he is keeping what he takes, and what he plans to do with it.

Because he doesn't reciprocate – not really. Bee thinks that they are equal partners, but only because she wants that so desperately. Yet what she really needs is to be cared for, to be looked after.

And that's what I want for her too and if I cannot be the person to do it, then please don't let her fall for him because he's not capable.

He just wants to see himself reflected in her worship; he wants some silly, vulnerable girl to adore him and make him feel good about himself. He just wants the total adoration that he receives in return for the few crumbs that he throws for my wonderful, foolish girl to peck at.

And I know this because I did the same. And I paid a heavy, heavy price for it.

If there is a God – which I seriously doubt, as I am still here in this limbo – then please let Him or Her not allow Bee to make the same mistake as I did: to fall for a narcissist and have it ruin her entire life, to fill her with so much regret that she will never be able to move on from it.

No. I do not like thee, Adam Wilson, and whatever your game is.

And it seems that my daughter's stepmother doesn't either, if Bee's vociferous complaints and rages following her last visit to that place that they moved away to are anything to go by.

Which is odd. As I always saw her as an arty type too, just like Wilson.

And interesting, because I thought that she didn't care for my child – that she stole Bee from me only as part of the package that ensured her Ed.

But if she hasn't welcomed Wilson into her home, if she disapproves, as it seems she does, then something has happened that I never thought possible. That there is now something else, apart from my husband, that we have in common. That if there is trouble ahead – as I fear there may be – I may have an unlikely ally.

SEPTEMBER 2020

Rowan

When she thought about it afterwards, Rowan could have sworn that someone – it was a woman's voice – shouted at her to "*Wake up!*" She had thought it must be one of the children at first, Clemency perhaps – the voice was of someone a little older than the others. She then reasoned that it must be Claudia herself. It had to be *someone*, urging her to rise out of her slumber.

But no. The dawn breaking silently through the gap in the curtains of the house in Cambridge illuminated the room sufficiently for Rowan to see that she was completely alone. For an instant, she was sure that she heard breathing, but soon realised it was her own. Her heart pounded.

For as soon as she woke, she was instantly filled with a sensation of dread. Something, somewhere, was terribly wrong. She was sure of it.

When Claudia rose at six, she found Rowan in the kitchen, her gaze directed over the pocket-handkerchief-sized garden of the house – all that remained from the once long and lovingly planted oasis which every year was claimed, piece by piece, by the river.

Claudia coughed as she entered the room and Rowan, holding a cup of tea which sent wisps of steam up into the air, turned to look over her shoulder, forcing a weak smile. In the harsh sunlight of the morning which streamed into the kitchen, Rowan was struck suddenly by how old she looked without a comb run through hair, or a face washed, never mind the absence of her armour: her make-up which she applied carefully several times a day with little deviation from the dramatic 1950s' style that she had always worn. Rowan knew she herself must look just as worn but she was still taken aback for a moment at the sight of the crow's feet around Claudia's penetrating green eyes, at the paleness of her skin.

There was a silence between the women while Claudia switched on the kettle, yawned and stretched and then reached into a cupboard for an old-fashioned tin. "More tea?" she asked Rowan casually.

Rowan shook her head.

"What has you up so early anyway?" Claudia finally enquired. "You were exhausted last night when you got here – I thought you'd have a lie-in this morning?"

Rowan turned from the window and slid onto a chair at the dining table behind her. "Oh, I think it was around five when I woke," she said dismissively.

Claudia's eyes widened. "Five!" she exclaimed. "Hell's Bells – that's the middle of the *night* round here! We don't even get up that early on Christmas morning! What on earth had you up at five?"

Rowan shrugged again. "Oh, nothing," she muttered quietly, thinking hard how to change the subject, but suddenly weighed down with her own negativity and the niggling sensation that she just could not shake the feeling that something, somewhere, in her life, was horribly wrong.

Claudia looked at her with a puzzled expression as she joined her at the table.

"What is it, Ro?" she enquired softly. "Not still that stupid row with Bee about her boyfriend, is it?"

Rowan nodded.

"But I thought you and she . . . I thought things were getting a bit better between you, no? Since she went away to college – absence making the heart grow fonder and all that?"

Rowan snorted and rolled her eyes. "They were," she replied. "Better. Until she met that guy. She's completely jumped in head first with him. And he's sweet-talked *her* into dropping out of her set design course – that she positively badgered Ed to let her do – and applying to another – at Darvill's College, of all places, where Ed went. Except now it's a super-trendy fashion college with a Beckham on the board and a waiting list that's more exclusive than the nightclub at Battersea Power Station – and I know it sounds harsh, but I don't think for a second she has a chance of getting in. I never even knew she designed *clothes* until she flounced home and started talking nineteen to the dozen about it – and about this Adam bloke . . . and I think he's making a fool of her. Worse, I think she's making a fool of *herself* – but she's completely blind to it all. But since she overheard me say all this the last time she came down to the Acre, she's taken up arms against me again – gone back to being how she was when I first met Ed, practically, and we all remember what a glorious time that was."

Claudia grasped Rowan's arm suddenly. "Breathe," she urged. "That's it. Slow down. Calm . . ." She was stunned to see tears form in the corners of Rowan's eyes, to hear her voice waver as she spoke again.

"Maybe I'm taking it all too personally, but he's her *lecturer*, Clauds. Her *teacher* . . ."

She didn't have to say any more. Claudia knew what that meant to Rowan, understood immediately why she was so concerned. Claudia reached out to her friend and enveloped her in a tight hug as Rowan finally broke down and cried the tears she had felt pricking at her eyes since Bee had first told her about Adam.

Of all the things, she had thought. All the coincidences.

"You'll have to make the first move, Rowan," Claudia urged eventually. "Maybe this is the right time to finally tell them both – to tell Ed, at least. Although I think maybe this time Bee deserves to know why you're so het up at her – why you're so worried?"

Claudia withdrew herself from the hug as she saw Rowan's expression fill with alarm.

"I don't mean *all* of it, Rowan," she said quietly. "Just the part that's making you crazy about all of this. Maybe reach out to her by letting her know that you identify with what she's going through – maybe somehow let her know that you'll be there, if she needs you."

Weakly, Rowan had eventually agreed with Claudia. She was right. She had carried one secret too far with her into her marriage, into the family life that she found herself part of.

It was beginning to affect things with Ed, too, she had to admit. After all, why was she here on yet another weekend in Cambridge with Claudia when she should be at the Acre, helping out as the soft furnishings arrived for the first self-catering apartment?

Avoiding him, that's what. Avoiding his worried expression, avoiding his disappointment that even now, when they were both grown adults, she simply couldn't manage to get on with his only child.

And it was that thought more than anything – Ed's disappointment in her – that was the deciding factor in Rowan's decision to pack her bags and leave her friend's house a day early. To tackle something that she probably should have done long before.

To get into her jeep and drive somewhere where she knew the reception would be at best frosty, where the door might well be slammed shut in her face. But something – she knew not what – drew Rowan in the direction she took, not knowing what would greet her on arrival, but just knowing that it was the way she should go.

With a wave goodbye to Claudia who stood on her doorstep, in a hesitant voice Rowan instructed the sat nav to take her to Pilton Gardens, Fulham.

SEPTEMBER 2020

Jenny

Oh sweet Jesus, this cannot be happening to me – cannot be happening to her!

Why has she done this to herself? Why can't I stop her? Why can't I just be there for her? Be a physical force instead of this useless observer? Why can't I even pick up a phone and dial 999?

Why can't I even take her in my arms – why can't I help!

Is she okay? I can't tell? I can't feel her – can't take a pulse – I think she's breathing, but I can't be sure.

I cannot bear this. Every time I say that I think I have reached my limits there is always another one – another challenge, another hellish nightmare thrown at my useless form.

If it were to happen I should surely cease to exist in any form. Wouldn't I? Surely I would have to just stop, to just dissipate, to vanish – surely that's what would happen?

Because I just could not do it. I could not lose her. Could not bear to see her go, to see her last moments – to see her stop breathing, for heaven's sake! To see her cease to be, and with her all of her beauty and potential and future and all of the love that I know she contains inside.

How cruel must God be to put me through this? All the years I have spent watching are forgotten – I would have them ten times over, so long as she hangs in – so long as she stays with me. If it meant that my death was worth something then I would gladly stay like this forever – watching the pain, watching the mistakes, feeling the concern like tiny pinpricks throughout my entire soul.

I will do anything in my power or out of it to change places.

Anything, if she will just wake up.

Anything, so long as I don't lose her.

Anything, so long as I do not have to see my baby die before me.

Wake up, Bee!

Please . . . Wake up!

SEPTEMBER 2020

Bee and Rowan

Rowan knew that something was wrong the minute she parked her jeep outside the house. It had begun to rain heavily on the drive up from Cambridge and the morning – or early afternoon as it was now – was dark. Dark enough for the streetlights to have come on for a time. The lights of 17 Pilton Gardens, too, glowed from each of its windows as Rowan stepped from the jeep and stared up at its façade. All of the lights on, in every room, Rowan noted, a chill running through her at the sight.

A memory of the Saturday morning, only a few weeks ago, at the Acre, when Rowan had found Bee packing cases into a taxi, an expression of pure rage on her face, flashed across Rowan's mind. Bee had driven off in complete silence, with no goodbye for Rowan, Adam sheepish in the passenger seat. She understood only later when Ed explained what Bee had tearfully informed him first thing. That she was leaving because of what she had overheard the previous night of the conversation that Ed and Rowan had in the dusk of the garden.

And now, standing outside the front door of her old home, Rowan was nervous of the reception that she would receive. As she rang the doorbell, the rain pelting against her shoulders and back, it suddenly struck her that she wasn't even sure what she was doing here, what had forced her to come this way at all, instead of heading home? Did she really think that she could solve everything by turning up on a doorstep with a confession? With a cautionary tale from the past? Was her gut right? Was there something really wrong somewhere? And if so, how could she be sure that it was here and not back at Judith's Acre? What if Ed had hurt himself, ambling around the place with that confounded pig and needed help of some sort? And yet here she was, standing on the doorstep of a girl who despised her, who was certain to tell her to leave straight away.

Rowan swallowed hard and rang the doorbell again. Still no answer. Reluctantly, but unwilling to just leave having come all that way, she rooted through her satchel for the door key which she still always carried.

To her surprise, however, it wasn't needed. The door suddenly and unexpectedly flew open before her, pulled with such force from the inside that she stepped backwards in alarm. Her heart sank when she saw her stepdaughter before her. She had known that she would be unwelcome, but she hadn't expected quite such an expression of rage on Bee's face.

"Bee!" she said, startled. "I just wanted to –"

The fury of the response shocked her.

"What the *hell* r'*you* doing here?" Bee screamed in what Rowan could only think of as childish temper.

She stepped back again.

"I told my father that I never, *ever* wanted t'see you again. Do you hear me? *Do you hear me?*" Bee roared at the top of her voice.

Rowan glanced left and right quickly to ensure that there was no one else listening. Bee, of course, picked up on this.

"'*Shamed*, are you? Case I show you up in front of th'neighbours?"

Rowan swung back to face Bee. She studied her intently for a moment, noticing her wild hair, the stains on her top, the crumpled, dishevelled state of her appearance. Her stance, too, wasn't right. Bee had a firm grip with her left hand on the internal handle of the front door, but instead of just holding it, Rowan noted, she leaned on it, using the door to support her full weight, to keep her upright.

Bee suddenly staggered backward, letting go of the door handle, her hands flailing as she tried and failed to keep her balance. Instead, she crashed awkwardly into the hall table and slumped to the ground, her eyes rolling and head lolling.

Rowan used the opportunity to quickly step inside and shut the door behind her, isolating her with her very drunk stepdaughter. She glanced at her watch. It was almost twelve thirty. What the hell was Bee playing at, being this drunk, this early in the day? She had been right to follow her instinct here. Something had to be terribly wrong for Bee – whom Rowan hadn't seen drunk since the police brought her home a few times when she was thirteen or fourteen – to be slumped on the hall floor before lunch.

"Bee," Rowan said softly, reaching down to give her a hand up. "What's the matter? Is something wrong?"

She was rewarded with having her hands smacked away violently and had to stand back to avoid being hit on the face by Bee who flapped her arms wildly.

"Ev'rything's fucking *wrong*," Bee slurred angrily as she managed to push herself into an upright position, standing up before again staggering backwards, into the stair-post this time.

"Where are Sasha and Matilda?" asked Rowan, trying her best to keep calm, to take control.

Bee looked around her, as if she expected to see her cousins standing there. "Gone," she said with a limp wave of her hand when she realised that they weren't.

It was Saturday morning, reasoned Rowan. They could be shopping, or gone to the gym or gone away for the weekend perhaps. They must be gone – even if they had been asleep upstairs, then Bee's screaming couldn't have failed to wake them. She concluded that they were definitely alone.

Rowan looked back at Bee who was having difficulty focusing as she hung onto the bottom post of the stairs for support.

"What's gone wrong, Bee?" Rowan tried again.

Bee appeared not to hear her – or see her for that matter. Instead she lurched violently toward the living-room door and staggered in, weaving from left to right. Rowan hurried after her, arms outstretched, waiting to catch her in case she stumbled again. She noticed the state of the living room as she did – a barely-touched takeaway pizza on the coffee table, the TV tuned to a black-and-white movie but muted – two, no, three, empty wine bottles on the floor along with an upturned glass which had leaked its burgundy-coloured contents onto the wooden floor. A single church candle burned on the hearth. The air stank of alcohol and sweat.

Bee finally halted in her erratic passage across the room by reaching out to the mantelpiece to steady herself. She then made a final lurch to the sofa opposite and threw herself on it heavily, sinking into it at first before pushing herself upright and sitting forward with her elbows resting on her knees.

It became apparent to Rowan that Bee was trying her hardest to glare at her but was finding it difficult to hold her head steady to do so. Rowan watched her in alarm. She had never seen her like this. What should she do, she wondered?

Water, for starters, she decided. If she could just try to sober her up a little bit, then maybe they could talk and maybe she could get to the bottom of what was going on.

"Bee," she said loudly and clearly, "I'm going to get you a glass of water from the kitchen, all right? Can you stay here? Are you okay to do that?"

She expected nothing in return – no response – not a coherent one anyway. She knew that Bee had no intention of making this easy on her.

The last thing that she expected, however, was Bee's reaction to the suggestion: "*No!*" she screamed loudly, suddenly struggling to stand up. "*Can't!* Don' gwin thur . . ." Her eyes were ablaze as she tried to push herself upward.

Rowan frowned. "Why ever not, Bee?" she asked, her heart still racing, the shock of the unexpected response mixed with alarm at whatever Bee's reason was for her not to go to the kitchen.

"Jus' don'. *Warning* you," Bee said, an air of menace to her tone.

"Why *not*, Bee?" Rowan asked, a little firmer this time. On top of her fear and uncertainty, a familiar sensation of exasperation had begun to creep in.

"Jus' don'" Bee replied. "'N'fac' jus geddout. Interfering always

. . ." She pointed an unsteady hand at the living-room door as an indicator of where she wanted Rowan to go.

"I shan't, Bee," Rowan replied. "I want to know firstly what's wrong. Secondly, why you're drunk at lunchtime on a Saturday – you've been up all night, haven't you? – and thirdly I want to know why I shouldn't go into the kitchen."

Rowan was unsure how wise it was to have said everything that she had just said, considering Bee's condition and temperament. Her chest rose and fell rapidly as she waited for her stepdaughter's reaction. It was, as she feared, irrational.

Bee managed to stand, suddenly, and lunged at Rowan.

"*Jus' leave me alone!*" she cried, a desperate, impatient, pleading tone to her voice this time. "I jus' wanna be *'lone*. I'm gonna sort this out and I don't need you to come in here an' start crissicising me for stuff. Dad's money's safe, *okay?*"

She stared Rowan full in the eye and Rowan recoiled a little at the glare that came her way.

"I don't understand what you mean, Bee," she replied hesitantly. "What has Dad's money got to do with it? I only want to help –"

"You *don'!* Thass jus' it – you don' wanna help! You wanna gloat 'cos you were right an' I was wrong and I'm not good enough. Not for *an'thin'!* Not for Adam, or for college . . . *she* didn't even want me. I'mma stupid was' of space – don' you *geddit?* You don' *have* to tell me! I *know!*"

She staggered again, and looked for a moment as if she might topple over. Rowan caught her arm to steady her but was immediately shaken off. Rowan felt as though her knees were about to give way. She took a deep breath to steady herself.

"I don't understand what's happened, Bee," she said calmly. "But look, let's sit down and just talk, eh? I'm not here to gloat, and of course I think you're good enough. Just let me get you a glass of water – that's all I want to go to the kitchen for."

Her gentle tone, the calm urge in her voice only seemed to madden Bee all the more.

"You're *such* a liar," she panted, her voice a low whisper as she peered at Rowan with disgust. "Is it som'thin' my dad goes for in women? Cos she was one too. *Liars!*"

"I don't know what you're talking about, Bee," Rowan responded through gritted teeth. She was growing tired of this. She had never had vast reserves of patience with Bee when sober, and drunk she was trying every last ounce she had. "Who's a liar? What's this got to do with your dad?"

Rowan gasped as Bee reached out to shove her, her face again red with rage and hurt. Rowan saw, up close, that Bee's eyes were red from crying and fresh tears glimmered at their corners. She braced herself for the attack, hopeful that Bee's lack of balance would somehow give her the upper hand, yet nervous at the same time that being drunk and so fearless would imbue the girl with extra strength. She was stunned when nothing came, when Bee suddenly seemed to fold, limp, back onto her seat on the couch, landing awkwardly on its arm and slumping down onto the seats where she lay, her hands covering her face, sobbing.

"*My mother*," Bee said, before falling silent save for the occasional, hysterical sob.

Rowan stared at her for a moment before deciding to take her opportunity. What exactly had Bee been so desperate for her not to see in the kitchen? Fear suddenly coursed through her. What if there was someone else in the house after all? What if they had come to harm? Matilda? Adam?

With a final, worried glance at Bee's crumpled form, Rowan suddenly fled, gripping the doorpost to steady herself as she rounded it out onto the wooden tiles of the hallway and down toward the kitchen, stumbling on the first of the steps down before steadying herself and coming to a halt on the bottom one.

It was clear what Bee had been trying to hide. They were all over the kitchen table. Rowan was stunned and suddenly filled with terror. She turned as abruptly as she had arrived and took the steps in one, throwing herself back along the hallway, back around the door to the living room to the now-still form of her stepdaughter. She rushed to her, kneeling down beside the couch and pulling Bee's reluctant fingers from her face.

"How many have you taken, Bee?" she cried. There was no response. Rowan shook her violently: "How *many*?" She felt some relief as Bee finally responded with a miserable sob and shook her head weakly. Rowan shook her again. "*Bee!* This is important. How many have you taken? I'm going to call an ambulance. Do you even know *what* it is you've taken? *Bee!*"

Bee shook her head harder. "*Nothing,*" she sobbed, finally removing her hands from her face and turning toward Rowan to reveal the snot-covered grimace underneath. She righted herself on the couch, sitting up straight. "I took *nothing,*" she said. "I din't have *time* 'cos you rang the doorbell an' I though' it jus' might be Adam. But it wuz *you* an' I din't want to see you. I just wanted to sort it all out – just finish it. 'Cos you're all liars, you hear me? *Liars* . . ." Bee sank back against the headrest and swiped her face with her hands, causing a stream of mucus and tears to spread all over her cheeks like a child.

"Do I need to ring an ambulance, Bee?" Rowan said, cautiously. "Do we need to go to A & E?" At four hundred pounds per visit, she sincerely hoped not.

Bee gave a long sniff and shook her head again. "Swear," she replied quietly. "I din't do an'thin'. Yet. Jus' some booze. Between not getting the course an' Adam . . . I jus' couldn't sleep, so I had a drink and then some more, but I din't do an'thin' with the pills. I'm jus' so sick of bein' lied to. I thought my *mum* . . . thought she was a good person. But even she wasn't. No one cares 'bout me. I thought she did, but no. Even she wanted to leave me . . ."

"Bee, what are you *on* about?" barked Rowan suddenly. Where was all this nonsense about Jenny coming from? It was looking like she'd need to take her to a hospital after all.

"Th'letter," said Bee, her tone exasperated yet suddenly tired. "Arrived yessaday. Like ev'rythin' else hadn't gone wrong. What's the point? You're all interferin' *liars.*"

Rowan sighed, exasperated. What letter? What was Bee talking about? Who could possibly have written to her to make her react so? To make her rant about her mother – a woman who had been dead for over twenty years, who she had never known? Rowan sank back into a sitting position on the floor, confused. She took a breath but suddenly found that she had to jump to her feet again as Bee suddenly retched and vomited helplessly down her top. All else forgotten for a moment, Rowan ran again toward the kitchen to grab a basin and a tea towel as Bee continued to vomit.

It was as she passed the table, covered in pills, that Rowan saw the letter and the envelope lying there. She reached out to pull it toward her, but stopped as she heard Bee suddenly lurch out of the living room and up the stairs toward the bathroom. Rowan felt too exhausted to move suddenly. Let her clean herself up, she though wearily, the basin and cloth still held in her hand.

Suddenly frozen to the spot with exhaustion, she glanced down at the collection of capsules and pills that were scattered everywhere – at what seemed to be everything from the household medicine cabinet.

Bee had emptied everything from the containers and mixed them together but had left the tubes lying scattered on the table. Rowan picked them up one by one. Paracetamol, she read – you could only buy five at a time by law, however, and there was only one empty tube on the table. Arnica, another said. Milk Thistle, Viagra – how odd – but nothing lethal from what she could see. A wave of relief washed over her. Just the alcohol poisoning to worry about, then, she thought to herself. The sounds of the violent vomiting from upstairs, however, seemed to indicate that Bee's body had thankfully decided to take care of that itself.

Rowan wasn't sure how she managed it but, once Bee had finally ceased to throw up, it only took the guts of half an hour to shower her and dress her in clean pyjamas before finally putting her to bed. She lay there, helpless as a child, her face red and her skin mottled from crying and purging. Rowan could see the tiny red pinpricks of burst blood vessels around her eyes from the strain. Bee allowed herself to be turned on her side and tucked in by her stepmother who placed a basin on the floor beside her bed, along with a stack of fresh towels and some face-wipes that she found. Bee was sound asleep by the time Rowan headed downstairs, the door left ajar so that she could hear if Bee should be sick again.

She would stay, of course. Until Bee woke and then maybe they could talk it through, whatever had upset her so. She gathered that Adam and the course at Darvill's were both gone by the wayside. But had that been enough to prompt Bee to such a response? To contemplate taking the contents of the medicine cabinet? To drink herself into oblivion?

There had to be something more, of course. All this talk of her mother . . . and a letter . . . It was of Ed that Rowan thought as she made her way back to the kitchen table to retrieve the letter she had seen there. She'd have to tell him everything, of course, but not yet. Not until she had a clearer picture of the facts. Not until she had read this mystery correspondence. And definitely not until she had spoken rationally – or tried to at least – with her stepdaughter.

It was with this plan in mind that she swept the collection of pills off the table surface and into the waste bin, clearing a space to finally sit down and at last begin to solve the mystery, and to acknowledge that her gut instinct had been all too correct all along.

* * *

June 29th, 2020

Beehive Lodge
Green Valley Road
Franschhoek 7780
South Africa

My darling Jenny,

There is so much uncertainty inherent in sending this letter that I barely know where to begin: I am uncertain if this will reach you – whether this address is correct in the first instance and also if you actually still live there.

I am uncertain as to whether or not you will even read it. Uncertain as to whether or not you will care to know what I have to say. Uncertain whether or not you have allowed yourself to remember me. If not, then this is who I am. My name is Guillaume Melesi and I once loved you more than life itself. But you didn't love me enough in return to choose to come with me when that was what I wanted more than anything in the world, so I had to let you be.

When I left England alone in December of 1997, without you, I made the conscious decision to let that be an end to my life there. I had plans for how my life would be – how our life would be together once we left – but you didn't come. So I drew a line in the sand: cut all communication – incoming and outgoing – with everyone back at home.

You were all that I wanted, so without you I left myself behind in England – threw my mobile phone in a litter bin at the airport – and have since – as I'm sure you know – never once sought contact or information from my life there. Cast off one skin and grew a fresh one here, in South Africa.

I understood when you didn't come to my flat that day that you made the decision to stay with Ed and little Bee. And I couldn't blame you for that. But it meant that I was a broken man and the only way I could survive was to cut away completely everything that I associated with you and our time together.

I can still picture you very clearly, however. Your auburn hair and those green eyes. You come to me in my dreams still, even after all of these years. Smiling your wide smile, making some pithy remark, or growing teary-eyed over small things and needing the comfort that it made me feel strong to give.

It's funny that for all the years I have spent in Africa – a lifetime – every time I hear the beat of the ngoma drum, that I hear the voice of Miriam Makeba or the Tuareg melodies played on the shepherd's flute and the imzad, it isn't Africa that I think of. It is you. In my dreams, I still feel your skin against mine. I hear your voice speak to me, hear you tell me that you want only me and that you will give up everything to be with me. I see your face look back at me – your lips apart, your cheeks flushed, as I tell you about Africa. About the exotic flowers, the dramatic, sharp mountains, the way the air is warm and sweet. About the gold of the desert and the white sands of the coast. I smell your beautiful clean cotton scent. I wonder how life would have been had you kept your promise and come to me and we had embarked on this adventure together. The adventure that was never to be.

I also loved Ed. He was my wing man, my partner in crime, my brother. Looking back with the clarity of years, it pains me that I could have hurt him so. For a long time I have wanted to say sorry.

I sat down to write to him, to e-mail, a hundred times over the last twenty-three years but every time I tried to say something, I couldn't. At first, it was because of your rejection of me. This love that I have carried for you burned so strong inside me that I simply didn't know what to say. I found myself angry with him, simply because you had chosen him over me. Because he had kept you, trapped in grey London when all the colours of the rainbow were here for your taking in Africa.

After a time, I was no longer angry. I was sorry. Never sorry for having loved you – for still loving you – but for having almost taken you away from him. After a time, it became easier to keep him from my mind and harder to find the courage to reach out to him. It was better that I left you all alone. My silence was for your good.

I waited for you in the flat that afternoon. At the airport, I kept glancing over my shoulder, expecting to see you rush in through the doors, coming in search of me. I really believed that you would. It broke me a little inside that you didn't.

I am a selfish man, Jenny. I have had plenty of years to reflect on that. I have no doubt that it took me a lot longer to come to that conclusion than it probably took the people I left behind.

Vicky, for one. How callous of me to desert her, pregnant. That decision was reprehensible – I see that now, but in my heart and in my head – and you can choose to tell her this if you wish – she and I were completely finished. I think she knew this too. I had no interest at that time in becoming a father and I knew that she knew my interest in her had waned. It didn't cost me a thought to just leave and never to get in touch with her again, despite the fact that she was carrying my child. At the time, my head and my heart were so full of you that there was no room for anyone else.

I look back now and see the chaos that my cowardice must have caused, yet I thought nothing of it at the time. But now the time has come to beg for forgiveness. It is so much to ask but if you ever loved me, Jenny, can I ask you to give this message to Vicky and her child – my child – to Ed, to their family and to your Bee. I am sorry.

I stayed in South Africa. My Christmas with my parents that year was extended to a month, then six months. And then my father got sick so I stayed until he died and then stayed longer to nurse my mother who followed him not long after. I became a hotelier eventually. Married a wonderful Danish woman called Grace and we built our own business here in the Winelands – a guest lodge with a spa and a small winery. Every morning, I rise here at Beehive Lodge and my breath is taken away by the sheer drama of the mountains that surround us. I walk among my vines, greet the guests, eat the finest foods and breathe in the unspoilt pure air. It is not the adventure I once bragged about. I lost the appetite to sleep in a Bedouin tent, or to dive with sharks, to win countless accolades, to change the world, but I am content here with my wife. It is beautiful. I should love you to come to see it some day. Please do.

It's Grace who will have mailed this letter to you. Because if you are reading it, it means that I am gone. I write this to you not knowing what time I have left, fearful of, yet resigned to the fact that it isn't long. I have fought lung cancer as hard as I could for as long as I could – I won't bore you with the details other than to say it is winning, even with everything that science can do nowadays. It seems that we Melesis were never built for the long haul.

With death, of course, come loose ends which must be tied. You and Ed were kind enough to allow me to be Bee's godfather – a job at which you cannot say I excelled! In reparation for the downright shoddy fist I made of the task, I have enclosed a cheque for her. I would like it very much if she were to use it to have an adventure for herself, or to further her education to do something that she loves – or just to live well, as I have done. There is no easy way to say sorry – all that I can say is that I almost changed her life for the worst once by taking her mother away. I would like, in some way, in passing, to try to change it for the better. To do some good for a change.

You will see another cheque attached. It is made out to Vicky, but it is for her child. A bit late for that, I hear you say in your sharp tone, but I wish for the child to have this money nonetheless. If Vicky has not changed, then I doubt she will refuse it because I deserted her. Call it a guilt payment if you will, but in the absence of being a father, money is all that I can offer.

The Lodge will go to Grace and then she will pass it on to whomsoever she chooses – I have specified that in my will. It's just *that I know Vicky will ask . . . (now, in my mind's eye, I see you smile!).*

And so I draw a line under us, Jenny Mycroft. You drew yours a long time ago, I think. On the 23rd of December 1997 when you chose to stay and I chose to go. Much as it still breaks my heart, you did the right thing. I hope that you have been happy, as successful as you would have wished, and that you went on to have a large family and are enjoying a long life still with Ed. You both deserve it.

As I write, Jenny, I can see you. You're sitting in your garden under coloured light-bulbs strung between the trees on a London summer evening, your face lit softly by candlelight. And you are smiling at me. I have made a photo album in my heart to take with me when I go and this is the picture of you that I have placed in it. The image of you that will be with me when I go, along with all of my other treasures.

Perhaps there is one more thing that you can do for me now. Try to picture me. As you knew me. As you saw me the last time you saw me, when maybe you still loved me. As I write, I am looking out over a small lake at the back of our property. Two black swans live there, slicing through the water, making a fleeting shape of a love heart with their bowed heads and long necks as they pass each other before continuing on their individual courses. Over me is blue sky, over you is most likely grey, but remember, it is the same sky all the same.

We have a blessing in South Africa that goes like this:
Walk tall, walk well, walk safe, walk free
And may harm never come to thee.
Walk wise, walk good, walk proud, walk true
And may the sun always smile on you.
Walk prayer, walk hope, walk faith, walk light
And may peace always guide you right.
Walk joy, walk brave, walk love, walk strong
And may life always give you song.

Goodbye from one who loved you fiercely,
Guillaume

SEPTEMBER 2020

Jenny

So that is what became of him.

Guillaume. The name that I have buried underneath everything else in my mind for twenty-three years. The name that I would bat away the second it dared to float up into my line of consciousness. For him I gave up everything – almost gave up my child, for heaven's sake. Almost gave up Ed. Instead, I lost them. All because I thought that I owed it to Guillaume – the name is sharp in my thoughts – to tell him face to face that things were over between us, that I wasn't going to go to South Africa with him, that I wanted to stay with my husband and child and grow my family and be a better person.

Because of him I died. And yes, it was my own fault – there were all those things that I could have done that day that would have meant I would still be alive – whether or not that meant I was still with Ed doesn't matter now.

But I read that letter in the silence of the house over and over again. I should be watching over Bee to make sure that she isn't sick again and does herself harm, the stupid thing. But I can't go up to her room, I can't face her because this letter has changed how she thinks of me forever. This is the ultimate irony: that for all her life she has grown up thinking that I died blameless in an accident while I have blamed only myself for leaving her.

But now, as I see his words, see his turn of phrase, read what he has said – I finally understand that while now she sees my fault in everything, I can see that I was not alone in causing my death and thereby changing the direction of my daughter's life forever.

Sure, I was driving the car when I shouldn't have been. Sure, I was on my way to see him. Sure, I was stupid and bored and gave in to selfish desires, looking for something external to reward me when I had it all on the inside in the first place. Sure it's all textbook cliché stuff. But it's true.

But I was not alone in my selfishness. Guillaume was selfish too. And how. Look at his words! His admission that he loved me – he never loved me! How could someone who was selfish enough to make a move on the wife of a man he called his 'brother' be capable of loving anyone but himself? How could he even begin to comprehend the sacrifice of love when he has spent his life in self-imposed exile, convincing himself that he left behind the greatest love of his life when, in fact, he sees that love every time he sees his own reflection?

'I am selfish,' he admits. Calling him selfish is like . . . like . . . calling the end of the world a minor interference with plans! Why have I never seen this before? Why have I needed the filter of such a long time to give me such clarity, such perspective? Selfish! A man who flitted in and out of life in search of satisfaction only for his own needs. A man who deserted his own child willingly – as he thought – just because he had grown tired of its mother. A man who could slice his life off with such ease and start again, thinking that he was reinventing himself when he was not. When he's just keeping calm and carrying on, as they say, exactly as he was before, with only himself at the centre of his universe.

And how could there have always been a piece of me, since I died, that felt guilty for not going with him? Even though my own stupidity over him cost me my life and ruined my family's lives, there has always been a part of me – and I can see it now as plain as day – that has felt I owed him something. What? An apology? A piece of me? The regret and worry that I've carried around with me like such a heavy burden in my soul for all this time? Seeing all of this now – seeing Guillaume in this light, seeing how I felt about him – stupidly, but temporarily, besotted – is like suddenly finding out that my overstuffed suitcase was too heavy because there was an anchor in it, hidden from my sight. And by throwing that anchor out I can finally see the truth.

I didn't love him.

I didn't even really love having an affair with him. I just convinced myself that it made me come alive. I changed myself – how I looked, how I acted, how I felt about my husband – when it suited me. Because I was bored with myself, because I hadn't figured out that I deserved what I had all along.

He didn't love me. He loved the chase, the clandestine nature of what we were doing. He loved that I was besotted with him. He loved to see himself reflected in my adoration.

Stupid, stupid woman. And stupid, selfish, self-centred, vain man. A man who deserted everyone who cared about him, who shirked his responsibilities and has since convinced himself that everyone was better off without him.

Well, they were, I suppose. But the damage was done by then. I paid too high a price for my stupidity, but at least I know who I am and what I should have had. Guillaume will never know – that much is clear from those words, from what he thinks is a sincere love letter to me but is instead just a love letter to himself on his deathbed. I hope it came peacefully for him.

But now, there is more damage to be cleared up. Now Bee knows that I wasn't the faithful, virtuous mother that she had built me in her mind to be.

And maybe that, too, is a good thing. For starters it is the truth. And now maybe she can carry on with her life free from the idea that I was some sort of saintly figure. Maybe now she can carry on and live in the present, instead of always leaving a bit of her heart in an unknown past.

Maybe that selfish man has done us a favour and set us both free from something. Set my daughter free from the burden of an untrue history. Set me free from carrying such heavy guilt around with me. Yes, it was my fault. But now I know why. I understand what I did and why I did it and that it meant little. It makes me know that I have punished myself for long enough – and yes, it's true that my death and the ripples it set in motion were disproportionate to my crime but that somehow, I can finally stop punishing myself for it.

Knowing that deep down what happened with Guillaume meant so little makes my heart purer again. Fills me with the knowledge that my love for Ed and for Bee was absolute and that he was never a real challenge to that, despite the niggling doubt I have carried with me all this time.

Now that the truth is known, that Bee is set free from me and me from the shackles of my guilt over Guillaume, I just hope that some day she will realise that my love for her would always endure. And that I am truly sorry.

But with all of this, I feel that finally I have served my time. No more of this punishment.

SEPTEMBER 2020

Bee and Rowan

It was almost half past eight the following morning when Rowan heard footsteps descend the stairs and Bee enter the kitchen behind her. She stood at the window, mirroring the position that she had stood in only the previous morning in Cambridge. At the sounds of shuffling footsteps she turned and saw her stepdaughter: pale, dishevelled, her hair matted together where it hadn't been properly dried, despite Rowan's best attempts before she got her to bed the previous day.

Bee moved slowly from the hallway door down onto the stone tiles of the kitchen. Her gait was that of someone who had been physically injured. She was stooped a little, as if she had been punched in the stomach, and she held herself just below the ribs. Rowan knew that the violent vomiting she had sustained yesterday would leave her in discomfort for a couple of days yet.

Rowan cleared her throat nervously, unsure what would happen next. Bee remained silent, one hand leaning on the back of a kitchen chair to support her, staring at the floor, her hair hiding her face. The silence in the kitchen was electric.

It was Bee who broke it. But gently. "You up long?" she said in a low, rasping voice. She looked up as she spoke and Rowan saw her swallow and wince. She turned quickly and filled a glass with water before handing it to her. Bee accepted with what Rowan thought might be a look of gratitude. She couldn't be sure.

"Since about seven," she answered. "I didn't sleep very well on the divan in the study. Forgot how hard that thing was after all these years." She laughed nervously, allowing the laugh to die on her lips as she watched Bee pull out the chair she leaned on and gently lower herself down on to it.

Bee looked up at Rowan's silhouette, her eyes narrowing to slits against the glare of sunlight from the kitchen window. "Why didn't you sleep in your old bed?" she asked. "Sasha's gone away to a wedding fayre – with a 'y'. . ."

Rowan smiled. Typical Bee.

"And Matilda's at Vicky's. She'll be back later, though."

Rowan shook her head. "I wasn't sure if they were coming back or not. And besides, I didn't want to sleep in someone else's bed."

"Not like my mother, then," said Bee suddenly, her voice gaining strength, her tone bitter.

Rowan's stomach sank. Good God but she wasn't ready to get into this. She sighed nervously and then took a deep breath, reaching out to switch on the kettle as she did.

She paused a moment to compose herself.

"I read the letter, Bee," she admitted softly, waiting for the accusation of invasion of privacy. None came.

Bee shrugged and examined some chipped nail polish on her left hand.

"I tidied a little . . . it was on the table and I . . . I knew it might have upset you . . ."

Bee glared at her stepmother. "I don't care that you read it," she said flatly. "God knows, it probably meant more to you than it did to me. I mean, who *is* that man anyway?"

Rowan focused her attention on a jar near her on the countertop. She pulled it towards her, extracted two teabags and placed them in two mugs that she took from the draining board just behind her. It was as far as she got, before sighing again and leaning back against the kitchen sink, folding her arms.

"I don't know much about him either, for what that's worth," she began. "Your dad, rather pointedly, never talks about him. I understand that he was his best friend for years. Then Guillaume had a fling with Vicky and did a bunk when she got pregnant. It turned out, of course, that Matilda wasn't his but he was long gone by then – so he still thinks, or thought rather, that there was a child of his running around London. Your dad's theory on his disappearance was that Guillaume did a bunk because he wasn't a particularly paternal type and valued his freedom too much."

"But how did they know for sure that Matilda wasn't his?" asked Bee. "Did they do a DNA test or something? Surely he had to be around for that one?"

"Matilda's white," Rowan shrugged. "Guillaume wasn't."

Bee nodded faintly and formed her lips into a pout as she digested the information. "Nice guy," she observed, drily. "Does a runner on his pregnant girlfriend, turns his back on his best friend, and then writes love letters to said friend's wife on his deathbed. Does he really not know that Mum's dead?"

It was Rowan's turn to shrug. "It appears not," she said, nodding toward the letter which had been returned to its envelope. She had left it out on the table, unsure exactly what Bee intended to do with it.

There was silence for a moment.

Rowan looked awkwardly at the ground, before remembering suddenly that she had been about to make tea. She busied herself with the task, glad of something to occupy her hands. She had just poured water into the two cups when she heard a loud sniff and turned again to look at Bee who was holding her head in her hands, crying at the kitchen table. Her shoulders heaved silently and a whine escaped, before she sniffed and then began to cry properly. Huge sobs escaped her as Rowan watched from across the room, unsure what to do.

In the long run, she did the only thing that she could think of. Something, oddly, that she had never done before, that she had always left to Ed because she didn't feel she had the *right*. She crossed to the kitchen table and placed her arms around the heaving figure of her stepdaughter and hugged her. It surprised her that Bee didn't immediately pull away. Surprised her even more when Bee leaned into her, pressed her head against Rowan's chest and allowed herself to be enveloped completely while she cried herself out. Rowan rocked her softly from side to side, making the comforting shushing sound that one might make to soothe a child. It felt strange, yet at the same time completely natural.

After a time, Bee stopped crying and pulled away, to rummage in her dressing-gown pocket for a tissue. She blew her nose loudly and Rowan took the chance to pull the chair opposite out from the table and sit down, leaning across, her face sympathetic.

"What's happened with Adam, Bee?" she asked softly, knowing that she took a chance by asking but if they were to sort out the events of yesterday then she felt sure that she had to start from the beginning.

Bee gave a little groan and rubbed her eyes hard with the base of her palms before joining her hands as if in prayer and resting them on the table before her, thinking hard.

"I know that you think I've been stupid," she said quietly. "I thought you were just being a bitch. That my . . . situation, with changing college courses and that, was interfering with your plans."

Rowan frowned, puzzled, but kept silent.

Bee looked down at the table and Rowan heard her voice tremble as the tears began afresh. "It's all fallen apart, Rowan. I didn't get into Darvill's. In fact I was so off the mark, *so* not suited that I'm sure they were laughing at me at the interview." She paused to compose herself. "It was awful. So humiliating. They were so mean to me. I couldn't wait to get out of there. At least I have Adam, I thought. At least *he's* not gone – not all the good bits of my life are gone. But it seems that he's more like that Guillaume man than I thought. Because he's done a bunk. Well, he's dumped me."

"But *why?*" urged Rowan. "Because you didn't get into Darvill's? That's ridiculous."

Bee sniffed and took a deep breath before looking toward the window. "That's part of it," she replied, her eyes wet. "You see it would have looked good for him professionally if he'd placed a student on that bloody course. It would have boosted his reputation to spot a talent big enough to get into Darvill's. But that talent clearly wasn't me, even though he swore to me that I was good enough. And because I was so gloriously awful, in fact, well, it's reflected rather badly on him, as it turns out. And needless to say, that's my fault. Along with . . . *everything else*."

"Oh Bee, you poor thing," said Rowan, her lip curling in disgust at the shallowness of the man. She'd felt in her gut all along that there was something about him and she was right. Something in Bee's expression, however, put her on high alert. She felt alarmed suddenly. What *did* 'everything else' mean? Wasn't it enough that he had used Bee as a pawn to service his own professional vanity? Had strung her along and then blamed her when his plans hadn't come together?

"What do you mean 'everything else', though? What other stuff has he done? Did he hurt you?"

Her heart stopped when she saw Bee's tear-streaked face look back at her with an expression of pure sorrow.

"Bee . . ."

"Turns out that the situation is rather similar to the one which that Guillaume man found himself in," she whispered. "Except in Adam's case, there won't be any doubt over skin colouring, or DNA or anything . . ." Her voice trailed off as she was overwhelmed with more tears, silent this time.

It took a moment for the information to sink in but as it did Rowan's eyes widened. "How far gone, Bee?" she asked softly, reaching a hand out across the table for her stepdaughter to take.

Bee kept her fingers firmly laced together.

"About six weeks, I think," she whispered. "I thought he'd be *happy* – I didn't think that it would matter because it was his and I thought we were going to be together, that he was going to stay with me."

Rowan stared at her, her lips set in a firm line. She had to take a deep breath to control herself, to keep her temper way down inside her. That bastard, she thought. That shallow, selfish, irresponsible bastard. She forced the rage back down inside her, forced herself to change tack.

"We need to get you to a doctor," she managed. "After yesterday. All that alcohol. We have to get a scan done and make sure that everything's as it should be. Did you take any of those pills, Bee? Answer me properly this time."

Bee's face filled with sudden horror and she clamped a hand over her mouth as she gasped. "The pills," she mumbled. "I completely forgot . . . oh God, Rowan, I was a mess – I'm so sorry!"

"But did you take any?" urged Rowan, a trace of temper escaping.

Bee shook her head vigorously. "God no," she said. "I had a ton of booze and then completely passed out on the couch for a while and then just carried on when I woke up. But none of the pills. Anyway, most of them were harmless. Vitamins and stuff, weren't they?"

Rowan's body slumped against the back of the chair with relief. "Good," she said. "That's one thing at least. Thank God you're the worst student house in London and didn't have anything more sinister in stock than paracetamol."

Bee smiled faintly. "And *Viagra*. Wasn't there Viagra or did I hallucinate that?"

Rowan smiled back: "There was, actually. Why the hell was there Viagra in your medicine cupboard?"

"Mike, I reckon," replied Bee. "I think he's been having it away with the lady in Number Eleven the last few weeks. That's pretty disgusting now I think of it."

Both Rowan and Bee suddenly dissolved into unexpected laughter. It felt good, even if there was a touch of the hysterical to it.

"*Mike!*" repeated Rowan in disbelief through the mirth. "Of all people. My God, if Betty finds out! Everyone's got their secrets, haven't they?"

The smile faded suddenly from Bee's lips. "Like my mother," she said suddenly, the previous tone of bitterness creeping back into her voice. "My sainted dead mother. That I thought the world of. My lovely, dedicated mum who gave up everything to look after me. Who broke my dad's heart when she died. She had a pretty big secret, Rowan, wouldn't you agree?"

Rowan sat upright.

A growing tone of anger was building in Bee's voice and her eyes flashed. "For years Dad's told me how I was her heart and soul, how I was what mattered to her most in the whole wide world. And now – that letter – telling me the opposite in black and white. That she was not only cheating on my dad but that she was going to leave me. To run off to South Africa with that man . . . her sister-in-law's boyfriend . . . her husband's best friend . . . my *godfather*? That's some secret."

Bee was panting slightly as the passion and hurt rose within her. Rowan tried to diffuse it: "But she didn't go, Bee. All the way through the letter – he's regretful, says that she did the right thing by staying . . ."

"The date, Rowan." Bee cut her short, her eyes cold as she fixed her in a steady glare. "He mentions the date in the letter that she was supposed to go. That she was supposed to meet him."

Rowan was blank. She stared back at Bee, confused.

"December 23rd, 1997," stated Bee.

It still meant nothing to Rowan.

"The day she died," Bee finished. "The day of the car crash – that's where she was going. To meet him. To run away with her lover and leave me and Dad in the lurch. The only reason she didn't go with him was because she was killed on the way."

Rowan paled. She shook her head in disbelief. "She could have been going anywhere, Bee – I mean if she'd been running away then surely they'd have found a case in her car? Plane tickets maybe? Some evidence of where she was headed?"

"The car went up in flames," said Bee, exasperated. "Dad told me. A passer-by managed to pull her body out before it all went on fire. There was barely anything left. So no. It's not like we'd have found evidence that she was running away."

Rowan was silent for a moment. She knew none of this – Ed always preferred to mark the anniversary privately despite her insistence that he didn't have to. The date of Jenny's death wasn't something that she could have rolled off the top of her head. These were details of something that had happened well before her time, something that she did her best not to think about.

"Bee, come on," she pleaded again. "She could have been going *anywhere*. To the shops for some last-minute stuff – it was Christmas, after all."

"Or just as easily to run away with her boyfriend. Who never bothered checking out why she didn't come. Who was *so* concerned for her that he went anyway and lived blissfully on the other side of the world for twenty-three years without knowing that she was dead, while her husband – while my father *broke* under the strain of it all. What am I supposed to tell him, Rowan? That after all these years the woman he loved was a liar and a cheat? With his best friend? What was that man thinking writing that letter? Selfishly dragging it all up to cleanse his soul or whatever before he shuffled off? What am I supposed to do with that information, Rowan? I mean, that letter was addressed to Jenny Mycroft – I was going to bring it down to Dad for him to open, but curiosity got the better of me after, oh, about the third glass of wine. What would have happened then? If Dad had read that letter and found out for himself about this . . . deceit? These horrible, horrible *lies*!"

There was silence between them for a few moments as Rowan tried to think of something to say but couldn't.

It was Bee who spoke first.

"Anyway," she said flatly, "in case you think that I'm going to sponge any more money off my dad to bring up Adam Wilson's kid, then you can forget about it. I won't interfere with your plans any more than I have to."

Rowan frowned. "What do you mean, Bee?" she asked.

Bee rolled her eyes. "I'm going to get rid of it. Have an abortion. Today, in fact. Although with any luck I mightn't have to after yesterday."

"*Don't!*"

Bee jumped at the ferocity of Rowan's tone. She stared at her for a moment, part of her wondering had she actually just heard her stepmother bark at her like that? Was Rowan actually capable of speaking in that tone of voice or was it her subconscious instead?

Rowan's face, however, was proof enough that it was she who had spoken. She was suddenly pale, her face as white as Bee's. Her chest rose and fell rapidly, although her breathing was silent. Bee flinched again as Rowan stood abruptly and went to stand at the window, her back to the table where they had been sitting. Bee couldn't have been positive – it was difficult to see against the glare of the morning sunshine that flooded in through the window – but she thought that her stepmother was trembling.

Rowan's voice came more quietly now. "Please, Bee . . ." she managed before her voice trailed off.

Anger suddenly flooded back through Bee. "I'm so sorry, Rowan, if this offends your pro-life sensibilities –," she began.

"That's not it."

"But seriously, what do you expect me to do? Have a *baby*? On my *own*? Because it's not like Adam's going to have a change of heart any time soon and come skipping home to me to change nappies. Are you out of your mind, Rowan? All these years I've studied – surely you of all people want me to finally start making my own money so you can get me off your back? And I've got a little bit of planning to do on that front seeing as how I was made to chuck in the course I was doing in order to free myself up to do something that I got – that I got *duped* into doing. I didn't make any of this bloody mess but I'm damn sure not going to get out of it if I'm saddled with a *kid*."

Rowan's voice came in a low growl. "Bee, are you *ever* going to grow up?"

Bee was stunned into silence again. Her headache and nausea – she blamed the hangover but she had a sneaking suspicion that morning sickness had begun to set in also – were forgotten as she stared at the silhouette of the older woman as she turned to face her.

"I'm perfectly grown up, thank you very much," she retorted bitterly.

It was an attitude that Rowan was familiar with from so many years before. "You're grown up, are you?" she replied, still in the same low, quiet tone. "Grown up because you don't live with me and your dad any more? Grown up because you're in college and you can just about manage to get yourself in on time in the morning? Grown up because you had a boyfriend? Because you can drive a car? Because you're twenty-five years old? Is that why you think you're so *grown up*, Bee?"

Rowan paused for a response which didn't come.

"How about you try the real stuff though? What about – oh, I don't know – taking *responsibility* for your actions for a change? Is it only Adam's fault that you chucked in your course and believed that you'd get into Darvill's? Is it only his fault that you got pregnant? Only up to you to keep it if it's convenient for you? Does the fact he doesn't want to be involved somehow absolve you from everything, conveniently enough? Don't you have *anything* to do with all of this?"

Bee stared at her stepmother, open-mouthed with outrage.

"How *dare* you?" she spat. "How . . . *dare* you! None of this is your business, you interfering old cow! I'm sick of you sticking your nose into my life when you're *nothing* to me, do you hear? *Nothing!* Except a control-freak gold-digger who's had her claws in my dad from day one. Who wasn't happy until she got everything to go her own way – until she *imprisoned* him in the countryside to keep a good hold on him. Who took him away from his family and friends so that she had the upper hand at all times –"

"Who took you away from those scumbags that you hung about with, more like," retorted Rowan. "You've always resented me, Bee. But you cannot for a second say that I am nothing to you. All your life I've looked out for you as best I could, no matter how difficult you've made it for me, but if you think that you'd be where you are today without the decision that your father and I made to take you out of London then you're very, very wrong."

"Where I am today?" squeaked Bee, her eyes wide with anger and disbelief. "What, like out of a college place with no idea what to do next with my life because someone lied to me? Sharing a house with my cousins and their overbearing family? *Pregnant* and alone?"

"I mean *alive*," snapped Rowan in return. "With no prison record, or addiction problems. The crowds you were running around with – they had knives and drugs and they knew what to do with them and a spoiled little brat like you wouldn't have lasted two minutes if things got serious. We took you out of London for your own good – your father was worried sick about you. At least he's had some peace since we moved to Somerset."

"So much peace that he's half dead with boredom," countered Bee.

Rowan raised her palms to heaven in exasperation. What planet did Bee actually live on?

"Wandering around the farm all day with that bloody pig for company. Hardly able to sustain a conversation."

"Not with you anyway on account of how it's impossible to get a word in edgeways about anything that *isn't* you, or Adam the last time you came to stay. Your father's *happy*, Bee. He's content – just ask him. Why wouldn't he be? He's got a great show on TV, he loves the farm and he bloody loves you too but you wouldn't know that because you never bother to talk to him, just *at* him. And listening – well, we can see now that that's an alien concept to you. How many ways does a parent have to tell a child to be careful, to look after herself?"

"I'm hardly a child, Rowan."

Rowan shook her head. "Well, then why couldn't you manage simple contraception then? Why are you now going to wreck your life having an abortion?"

Silence fell for a moment as Bee sneered at her stepmother. "Like having a baby wouldn't wreck my life?"

"It might bloody teach you to grow up a bit," Rowan jabbed back.

Bee set her lips in a thin line before speaking again. "Look, Rowan, I think you're crossing a line here. What I choose to do with my body is absolutely none of your business. I *cannot* have this baby, do you hear me? I don't want it and you can't tell me what to do. I don't fall under your spell like my dad does. You can't control me any more the way that you've controlled where we've lived, and what jobs my dad did and everything that we ate and wore and where I went to school. It's nothing to do with you, Rowan. You're not my mum!"

Rowan stared at Bee, her mouth twisting for a moment into an incredulous smile that fell away as quickly as it had formed. She shook her head again in disbelief.

"Bee, I have no *clue* where you get your ideas, do you know that? I'm not a control freak, nor do I have any sort of master plan like you seem to think. I'm no gold-digger – in fact, if you want proof, in the early days of *Lila and Vulpo* it was *me* who supported us, who paid all the bills. Not that it's your business, but I have *never* asked your father for a red cent in all the time we've been together and I have no plans to start doing that now – and I'm damn sure I'm not eating into anything that you have a right to. Don't you even *know* your dad? I couldn't manipulate him if I tried – and I haven't, before you accuse me of that. But do you know something? You're right. I'm *not* your mum. Very far from it, in fact. For example, I've been faithful to your father for twenty years. I adore him and he adores me. And I have always, *always* done my best by you, even when you made it nigh on impossible. And something else, Bee – I'm here. Here for you in this big mess. And I'm not planning on going anywhere."

"Holding back my hair while I throw up doesn't make you a parent," spat Bee, her face red with fury. "How dare you get all sanctimonious and superior about my mother when you know nothing about her!"

"You're the one who was calling her a liar not ten minutes ago! It strikes me that you don't know very much about your mum either, except some idea of a saint that you've formed in your head."

Bee responded by throwing her hands in the air and suddenly standing, making as if to walk away but at the last second changing her mind and turning back to Rowan.

"This conversation ends here, Rowan," she said flatly. "I don't know why you're here in the first place and I don't care. All I know is that I don't need you, do you hear me? I don't need you interfering with my life and my decisions. I don't need you to preach at me to keep this baby because it's not something that I'm going to consider. And I don't want you ever to mention my mother to me again. Is that clear?"

Rowan stared back at her for a moment. Tried to think of a response. Tried to think what she could say to change Bee's mind. Thoughts flooded through her mind, too fast to rein in and make coherent sense of. Her body tingled as she longed to grab the younger woman and shake the nonsense she was spouting out of her. Instead, she remained silent. Her body deflated suddenly. What was the point?

"Is that *clear*?" snapped Bee again.

"*Yes*," replied Rowan sharply. "Have it your way, Bee. Think your crazy thoughts. Live your stupid, irresponsible life. You don't need help after all, do you?" She shook her head again and on impulse stood, reached out and grabbed her keys which lay on the kitchen countertop, beside Guillaume's letter. "Good luck with it all then, Bee. And go ahead and have your abortion. You're right – it's none of my business. But for what it's worth, I have a bloody strong feeling that it's going to create more problems for you than it solves."

She brushed sharply past Bee as she made her way out of the room.

Bee stepped aside and watched her go, her face still sullen and resentful, her expression hard. It softened a little as she heard the front door slam behind her stepmother and she was left again entirely alone.

SEPTEMBER 2020

Jenny

She's right.

That bloody woman is absolutely right.

I *watch as my daughter falls apart* yet that woman I have despised for so long tries to put her back together.

I *watch as my daughter spouts nonsense*, blames the world and lives in denial when she is old enough to start to think for herself, to take responsibility, and that woman tries her best to set her straight.

I *watch as my baby cries* because she is going to have a baby herself.

And I don't know what to say or do.

But that woman does.

She doesn't know that she is doing everything right but she is taking over my job. Acting like a real mother.

And I realise that even if I were there to do that job myself, I am not entirely sure if I would know what to do.

More than anything, I realise that Bee is moving away from me. That not only is her mental image of me shattered, but that I am of no use to her now in the slightest.

She needs a real mother. Someone of flesh and bone and wisdom and it seems that this woman is all of those things.

I am losing my daughter to someone else.

But of that I am suddenly and strangely glad. Because she needs to be nurtured, to be protected – all of those things that I once thought were my responsibility.

It turns out that they're not any more. The time has come for someone else to be a mother to my child.

SEPTEMBER 2020

Bee and Rowan

Twice Bee thought seriously of asking the cab driver to stop and let her out so that she could be sick. Twice she managed to keep it under control. It was the timing that was crucial, she knew. She had to be at the Mayberry by two, a little earlier even. Her appointment wasn't until three, but that wasn't the time that she had given Adam.

If she just had him for an hour to herself, she knew that she could talk him round. It had come as a shock to him, she knew that. And on top of her letting him down so badly at the Darvill's interview. But they'd had a few days apart to cool down and she knew that deep down he still loved her. All those times they'd spent together – they couldn't stand for nothing, could they? All the times they'd talked about the future, being together – she consoled herself with memories like this. They made her feel safe. Made her sure that he'd come back to her and they'd carry on being as happy as they had been. Made her sure that he'd turn up today.

As the cab pulled up, she looked toward the dated façade of the building. She had been born here, she knew. It had been a state-of-the-art maternity clinic then, her dad had told her once as they passed it. It was shabby now. And more multifunctional, of course. The entrance that she sought wasn't at the front but in a more discreet location around the side. In an effort to keep the heavily pregnant mothers separate from the others. From people like her, who came to end life rather than start it.

Bee gagged again at the thought and she immediately squeezed her eyes shut to block it. She couldn't for a second think about the abortion. She wasn't going to have to go through with it anyway, she was sure of that. Adam would turn up. It was going to be fine. The next time she came here it would be through the front door, she knew it.

She managed to collect her thoughts and accepted her change from the taxi driver in silence before stepping down from the cab onto the pavement, glancing around her to see if perhaps he was there, waiting already.

He would approach her straight away – arms outstretched, begging her not to go through with it and they'd collapse, happy, into each other's arms, aware of all that they might have lost, before turning their thoughts to the bright future they were going to have together.

Her cousins would have to move out of Pilton Gardens, of course. And then it would be perfect. Then they would plan the nursery and redecorate – put the baby in her old room. Just like her mum and dad had. Bee blocked that thought from her mind as soon as it arrived, too. She couldn't think any more about her mother now. That was another day's work.

With a sigh, Bee stuffed her hands in her pockets and sat on the edge of one of the raised flower beds to wait – her dad had said that they were fountains once, but nowhere in England had fountains these days unless under very special dispensation from the government. Even the king had had to apply, just like everyone else. Odd really, when flooding was so severe, that they couldn't somehow just fathom a way to channel it into fountains, to make something beautiful out of disaster. Like she was going to do. She knew it.

She tried to keep an eye on everyone who passed at first, turning this way and that to catch better sight of a familiar navy-blue blazer or the tip of a blond head. She grew tired of this after a while, however. Decided in herself that no good would come of looking too eager when Adam did, eventually, get there. Anything could have delayed him, she thought, glancing at her watch which read two fifteen. She had no doubt in her mind that he was currently on his way, making a dash across the city to get to her before it was too late. And then all of this anxiety would stop. This awful feeling of being unsure. She knew it was going to be fine, of course. She just needed to hear him say it.

When she saw the glint of sunlight reflect off the black cab as it pulled up, she thought that she might actually faint with the wave of relief that flooded over her. *He's here*, she thought, her heart pounding so quickly that she feared it might seize up. Finally. *He's here*. She watched the door open slowly, gripping the insides of her jacket pockets to still her trembling fingers, positive to her core that it was a matter of moments only before she would see his face, and then everything would be fine.

But it wasn't fine. It was far from fine, in fact. Yes, the face that emerged from the cab and looked wide-eyed around the piazza outside the clinic was a familiar one. But it wasn't Adam's. It was, in fact, the last face that she wanted to see. Hadn't she told her stepmother as much only a couple of hours before?

Bee contemplated hiding. She glanced around her hurriedly to see if there was a bush or a tree perhaps, or something she could position herself behind until Rowan went away. What the *hell* was she doing here? How had she found out? Or was this some horrendous coincidence? Bee's heart pounded faster as she observed that there was nowhere to hide. She glanced at the door of the clinic through which she would have to enter in a little over a half an hour and a wave of dread hit her. She brushed it aside, contemplated making a run for it in through the door before realising that it was too late. Rowan had seen her and was approaching fast, half walking, half running, her face filled with unwanted sympathy.

Bee took a deep breath, tried to quell the growing sense of panic that was mixing with the anxiety and terror that she already felt.

"Go away, Rowan," she warned, when the older woman was still a good few yards away. It didn't stop her approach.

"Bee . . ." Rowan began, coming to a halt before her, slightly out of breath.

"Rowan, seriously – this is none of your business and I do not want to see you."

"Bee, please, let me talk to you for five minutes."

"*No.*" Bee glanced around her frantically. Adam would be here any minute and she couldn't risk him seeing her horrendous stepmother and then disappearing again before she'd had a chance to talk to him. What was Rowan playing at? She could *ruin* everything.

"How did you know I was even here?"

"I guessed, Bee . . . geography and that . . ." She glanced up at the building with trepidation. "It's closest to home. I've been here before."

Bee wasn't listening. "Rowan, get out of here, okay? I really don't need to be seen with you."

Rowan was taken aback. She followed her stepdaughter's frantic, frightened stare around the piazza for a moment before realising that she was looking for someone.

"Is someone coming to be with you, Bee?" she asked softly. "Are you expecting someone? A friend? One of the girls?" She paused. "Is it *Adam*?"

Bee sighed with frustration. "What does it matter to you, Rowan? Now just leave me alone – I don't want you interfering in this too."

"I came to say I'm sorry, Bee," Rowan said suddenly.

It was the last thing that Bee had expected to hear. She stopped suddenly in her frenetic search of the square for Adam and focused on Rowan who took advantage of the unexpected attention.

"I'm *sorry*," she repeated. "About this morning – I didn't want to fight with you, and you're right – this is absolutely none of my business and it's completely within your rights to do this – to have a – a termination. It's just your Dad, Bee. It's not my place to tell him about this – and I don't know if you plan to – but I've been thinking and if he finds out, and if he thought for a moment that I had just left you alone to do this then he'd never forgive me – can you understand that, at least?"

Bee remained silent, her lips pursing together in that sullen expression that Rowan knew so well.

"*Have* you got someone coming? To be with you?" Rowan asked.

Bee cast her eyes again around the square, a look of despair growing on her face as she saw still no sign of Adam. The despair turned to panic, however, as she suddenly spotted a small group of people appear around the side of the Mayberry building, walking toward where she and Rowan stood. "*Shit*," she muttered.

Rowan swung around to look in their direction: "What is it?" she asked.

"Protesters," replied Bee, her whole body tensing as she took in the megaphone and the large portfolio which one tall young man, wearing a thick cross around his neck, carried. She knew that they'd have the posters in that. And she couldn't see them. Couldn't see those pictures – couldn't think about what she was going to do. Where the *hell* was Adam? Why was she still alone? Was she actually going to have to go through with it? What if those protestors sniffed her out – which they were sure to do? They'd target her, condemning her to all of London through their megaphones. They were notorious – they'd photograph her for their infamous *Name and Shame* website which the government still couldn't manage to shut down, despite years of legal cases. Bee was filled with even more panic than before and she made to run, although she wasn't sure where.

Rowan sensed her panic and grabbed her suddenly by both arms. "Calm down, Bee," she said quietly.

"But they'll target me!"

"They won't." Rowan pulled Bee closer to her and whispered into her ear. "If you don't panic, if you don't show fear, then they won't. They're like rabid dogs. Look!" She glanced upwards as a familiar sound became audible and a police drone appeared around the same side of the building that the protestors had come.

"There's one of those infernal drones. The law only allows them to gather for fifteen minutes in total. Any longer than that and the police will be here – the drone will alert them. Here . . . let's just go inside while they're distracted, setting themselves up. We can hide out in there – have a cup of coffee or something."

Rowan didn't wait for Bee to respond. Instead she just took her firmly by the arm and half-guided, half-pulled her up the steps to the unmarked revolving door which led into the terminations clinic. There was a muffled "Oi you!" as they ducked in. They had been spotted. Too late, thankfully. They were inside.

The nausea hit Bee in a fresh wave as she blinked, her eyes assaulted by the perfectly ordinary scene before her juxtaposed with the thought of what she was actually here for. She was going to have an abortion. To kill her baby. Bee's knees buckled.

If Rowan noticed, she didn't say. She just kept a firm grip on Bee's elbow as they looked around, spotting an open-plan café area directly to the left of the front door. Without a glance at the receptionist behind the plain wooden desk directly in front of them, she steered Bee toward a table where Bee sank into a sitting position, her eyes wide and glazed with fear. Still, Rowan bustled about her, chatting in a low tone all the while.

"Bloody pro-lifers," she hissed, removing her jacket and the shaggy scarf she wore and draping it on the seat behind her. "Like it isn't hard enough to come through that door without being driven in by their nonsense. Would you like a cup of coffee, Bee?" She raised her voice for the last sentence, unsure if her stepdaughter could even see her, never mind hear her. Her heart felt a pang of sympathy for the pale young woman across from her, transfixed with fear with the realisation that she was actually inside those doors. Rowan wanted to reach out and hug her again, but she didn't, for fear of the response. "I can see the front door from here," she continued as she searched her knapsack for her leather wallet. "And you can be seen too – in case your . . . friend arrives."

This registered with Bee and she glanced at Rowan with a weak smile. Adam would see her when he arrived then, she thought. Because he *would* arrive, wouldn't he? She looked at her watch suddenly. Two twenty-five. He was almost half an hour late for the time he would have thought the appointment was at, Bee realised suddenly. Helplessly, she turned her head and glanced at the reception desk behind her, hopeful suddenly that he would be standing there and that it would all play out the way she had planned. The way it *had* to.

Rowan watched her sympathetically as she did so, before

hesitantly walking over to the coffee machine where she selected two cappuccinos and paid in coin rather than with her Myriad Card. She wanted no receipt of her visit to this place.

Bee barely noticed when Rowan returned with the coffee and placed it down on the table in front of her. She was too busy craning her neck to see over her shoulder back to the clinic entrance. When Adam arrived, she simply couldn't miss him.

Rowan watched for a few moments before speaking, filled with a sudden clarity, a fear but a deep certainty nonetheless, that what Bee watched for was never going to arrive. She took a sip of her coffee before clearing her throat.

"You were born here, you know," she began.

Bee didn't answer. She was too distracted.

"Bee, why don't you have your drink? Calm down a bit after the protesters. I can see the door here – when your friend arrives, I'll tell you that he's here, all right?"

Bee turned and sighed, nodding weakly before taking a noisy sip of her coffee and placing the recyclable cup back on the table before joining her hands together on her lap and jigging her knees anxiously.

Rowan tried again. "You were born here," she repeated. Bee nodded. "Your dad told me once that he had one of the happiest moments of his life here." She watched Bee to see if she could win over any more of her attention. "When your mum had her first scan – when she saw you for the first time. She had been nervous about being pregnant, he said. They both were. But one day she thought she was going to lose you and she rushed here and it turned out to be fine. Your dad came to collect her after her scan – he was terrified when he heard what had happened. He said afterwards that was the day that they both realised that they wanted you more than anything in the world. He said that he became a new man after being here on that occasion. Of course, all the other times . . ."

Bee finally took notice.

"What do you mean 'all the other times'?" she asked. "Did he and my mum try to have more kids?"

Rowan sipped her coffee. "No, your dad and I did," she replied, unable to conceal the hint of surprise in her tone.

Bee was suddenly still, instantly gobsmacked, which in turn surprised Rowan even further.

"What?" she asked. "Didn't you notice? All those times I had to go to hospital over the years?"

Bee shook her head. "No," she said. "I guessed you had just gone to Cambridge or something. I always assumed that you didn't want any." She resumed the jigging under the table, and glanced at her watch.

Rowan took a deep breath and sighed. "I thought you knew. That your dad might have said something. Or at least that you might have picked up on it."

"You say my mum nearly lost me?" interrupted Bee.

Typical Bee, bringing it back to herself, thought Rowan. Still. At least she was communicating.

She nodded in response.

"Dad never told me that."

Rowan shrugged. "He probably didn't feel that he needed to. Miscarriages are unfortunately still very common things."

"Seems a funny story to tell your second wife," said Bee.

Rowan frowned. "Why do you say that?" she asked.

"Well, you said that he didn't tell you stuff like about that friend of his, and that you don't talk about Mum much. It just seems odd that he'd tell you something so *personal*."

Rowan sighed, trying to suppress the annoyance that flickered through her again. Calm, she thought. Calm.

"Your dad and I have been together for twenty years, Bee," she pointed out. "It would be odd if he'd never ever spoken about such a huge event in his life, wouldn't it? Besides – babies. Now that's a topic that we've talked a lot about. And we've spent a lot of time in this hospital too – albeit the maternity section. Doesn't mean we walked out with a baby though."

Rowan's face grew serious, the sadness in her eyes clearly visible.

Bee sat up. "How many times have you been pregnant?"

"Six," answered Rowan quickly, the figure always just on the tip of her tongue. Six babies. And none of them stayed.

Bee gasped. "Jesus Christ, Rowan? More of your bloody secrets. *Six*? Didn't anyone think to tell me any of this?"

Rowan sniffed. "It's not that straightforward, Bee. We desperately wanted a brother or sister for you – more than one if we could. And after the first time we didn't want to upset you – you were still very young – so we said nothing, thinking that the next time we'd have good news for you. A scan picture to show you, maybe. And we thought that the next time, and the next time – all five times – until we just had to make the decision to stop. We had to draw a line underneath it because it was going to kill us both. We were worn out from tests, from scans, from . . . from just pure grief every single time." Rowan hung her head for a moment as she tried to gather herself together. She hadn't spoken about this to anyone other than Claudia in a long time, not even Ed. "Some women have the balls to keep trying year after year," she said quietly. "I didn't. I couldn't face any more and neither could your dad." She looked back up at Bee. "We decided to count our blessings. We had each other, a beautiful home, a whole new life to live." She paused: "And you. We had you and you brought us such joy. Such pain too, mind, but mainly joy."

The two women sat in silence for a few moments, Rowan looking down at her hands, Bee staring at the top of her head, reeling from the past few moments. She felt very tired suddenly. All these revelations – had it only been twenty-four hours since she'd opened that letter? And now this, all on top of what she was doing today anyway.

"Wait," she said suddenly. "You said you were pregnant six times but just now you said that you and my dad lost . . . five times . . . you just said."

Rowan didn't move for a moment. When she did, her face was drawn and tired under her curls. She said nothing in response to Bee. Couldn't think of how to say it. Instead, she cast a glance at her surroundings, suddenly sick at the memory. So long ago now, but still so fresh in her mind.

Bee gasped, suddenly understanding what Rowan's silence was telling her. "You said you'd been *here* before," she said.

Rowan looked up and then down again, shaking her head as she did. "Not here, exactly. Not the Mayberry. I went . . . to a different clinic."

Blood rushed to Bee's head. "Was it Dad's?" she blurted, reddening at the thought.

Rowan shook her head emphatically. "No, Bee. Absolutely not – oh God, maybe I shouldn't have mentioned this. Maybe it's a bad idea after all – you have enough on your plate . . ."

"No, Rowan," Bee sighed wearily and glanced at her watch. Two forty. She hadn't much time.

"You can't just tell me something like what you've told me, after the day I've had. You told me earlier – no, you *yelled* at me earlier not to go ahead with the – with *this*. I need to know why. I've only got a few minutes and I've never spoken to anyone – never met anyone, that I knew of, who went through this."

Bee glanced back around at reception suddenly and then back to Rowan who was looking at her in alarm.

"Didn't they give you counselling . . . when you spoke to them?" Rowan asked, aghast.

Bee looked at her disparagingly. "This isn't 1990, for God's sake!" she snapped. "You don't get *counselling* any more – you just ring up and book. Like getting your hair done, or your nails. If you need *counselling* then you sort it out yourself afterwards. Tell me, Rowan . . . before I go upstairs . . ."

Rowan took a deep breath. "Bee – if I tell you, then you're not going up there with a balanced viewpoint on things. I only have my own experience – I only have what *I* know and that's not what *everyone* knows."

"Just *tell* me, for Christ's sake." Bee looked again at her watch, her face filled with panic.

Rowan was suddenly lost for words. This – this was what she had wanted to share with Bee all along, but after all she had been through she couldn't give Bee the impartiality that she needed. It made her no better than the group outside with their banners and the hideous photographs and their megaphone.

"I . . . I was in college too," she said quietly, searching for the right thing to say. Bee glanced again at her watch and Rowan felt her heart race with panic. "I was like you, Bee. All innocent and unafraid and in love. With one of my lecturers too, as it happens. I studied art and computer design – he zoned in on me like a bee on a flower. I was in second year – had two more years to go but I couldn't concentrate on studying. He made me totally fall for him so that when I found myself like . . . like this, like you are today, I was also alone. And I went through with it and I've regretted it every day since . . ."

Bee's face reddened again at Rowan's words. "You *hypocrite*!" she hissed, glancing at the surrounding tables to see if anyone had heard. "You complete *hypocrite* to lecture me on responsibility earlier – when you're just laying the blame on this guy – this – this lecturer. Like it was all *his* fault and you had nothing to do with it except to be the victim."

"But I *was*, Bee," Rowan said, her tone pleading.

Bee was shocked as sudden, silent tears began to trickle down Rowan's cheeks. She was momentarily annoyed. She didn't have time for this. She had to get up for her appointment. She reached down beside her seat for her handbag on the floor. Screw Rowan. And screw Adam for not turning up. She'd bloody show him. Although, there was still time . . .

"I was very young," Rowan went on. "And naïve – just a country girl. And he knew that I was weak in some ways, but I had very strong morals in others. He invited me to his rooms for a private tutorial and it all happened there. He spiked my drink . . . I barely remember it . . . but I had an abortion . . . because I was raped, Bee."

Bee froze. What had Rowan just said? Had she heard correctly? She straightened in her seat and looked Rowan full in the face. Her stepmother's eyes were squeezed shut now, trying to staunch the flow of tears that streamed from them. Her face was etched with pain.

"Sweet Jesus," whispered Bee, and flinched as a sob escaped Rowan's lips.

"I didn't want to," Rowan sobbed quietly. "But I couldn't have faced childbirth – couldn't have looked at that baby every day of its life without seeing . . . without experiencing what he did to me all over again."

She paused, tried to control her breathing.

Bee watched her, transfixed, taking it all in, yet feeling like this scene was being experienced by someone else.

"Like I said, I wasn't one of the strong ones. So I went ahead and did it. I killed that baby and I've paid for it every single day since. Every day of my life it haunts me. *That's* why I didn't want – why I don't want you to go through with today – but it's none of my business after all."

Bee blinked. Everything forgotten. The time. Adam. She watched Rowan's face change with the tears and realised that she had never seen her cry before. Never properly, like this. She'd seen her red-eyed, occasionally, or seen her well up at the end of a sad movie. But she'd never expected *this* of her. Hadn't thought her capable.

"That's why you're so controlled," she said suddenly, regretting it instantly.

To her surprise, Rowan nodded as she rooted in her jeans pocket for a tissue.

"Perhaps it did affect certain things. I certainly can't face alcohol in any quantity," she said with an unexpected, bitter smile. She blew her nose loudly and wiped it repeatedly with the tissue. "I had to leave college," she went on. "I lost out on my course – never got my degree which is why I ended up working as a receptionist in a graphics firm. When I left college, I moved back to the Acre. After a while, I couldn't leave. I was afraid that everyone knew, that they'd talk – that they'd blame me for it all. I was sure it was all my fault – what Rex – that was his name – had done to me was my own fault and that I was stupid and worthless. I lost years of my life because of it all. Eventually, I saw a counsellor and it took a long time but I felt okay again. And then I met your dad. And we planned a family but we couldn't have one. I was a failure again. I'd had an infection after the abortion, you see – it obviously screwed things up – if I'd only known that baby was to be my only chance at being a mother then I'd have done things differently, Bee. But I don't have the luxury of time travel. I can't ever put things right."

Bee was herself close to tears as she heard her stepmother speak. "I'm so sorry, Rowan," she offered, reaching out slowly across the table to touch her hand. She jumped when Rowan withdrew it suddenly.

"That is just my experience, Bee," she said, her voice suddenly filled with panic and regret, her eyes with shame. "Your life is *your* life and you *must* make your own decisions. Our circumstances are different, Bee."

Bee was shocked to see her stand suddenly, grasp her jacket and handbag under her arm and begin to move away from the table.

"Rowan, please . . ." she began, looking in panic at her watch again as her stepmother made to move past her. Two fifty.

"The time . . . it's time . . . can you . . .?"

Rowan stopped dead in her tracks and paused for a moment before turning back to Bee, reaching out and running her hand over her hair and down along her cheek, all the while slowly shaking her head. "No," she sobbed, fresh tears staining her face. "I *can't*, Bee. Anything else that you would ask of me . . . *anything* . . . but I can't stay for this . . . please understand that I can't."

Bee began to cry, gazing up at Rowan's face. At the face she had looked at so many times she barely saw it any more. The face that, throughout most of her life, had dealt out admonishments and punishments, urges to eat her vegetables, instructions to stay in and study. All that stuff that she had resented. Her wicked stepmother. The woman who had taken her away from everyone and everything she loved. And all that time all that pain, that loss that she endured without ever letting on. Grief suddenly washed over Bee in a flood as she saw through to the vulnerability that filled every corner of Rowan's face. At the fear of being reminded, of being taken back. Anything, she said. Anything except what Bee was about to do.

"I cannot do this, Bee," whispered Rowan fiercely. "But whatever you decide, I am there for you, I swear. To hold your hand, whatever you're going through – whatever we've already *been* through. I'm sorry if you don't feel the same way about me, Bee, and it's late to say now that I love you. I always have. And I will *always* be here for you like I have been. Just not now . . . not this."

With that, she was gone. Bee swivelled in her chair and watched Rowan speed through a small party of people who had just come through the door and then disappear outside, leaving Bee completely alone.

NOVEMBER 1992

Rowan

Judith didn't even flinch at the sound of the back door creaking open and closing again, at the sound of a rucksack being dumped on the floor. As Rowan entered, she was greeted by the sight of her grandmother's back hunched over the kitchen table. Rowan could tell by the empty bowls around her and the vigorous movement of her arms that a cake was being mixed. Feeling very small all of a sudden Rowan paused where she stood, unsure what to do next.

"Oh, you're back then, are you?" asked Judith, continuing to whisk the contents of the big beige-coloured mixing bowl.

The movement was so familiar to Rowan who had watched her make cakes for years. Everything on the table – she recognised it all as everyday things, as the stuff of her childhood. It should have felt familiar. But it didn't. Nothing did. Nothing in this room was the same as it had been before she'd left. Everything was different. Now, and from now on. Nothing would ever be the same.

And still Judith stirred, pausing to add in a shake of flour before resuming her task.

"How was the concert?" she asked casually. "Only I didn't think you were a fan of *Take This*."

"*Take That*," Rowan corrected, the voice she spoke with coming from deep inside her. Coming from someone else.

"It was good. *They* were good," she managed.

"Earl's Court, wasn't it?" continued Judith.

"Hammersmith Apollo," corrected Rowan, staring around the room, trying her hardest to place herself, to find something familiar with which she could make a connection, something that might settle her.

"Hard to find?" asked Judith.

Rowan shook her head. "No," she replied. She had researched it all meticulously. "There's a Tube station there."

There was no need for her grandmother to know that she hadn't been to the gig. That she hadn't, in fact, even been to London.

"Did your friend Ellen enjoy it?" asked Judith.

Rowan focused on her suddenly. She longed to scream at her. To rush over there and push her out of the way and upend the table so that everything on it would smash and break and there would be chaos.

"Yes," she answered meekly, still standing stock-still on the doormat just inside the back door.

"I think I've raised you wrong, you know?" said Judith suddenly.

Rowan's heart sank suddenly. She could feel her cheeks colour and start to burn. She knew. Judith knew. She had to. And she'd blame her too, tell her it was her own fault for being so stupid. For allowing herself to get into that stupid situation in the first place. She only had herself to blame, after all. What did she think made her so special? Made her think that bad things still couldn't happen to her? Made her think that losing her mum and dad was the only bad thing that would ever happen in her life?

Rowan's heart pounded as she waited for Judith to speak.

"I mean, why Take That? Four or five little wazzocks skipping round a stage singing about love like it's candy floss and heart-shaped sweets." Judith continued to whisk, shaking her head as she did so.

"I mean, whatever did I do wrong that you won't listen to Dylan? Or a bit of Billy Bragg, even? He's more your generation surely? What's wrong with a song having a message? A purpose to it? Instead of that manufactured boy-band nonsense? I despair of you sometimes, Rowan. I really do."

How could she, Rowan wondered, her grandmother's voice falling to a faint hum in the distance. How could she not know? Maybe if she turned around? Maybe if she saw her face then she'd have to know? She'd have to realise that something was terribly, terribly wrong. She'd be able to tell instantly that Rowan hadn't been to London. That she'd only been as far away as Clevedon for the past few days. That she hadn't been to see a 'manufactured boy band' in concert with her college friend Ellen at all. How could she not be able to tell this just by the sound of Rowan's voice? How could she not know to turn and *look*?

Maybe it's because she's not my mother, Rowan reasoned. Maybe if she was then she'd just *know*. Then she couldn't, surely, leave me to do what I did alone? Then I wouldn't feel so isolated in all this. If I had a little girl, I'd never let this happen to her. I'd never just leave her to her own devices – I'd be *there*, *with* her, holding her hand, keeping her strong, keeping her in my arms where she was safe forever more.

But for me – now everything is changed. Everything's *broken*. I can't go back to college – I can't face seeing him again – can't face everyone *knowing*, everyone *looking* and *pointing* and *whispering* about me. *There's that girl who threw it all away . . .*

Well, there were things that I shouldn't have done.

I shouldn't have allowed myself to feel so strongly for him. To become so besotted with him that I allowed what happened to happen. I shouldn't have gone to his rooms alone. Shouldn't have accepted that glass of wine. And now I can never shake him off me.

And maybe I shouldn't have done what I did in that clinic in Clevedon. But what other choice did I have? Maybe other women are strong enough but I couldn't . . . I couldn't carry it inside me, couldn't look at *it* every day of my life for fear that *he'd* be looking back at me. *Come to my rooms for those notes, Rowan. Have a little drink, Rowan. You like me, Rowan, don't you? I've seen how you look at me in classes . . . we shouldn't really . . .*

How could I have been so *stupid*?

And why can't I tell her? Because then she'd feel like it was *her* fault too. I can't make her feel that way – this is *my* doing, *my* fault. No one else's. I can't burden anyone else with this – not ever. It's in me now. Locked inside me. And I can't let it out. Can't lose control and let it slip, ever. I must make it go away, or else I might die . . .

"Now Pete Seeger – couldn't you root out some of his records? There's plenty to be learned from Pete –"

"I think I might go up to bed, Gran, if that's okay?" interrupted Rowan suddenly.

"Oh fine. Do what you please," came the reply. "You generally do anyway."

"I'm just a bit tired," said Rowan, picking up her backpack, closing her eyes and holding herself steady at the doorpost as she swooned a little. She leaned against the wall for support while the moment passed. "Late night and all that," she continued, feeling steadier.

"Off you go then," replied Judith. "I'll bring you up a cuppa and a slice of this in a couple of hours. Oh, and Rowan?"

Rowan stopped, looked again at her grandmother's back, hoping, praying that she might turn. Longing with all of her heart to be taken in that great embrace, to feel safe, and loved, and wanted. To forget. Just for a moment.

"What?" she replied.

Judith didn't turn. Instead she poured the last of the flour into her mixing bowl and resumed the energetic mixing.

"Don't call me 'Gran', love, all right? I've told you a thousand times if I've told you once – I'm not a gran, or a granny or a grandma or anything. I'm just Judith, all right? That's my God-given name and the one I'll use till the day I die. It's just me, all right?"

"All right, Gr– Judith," replied Rowan meekly before passing through the door that led to the winding staircase to her room.

But once she reached the stairs, she found that she couldn't go any further. That she didn't have the energy to even lift her foot onto the bottom step. Frozen, she turned to look back at the familiar sight of her grandmother at work in the kitchen and was instantly drawn back like a moth to a flame.

"Judith," she whimpered.

"That's more like it."

"Can you sit down for a bit? I need to tell you something. I've been keeping a secret . . ."

SEPTEMBER 2020

Jenny

*I am waiting on the stairs as I hear the key turn in the front door.
I watch as my poor, beaten Bee enters first, her shoulders slumped,
her steps careful. Behind her comes the woman, guiding her, placing
a hand in the small of her back to make sure that she doesn't trip.*

*They are silent. The front door is closed with a gentle, reverent
click, instead of the loud slam that usually echoes through the
house when Bee arrives. She is normally so full of energy, such a
human whirlwind – so alive. But not today. Today she is a shadow
of herself. Today she is almost as much a ghost as I am.*

*I watch them chat briefly in the hall. Watch as the woman asks
Bee if she would like something to eat and Bee replies something
about getting a drive-through Jamie Oliver once they are on the
road. She doesn't want to stay a minute longer in this house, she
says, and the woman nods and agrees and says that's a very good
idea. She says that she will pick up some things from the kitchen
while Bee packs a bag for herself.*

*Bee takes the stairs one step at a time, climbing them with her
back hunched, the weight of her worries on her shoulders.*

*Yet I want to grab her and dance with her, to be joyous and
celebrate. Because she is still here. And because she has someone to
take care of her. Someone real, someone physical.*

I watch Bee in her room as she throws handfuls of clothes into a duffel bag. She isn't even aware of what she's doing. She forgets her hairbrush, her dressing gown. And there are other things that she deliberately doesn't pack. The sketchbook – my sketchbook – which she thought was such a source of inspiration. She can't even bring herself to touch it now, seeing it as the symbol of all that has gone wrong for her.

I watch as she slopes back down the stairs, laying the duffel bag on the hall floor before wandering into the kitchen where the woman stands, holding Guillaume's letter in one hand and the two cheques it contains in the other. They are substantial. Guillaume cannot have wanted for much if he can leave that amount to the daughter of a woman whose life he ruined and a child that he has never met. It would probably be more honest to send the cheque for Matilda back to his wife – Grace – at the address on the letterhead, but how much does Grace know? Will sending it back make her aware of something that will haunt her for the rest of her days somehow? Far better that the cheque goes to Matilda, even though she isn't Gui's child. But with it, she could finally achieve her goal. It's enough to fly her far, far away and set herself up for a very long time, should she choose to do that. Or to invest in something that will make her a fortune. Either way, the money will make Matilda a very happy little girl. No one will ever call her 'Poor Matilda' again.

The woman slips that cheque in her handbag – it's made out to Vicky, but I know that the woman intends to make sure Matilda gets it. Matilda's in no rush yet – there's a while to go for her to finish her degree, and for her to plan, plan, plan whatever it is that she is going to do.

She holds the second cheque out to Bee, who shakes her head in refusal. I want to physically urge her to take it, but I need not worry. The woman is on the case for me, singing the same tune as I would have sung.

"Take it," she urges. "You'll need something to tide you over while you get through all this. You don't have to spend all of it, but what good would it be to send this money back to a woman who might not even know you exist? Who doesn't need to know the

335

reason that her husband sent you this money in the first place. Just take it, and keep it safe. You'll need it."

And she does.

Bee reluctantly takes the piece of paper and glances at it for a second before folding it carefully and placing it in her pocket.

The woman immediately admonishes her. "Take that out of there," she urges sternly. "It's not much use to you once it's been through a hot wash, now is it?"

And it is then that I see Bee smile. It's a flicker, a hint, a trace of what it should be like. But it is there nonetheless. There is hope.

They leave in the same silence that surrounded them when they came in. Bee's head is down and she walks like a robot to the car while all the while the woman chats to her in a gentle voice, talking about banal things: what they will eat when they get 'home' as she calls it, what's on TV that night, how Bee shouldn't yet mention the letter from Guillaume to her dad. They won't keep it a secret, she says, but she needs time to clear her mind before she decides what – and how – to tell him.

"Maybe it's best not to tell him anything," Bee suggests.

The woman doesn't dismiss the thought. And in my selfish way I hope that they don't. Not to save my own gutless hide, however, not to preserve me as the tragic lost love of Edmund Mycroft forever, but to save him from more shattered dreams, more disappointment. To allow him to see out the rest of his days – and face what is to come when he is told Bee's news – protected from information that might just break him all over again, when he is at last content.

I admit that I didn't think I would ever feel peace at thinking that. Up until now, I still wanted him to miss me a little, to long for me sometimes, to think that nothing compared to me. But now that I know that he is finally happy, I feel some happiness too. And I am prepared to be forgotten by him if it means that he is spared the news of my stupid infidelity. If that is the price that I must pay for his happiness – to no longer exist for him except as an occasional, dim memory – then that is what I want.

I would like Bee to forgive me, of course. To somehow realise that I am not as dishonest as she has come to think over the past –

is it only a matter of hours? A couple of days? She has too much to deal with now. She needs to go with the woman to the countryside. I didn't think that I would ever feel this either, but she needs to be nurtured by someone, brought back to health. She needs help to regain her strength and make decisions for herself and move on.

Mostly, I just want her to be happy too – at whatever cost. It doesn't matter now, anyway. She will come to realise over time that I loved her – that I truly loved her. That it's impossible not to. But that she has someone else to watch over her now. Someone who already loves her too, and who will come to love her even more, I am sure, until she loves her as much as a real mother could.

The woman casts a final glance around as she pulls the front door shut behind her. She glances up to the ceiling above, around the walls, and finally to the stairs, where I sit on the bottom step. And for a moment her eyes linger, for just a split second too long. And I wonder if she can see me. If, after all these years, someone can really see me.

Then again, maybe she can't. She pulls the door suddenly behind her and it closes with a loud click. I am alone again.

And I know for certain this time that they will not be back again.

JUNE 2021

Jenny

I'm sitting at a garden table. It's Saturday morning and it's glorious, the sun is warm and a balmy breeze flits across my face where I sit, slightly shaded, every now and again. The sky is cloudless. A fat bee bothers some lavender beside me, lavender so thick that the pot in which it is planted can barely contain it. A robin, of all things, trills its song from the branch of a magnolia nearby. She and I have much in common, I think. Both of us watchers, both of us unseen, keeping a close eye on this moment.

I am watching a man and a woman. They sit a few feet in front of me, side by side on a wooden bench which looks out over a small courtyard lined on either side by pots of flowers and herbs. The man gently bounces a child on his knee. I cannot see his face, but I know that it is a picture of bliss; the woman, the same. Their voices, their laughter rises and falls into the still summer air to be caught by that teasing breeze and carried out over the valley below.

I am unsure how I am here. Since the house where I spent my life and my death was sold a month ago, I have been somewhere and nowhere at the same time and now I am here. It feels odd to be outdoors after so long. I grew so used to the walls of 17 Pilton Gardens that I didn't think anywhere else existed any more, not really. It feels good too. I feel more solid, somehow, as if I am something again. As if I am somehow a person. If I concentrate very hard I can feel a tingle on my skin, the tickle of the air rushing by. It can't last, this feeling, of course. I know that – I understand it. Because along with the sense of being again, comes a weariness with which I can barely contend. The exhaustion of every heightened emotion of twenty-four years spent watching.

If I were alive, I would be middle-aged. How odd to feel it, yet to have no idea what it would look like. In my head, I am still twenty-seven years old – I am twenty-seven years old, but with the wisdom and pain and joy of the fifty-one years that I have existed coursing through my veins. Before now everything was unfinished but being here – finally leaving the prison of my death and being here, with them, where they all are – my family – the sense of completion becomes clearer and clearer.

The robin gives another sharp trill in the tree as if demanding attention. She succeeds as they turn their heads to seek and find her and point her out to the child. "Look, Judith," they say. "Look at the birdie." But at two months old my granddaughter is only interested in the warmth of arms and the taste of sweet milk.

My granddaughter. Judith Rose, Jennifer Mycroft. The Jennifer is for me, the Rose for my mother, and Judith, not after the woman, but after the place, Judith's Acre. Where my daughter has thrived. Where she has been happiest.

My beloved Bee. My darling. My beginning. My end. She'll be back soon, I heard Ed say. Gone to the village of Watchet – "Watch iiiit!" he warns the woman in jest, in what seems to be a familiar joke – to meet her friends from school for coffee. He laughed about how once they couldn't keep her in but since Judith's arrival they cannot get her out. I understand that too. The love, the sheer adoration that you can feel when your child finally leaves the sanctuary of your body and you are torn between wanting her to go back where it's safe, and the want – the need – to look at her beauty every hour God sends. To drink her in, to find looking away unbearable in case you miss something, the tiniest thing, to need to touch and smell and nuzzle and nurse. After that, there is nothing that can make you as happy again. I know that my Bee understands that now too. That she knows that this is instinct. That this is how every woman feels about her daughter. How I felt about her.

Ed and I dreamed of this too. Of sitting side by side in the sunshine. Of grandchildren. Of love. Of contentment. If I had to die again, then this is how I would want to do it. In the arms of my family, peacefully. On a Saturday morning when the world is at rest, going about pleasurable business.

I look at Ed. My husband. Still my husband, despite all of the changes of the years. He beams at his grandchild beatifically. How must it feel, I wonder, to hold an infant in your arms after wanting to for so long? To inhale the scent that you wish was the only air that you ever had to breathe, to feel the silk of the skin, to run your finger the length of the miniature hand and marvel as the fingers unfold like exotic petals just for a moment before they curl again. I am awash with love for him. My being is made up of love for this man, after all these years, after the betrayal. My body feels like a light – a coloured beam that suddenly changes to another shade as jealousy flashes through me – my old companion. How I want to hold that child! How I want to be the woman who sits with him at this very moment in time. Who laughs as he kicks his foot out at a pig that wanders up to him, snuffling at his feet. Who takes the child delicately from his arms as he reaches down to the animal to make an apology and is rewarded by sniffs and grunts. How I want to have lain beside him every night for all these years, to have mothered more of his children. How I want to die beside him – I am reminded suddenly of a song that my mother liked. 'Bist Du Bei Mir' it was called. She translated it for me once:

"If you are with me, then I will go gladly
unto death and to my rest.
Ah, what a pleasant end for me,
if your dear hands be the last I see,
closing shut my faithful eyes to rest!"

That. That is what I want. I burn with longing for what I have missed. Ache as I watch the woman – I should call her by name: Rowan – place my granddaughter over her shoulder, pressing their cheeks together. I can see my granddaughter's face now as she turns her head gently into Rowan's neck, nuzzling, hunting for food. The tiny wrinkled nose, the eyes screwed shut as she yawns, long and *thoroughly, the two tiny fists under her chin, propping her head up to enable her to get a better look at me when she finally deigns to open those eyes and look. She can see me, of course. They say that babies can – I never believed it when Bee used to stare in the direction of my mother's favourite armchair and my father used to tell me that she must be there, watching over her. Now I know it was true. Tiny Judith will never remember this moment but it is good enough for me. She has seen me. I am sure of it. And with that comes another release. I can be of no use to her, of course. Will never know her, will never hold her or talk with her. I am not the woman for the job, I know. That is Rowan's task. She is her grandmother now.*

I think I might have grown to like Rowan if I had known her. If not like her, then admire her. Admire her resilience and her strength. Admire her kindness and patience. Admire the way in which, while she couldn't have stayed to watch, she waited right outside the door of the Mayberry abortion clinic that day and gathered Bee in her arms the instant that she emerged, unsure as to whether or not Bee had gone through with the procedure. Admire the way she took her away for good advice and tea and dry crackers and love. I am jealous of her, yes. But I do not begrudge her what she has just because I myself can't have it. She has had a hard life. She deserves the love of the man she has stood by and adored all of these years. She is a better woman – a better wife, I know, than I could ever have been. I am filled with a longing to embrace her, to say thank you, to say sorry. This woman who has taken the family that I broke and repaired them one by one with her love.

I look at Ed. He turns to smile at his wife and I see him again as he was over thirty years ago when he first smiled at me. When we started our adventure together. If I had lived another life then at this very moment in time I might be enfolded in his arms, inhaling his scent, feeling the roughness of his chin against my cheek. I have been enshrouded all of these years by guilt and regret every time I have looked at him. It is only now that I watch him reclaim the child and cradle her to his chest that I can somehow cast that shroud aside and feel at last happy for him. Feel his contentment, his bliss, his complete peace.

There is a sudden flurry of excitement as the sound of a distant engine grinds closer, climbing the hill to the house behind where we sit.

"Mummy's home," they tell Judith.

How strange that feels, to hear my baby Bee called that. Exhausted as I am, I can see her now, coming around the side of the house and my heart leaps so hard that I think it will burst from me, that I am sure that I must be alive again, reincarnated by the thrill of her presence. As I have done her whole life, I watch her. See her hair wild and ablaze in the sunlight; she wears it loose over her shoulders today, her errant curls nudged by a breeze that catches her as she stops and bends, her hands on her knees, her face alight as her father holds Baby Judith up to show her that her mother has returned.

"Well!" gasps Bee. "Have you been a good girl?" She reaches out – that blissful second of anticipation, of empty arms that know they will soon be full. "Mummy's home," she says herself. There. I've heard her say it. That word. 'mummy'. One last time. Not 'mum' or 'mother' but 'mummy'. My name.

I watch as mother and child are reunited. I follow the familiar pattern of the little kisses, the embrace loaded with the relief that comes when two pieces of the same thing have been rightfully fitted back together. I close my eyes and try to imagine how that might feel. To hold someone. My child. And suddenly I can. I feel warmth as if my arms were wrapped around another being. And I feel their arms around me in return. I am unsure if it is memory, or an illusion created by longing, or someone who has come to take me, but finally, I can feel again.

And it is surrounded by this bliss that I open my eyes and look at them all one more time. Tiny, perfect Judith, good and kind Rowan, my wonderful Ed and finally Bee who is lost in her own bliss, her daughter cradled warm and safe under her chin, crooning a tune that only the child can hear. Singing her to sleep. This is all that has ever mattered, I know. All that will ever matter again. They are my family and they are together. And I am with them. This is why I have stayed awake for so long but now it's all in place, all complete.

I can go now.

ACKNOWLEDGEMENTS

My thanks go to:

Paula Campbell for her wisdom, encouragement and support – thank you, as always, for the amazing opportunity to write.

The team at Poolbeg – Ailbhe, Sarah, David – for such hard work and constant support.

My editor, Gaye Shortland, who takes the efforts that I serve up and turns them into something that somehow works!

My former teachers at the Brigidine Convent, Mountrath, especially Mary Holden who gave me the first taste of seeing my name in print.

My parents, my in-laws, my family near and far, and my friends who are always behind me.

The readers – the buyers, the borrowers, the Tweeters, the Facebookers – thank you all so much.

And to Daryl, Daisy and Florence who are my world.

Now that you're hooked, why not try
The Dark Water Chapters one and two,
also by
Helen Moorhouse, as a taster!

THE DARK WATER

CHAPTER 1

October 29th

Silently, the intruder slipped into the apartment and stayed a while in the hallway, listening, contemplating his next move.

He was drawn to the living room – had been since the first time he'd come here, unnoticed and silent. He moved so stealthily that it was hard to tell if he walked or floated down the corridor. Once there, he moved the living-room door at the very end of the passage and it squeaked defiantly, causing him to pause a moment, to listen for sounds of movement from the room on his left – the one he hadn't dared visit yet. There was only stillness. He proceeded, entering the room and beginning the familiar walk-around.

He walked by the first window, a shadow crossing past the amber glow from the streetlight outside. Next, to the writing desk which fitted into the space between the two long sash windows. He riffled through a book open on the desk – *The True History of Edinburgh's Vaults* – losing the page that had been left open. Beside it, a notepad – should he try to leave another message? The last one had been so difficult. And it had taken so much of his energy. He decided against it tonight.

The intruder moved to the mantelpiece of the tall fireplace, grasping its edge momentarily, leaving four fingerprints behind in the dust. He then ran a forefinger along the mantel, leaving a trail, pausing at the end. At the picture. Gently, he turned the frame toward him, to see it better – the black-and-white photograph of a boy in swimming trunks – nine or ten years of age – he couldn't remember precisely. The boy stared back at him, a familiar broad, proud grin across his face, holding a brick, of all things, under his left arm and in his right hand, thrust toward the camera, was a medal on a piece of ribbon.

The intruder stared at it a long time, lost in the face of the beaming child, thoughts and memories rushing through his head, so many that they hurt. He turned away, unable to sustain the energy that they needed. He wanted to go, but knew that he couldn't leave yet. He had a job to do and he was determined that tonight he was finally going to do it.

He glanced around the rest of the room, at the belongings of the man. Empty teacups, a half-drunk bottle of Bell's, a glass left with a sticky stain on its base where the last drains of a drink had congealed. A long black coat was slung over an armchair, the pocket pulled inside out. Dirty dishes were scattered throughout.

The intruder moved toward the door again.

This time, he didn't pull it toward him to open it, or pull it behind him to close it. Instead, he stepped silently around it, despite the fact that he seemed too big, even for a small person, to negotiate the space. In a second, he stood outside the next door to the right. In yet another second, having summoned all of his energy, and as quietly as he possibly could, he stood on the other side of it, taking in his surroundings: the wardrobe and tallboy, the bedside lockers, the vast bed. And in it, the man he desperately needed to see. The one person who could maybe help him. The one person that he needed to know.

In his sleep, Gabriel McKenzie dreamed that someone had entered his room. They hadn't used the door – he hadn't heard the handle turn – but they were in there with him all the same. Gradually, he found himself swimming up from deep, deep sleep, to something verging on consciousness. Half-awake, he became gradually more aware, his heart starting to beat faster, his breathing audible as he surfaced from his slumber. There was someone in his room, someone standing at the end of his bed, watching him.

Gabriel didn't want to, but he knew he had to. He gasped with fear and expectation, forced himself to sit upright, ready to confront who was there. He subconsciously sought words – a 'who the hell are you?' or 'get out' or 'don't hurt me' – he wouldn't know until they came out of his mouth.

But there was no one there.

Gabriel's heart raced as he scanned the room, his eyes darting from right to left and back again to the end of the bed where he'd felt – no, known – that someone was watching him, but the room was empty, the only sound his own ragged breathing. Not again, he thought.

CHAPTER 2

October 31st

"Come on, Martha, it's starting!"

Martha Armstrong glanced impatiently at the clock in her kitchen, two empty glasses in one hand and a chilled bottle of wine in the other. She had to resist shouting back to Sue in the next room, to let her know that she was on her way. She jigged a little from foot to foot and forced herself to look at the screen that Will was studying intently, his elbows resting on the granite-topped island where they both stood, staring at his laptop.

"There!" he said, pointing at the screen. "What do you think?"

Martha stared at the screen. It showed a large room in darkness, visible only in the green tinge of night-vision cameras. The shot was focused closely on a grand piano to the left of a marble fireplace. Suddenly, what seemed like a small, flickering ball of light rose directly up from the closed lid of the piano, hovered for a second or two and then appeared to double – a second, identical ball of light appearing to imitate exactly what the first did – before they zoomed off the screen and disappeared.

"Orb?" asked Will, leaning on his elbows and turning toward Martha, his face intent and hopeful. Martha couldn't help but smile and resisted the urge to lean forward and kiss him. "Moth, my sweet," she grinned and put the glasses and the wine bottle down on the kitchen island before reaching for the computer mouse.

Will sighed. "Are you sure?" he said, frustrated. "The Leith Street Group sent this to me, positive that there was something in this particular piece of footage."

Martha shook her head. "Watch," she said, returning to the beginning of the segment of video and playing it again. "The movement is fluttery, I suppose you'd call it, exactly the same as a moth or a butterfly, and the hovering is just too similar to the movement of a flying insect to conclusively prove that it's paranormal – you're always saying yourself that it can only be paranormal if you can't in any way, shape or form prove that it's normal – and this is just too normal for me."

She reached again and picked up the wineglasses, intending to move away.

"But it splits in two!" Will said, exasperated.

Martha sighed and put the glasses down again with a clink. "Seriously, Will – you don't even believe in orbs being the first stage of a spirit manifestation. You told me that you thought they were only ever insects or dust or reflections of passing lights or whatever – I didn't pick my cynicism up off the side of the road." She was growing increasingly impatient. So many conversations with Will were like this these days.

"The footage is very grainy but, look, there's a mirror on the mantel up above the fireplace, and my guess is that the edges are bevelled – hence our moth, or insect or whatever, fluttering about, looking for a way out, reflected in the light from the camera, suddenly doubles up, one becomes two – its own reflection – and then zips off about its business. The mirror is unframed, and the angle of the shot, up that close, makes it difficult to get a clear view of the scene as a whole. It's a simple mistake to make though, especially for believers in orbs. Which you're not, right?"

Will knew she was correct but Martha could tell it didn't make him happy. He so desperately wanted evidence these days to prove absolutely that there was something out there. He knew it, and she of all people knew it but proving it was the elusive dream for people like him, and hundreds of thousands of people before him. When he'd had Gabriel to bounce off, he'd been less disheartened every time something proved inconclusive but now he relied more and more on her, and his own desperation. Obviously his age didn't help – approaching his late thirties might well have catapulted him into a mid-life crisis and a need to make a significant mark in his field before it was too late.

For that matter, at the age of thirty-seven, perhaps she was in premature mid-life crisis too.

"Shit," he said simply.

Martha tried to avoid eye contact with him and continued to stare at the laptop. She knew it was ridiculous but sometimes she felt that he almost wanted to blame her when something could be explained rationally and she was the one doing the explaining.

Will went and picked up his waxed jacket from a nearby chair and slid his arms into it. "Shit, shit, shit!" he said, and ran a hand through his hair. "Of course it's a moth!" He rolled his eyes upward. "It's so stupid of me to think otherwise but you're right – I need to get a grip and get back to using my head when it comes to these things. It's just so frustrating sometimes . . ."

"Here, Will, what's this?" Martha suddenly interjected.

"What?" He was back at her side in a single step, as she leaned closer toward the screen, dragging the mouse across to take the footage back a few moments.

"Watch this," she said, leaning back to allow him a closer look.

They stared as the camera automatically pulled back – it was a static night-vision camera, fixed on a tripod but with the facility to focus automatically if it sensed movement or needed to expand its view to allow a shift in light or mass to fit the frame. The shot was much the same as before – the grand piano, the fireplace, the mirror now clearly visible, reflecting the wall just above the camera, faintly lit with the glow of the infrared light from the piece of equipment. The movement was so fast that had they not been staring intently at the screen, they might never have seen it but, as they did, Will gasped, and grabbed the mouse in his right hand to watch it again.

It was definitely the shape of a person. It moved in a flash across the wall, as though walking quickly from left to right. What thrilled Will most was that, as the shot took in the mirror, they could quite clearly see that it wasn't a shadow caused by a reflection. There was nothing to reflect.

Will watched it several times in a row, each time his face becoming more animated and the beginnings of a smile creeping across his features.

"Good?" asked Martha tentatively.

He turned to her and beamed. "You bloody genius!" he exclaimed and straightened, grabbing her in a bear hug.

It wasn't comfortable – he squeezed too hard, and his jacket smelled musty, the wax slimy – but Martha allowed herself to be crushed in the embrace and smiled at his enthusiasm, closing her eyes for a moment.

"It's clear that the shadow isn't caused by a person – we'd be able to see anyone crossing the room in the mirror! How did I miss this before?" he said, breathless, releasing Martha and turning back to the screen to watch it again.

Martha glanced at the clock – eight fifteen. "You were looking too hard?" she offered, smiling. "C'mere, didn't you say you'd meet the guys at half eight?"

"Hmm?" he asked, preoccupied.

"Only it's a quarter past now," she continued, "and you've got to get all the gear set up and it's Hallowe'en and there's a caretaker waiting at the house for you . . ." She allowed her voice to tail off as Will glanced at the time at the bottom of the computer screen.

"Oh Christ, you're right," he said, and hurriedly snapped the laptop shut.

He was going on an investigation he'd been excited about for weeks – a recently renovated former tenement house in Edinburgh's Old Town. Will and his group from the university were to be the first to investigate it for signs of ghostly activity and they were hopeful of concrete evidence, based on the reports they'd received from the new owners and their workmen – a ghostly apparition of a priest coupled with odd noises and knockings in the dead of night.

Martha picked his keys up from the table and held them on her forefinger, clinking them gently from side to side to make it obvious, as he searched around the kitchen frantically for them, patting the many pockets on his jacket as he did so. Will smiled as he finally turned and saw them dangling there. He grabbed them with a grin, leaning in to kiss her softly as he did.

"You know I love you to absolute bits?" he said quietly so that Sue, waiting in the living room, wouldn't hear.

"And so you should," she grinned and kissed him back. "Now please be careful tonight, don't bring anything back with you, and don't trip over stuff. And drive safely."

"I promise," he said and pocketed the keys before tucking the laptop under his arm and leaning in for another kiss. "Seeya, Sue!" he called into the living room as he strode out of the kitchen, turning briefly to give Martha a warm smile of parting.

She followed him out to the hall to watch him head out into the dark evening, feeling the blast of cold air that gusted in through the front door before he closed it softly behind him.

"Is he bloody well gone?" called Sue from the couch.

Martha grinned before retreating to the kitchen to pick up the wine and glasses. "Finally!" she answered and flicked off the kitchen light before joining her friend in the cosy living room and closing the door behind her.

"My God, I thought he'd never leave!" said Sue, reaching out to grab some cashews from a dish on the coffee table. A fire crackled in the grate and the TV hummed low in the corner. "I set it to record so we didn't miss a millisecond – the Hallowe'en special is going to be too bad to be true!"

Martha smiled as she settled herself in an armchair and began to pour the wine. She felt guilty at being so excited about what they were going to watch, but Sue was right – it was terrifically bad TV. If Will caught the two of them about to gorge on a two-hour special, he'd go into one of his sulks. "Right then," she said, "Hit it!"

Sue jabbed her forefinger dramatically at the remote control on her knee and immediately green footage, much like that which Martha had been watching moments before on Will's laptop, filled the screen.

A theremin played a 70s' science-fiction-style theme tune, just audible under a deep voiceover which announced that the next two hours would most likely change the lives of those who watched, and prove without a shadow of a doubt that life after death existed.

Sue mouthed aloud along with the final few sentences which were part of the credits each week: "'They're young, they're ready for anything, and they believe. We are ghosts . . . ghosts are them . . . Ghosts R Us!'"

The theme tune grew louder and the 'cast' of the newest ghost-hunting show on TV flashed up one by one on screen, all in their early twenties and equipped with various cameras, thermal imagers – the sort of equipment that Will used on his investigations – all captured in various states of what seemed to be terrible fear. And at the end, one last 'character': the resident psychic medium who accompanied the team every week. Gabriel McKenzie.

≡≡≡ WARD RIVER PRESS
titles now available and Autumn 2014

The Friday Tree by Sophia Hillan
now available

Ruby's Tuesday by Gillian Binchy
now available

Into the Night Sky by Caroline Finnerty
coming Autumn.

The House Where it Happened by Martina Devlin
coming Autumn.

Levi's Gift by Jennifer Burke
coming Autumn.

Also published by Helen Moorhouse

The Dead Summer

Leaving behind a broken marriage and a city life she no longer wants to lead, Martha Armstrong takes her baby daughter to start again in the beautiful English countryside. Living in a tranquil cottage in the heat of a perfect summer, it seems that all her wishes have come true.

Until the noises start.

Plagued by mysterious footsteps, scratchings, and crying in the night, Martha is at first unnerved and then terrified. What is happening to her idyllic existence? Is it all her imagination or is someone persecuting her?

Little does Martha know but the cottage has witnessed terrible hatred, fear and pain in the past, when two young Irish sisters lived in it. The fate of these girls and the baby born there now casts a dark shadow over Martha and her daughter.

Martha begins to unravel the story of the cottage's past, and uncover the terrifying secret that still haunts it. But can she discover the truth in time to keep herself and her little girl safe from the evil that threatens them?

ISBN 978-184223-503-4

If you enjoyed this book from
Poolbeg why not visit our website:

www.poolbeg.com

and get another book delivered straight
to your home or to a friend's home.

All books despatched within 24 hours.

POOLBEG

Why not join our mailing list
at www.poolbeg.com and get some
fantastic offers, competitions,
author interviews and much more?

@PoolbegBooks